LIPSI'S
DAUGHTER

ALSO BY PATTY APOSTOLIDES

Helena's Choice

The Greek Maiden and the English Lord

The Lion and the Nurse

Candlelit Journey: Poetry from the Heart

LIPSI'S DAUGHTER

BY

PATTY APOSTOLIDES

ACKNOWLEDGEMENTS

I would like to thank all the wonderful people who helped make this book a reality: Alex Alexandrou, Matt Barrett (Athensguide), Jacqueline Freeman, Mary Jo Gileno, Linda Morelli, Marilyn Rouvelas, Mary Schaller, and Vivian Gilbert Zabel (Writing.com).

Special thanks go to my parents Christos and Anna Koumoundouros, who showed me love and support all through the years, and who gave me the gift of loving, and to all my sisters, Rena, Manuella, Sylvia, and Helen, who through their loyalty and love, gave me the gift of sharing.

Last but not least, I give my heartfelt thanks to my late husband Tony, for all those times he read my manuscript into the night, giving constructive criticism, and Tony Jr., for all the times his bubbly personality made me laugh. You showed me how blessed I am.

CHAPTER 1

Did time stand still when first we met
As did my heart that saw you yet?

The yacht heaved headlong into the black night while the howling winds and heavy rain pounded the ship. Tony left his quarters; pelted mercilessly by the rain, he stumbled toward the Captain's steering room.

"Mr. Plakis. Thank God you came!" Captain Haris shouted, trying to steer the yacht. "We can no longer fight the storm. One of our engines is down."

"Where are we?" Tony asked. He battled with the door, trying to shut it against the forceful wind.

"We are near Lipsi Island. It is safer to dock there for the night."

Ipatia stood in the courtyard, gazing at Lipsi's sun-splashed rolling hills and deep valleys. The vibrant greens of the cypress trees dotted the lime-green landscape, and the whitewashed houses, so pure in color, appeared almost saintly.

Beyond, the calm Aegean Sea glistened under the sun's rays.

Last night's storm had unleashed a fury that pounded rain and wind upon the island, forcing the islanders to remain secured inside their homes. She had learned a long time ago that the sea could turn treacherous.

Today, everything seemed normal as several white fishing boats studded the sea.

"Come, Kitso. *Pappou* (Grandfather) wants us to get bread before the bakery closes," she said, patting the donkey and straightening his red silk tie until it hung gracefully from his neck. "There, you're the handsomest donkey in town."

Mistakenly bringing home the wrong donkey years ago, Ipatia's mix-up had caused much confusion. She had solved the problem by having Kitso wear her father's red tie. At first, her grandfather grimaced at the gesture but learned to accept it over time. The tie had become a part of Kitso, identifying him from the other donkeys.

They ambled down the narrow stone path, down the steep hill past her grandfather's lush vegetable garden and olive orchards, and past the open fields with stone boundaries. A gust of wind pulled her braided hair loose and played havoc with her black skirt. Used to the capricious island breeze, she absentmindedly tucked the golden strands of loose hair behind her ears.

Her thoughts turned towards the trip tomorrow.

This would be the first time she was returning to Piraeus, a main harbor in Greece, after her parents' death. Her aunt had inherited their house and Ipatia planned to live there with her. Ipatia also intended to study at the university in Piraeus. The fact that her aunt had not replied to her letter dampened her growing excitement at the impending trip.

The plodding donkey's steps stopped in front of the Tsatsikas house. Ipatia's trips to town often included stopping to have a chat with her godmother, Katerina Tsatsikas, whom she called *Nona*. Her godmother usually had some juicy gossip to deliver over a cup of coffee and a *koulouraki* (Greek cookie). Afterwards, Ipatia would treat Kitso to the tasty, leftover morsels, and he would smack his lips with satisfaction.

Kitso turned his head and gazed expectantly at the shut door. *A shut door indicated that the family was probably napping or gone.*

Even if the family were home, Ipatia could not stop for a visit. She was already late.

"You'll have to wait for your treat," Ipatia said, laughing and nudging him onward with her feet.

They reached the bottom of the hill and entered the main road.

Soon, Ipatia spied the magnificent domed church of The Virgin of Haron. Last week, thousands of tourists had arrived on Lipsi Island to witness the miracle of the Virgin Mary icon and join in the parade and festivities that lasted several days.

As she rode by the church, Ipatia reverently made the sign of the cross. A forceful, howling wind smacked her face. She pulled the strands behind her ears, and then heard a banging sound coming from the church

Ipatia spied its door swinging back and forth from the wind. *The wind must have pried the door loose.* Stopping, she hopped off the donkey and sprinted up the ramp to the entrance. She peeked inside. A strong scent of incense tickled her nose.

"Hello?" she called out.

The place was empty except for the icons that observed her quietly. She would have stayed to light a candle, but she was late.

Ipatia shut the door firmly.

"Come, Kitso. We must get to the bakery before it closes," she said, getting on the donkey. Clucking loudly, she sped past the waist-high boundary walls made of rocks and stone that guarded the old almond trees with their knobby branches, olive orchards, and fig trees.

Ahead was the village water basin. Kitso slowed considerably.

"We'll stop by on the way back," Ipatia promised him, patting him reassuringly on the back.

They reached the outskirts of the town-square.

Ipatia jumped off the donkey, tied him to a post, and briskly climbed the whitewashed steps of the alley, intent on her task. The slope was steep, and she was panting by the time she reached the bakery.

To her dismay, Ipatia found the door locked. She tapped loudly on the window hoping someone would be inside. She tapped it again.

Mrs. Poulos, the baker's wife, opened the door, smothering her with the scents of warm, baked bread. Her wide, friendly face broke out into a grin as she gestured Ipatia inside.

"Ipatia, come in. I was just closing up the shop."

Ipatia thankfully chose three loaves of warm, crusty bread, and placed them in her canvas bag. She took the drachmas out of her skirt pocket and began counting the coins.

"No, no, my good girl. This is my farewell gift to you," Mrs. Poulos said, brushing off the proffered hand. She warmly hugged Ipatia, enveloping her in a soft cushion of human kindness.

"Thank you. I will miss you and your family," Ipatia said, feeling sad as unexplained emotions surfaced. It had been a long time since anyone had hugged her.

Mrs. Poulos dabbed away the tears that had formed in her reddened eyes.

"I remember when you used to play with my daughters. Although you were the youngest, you were the best behaved. When they married and left the island, I was sad. Now you are leaving us, and I am sad again."

"Don't worry, Mrs. Poulos, I'll return some day and visit you."

On the way home, guilt feelings threatened to overwhelm Ipatia. *This island isn't so bad after all. At times, I felt sad because I missed my parents, but the kind people here have helped me in so many ways. And what about Pappou? He is all I have, and I will miss him dearly. Besides, he is getting on in years. He needs me here. Oh why, why do I want to leave?*

Her troubled thoughts continued for a few minutes more. Then she remembered why she wanted to leave.

"There is no future for me here except marriage," she said aloud. She sat upright on the donkey, and her back became stiff as a rod. Her determination to leave the island had returned. For some odd reason, she began to feel cheerful. Was it because she would be in Piraeus tomorrow and closer to getting her degree?

They reached the water basin; the donkey stopped, planting his feet firmly. Ipatia laughed as she watched him sipping water under the shade of the old, gnarled olive tree.

He might be a while. She glanced around. There was no one in sight.

Impulsively, she hopped on the edge of the basin and, reaching for the branch, pulled herself up; scrambling for a moment, she finally settled against the crook of the tree. This would be the last time she would sit in her favorite, secluded resting-place, reading her favorite book.

Ipatia pulled out the slim English novel from her skirt pocket and began reading it aloud. An old present from her English tutor, its worn edges were a testimony of the many times that she had read it. Several months had passed since she had last cracked the book open, for she had been too busy. With only a few pages left before the ending, Ipatia laboriously attempted to translate the text into Greek.

How will the heroine in the novel get out of her predicament this time? Ipatia received the answer. The heroine finally declared her true feelings to the man that she loved.

"I love you. I have always loved you," Ipatia announced in English. Her voice sounded loud and triumphant. The hero declared his love in return and promptly proposed to the heroine.

The End.

Feeling oddly dissatisfied, Ipatia shut the book. Her recent decision to pursue a college education over marriage clashed with the story's ending. She sighed. *Have I outgrown the book?*

Something rustled above her, and she glanced upward, thinking it might be a bird. Her breath choked in her throat. She froze. A large, black snake slowly slithered down the trunk of the tree heading towards her. Terrified of snakes, she scrambled blindly to get away. Ipatia pushed her body off the thick branch, expecting to hit the ground. Instead, she found herself floating in air. It took her a moment to realize what had happened. Her long skirt had caught on the branch, and it was holding her up. She twisted her head desperately around to see if the snake was slithering toward her. *It was moving closer.*

Panicking, Ipatia flailed her arms and legs, trying to extricate herself from the branch. Her heart racing with fear, she cried out, "Help! Help!"

A man appeared out of nowhere.

●•———◆ ●•———◆ ●•———◆

Tony's first reaction had been to laugh at the comical scene in front of him; the girl swinging from the branch like a monkey, her arms flailing, her stockinged legs crisscrossing like scissors

Yet when he saw the snake, Tony went into action. He grabbed a branch from the ground and ran toward her.

"Don't move. Don't say anything," he said to the girl, his eyes intently watching the snake.

The girl stopped moving. As if sensing danger, the snake also stopped its movement. Tony reached up and poked the snake. It moved swiftly toward the girl. With a quick, forceful jab from his stick, Tony flung the snake powerfully in the air. It fell with a thud to the ground and slid quickly away, vanishing into the nearby bushes.

Tony jumped on the basin, untangled her skirt, and plucked her off the branch like a ripe apple. Her soft body nestled in his arms, giving him an exhilarating feeling. She opened her eyes. "You are safe now," Tony said reassuringly, gazing down at her beautiful face.

Shivering uncontrollably, the girl pushed herself off his firm chest, toppling ungracefully on to the ground like a sack of potatoes. "Ow," she sputtered, scampering up. She dusted the dirt off her face and arms.

Tony lost his balance from the force of her push and landed in the water with a splash. Trying to stand up, he faltered and slipped back into the water.

"I, I thank you. I have to go," she stammered. She grabbed the donkey's rein and slapping his behind, yelled, "*Ante (Go)."*

"Wait. Wait just a minute," Tony shouted, getting up.

The donkey broke into a trot, pulling her along with him.

Tony watched the fleeing girl as her long sun-kissed tresses streamed behind her. She reminded him of a frightened deer.

He climbed slowly out of the basin, holding steadily on the side for support. His white, cotton shirt and black, cotton pants were drenched. He shook his legs to get rid of the water, removed his soaked shoes, and poured the water out of them. He swore silently. Not only did the girl run away, but she also had the audacity to push him into the water.

Let's be honest. This was the first time a girl ran away from me, and I didn't have a chance to talk to her. She has bruised my ego. In all my twenty-nine years, my good looks always had girls flocking to me. Even my nanny adored me.

His glance fell on the brown book on the ground. The girl must have dropped it. He picked it up, mindful of his wet hands.

"An English novel," he said, somewhat surprised at the discovery. Curious, he opened the cover. On the inside it read, "To Ipatia Kouris, may you enjoy this book. I wish you success and happiness all your life. Love, Mrs. Rodos."

He leafed through the pages, noticing the scribbling along the sides. A piece of paper fluttered out of the book. The large, clumsy handwriting, evidently that of a child's, was shaped into a poem titled "To My Father, Captain Manolis Kouris." Its simple stanzas revealed the admiration and love of a daughter for her father. Tony paused, deep in reflection. The name was familiar.

Could this man be the same Captain Kouris who had once worked for Father?

Tony remembered feeling overcome by a bout of sadness when he learned of the captain's fatal journey with his family. Could this elusive girl, this precocious, tall girl be the surviving daughter of Captain Kouris? The fact that she still wore black clothes several years after their death was a sign she had not gotten over her mourning.

An odd feeling filled his chest, followed by an unexplained yearning to see her again. Tony tucked the poem carefully back into the book trying not to wet it. He checked his watch. He was to meet Michael in front of the yacht at five o'clock.

His sightseeing for the day had ended.

Ipatia ran with Kitso until they reached a safe distance from that man. Panting, she slowed to a walk.

She scolded Kitso, saying, "Why did you have to be so thirsty? If we hadn't stopped at the water basin for you to drink, then I wouldn't have gotten in this mess."

The donkey's large, trusting eyes looked at her sideways.

Feeling guilty, Ipatia patted him on the head and sighed, saying, "I'm not mad at you. I am mad at myself. I should have known better than to be climbing trees."

She recalled that time when she was nine years old and had fallen from the same tree and sprained and cut her ankle. Her grandfather had scolded her and had prohibited her from climbing that tree again. Her impulsiveness had surfaced once again, as it had done in the past.

Ipatia replayed the chain of events in her mind. After she tried to flee from the snake, she found herself hanging from the tree like a bat, flapping her arms in the air and squealing for help.

Giggling nervously at that awkward scene, Ipatia combed her fingers through her unraveled strands and braided her hair once more. The handsome stranger had arrived just in time to save her from the snake. She must have fainted for she didn't remember anything after the man jabbed the snake. One minute she was hanging from the branch, and the next minute, the man was holding her in his arms.

Feeling grateful that he had rescued her, yet apprehensive that he had held her so close, Ipatia didn't know what to think. *What would people say if they had seen me in his arms?*

Daydreaming about being in the young man's strong arms, she succumbed to the emotions coursing through her body. A part of her had wanted to remain snuggled against him, while another part had scolded her for being so bold. *Did I push myself away because of Pappou's strict rules about boys, or was it because I didn't trust my own feelings? Was I afraid that I would fall in love with him?*

"Ipatia Kouris, how could you stoop so low into thinking that because someone saves you that you will fall in love with him?" Ipatia whispered fiercely, realizing her emotions were betraying her resolve not to engage in any relationship. *Yes, but this isn't just anyone. I've never been in a handsome, young man's arms before.*

CHAPTER 2

Rolling hills and deep blue sky,
The sea stood still so I could fly.

Catching glimpses of the calm, blue sea to his left, Tony strolled down a cobblestone path. He had made a good choice for this led to the main road. Both the inviting sun that beamed down on him and the island breeze that ruffled his dark hair had quickly dried his clothes.

This beautiful island was such a different world from the stolid classrooms of Oxford. Here was a magical world where people like Ipatia, once thought dead, came alive.

Tony's thoughts turned to Captain Kouris whom he had met when he was a teenager. Tony's father had wanted him to work in his shipping business and eventually own the company. Determined to attend the university instead, Tony had resisted. His father threatened not to pay for his education unless he first took a voyage with one of his cargo ships. In a last attempt to appease his father, he had conceded to going on the trip. That trip, imprinted in his mind as though it happened yesterday, was how he met Captain Kouris.

Captain Kouris, tall and lean, had a black mustache and a handsome face. His charming manner and zest for life had appealed to Tony. The captain had encouraged Tony to be a member of the crew, believing that by working there, he could find out whether he liked this business or not.

Tony submerged himself in the day-to-day operations of the ship working alongside the men. The work was labor intensive and menial, and Tony became bored. Soon, he began daydreaming about the university instead.

Whenever the captain invited him to play *tavli* (backgammon) with him in the evenings, Tony jumped at the opportunity. He looked forward to those visits, not just for the game, but also for the stories the captain would share.

After a game of backgammon, Tony would ask the good-natured captain if he had any story to share. Captain Kouris would sit back in his chair smoking his pipe and thinking. Then he would inevitably prop his long legs up on the desk, signaling he had found a story. With a gleam in his eyes, he would weave a story so thick with adventure that oftentimes Tony secretly wondered if the captain was making it up. Nevertheless, he was an accomplished storyteller, causing Tony to escape for a few hours.

The day before they docked, the captain asked Tony how he liked the trip, and if he planned to enter into his father's shipping business. Tony confided in him, describing his plans for the university.

The captain listened quietly with a sympathetic face as though he understood. His advice had been "Keep your doors open, because you never know when you will need them."

As the ship pulled into the Piraeus harbor the next day, Tony stood by the captain's side, watching him position the ship expertly. The captain was in a particularly happy mood, talking about his family. He was proud of his young daughter's accomplishments and her love for music.

Once docked, Tony wistfully watched from the deck as Captain Kouris went on shore and kissed his lovely wife and hugged his blonde-haired daughter who was bouncing up and down with excitement. As the captain and his family walked away holding hands, Tony remembered wishing he had such a family. That poignant image had stayed in his mind all these years.

His father, a workaholic, had been too busy to notice Tony's accomplishments and had used money as a way of pacifying him.

Yet even with those troubling thoughts, Tony paused to remember Ipatia's plight; other than her aging grandfather, she had no parents, and he did.

He should be grateful for at least that.

On her way home, Ipatia decided to stop at the Xilouris house. Mrs. Xilouris had said that she was going on the trip to Piraeus tomorrow, and Ipatia needed to talk with her about traveling together.

The whitewashed house stood on the hill exposed to the searing rays of the sun. Ipatia jumped off Kitso and tied him to the gatepost.

Kitso snorted loudly.

"What is it, Kitso?"

Ipatia got her answer. She jumped when she saw the shiny scorpion, scurrying sideways towards them with its tail up in the air. Ipatia's lithe body danced agilely out of its path. *Earlier today, it was the snake and now it's the scorpion.*

She remembered when she was eight years old and visited Maria, her new friend; a huge centipede with thousands of legs had appeared in her path. Panicked, she sidestepped it and raced towards the house. Maria, who had been waiting for her by the door, laughed at Ipatia's frantic dash for cover.

The following day, Ipatia had learned that her parents had died at sea. *Was this scorpion another omen?*

Frowning, Ipatia hiked up the stone path toward the house. She was mildly surprised to find the door shut. Usually, it would be open, and someone would be home. She wondered whether the family were napping. As she turned to leave, she heard someone shouting her name.

"Ipatia."

She turned around.

It was Mrs. Xilouris. She appeared distraught as she hurried up the path toward her, pulling her young son. "Ipatia, I'm so glad you came," she cried, panting heavily.

Ipatia rushed to the thin, wiry woman. She was shocked to see little Nick's arm wrapped in a bloodied cloth and tears streaming down in his face. He had been crying.

"Mrs. Xilouris, what happened?"

"*Aachh*, my little Nick," Mrs. Xilouris wailed, gesturing frantically. "He fell and cut his arm badly on a piece of broken glass. I went to the Clinic, looking for Doctor Thanassis, but he is not there."

"May I see? I hope it wasn't a big cut," Ipatia exclaimed, feeling concerned. Her hand trembled as she took the boy's arm and removed the red-stained cloth.

She was shocked to see a big gash right below the wrist. It bled heavily.

"Oh." Ipatia swallowed hard, trying to ignore the sudden nausea that threatened to overtake her, but when she saw Nick's frightened face, she forgot her own feelings. *He needs help.*

"I'm afraid he will need stitches. We must stop the bleeding," Ipatia said. Recalling what she read in the medical textbook that Dr. Thanassis had lent her, she wrapped the cloth tightly around the wound and pressed firmly on it to stop the bleeding.

"Now press down, like this," Ipatia said to the boy, trying to remain calm. "It will help stop the bleeding."

He did what she told him, and she gently lifted his bandaged arm towards his chest. "Keep your arm up. That's a good boy."

"I don't know what I should do. My husband is in Piraeus, and I have no one here to help me," Mrs. Xilouris wailed.

"Doctor Thanassis might be down at the dock."

Mrs. Xilouris nodded excitedly. "Yes, that's where he probably is. We will go there."

Ipatia knew that Mrs. Xilouris did not have a donkey. "Why don't you let little Nick ride Kitso? It's too far for him to walk,"

Ipatia said, trying to reassure her. "If you like, I could come with you."

"Thank you, Ipatia. God must have sent you," Mrs. Xilouris cried, her face breaking out into a happy expression.

"The reason I stopped by was to see about the trip tomorrow."

Mrs. Xilouris did not reply. She was busy lifting Nick on the donkey and must not have heard her.

"*Ow, ow*," Nick cried, sobbing and looking frightened.

Ipatia patted his leg reassuringly. She turned and spoke to his mother. "Mrs. Xilouris, why don't you ride with him? I think he'll feel better."

Mrs. Xilouris thanked her and settled behind her son on the donkey, embracing him. "Here, lean against me."

Nick obediently rested his head on her breast and shut his eyes. That seemed to pacify him.

Ipatia walked alongside the donkey, singing a favorite tune and trying to cheer them up.

"You'll be fine, little Nick. Just remember to keep your arm up."

He opened his eyes and lifted his arm higher.

"That's right," Ipatia said. "You know, I cut my leg not long ago, and the good doctor took care of it. Everything is fine now. See how I can run with it." She broke out into a short trot.

When she returned, he rewarded her with a weak smile.

Mrs. Xilouris smiled at Ipatia's antics.

Tony approached a small square; its side alleys fanned out from it like spokes. A coffee shop sat at the corner alley and faced the square. It was shielded from the sun's hot rays by a large oak tree. Feeling thirsty, he decided to stop for a drink.

Tony peered inside the shop, his eyes adjusting to the darkness. "Hello?"

A potbellied man with bulging eyes came to the door. He yawned, scratched his stomach, and looked as though he had just woken up.

"Excuse me, but would it be too much trouble to order a drink?" Tony asked politely.

"Certainly, certainly. Stellios Pericles at your service," Stellios said, bowing and displaying his shiny bald, head. He took the order and vanished inside.

Tony sat at one of the tables outside, flexing his fingers and gazing around him. No one else was there. The natives probably had their coffee either earlier in the day or later in the evening when it was cooler. Small, round tables and delicate chairs graced the coffee shop's small courtyard. Painted ceramic flowerpots filled with beautiful red flowers lined the few stairs that led to the door.

A large, unusual vase stood next to the door. Its geometric lines and black figures appeared to be telling a story. The vase cast a spell of another era, its beauty mesmerizing him. Tony stared at it. His university art course had covered Greek art and the design of vases. If his memory served him right, the geometric style evident on this vase could prove to make it a very ancient vessel indeed, at least two thousand years old, if not older. *It should be in a museum.*

Mr. Pericles returned swiftly with a bottle of cold Coca Cola and a glass, saying, "With all due respect, did you have an accident?" He stared at Tony's damp clothes.

Tony had forgotten about his clothes. He chuckled. "Yes, they are almost dried." He guzzled down the Coca Cola, enjoying its fizzy coolness.

"You are not from around here. Your accent tells me you are from Crete, am I right, Mr.?"

Tony felt somewhat surprised at this man's acumen. Years at Oxford had blended the English with the Greek, resulting in his pronouncing Greek with a British clip. "Tony, Tony Plakis. Yes, I came with the yacht last night. We had to dock here because of the storm," he said. He peered at Mr. Pericles with half-closed eyes and ascertained that this man looked sincere enough. Yet he had learned a long time ago not to give out personal information freely, especially when one was wealthy. Wealth was like a magnet. It drew all kinds of people to him, particularly the needy ones; they usually wanted favors or money.

"Yes, the storm was a bad one, but we are used to them," Mr. Pericles said, nodding his head. "We get those around this time of year."

"Excuse me, but would you happen to know a person by the name of Ipatia Kouris?" Tony asked. "I have something which belongs to her."

"Yes, yes, of course. I know everyone here. I have been here all my life," Mr. Pericles boasted. "You see that hill up there, Mr. Tony?" He pointed towards a hill in the distance.

Tony gazed at that direction, shading his eyes from the sun and nodded.

"She lives up there with her grandfather, Christos Rodakis. He comes down every morning and stops here for coffee."

"Is it easy enough to go there?"

"You will need a horse or a donkey, and at least one hour to go and come back. Otherwise, it's a long walk," Mr. Pericles said, shaking his head knowingly as he glanced down at the young man's shoes.

"Oh, I see," Tony said. His boat shoes were not the best shoes for walking an hour on rocky paths.

His curiosity was provoked once more when his eyes fell upon the vase. "Mr. Pericles, where did you get that vase?" Tony pointed to it.

"A couple of years ago, Mr. Rodakis needed a horse. You see, I sell horses on the side. He's an old man, with limited means, and all he had was this vase to give me at the time. Since we are friends, we worked out a deal. I gave him the horse, and the vase was used as collateral until he came up with the money to pay for the horse."

"I see you still have the vase."

"Mr. Rodakis is old and doesn't have much money. He gets by with what little he has. Years ago, when his wife died, I found a buyer who was interested in his land, but last minute he backed out and decided to keep it." Mr. Pericles shrugged his shoulders. "Even worse, the horse I gave him has died on him, and he refuses to pay me for it. Now I am stuck with the vase. It's good only for plants."

"The vase should be in a museum."

"We have a small museum here on the island," Mr. Pericles said, nodding. "The priest oversees it, and it houses several interesting artifacts. He has shown interest in the vase, but I haven't gotten around to it."

"Is that right?" Tony asked. If he had more time on the island, he could visit the museum. "How did Mr. Rodakis come across the vase?"

"It was a present form his late son-in-law, Captain Manolis Kouris. He traveled all over the world, and whenever he visited Lipsi, he would bring him presents. Now Mr. Rodakis's daughter and son-in-law both are in the sea, God rest their souls."

Mr. Pericles bowed reverently while making the sign of the cross.

Feeling saddened by the story, Tony pulled out his leather wallet and placed a few bills on the table. "I must be going, Mr. Pericles. Thank you for your kind service."

Mr. Pericles picked up the bills, his large eyes bulging from the amount.

"Please, keep the change."

"Thank you, Mr. Tony," Mr. Pericles said, beaming.

"What time do you expect Mr. Rodakis tomorrow?"

"Around nine o'clock or so. Stop by then, Mr. Tony. We are more than happy to serve you," Mr. Pericles replied, shaking his hand.

CHAPTER 3

The book which did belong to me
Did change my whole life's destiny.

Ipatia trudged alongside Kitso, singing softly and holding on to his rein while Mrs. Xilouris sat quietly with her son on the donkey.

"Look. There's Mr. Pericles," Mrs. Xilouris cried. "Maybe he will know where the doctor is."

Mr. Pericles stood outside his coffee shop, his back turned to them. He appeared to be conversing deeply with someone.

Ipatia handed the reins to Mrs. Xilouris and ran toward him. "Mr. Pericles, Mr. Pericles."

"Why Ipatia, hello. We were just talking about you and-"

"Little Nick Xilouris fell and cut himself badly," Ipatia blurted, interrupting Mr. Pericles and pointing to the boy on the donkey.

"My God," Mr. Pericles exclaimed. He rushed towards the boy and his mother.

As Ipatia watched Mr. Pericles talking excitedly with Mrs. Xilouris and examining the boy's arm, she sensed someone's presence behind her. Curious, she turned to find a pair of warm, liquid brown eyes gazing at her. Her breath caught in her throat. *He was the same man who saved me earlier from the snake.* She blushed at the memory, embarrassed at seeing him again.

Ipatia fled towards the donkey and Mr. Pericles, not knowing what to say.

The man also had not spoken.

Partially hidden behind the donkey, she quietly assessed the stranger. For the first time, she noticed his exceedingly handsome demeanor. He was tall for a Greek and had an athletic build of Olympian proportions. His fine, noble nose and firm chin added to his handsome features.

He had turned his gaze on the injured child, his expressive eyes revealing a sadness that touched her inner being. Her knees became weak. The man's sad gaze reminded her of her father when he had looked at her in that manner, when she had injured herself as a child. Memories of her father came rushing to the surface. Her loss threatened to overwhelm her, and Ipatia brushed the tears from her eyes. Trying to remain focused on what Mrs. Xilouris was saying, she shifted her gaze to the distraught woman.

"Mr. Pericles, do you know where we can find Dr. Thanassis?" Mrs. Xilouris cried anxiously. "Little Nick has lost much blood, and I don't know what to do. Please, tell me. *Please*."

"He was here at the shop just this morning; he said he was going to Patmos to get medical supplies," Mr. Pericles replied, scratching his head and looking worried. "I don't know when he'll be back."

"He went to Patmos?" Mrs. Xilouris wailed, wringing her hands. "What am I to do?"

The handsome stranger approached them. "Madam, excuse me for intruding on your conversation, but I know a doctor who can help you."

"What?" Mrs. Xilouris said, looking up at him with a confused air.

"Doctor Michael came on the ship last night, and I am supposed to meet him at the dock. I can show you where he is," Tony offered.

Mrs. Xilouris looked at the stranger, and then at Mr. Pericles with a puzzled air as if to say, "Who is this man?"

Mr. Pericles made the proper introductions, smiling. "Mrs. Xilouris, this is Mr. Tony. He is a friend of mine. He will help you."

"Thank you so much," Mrs. Xilouris said to Tony, her voice full of emotion.

They bid Mr. Pericles farewell and headed down the sloping path toward the dock.

Ipatia stayed on the left side of the donkey, slightly hidden, while Mr. Tony walked on its right.

"Mrs. Xilouris, could you tell me a little bit about the island?" Tony asked, trying to steer the conversation away from the young boy's arm.

With a high-pitched voice that revealed her unsuccessful attempt to harness her emotions, Mrs. Xilouris informed him about the island. "In ancient times, this island, some claim, was called Calypso. It used to be much bigger than it is now. Divers have discovered a part of this island buried under water. They have found old vases and coins," she said, pointing towards the sea.

"Also, giant bones, this big, have been discovered on the island," Ipatia blurted. She stretched out her arms to the length of two feet.

Tony was surprised to hear this. "Really?" he asked, raising his eyebrows. "Are they human bones?"

"*Pappou* said they were giants who once lived here. Also, some farmers discovered pirate's treasures, gold, buried on their land."

"Ipatia, let's not get carried away," Mrs. Xilouris retorted, laughing nervously. "You know how rumors travel around here. Someone finds a gold coin and suddenly it becomes a pirate's treasure."

"Hmm, it sounds interesting anyway," Tony said, noticing the girl's subdued look. "How many people live on the island?"

"Oh, close to seven hundred, I guess, but we get a lot of tourists during the holidays and particularly in the summer," Mrs. Xilouris replied. "But for hundreds of years, this island belonged to the Monastery of St. John the Theologian on Patmos Island and the monks maintained the land."

"There's a cave on Patmos, halfway up the mountain, where St. John lived and wrote the Book of Revelations," Ipatia said. "The cave holds the lightning strike that the saint witnessed and there are indentations on the wall from when he would bow his head against the wall when praying."

"Amazing," Tony said. "So how did people end up settling on the island?"

"During the revolutionary war, in the 1800s, Lipsi became a refuge island. After Greece became independent from Turkish rule, many people who had come here ended up settling here, including my relatives. But once the children grow up, many leave the island, either for better work or to marry someone from another island," Mrs. Xilouris replied.

Tony was pleased that Mrs. Xilouris had calmed down; their conversation had diverted her attention from her son's injury. "How far are the other islands from here?" he asked.

Mrs. Xilouris scrunched her tanned face, thinking. "Patmos Island is northeast of here, and to our south is Leros Island," she replied. "Captain John's boat can make it in thirty to forty minutes to either island, depending on the weather. Most of our supplies come from those two islands. In the wintertime, due to the weather and high waves, travel is limited, and our fuel and supplies should last us through the winter."

Tony glanced at Ipatia, wondering if she would join the conversation, but she remained silent. "I hear you also have a few Cretans living here?"

"Oh, yes. My family is from there, and there are other families from Crete," Ipatia piped. "They came many years ago."

"Almost everyone here is related, either through marriage or by birth," Mrs. Xilouris said, tittering.

"Do you get many tourists in the summer?" he asked.

"Dear, yes. Many visitors are relatives, traveling from abroad, while others are from Germany, Sweden, or from other countries.

When the hotels are full, sometimes they come knocking on our door to get a room."

They passed a small church. Both women made the sign of the cross.

"For an island with so few families, it struck me that there are so many churches," Tony remarked.

"There are close to forty of them," Mrs. Xilouris said proudly. The monks from Patmos built churches, and since then, due to a number of reasons, many people have also built their own chapels."

"The main church on Lipsi is named after St. John, and is located next to the Plaka, near the harbor. We attend Sunday liturgy there, but not all the time," Ipatia said.

"Why not?" Tony asked, studying her lively expression. It seemed as if she were enjoying herself.

"When a saint's name day falls on a Sunday, then we attend the Sunday service at the church that is dedicated to that saint," offered Ipatia.

"Interesting," Tony said.

"A few churches are a good distance away, like Agios Spiridon and Agios Pandeleimon in Katsaidia. On a certain saints' name day, my grandfather and I would leave the house early just to make it in time for the service. Sometimes we'd leave two hours early."

"Two hours?" Tony asked. "I find that hard to believe."

"My grandfather rides the donkey, and I walk alongside him," explained Ipatia.

Tony combed his fingers through his wavy black hair, touched by the girl's respect for her grandfather and her strong faith. Should he mention that he visited the church of the Virgin of Haron earlier today?

Instead, Tony pointed to some site in the distance and asked, "Where does that lead to?"

"To Plati Yialo, all the way to the other side," Mrs. Xilouris said proudly. "There are no main roads, and it's rocky and far, so one usually goes by donkey. The water is very clear and shallow there, and it tends to be a favorite place for picnics. Often, we see tourists snorkeling there."

Mrs. Xilouris rambled on about the rest of the island, not needing any prompting from Tony. She covered the beaches at Liendou Bay, and when she started to talk about Katsaidia, which was located further away, she hesitated.

"What were you going to say about Katsaidia?" Tony prompted.

"There are two sides to everything," Mrs. Xilouris said. "The same with this island. We may have the churches, but we also have the nudists. Katsaidia, for some reason, attracts tourists who like to swim without their clothes."

"I'm afraid your island doesn't have a monopoly on them," Tony said, laughing heartily.

He caught Ipatia blushing and looking mortified. *She probably thought it improper of Mrs. Xilouris to be discussing this topic with me.*

Nick moaned, and Mrs. Xilouris stopped her chatter. She focused on him, speaking in a worried voice. "Does it hurt?" she asked him anxiously.

"The road is bumpy," he mumbled.

"Here, let us stop for a moment," Mrs. Xilouris said.

They stopped, and Tony remembered that he was carrying the little book he found earlier in his hand. He lifted the book, revealing the title to Ipatia's inquisitive eyes. "I suppose this is your book I am carrying, Ipatia?" he asked in English.

Ipatia's eyes became large when she saw it. "Yes, but how did you know my name, that I knew English, and that this was my book?" Ipatia asked in English.

"First of all, my darling girl, I happened to be walking down the road when I overheard your beautiful voice singing out from the tree," he admitted. "I think I heard the following words "I love you with all my heart."

She appeared startled.

"Of course, intrigued by what I heard, I came closer and discovered you sitting in the tree reading the book and speaking these words. Little did I know you would end up dropping your book to the ground, hanging from the tree, and needing to be rescued from a snake."

He was goading her and laughed heartily, enjoying her flushed cheeks and stormy eyes.

"Will you please give me back my book?"

"Where I come from, when people are rescued from snakes, the rescuer receives a token of appreciation, a gift," he teased. "Saving your life is not a small thing."

She was silent. "What gift would you like?" she asked timidly.

"I haven't decided yet, so until that time, I guess I'll have to keep the book as collateral."

He placed the book inside his shirt and started whistling. This book was a part of Ipatia, and he wasn't too keen on letting go of her yet.

They had arrived at the large dock. A young couple stood in front of the foreign yacht.

"That man over there is Dr. Michael Hatzis, a friend of the family. The girl next to him is my sister, Melissa," Tony said, pointing to them. "Please wait here a minute."

He left the group under the shade of a tree and approached the couple.

"Hi Tony," Melissa called.

"Sorry I'm late," Tony said, bending down to kiss his sister's cheek. He patted Michael on the back.

"Your little sister has been the perfect hostess and has kept me company during your absence," Michael said, smiling.

Melissa's blushing confirmed Tony's suspicion that his younger sister had more than a crush on his best friend.

"Where are all the others?" Tony asked, looking around expectantly.

"We left the parents behind at the hotel. Bonnie and Chuck, I mean Mr. Daras, went ahead and are waiting for us at the taverna," Melissa explained.

"You go ahead, sis. I need to borrow Michael for a medical emergency." Tony explained little Nick's situation to Michael.

"I'll need to get my medical bag from the yacht," Michael said. "He will probably need stitches."

"The Captain's cabin is available if you need it," Tony informed him.

Melissa's blue eyes focused on Michael. "Will I see you later at the taverna?" she asked sweetly.

"Yes," Michael replied.

"Don't be too long," Melissa said, tossing her blonde hair in a flirtatious manner as she sauntered away.

<HAPT<R 4

Whether by fate or by chance,
I will now take a stance.

While Ipatia and Mrs. Xilouris waited for Mr. Tony to get the doctor, Mrs. Xilouris reprimanded her.

"Ipatia, I didn't understand a word of English that you were saying to that man," she said sharply. "If your grandfather learned that you were conversing boldly with him in English, he would have a fit."

Ipatia felt her face heat up. She didn't have time to reply, for Mr. Tony had arrived with the young doctor.

"Mrs. Xilouris, this is Dr. Hatzis. He said he could help little Nick," Mr. Tony said.

"Thank you, Dr. Hatzis," Mrs. Xilouris said, bobbing her head up and down.

Michael nodded his greeting to her and then approached the boy, touching his arm and discerning his condition. "And what happened here, little Nick?"

Little Nick mumbled that he cut his arm with broken glass.

Michael turned to Mrs. Xilouris. "My medical bag is on the yacht. Let's carry him inside so I can treat him there."

"Ipatia, please come with me," Mrs. Xilouris whispered, holding Ipatia's arm tightly. "You know how people gossip around here."

Ipatia silently agreed, knowing that tongues would be wagging if they saw Mrs. Xilouris going into the yacht with this strange man.

"Here, don't be afraid. I will carry you inside so the doctor can help you," Tony said, lifting Nick gently.

Ipatia watched Tony, feeling a strong sense of security as though he were carrying her and not Nick in his capable arms. She tied Kitso to the tree. Mrs. Xilouris clutched her arm as they followed the men up the ramp and into the yacht.

Ipatia's eyes were wide with wonder at the size and luxuriousness of the yacht. They entered a carpeted lounge with large windows on each side. It held a white, leather couch with two matching loveseats, and two round tables with chairs and a wet bar. They walked through the lounge and into the dining room. It had to be the dining room, because in the center stood a large table with chairs that could seat at least twelve people. The Oriental rugs, Chinese paintings, vases, and Oriental furniture transported her into an exotic world.

They walked down a set of stairs and through a hallway with doors on each side. Ipatia almost slipped on the shiny, teak floor.

The doctor entered a room and returned, holding his black medical bag. They walked a few doors down and stopped in front of the Captain's cabin.

"Could you please wait out here? I will call you after I finish," Dr. Hatzis told Mrs. Xilouris and Ipatia.

"Thank you for your help," Mrs. Xilouris said. She kissed her son on the forehead, whispering tearful endearments before leaving.

"Your son is in good hands, Mrs. Xilouris," Tony said.

Dr. Hatzis entered the captain's cabin with Tony and the boy.

"You've been a brave boy," Tony said, placing the boy on the Captain's chair. He cleared the table and made room for Michael's bag. "Dr. Hatzis is a good doctor. You will receive the best treatment."

Dr. Hatzis closed the door.

The two women waited outside. Mrs. Xilouris shut her eyes and clasped her hands tightly as though she were praying.

Ipatia said a silent prayer for the boy. "How are your daughters, Maria and Joanna, doing in Crete?" she asked. "I wrote to Maria but haven't received a letter yet."

"Maria and Joanna? They are doing fine. My Maria is three months pregnant," Mrs. Xilouris said. "She probably didn't write to you because she's been having bouts of morning sickness and hasn't been feeling well. Joanna is helping her, though."

"Maria's pregnant. How wonderful," Ipatia exclaimed. "Will you be going to visit them?"

"I'm afraid it's not so simple," Mrs. Xilouris said, sighing. "My Nick is in Piraeus, and he was expecting me on this trip, but now I'll have to wait until little Nick gets better. Then we'll see about visiting the girls."

"Oh, I was hoping you'd be able to go with me tomorrow," Ipatia whispered, realizing the impact of the woman's words.

"I'm so sorry," Mrs. Xilouris said, touching Ipatia's arm apologetically. "Why don't you wait, and we can go together later?"

"It's not so easy. I wrote to my aunt that I would be leaving tomorrow," Ipatia said firmly.

"Let me ask you a question, my girl. Why are you going to Piraeus? Don't you want to marry one day? There are some nice young men here, like Stamatis."

"Stamatis, the balloon?" Ipatia blurted, remembering the nickname she used to give him when they were children.

"You should see him now," Mrs. Xilouris said proudly. "He returned from his studies, and they hired him at the post office as a clerk. He is no longer the boy who used to tease you and pull your braids. If he weren't my nephew, I would have wished him for one of my girls."

Ipatia shook her head. "I know you mean well, but I'm not interested in getting married. When my parents died, I felt much sadness and pain, and it took me a long time to get over that. I don't ever want to feel so much pain again if someone I loved passed away."

"I understand, but you can't go through life feeling afraid," Mrs. Xilouris said gently. "Your parents are somewhere in heaven, a better place than here. God took them for a reason although we don't always see it."

The clicking sound of a woman's heels interrupted their conversation. A glamorous looking woman, like one of those models Ipatia used to see in the international fashion magazines in Rhodes, approached them, her hips swinging.

"Is Tony here?" Bonnie asked. Her pale blue eyes flashed at the two women.

Ipatia nodded, gesturing towards the closed door. "He is in there," she said.

The woman's unexpected entrance, followed by that question dampened Ipatia's spirits. She observed her as she walked to the door. Her flawless skin was a golden hue and her straight, platinum blonde hair bobbed to her shoulders. The low-cut turquoise summer dress revealed an abundant bosom and shapely legs.

Bonnie boldly opened the door. "*Yiasas,*" she purred her greeting to the two men.

"Bonnie?" Tony asked, looking surprised. "Is everything all right?"

"Yes. Melissa told me what had happened, and I came to see whether you needed help," Bonnie said, leaning against the doorway seductively.

"It depends on Michael here," Tony replied slowly.

"Thanks, but everything is under control," Michael said, looking up briefly. "I need to work fast before the anesthetic stops working. Tony, you are free to go."

"All right, Michael. Thanks for everything," Tony replied. He turned to the boy and saluted him.

Tony walked out into the hallway. Bonnie sidled next to him and placed her hand possessively on his arm.

A burning desire to know what relationship this woman had with Tony consumed Ipatia. *Could this woman be his wife?*

She acted like it.

Mrs. Xilouris extended her arm to Tony. "Again, thank you so much for your help, Mr. Tony."

He smiled and shook her hand. "I am glad I could help, Mrs. Xilouris, but I didn't do much. It's the good doctor you should thank instead."

Tony's beautiful, expressive eyes settled on Ipatia. He looked as though he wanted to say something to her.

Ipatia also felt a need to say something to him, anything, even to ask him about her book, although she knew the answer. Her thoughts were interrupted by Mrs. Xilouris's sharp cough. *She was like a mother hen protecting her young.*

"Goodbye," Tony said, leaving with Bonnie.

Ipatia numbly nodded her farewell, watching them walk away. They made a handsome couple.

After they left, she felt empty and cold as though he had taken his warmth with him.

Dr. Hatzis called out loudly, "Mrs. Xilouris, could you please come here, quickly?"

She ran inside the room.

Ipatia peeked inside. The boy was wailing and kicking his feet in the air. Mrs. Xilouris went and held him, her calm tone helping to relax him and allowing Dr. Hatzis to finish stitching the wound.

Ipatia's stomach revolted at the sight of the blood oozing from the wound. Shutting the door, she leaned against it, feeling a bout of nausea overwhelm her.

●●————◈ ●●————◈ ●●————◈

Bonnie pressed lightly against Tony as he held her arm, leading her off the ship. The scent of her rich perfume was overpowering. With mixed feelings, he gazed at her. She was an attractive woman, and she knew it.

A strong gust of wind swept through the area, ruffling his hair and the water, causing the small boats docked there to bob up and down. The unsettling idea occurred to him that Bonnie was like this gust of wind, moving in and stirring things up.

He combed his hair back nervously, wondering what Ipatia must have thought when she observed Bonnie's bold entrance.

"I was surprised to see you," he began tightly.

Bonnie smiled. "I hope you don't mind my coming and offering you help. I needed an excuse to apologize for my outburst the other day," she said huskily. "With only a few days left before your return to England, I didn't want to spend the rest of the time with hard feelings coming between us."

"I accept your apology," Tony said civilly. "By the way, the disagreement was because you were complaining about my returning to England. I am not going to another planet. England is only a few hours away by airplane."

"The way you've been avoiding me since our argument, Tony Plakis, sometimes I feel you *are* on another planet," she retorted.

Tony winced at the reminder of their argument two days ago. Her controlling character had surfaced when she stated that she wanted him to remain in Greece and become involved in his father's shipping business. He adamantly refused, saying his intentions were to leave for England. Instead of going along with his decision, she continued, pressing her case. He resisted her controlling behavior, which reminded him of his father and doggedly repeated his desire to leave for England.

When Bonnie broke down crying, he had placed his arm around her, trying to comfort her. His weakness for crying women made him promise he would come and visit her in Greece. That was his undoing, for Bonnie took the opportunity to kiss him, declaring her love for him. Surprised by her bold action, Tony left abruptly.

He hadn't talked with her since then, avoiding her.

"I think there has been a misunderstanding between us, Bonnie. When you were crying, I was trying to comfort you as a friend," he said. "You see, I don't like to see women cry."

Bonnie remained silent for a moment, her eyes lowered. "I guess you don't feel the same way about me as I do you."

Tony decided not to reply to her statement, not wanting to get into another argument. Instead, he asked politely, "Will you be returning to the taverna?"

"No," she said shakily. "I'm not hungry, and besides, Chuck and Melissa are doing fine without anyone else there."

"Oh?" Tony asked. A wealthy ship owner in his early forties, Chuck Daras had been invited on the trip to discuss buying a ship from the Plakis Shipping Company. Tony hadn't considered him a possible match for Melissa since Melissa had been showing considerable interest in Michael for some time.

He wondered what developments his little sister was concocting.

"What are your plans for tonight?" Bonnie asked.

"First, I need to see Father, then I need to shower and retire for the evening," he replied wearily, gesturing at his wrinkled clothes.

"Do you mind if I join you?" she asked, taking his arm possessively. "We can make up for lost time."

They walked towards the hotel.

Tony was silent, feeling mixed emotions about this woman, contemplating on what to say. He was keenly conscious of her body leaning seductively against him. "You never told me what made you become a fashion designer?" he asked, making small talk.

"I always liked clothes, ever since I was a girl. When I finished my studies to become a fashion designer, I went to Paris. There, I modeled a bit and worked at boutique shops," she said.

"Ahhh, did you like it?" he asked, prompted by her silence.

"Of course, you darling man," she said, pecking him lightly on the cheek. "You see this dress I am wearing? I designed it after spending time in Paris."

She provocatively posed for him, turning slowly with her head at an angle, modeling her dress.

"It becomes you, but the neckline, isn't it a bit low?"

"That's the style, silly," she said, laughing flirtatiously. "I thought you liked low necklines."

He silently disagreed. Low necklines were not for public display.

They entered the hotel. Tony recognized Irene, the Greek American hotel manager, who stood behind the counter, chatting with Christina, his stepmother. Irene waved to him, and he waved back. She was an asset to the island, for she was not only friendly, but she could speak Greek and English easily.

Christina turned and saw them. When his father married the thirty-eight-year-old heiress four years ago, Tony had been shocked. He had assumed his father would never remarry. He could never think of Christina as a mother.

"Hello, you two," Christina said, going to meet them. "Tony, your father's been expecting you."

"I will go to him," Tony said, politely excusing himself.

Dr. Hatzis finished wrapping the bandage around the boy's wound. "All done," he said matter-of-factly.

"Thank you very much, doctor. May the good Lord and the Panagia bless you!" Mrs. Xilouris cried with tears in her eyes as she touched the shoulder of her son.

He smiled. "I am glad I could be of service. Is there any water here? A pitcher, maybe?"

Mrs. Xilouris found a pitcher of water on a small table and handed it to him.

He pulled a linen cloth from his bag and wetting a portion of it, started cleaning the blood stains methodically from the table. Next, he took a small bottle of alcohol from his bag and pouring it on the rest of the cloth, wiped the table again. Pulling out a clean handkerchief from his pocket, he wiped his spectacles.

Mrs. Xilouris opened the door and gestured to Ipatia to join them.

Ipatia hesitated before entering the room. She knew that Mrs. Xilouris didn't want to be in the room alone with the doctor, but at the same time, she wasn't sure how her stomach would handle the situation.

Luckily, little Nick sat quietly on the chair, and his arm was bandaged. Although his face was still wet from the tears, there was no blood in sight. Everything had been cleaned.

Ipatia relaxed.

"There is nothing to fear, Mrs. Xilouris. Although he lost some blood, little Nick will recover quickly," Dr. Hatzis said. Before putting his glasses on, he studied Ipatia with his cold, blue eyes. "Are you his sister?"

"No, I'm a friend of the family," Ipatia replied timidly, her breath catching in her throat under his scrutiny. He was studying her like some insect.

"I see," he said, smiling warmly. He put his spectacles back on and took a little bottle out of his bag. "Mrs. Xilouris, I stitched the wound and gave him a dose of antibiotics. Here is enough for a week. We don't want him to get an infection."

"Thank you, doctor," Mrs. Xilouris said, shaking his hand after he gave her the medicine.

"The local anesthetic will wear off soon. He needs to follow up with the island doctor."

"Yes, doctor. How much do I owe you?" Mrs. Xilouris asked as she carefully placed the medicine in her pocket.

He hesitated, then told her the cost for the medicine.

She searched her pockets. "Oh, my," she mumbled, turning red. "I didn't bring any money with me. Can I bring it to you in a few days?"

"That's all right. We are leaving tomorrow."

Ipatia dipped her hand in her pocket; retrieving the coins left from the bakery, she counted them. "Here is all the money I have," she said, firmly placing all the drachmas in the doctor's hand. "It's a little short, but- "

"Oh, thank you, Ipatia!" Mrs. Xilouris exclaimed. "I will pay it back to your grandfather."

Dr. Hatzis nodded, appearing pleased. "Thank you, young lady, that is sufficient. What is your name again?"

"Ipatia Kouris," she replied. He was staring at her again. She blushed.

"Ipatia?" he asked. "I think it belonged to a famous female mathematician and philosopher. She lived in Alexandria, around the year four hundred or so, am I right?"

Ipatia nodded silently, knowing the story. "Will Mr. Tony and his wife also leave with you tomorrow?"

At first, Dr. Hatzis appeared puzzled. "Yes, we will all be leaving together tomorrow, but Mr. Tony is not married," he replied. "What made you think that?"

"The woman that came earlier-" she began and stopped after Mrs. Xilouris pinched her arm.

"Oh, Bonnie. She is a good friend of his sister."

"Mr. Tony has been kind to us. We will never forget his helping our little Nick," Mrs. Xilouris said, beaming.

"Yes, he is a good man," Dr. Hatzis said.

Mrs. Xilouris bid the doctor farewell, thanking him several times.

Minutes later, Ipatia and Mrs. Xilouris lifted Nick back on Kitso; Mrs. Xilouris settled behind him.

"Let's use the main road," Ipatia said. "I need to hurry home since it is getting late, and I have much explaining to do."

CHAPTER 5

What matter all the wealth
If one doesn't have one's health?

Tony strode through the hotel lobby and up the stairs to his father's room. He entered the suite and went directly to the balcony where he found his father leaning against the handrail, listening intently to a worker who was speaking to him. Beyond the balcony, the blue waters of Liendou Bay shimmered like a Monet oil painting.

Gregory Plakis's observant eyes took in Tony's disheveled appearance. "Did everything go well with your tour of the island?" he asked, interrupting the man next to him.

Tony gave him a summary of the events that had occurred, mindful of the lanky worker who was listening to their conversation. At some point, the worker coughed politely.

Gregory pulled out his wallet and gave the man several bills, saying, "Here is payment for your labor and for the new part, Alex."

Alex thanked him and left.

"Did they fix the engine problem?" Tony asked his father, sitting down in a chair.

"No," Gregory admitted. "Alex told me the engine was affected by the storm and beyond repair, so we ordered a new part. The part won't be here for several weeks."

"What about the other engine?"

"It hasn't been working well, either. We have no other choice but to leave the yacht behind and travel back by ferry."

"I suppose no airplanes come by this way," Tony said dryly.

"Oh, no, no," Gregory said, shaking his head. "This small island doesn't have that capacity. We'll leave on the ship for Piraeus tomorrow afternoon."

"That'll do. I have to be in Athens by Tuesday to catch a flight back to England."

Gregory eyed his son skeptically. "Tony, why are you doing this to me? I don't want you returning to England. I need you by my side."

"You've done well all these years without me," Tony retorted.

The words came out quickly, catching Tony by surprise. Although relevant to the discussion at hand, these words held a deeper meaning for him. His father had sent him away to boarding school when his mother had died. He had never taken the time to attend Tony's school events and graduations because he had been too busy. He had sent money instead. This same father, when Tony had fallen ill, had sent a nurse to assist him and never visited him once in the hospital. Now, his father was not making a simple request. He was asking him to change his way of life.

"Let me be frank with you, my son. I have not been doing well with my health lately," Gregory said, rubbing his head.

"What are you talking about?" Tony asked, perplexed. This was something new.

Gregory became quiet. "Do you remember when I almost fell in the yacht's dining room a few days ago, and you caught me? I had given the excuse about tripping over something. That was not the truth." He sighed. "Lately, I've been having these spells, fainting spells, and I black out."

Tony stared at him, feeling helpless. He had always assumed his omnipotent father would always be there, managing the family business. Now his father was pleading for help, pleading for forgiveness. "Why didn't you tell me this sooner?"

"I didn't realize its importance at the time," Gregory replied, shrugging. "I talked with Michael this morning because I had another spell. He thinks I should see a doctor he knows when we return home. He says these severe spells might be caused by something serious."

Tony felt his stomach churn with anxiety. "Something serious? Like what?"

His father remained silent, staring out at the sea.

"Did he tell you how serious?" Tony insisted, his heart beginning to race. His father's continued silence threatened to destroy any peace that Tony felt. "Tell me, Father."

"It could be a brain tumor," Gregory finally replied, his voice low and heavy.

Having a brain tumor was like being given a death sentence. Feeling a foreboding feeling settle in his heart, Tony digested this unsettling news. "Maybe it's not as serious as that," he said hopefully.

"Whether or not it is serious, I'm going to be too busy with the doctors going through tests to be managing the business."

"Is that the reason why you've been asking me to join you recently?"

Gregory nodded and looked at Tony, his eyes reddened. "The company needs a head and what better one than my son."

Tony's heart filled with compassion for his father's plight. "I will help you," he said, his voice filled with emotion. In an unusual display of warmth, he went to his father and hugged him tightly.

"Good. I knew you would pull through." Gregory's voice shook as he patted his son on the back.

"I don't have much experience with cargo ships, though," Tony admitted, after the show of emotion subsided.

"If only you had listened to me when you were young. I would have had you managing the business years ago. But you wanted to get your graduate degree in Economics from Oxford," Gregory scoffed, shaking his head.

Tony nodded his head contritely, knowing that he could not afford to argue with his sick father. He didn't want to worsen his condition.

"Yet there is no need to worry. I will give you advice whenever I can," said, softening. "Also, there is plenty of help from others. Sarkalos, our fleet manager, does the day-to-day management. Spithas, our attorney, handles the legal papers, and several others on our staff are experienced and knowledgeable. They will help you."

Christina glided on to the balcony.

"Hello, honey," Gregory said, smiling fondly at her.

"Hello, dear," she said sweetly, kissing his cheek. "Shouldn't we join the others at the taverna? It might do you some good to eat a little."

"Who's at the taverna?" Gregory asked getting up.

"Bonnie told me that Chuck Daras and Melissa were there," Christina replied.

"And where's Bonnie?" Gregory asked.

"She went to her room. She said she had a headache."

"Oh?" Gregory asked, surprised. "Tony, what did you say to her this time?"

They all walked toward the door.

Tony shrugged his shoulders. "Father, I told you before you invited her on the trip, that she's not my type. She is nice to look at, but all she talks about is herself and her clothes. You didn't listen to me."

"This is your chance to marry into a rich family and the best you can do is say she's not your type," Gregory complained.

"Can you please stop this fussing?" Christina said.

"What's wrong with what I said?" Gregory asked, shrugging his shoulders. "Now I have Chuck Daras confiding in me that he is interested in Melissa. Do you know he owns several ships and is an expert in the shipping business?"

"So long as Michael is around, I don't think Melissa will marry Chuck," Tony said dryly.

"You may be right," Gregory replied, looking skeptical.

"Tony, will you be joining us for dinner?" asked Christina.

"I'm afraid not. I feel exhausted by the events of today," he said wearily.

"Then get some rest. We will continue our conversation at another time," Gregory said, nodding. He opened the door for Christina, smiling at her. She smiled back. He gently put his hand on her waist and left with her.

His father was still handsome and commanded a presence while Christina's attractive features complemented his.

They were good for each other.

Tony entered his own room which was next door and went and stood on his balcony. He gazed at the beautiful sunset, thinking about his conversation with his father and wondering what his changing world would hold in the future.

He stood there for a long time.

⋅⋅⋅⟶⟶⋅⋅⋅⟶⋅⋅⋅⟶

Ipatia trudged along holding Kitsos's reins while Mrs. Xilouris and little Nick sat on him. They reached the fork in the road that led to Mrs. Xilouris's house.

"Mrs. Xilouris, can you continue without me? I'm late and Grandfather will be worried. It's quicker for me to go through the fields."

Mrs. Xilouris dismounted and hugged her. "Thank you for all your help," she said, "I am sorry I cannot go with you on the trip."

"That's all right," Ipatia said. "Don't worry about me. You'll see, Nick will be all right, and you'll be in Piraeus with your husband soon."

"What about your donkey?"

"Please send Kitso back to our house when you are done with him. He knows the way."

Ipatia untied the bag of loaves from the saddle as Mrs. Xilouris settled back on the donkey.

"Have a good trip!" Mrs. Xilouris said. She held the reins and clucked to Kitso. He began to trudge forward. She turned and waved to Ipatia. Little Nick turned and waved to her also.

Ipatia waved to them and smiled. "Goodbye!" As soon as they were out of sight, she began running as fast as she could. Her agile, slim legs took her swiftly up the hill, off the main road. She ran through the fields, jumping over the stony walls, holding tightly to the bag of loaves.

Her legs continued their rapid pace. She reached the outskirts of their property in what seemed like record time. Her heavy breathing and tired legs were begging her to stop. *I'm almost there.*

She slowed down, trying to catch her breath. The sun was setting, bathing everything around her in warm colors. Even the whitewashed homes nestled up on the hills were a golden hue. The lazy sound of goat bells jingling in the distance was soothing to hear.

Ahead, her grandfather's straw hat bobbed up and down in the vegetable patch. He was working late today. She called out to him, waving to him. He peered at her from under his hat and waved back.

As Ipatia approached her grandfather, the sun cast a strange, golden glow around him making his face look deceivingly pleasant, although she had anticipated his anger at her lateness.

"Come here, Ipatia. Tell me why you were so late," he demanded.

"Mrs. Poulos had saved three loaves of bread for us," she said, her voice trembling as she tried to sound cheerful. She held up the bag of loaves. "She didn't accept money for them. She said they were a farewell gift."

"Hmm. I'll remember to give her a bottle of my wine next time I see her. What happened next?" he asked.

"Remember the tree near the basin on the way to the bakery, where Kitso always likes to stop and have a drink?"

He nodded impatiently.

"Well, Kitso was drinking from the basin and while I waited, I climbed the tree to rest in the shade. Then I saw a snake on the branch above me. As I hurried to get down, my skirt caught on a branch, and I was stuck there until a man came and saved me, and, and-" she babbled, and then broke down crying.

"Now, now, that's all right. You are still young, my Ipatia, and sometimes you do things without thinking," he said. He dug in his pocket and handed her a handkerchief, and then patted her on the back clumsily.

She wiped her eyes with the handkerchief, sniffling. "I'm sorry Grandfather. I should have known better than to climb that tree," she said contritely.

"You have a good heart and are righteous like your mother was, but I don't remember her being impulsive. It must come from your father's side. You've needed a mother's touch all these years, and I couldn't give it to you."

He took out another handkerchief from his pocket and wiped his hands and picked up the basket.

"Here, let me help you," she said, taking hold of the heavy basket with her free hand and sharing its weight. They walked together, holding the basket, heading towards the cottage.

"You said a man saved you?" he prompted. "Do we know him?"

"He's a tourist from the yacht that came in last night," she replied softly. "His name is Mr. Tony." She recounted the rest of the story and then finished by proudly saying, "Mrs. Xilouris said the Lord must have sent me to help little Nick."

"You did good by helping them, but you must remember to think before you do things," Christos scolded. "Climbing that tree got you into trouble, Ipatia Kouris, and wherever you are in life and whatever you do, remember, the one person you are always accountable to is God." He pointed to the sky.

She nodded. Whenever she heard him call her by her full name, she knew he was going to preach. And preach he did, all the way up to the cottage; he talked about praying and its importance, particularly when things did not go well, and even when things went well, the evil one made his entrance.

The sun had set and Ipatia's arm was aching by the time they reached the cottage. They laid the big basket of vegetables on the countertop. Her grandfather went into the bedroom to wash and change.

After warming the bean soup that she had prepared earlier in the day, Ipatia spooned it into the bowls hoping that Grandfather's anger would dissipate after he had his meal. Taking a loaf of bread from the bag, its wholesome aroma filling the room, she sliced it into hearty chunks.

After saying their prayer, Ipatia and Grandfather began to eat their meal.

Someone knocked on the door.

ᚲHAᛈTᛖR 6

All of this I leave behind
To follow fate, what will I find?

Christos went to answer the door, muttering, "Who could it be at this late hour?" He opened the door.

The chilly evening breeze caused Ipatia to shiver.

Katerina Tsatsikas and her youngest son Thomas stood at the door. Breathing heavily, Katerina greeted them with the customary kiss.

"*Koumbara,* welcome," Christos said.

Godmother's cheeks felt cool against Ipatia's face as she kissed them.

"You wouldn't believe this, but your donkey was standing in front of our house, so we fed him and brought him here," Katerina Tsatsikas explained. "With this opportunity, I also brought some of Ipatia's favorite *tiropites* (cheese pies)."

Katerina smiled broadly as she lifted the bag of cheese pies. Some of her teeth were missing, and she was a large woman, but for all her unattractiveness, she made up for it with her kindness.

"Thank you for the *tiropites,*" Ipatia said, receiving the proffered bag from her godmother. "Kitso always likes to stop in front of your house. He knows you feed him well."

"We were getting ready for dinner. Would you like to join us?" Christos asked.

"Thank you. We already ate. We will stay only a few minutes," Katerina replied.

They filed into the cottage, filling the small kitchen.

"Sit down, sit down," Christos said, pulling a chair for Katerina. Her large frame plumped down in the chair, causing it to creak.

Ipatia stifled a giggle, hoping the chair wouldn't break. There were only three chairs left, as *Nona* had broken a chair on her last visit.

"Here, Thomas, please have a seat," Ipatia said, gesturing towards her chair.

"I'm fine," he said, shaking his head awkwardly. He remained standing.

"This bag was tied to the saddle," Thomas said, handing it to Christos. "By the way, I already put Kitso in his stable."

Christos thanked him as he took the bag. Inside it were two, round, aged mizithras and a note. He read the note aloud, "Thank you for everything, Ipatia. I hope you like the aged cheese. Again, I am sorry we could not go with you on the trip tomorrow. Regards to your grandfather, Mrs. Xilouris."

"I'm glad little Nick is all right," Ipatia said.

"What happened to him?" Katerina asked, appearing surprised.

"I was visiting their house today to see if Mrs. Xilouris would be traveling with me to Piraeus, and I found out that he had cut his hand badly," Ipatia explained.

"Did Dr. Thanassis take care of it?" Katerina asked.

Ipatia shook her head. "He was in Patmos when it happened, and someone from the yacht that came in last night told us about Dr. Hatzis, who was traveling with them," Ipatia said.

"Dr. Hatzis? I seem to recall that name. Is he from Leros?" Katerina asked.

"*Koumbara*," Christos said apologetically. He knew about Katerina's insatiable curiosity and knack for gossip. "You know how people talk around here. Whatever Ipatia told you, will you promise me that it will remain here?"

"As I kiss the cross, you have my word on this," Katerina exclaimed, making the sign of the cross with her thumb and finger, and then kissing her two fingers, appearing flustered.

Realizing that she had said too much, Ipatia busied herself by serving her godmother a glass of water with a small dish of candied quince, a delicacy. Then she did the same to Thomas. He took them clumsily, almost spilling the glass of water.

Katerina eyed the dish. "Did you know that my oldest son, Alex was called this morning to see about fixing the yacht's engine."

"Hmm. Who does the yacht belong to?" Christos asked, twisting his mustache thoughtfully.

"Mr. Gregory Plakis," Thomas said, his Adam's apple moving up and down along his thin, scrawny neck. "When I went with Alex to work on the engine, I heard them speak his name."

Ipatia leaned against the kitchen counter, listening intently.

"I heard he was traveling with his family from Crete and stopped here because of the storm. More importantly, he is rich. Besides owning the yacht, he also owns several large ships," Katerina announced. She appeared to be enjoying the attention she was getting from her rapt audience.

"I used to know a shipowner from Crete. Who would have known that he would come to this tiny island?" Christos exclaimed.

"You should see the inside of the yacht," Thomas said, his eyes shining brightly. "It's like a king's palace, with all the shiny floors, beautiful furniture and carpeting. I wish I had something like that one day."

"Thomas, you're fantasizing again. These people are in a different class from us altogether," Katerina said, interrupting him. She gripped the chair to steady herself and stood up. "Well, we must be going. You eat your dinner before it gets cold."

Christos stood up. "Here, let me give you some wine." He went to his bedroom where he kept several bottles stored in a trunk.

Katerina turned and looked at Ipatia. "Now that Mrs. Xilouris won't be traveling with you, Ipatia, you might want to reconsider about going to Piraeus. You know how people talk around here."

Ipatia winced. Inevitably, her godmother, who had been like a mother to her all these years and protective of her, would be concerned. "I'll be eighteen in a few weeks, *Nona*, and when I traveled to and from Rhodes, I traveled by myself."

"Oh, well. Write me your news when you get there safely. May the good Lord be with you during the trip," Katerina said, gripping her in a bear hug.

"Have a safe trip, little sister," Thomas said affectionately, pecking her on the cheek.

"Yes, brother," she teased. He was two years older, and they had teased each other as far back as she could remember.

Grandfather had returned with a bottle of wine and handed it to Katerina.

Katerina thanked him. She had tears in her eyes as she went to the door. "Don't worry, Ipatia, we will keep an eye on your grandfather for you."

Ipatia nodded as she wiped the tears from her own eyes. She waved to them, watching their bodies blend into the night. She was going to miss them.

Her grandfather gently touched her on the shoulder, a reminder that dinner was waiting.

After eating her meal, clearing the table, and washing the dishes, Ipatia adjourned for the evening. While resting in bed, her thoughts churned over the events of the day. She had not had so much excitement packed in one day before. It took her a long time to fall asleep that night.

•◦———◇ •◦———◇ •◦———◇

Ipatia felt the goose bumps rising on her thin arms as she finished buttoning her sweater in the early morning darkness. Was she shivering from the cold or was it in anticipation of today's trip?

She eagerly went into the kitchen and grabbed the large pot. The crisp cold wind greeted her with a resounding smack as she closed the door behind her. Burying her face into the warm fold of her sweater and carrying the pot, she ran down the path blindly, her feet leading the way. Having done this for years she reached the goat stall with no problems.

The two mother goats were straining against the wooden fence, bleating loudly, complaining.

"Hello, my loves," she said, entering swiftly and shutting the gate behind her.

Their warm, fuzzy faces nuzzled against her shivering body. She pulled the small stool towards her and sat down to milk the goats.

"Today I am going far away," Ipatia said in a soothing voice, rhythmically squirting the frothy warm milk into the pot. The dawn shed some light, enough for her to see, and she noticed her hands. She bit her lips. Before she came to the island, her hands were soft and clean, used for light tasks, such as playing the piano or putting ribbons in her hair. Now, years of hard work and toil had made them rough as the bark on the trees, with jagged, dark nails. Her fingers tightened. No more. She was going back to Piraeus where there was heat in the winter and people bathed often with warm water.

The goat responded by turning her head towards her, looking at her with a worried expression.

"Don't worry, I won't forget you. I'll return after I get my degree, you'll see," Ipatia said, laughing and relaxing her hold. The goat stood motionless, looking content. The second goat was equally still.

Satisfied with the results, Ipatia shooed the goats to the next stall where their baby goats were waiting. The kids sucked hungrily, reminding Ipatia of her own breakfast.

She quickly made her way back to the cottage. The heavy pot threatened to spill its contents as the strain on her arms became unbearable.

The door magically opened before her.

"There you are, already here with the milk. You should have waited for me to do it," her grandfather lightly scolded her. He lifted the offending pot from her aching arms as if it were a loaf of bread.

"That's all right, *Pappou*. I had to say good-bye to the goats," Ipatia replied, removing her muddied shoes outside the door.

Christos Rodakis peered into the pot and nodded his appreciation. "This will last for a while. You are a good girl, like your mother was."

He placed the pot of milk on the gas burner and began stirring while Ipatia sliced the bread into thick chunks, then the *Mizithra* cheese.

"Bring the cups," Christos ordered, nodding towards the cupboard.

He maneuvered the spoon, skimming the froth off the creamy white surface. Satisfied, he poured the warm milk into the cups. The cottage became cozy with the scent of the heated milk. Once seated, they bowed their heads and recited the Lord's Prayer. Ipatia dipped her bread in the warm milk and ate it with a spoon.

The rooster crowed in the distance, a reminder of the new day ahead.

Ipatia looked at her grandfather impishly. "The rooster is tooting his horn again."

Her grandfather chuckled, wiping the milk off his mustache. "Yes, and I remember when you crowed outside the door not long ago, and I ran outside, thinking the rooster had gotten loose."

He went on to recount the number of mischievous acts she had performed throughout the years. They talked about the time she hung the red tie on the donkey's neck, parading him around and making him the talk of the town. Another time, she buried herself in the sand with a large hat covering her head, and when unsuspecting tourists came to bathe, she turned her head to have a look. When they saw the hat moving, it alarmed them. Laughter erupted in the small kitchen, making it cheerful.

After breakfast, Ipatia cleared the table, humming a favorite tune.

"Ipatia, my girl, we need to talk about your trip," Christos said seriously, folding his arms and leaning back in his chair.

"Yes?"

"I am worried that your aunt hadn't replied to your letter. What if you go there, and she's not there to receive you?"

"We talked about this already *Pappou*. I sent Aunt Sophia the letter over a month ago," Ipatia said. "She probably replied, but the mail tends to be slow this time of the year because of the weather."

"Your godmother raised a good point last night – you shouldn't be traveling alone."

"I was much younger when I traveled by myself to Rhodes to go to school there, and I was fine."

"You were just as stubborn then, wanting to attend the school in Rhodes, even after I said no. Fortunately, your cousins were kind enough to house you. Now, you want to leave me once more." Christos became silent, lost in deep reflection.

"I've been planning this trip the whole summer," Ipatia insisted. "Grandfather, don't worry. Everything will turn out all right."

"In a month you will turn eighteen, going on nineteen. Your mother was married at eighteen. Remember, there's more to life than school," he said gruffly. "There are fine young men, like Tom Tsatsikas, ready to start a family."

"Tom is like a brother," she said, sighing.

"I'm getting on in years, and when I'm gone, I plan to leave all my land to you."

Ipatia knew about the land. Decked with fruit orchards, one hundred olive trees, several dozen fig trees and lemon trees, it provided sustenance for most of their needs. Closer to the house was the vegetable patch, the chicken coop and goat stall.

"*Pappou*, please don't talk that way. You'll be here for many years."

"Promise me this," he said sternly. "That one day, God willing, you marry. I want to die with the peace of mind that one day this is passed on to your children." He stopped abruptly, breathing heavily, trying to catch his breath.

"Yes, *Pappou*," she said meekly, knowing she could not change his mind. He had given this speech several times before and no matter what she would say, he wouldn't listen to her.

He arose slowly, partly due to old age and partly due to sadness and reached for his jacket hanging from the peg on the wall.

"Now I must see about the supplies. Your ship for Piraeus arrives in the afternoon," he said heavily. "I will be back to take you to the dock. Have you finished packing your trunk?"

"Almost."

"Later, I will give you your legal papers and some things to give to your aunt," he said, his voice cracking midway. He silently wiped the moisture from his eyes.

"Please don't cry," Ipatia said. She hugged him, comforted by the familiar mountain scent that clung to his jacket.

He patted her gently on the back, causing her tears to flow readily.

"I don't have to leave. I can stay here with you," she said, sniffling. She wiped her wet face, feeling sad.

"No. It will do you good to be with your aunt. You need a woman's guidance."

She followed him outside and watched him attach the small wagon to the donkey. "Oh, I almost forgot," Ipatia cried. "Can you be sure to give Dr. Thanassis the medical book he lent me?"

"Dr. Thanassis said you can keep it as a going-away present."

"When did he say that?"

"Yesterday, when I saw him going down to catch the boat for Patmos. He stopped at the coffee shop and told me."

"He is such a kind man."

"Try to do as much as you can," he said before leaving.

Ipatia stood there, watching her grandfather maneuver his wagon around, its old wheels creaking. The wagon slowly ambled down the winding path, heading towards the harbor.

CHAPTER 7

The gift that I do give to thee
When I am gone, remember me.

Ipatia watched her grandfather's wagon going down the hill until it became a dark speck against the lime-green landscape.

In the distance, the sea appeared calm. She wanted the sea to remain calm for her trip in the afternoon.

I will light a candle in the church and pray for a calm sea. She still had time.

As Ipatia marched down the hill towards the *Panagia tou Harou* (Virgin Mary of Death) church, she could see people working the Tsatsikas land. Her godmother's large frame stood out among the fruit trees, moving slowly.

Moments later, Ipatia entered the cool, empty Byzantine church, enjoying the faint scent of incense that lingered in the air. Someone must have been here earlier.

She gazed lovingly at the Virgin Mary icon that the domed church was named after, depicting the image of the Virgin Mary holding her son, the crucified Christ. The icon, known for its miracles, was covered with glass that encased the miraculous lily. It brought many visitors to the island annually. The lily, withered and dried throughout the year, miraculously bloomed under the enclosed icon's glass during this period in August.

Ipatia prayed for guidance and kissed the icon, reverently making the sign of the cross and feeling peaceful. She lit a candle and placed it in the candle holder. Lighting the charcoal with her candle, she dropped it into the burner and placed a few pieces of incense on the hot charcoal. The heat from the charcoal warmed the incense rock and a sweet scent filled the air as she prayed. She lifted the incense burner and, making the sign of the cross several times, moved around the church praying.

"May the Lord bless my grandfather, my deceased parents, my godmother and her family, and my aunt," she said. "I also pray I get my book back, because Mrs. Rodos gave it as a special present."

Ipatia stayed there, praying for a while longer. "Help me have a safe journey," she finished.

She left the church, and the sun's rays warmed her as she trekked up the sloping path towards the cottage. When Ipatia reached the courtyard, she stopped and turned to gaze at the serene view beyond. The rays of the sun made the sea shimmer like millions of diamonds. Diamonds. Stones. Why *not give Mr. Tony the gemstone?* It was a gift from her father, from one of his journeys; it would make a good present for the book he returned to her.

Ipatia took in deep breaths of the fresh air, enjoying the island breeze. She noticed the pots of crimson colored geraniums lined up against the wall of the cottage. The flowers' delicate red petals appeared exceptionally beautiful today, contrasting well with the white walls of the cottage. She watered them.

Filling a bucket with water, she entered the cool, dark cottage and washed the dishes. Afterwards, she went into her bedroom. A bright-orange blanket lay on the small cot. Knitted by her mother, it added a welcome splash of color into the drab room. A small water basin sat on the table. Next to it stood a framed picture of her six-year-old self, holding hands with her parents.

Ipatia opened the window, allowing the breeze to flow into the room.

On the wall was an icon of the Virgin Mary holding the baby Jesus. They were witnesses to Ipatia's many tears and sleepless nights after her parents' untimely death. She opened the trunk that stood against the wall. Everything that belonged to her was stored inside the trunk.

Ipatia's black blouse and long black skirt lay on top. She removed them, intending to wear them on the trip. Although Grandfather had scolded her often for wearing the black clothes, she continued to wear them in memory of her parents.

The medical textbook lay beneath several layers of clothes. She touched its brown cover and then retrieved it reverently. The book had inspired her to pursue an education in health. She placed it back gently.

"Where did I put that gem?" Ipatia asked aloud.

She found the treasure box her late father had given her when she was young. Inside were several pieces of jewelry. Something glittered at the bottom of the box.

"Here you are," she exclaimed. A gift from her father, she remembered how fascinated she had been when the stone had changed color from a light green during the day to a red in the evening. She placed it in her purse. *I must see Mr. Tony today before I leave. I will give it to him so I can get my book back.* She began daydreaming about him as she returned everything into the trunk.

She bent down, searching for her hatbox under the bed. Her godmother had given her a new hat as a present to wear for the trip. As she pulled the hatbox towards her, it hit against something else, bringing it forward. It turned out to be her photo album. She had forgotten all about it.

Sitting on the bed, Ipatia leafed through the photographs, gazing at them nostalgically. She recognized the black-and-white picture of her handsome father, sharply-dressed in a uniform, standing in front of a large, majestic ship. It reminded her of the times she and Mother would go and greet him upon his return. Another picture showed her standing with her parents and Aunt Sophia in front of the two-story house in Piraeus. She was probably around four or five at the time. It must have been a Sunday, for they were decked in Sunday clothes, elegant hats, and white gloves. Her parents made a handsome couple. *Too young to die.*

Ipatia wiped back the tears as the memories washed over her like a spring shower. She missed her parents. Their memory would always remain a part of her.

She had spent her first eight years with her parents and Aunt Sophia in their home in Piraeus. She would be returning there. How would it feel without them? She hadn't thought about it until now. At least she would have Aunt Sophia.

She gazed at a photograph of herself wearing a pink dress and a large, white bow atop her head as she sat on the bench playing the upright piano. After Father had given her the piano when she turned five, she began taking lessons. Her piano teacher often patted her on the head and claimed she had much talent and should continue her lessons, but after her parents died, she stopped playing the piano.

Ipatia sighed, wondering if she would remember how to play the piano again. It felt so long ago.

Next, she saw a picture of her English tutor, the prim Mrs. Rodos. Wearing wire-rimmed spectacles, Mrs. Rodos held a book protectively against her chest. She had given Ipatia this picture as a present along with the English novel for her eighth birthday. Ipatia knew that underneath that stern exterior was a warm and caring heart.

After gazing at the photos for a while, she placed the album in the trunk and locked the trunk. She couldn't help feeling that even though she lost her parents, other people in her life had stepped in and helped her; her grandfather, her godmother, and her friends.

Slipping into her work clothes, a navy-blue cotton blouse and dark pants, Ipatia caught her reflection in the mirror mounted on the wall. The light coming in from the window made her eyes glow; they were the color of green olives with specks of sliced almonds. She pulled on one eye, trying to see how many yellow specks it had. She wondered what color they were the time Tony saw her.

Ipatia glanced down at her slim body. Although slow to develop like the other girls, her blouse was becoming snug. She tugged at it, realizing that she could no longer ignore the fact that she was slowly but surely becoming a woman. Even the work pants she wore - that had aroused her grandfather's anger when her godmother presented them to her as a gift two years ago, because he thought women should not be wearing pants - were now an inch short and were becoming tight on her.

She went outside to feed the rooster and chickens. The rooster chased her in earnest, delineating his territory while the chickens cackled.

Mindful of the time, she bundled the linen and dirty clothes and took them out to the courtyard. Filling the round, metal basin with buckets of well water, she pulled up her sleeves and began to wash the clothes.

She worked diligently, scrubbing the clothes with the olive soap, scrubbing her fingernails, scrubbing her life clean. Then she rinsed them. At one point, Ipatia noticed her clean fingernails. They looked much better. Later she should remember to put a little olive oil on them to soften them. The sound of bells jingled softly in the distance. At the bottom of the hill, she could see a shepherd with his flock of sheep, moving slowly. *Pappou* should be returning by now.

She was almost finished.

Her eyes periodically combed the horizon for her grandfather, and she was reminded of the time she had stood in this same spot, searching for her parents' return that fateful summer.

Every summer, as far back as she could remember, Ipatia and her parents left Piraeus and visited her grandfather on Lipsi Island. It was like stepping back in time and enjoying nature and the good people. However, shortly after they arrived that fateful summer when she was eight years old, they received news that her father's father in Crete was deathly ill. Her parents told her that they needed to go to him right away. They kissed her, promising her that they would return soon.

Each day after they left, she faithfully stood outside, looking for them and waiting for their return. As the days turned into weeks, her small body began to pace anxiously, hoping for a welcome glimpse of them.

A month had passed when the priest, dressed in his black garb, rode up the hill on his donkey to pay them a visit. He gently told them the news; her parents' ship was caught in a storm and there were no survivors. He told her that they were with the good Lord and would never return. She would live with *Pappou* from now on. She had wailed in his arms, clenching her small hands angrily, not wanting to accept the news about her parents' death.

Ipatia wiped the sweat from her face or was it tears? Squeezing the water out of the last shirt, she quickly hung it on the clothesline with the other clothes. Time was passing. She must hurry and finish the rest of her work.

Within minutes, she was on her hands and knees scrubbing the kitchen floor.

••——◈ ••——◈ ••——◈

Tony woke early that morning. The peaceful stillness of the room seemed pleasing to him. He lay in bed, savoring the moment. The clock showed seven o'clock, too early for anything.

He rolled over, adjusting the soft pillows and burying his head in them. Then an annoying thing happened. He could not return to sleep. Instead, numerous thoughts raced through his head, competing for attention.

Yesterday, for the first time in his life, he had seen his father with different eyes. After the news about his illness, Tony felt more compassionate and caring towards the very person who had been cold and aloof from him all his life. He felt as if a role reversal had transpired; he was acting like a father to his father.

A bothersome thought entered his mind. *I know Father is shrewd and manipulative. Everything he did in the past was for*

Gregory Plakis and no one else. Don't assume because he is sick, that he will change overnight.

Could it be possible that Father was using his illness to manipulate him into joining the family business and marrying Bonnie in order to bring in new money? Tony's jaw tensed at the thought. *But I gave him my word. I can't go back on my word. Not now.* No matter what his father's intentions were, he was his only son and was committed to helping him, he told himself.

Then he thought about Ipatia, the beautiful island girl and her book. She had appeared so helpless hanging from the tree, and he had much satisfaction in rescuing her from the snake. He admitted, when he held her in his arms, the temptation to kiss her had been strong. Then he remembered her stormy, light-green eyes when she found out he had her book. *The girl obviously wants her book back, and I, Antonios Plakis, should return it to her.*

An hour later, Tony slipped out of the hotel, feeling vibrantly alive and whistling softly. He carried the slim book in his right hand. He walked down the paved hill. To his right, below him, an older, tanned man stood on a large boulder, beating an octopus against some large rocks to make it tender. On the rope hung several octopuses to dry.

Tony's mouth watered as he remembered the succulent taste of grilled octopus from the past. This arduous task was well worth the effort. The man waved to him, and he waved back.

Ahead, Tony spotted his father's stout frame standing by the yacht, speaking to the captain. By the time he reached him, his father was alone, deep in thought.

"Good-morning. Why so early?" Gregory asked, patting his son affectionately on the back.

"I wanted to see more of the island, so I had an early start," Tony replied. "How are you feeling?"

"Fine, right now. The difficult part is I never know when it will hit me," Gregory said. He looked curiously at the book. "What do you have there, a book?"

"It belongs to Ipatia Kouris, the daughter of the late Captain Kouris."

"Is that right?" Gregory asked, looking surprised. "How did you come by it?"

Tony explained the story while his father chuckled.

"I'm planning to meet her grandfather, Christos Rodakis," Tony admitted. "Although he doesn't know I am. I learned that he visits the coffee shop in the mornings, and I'm hoping to catch him there."

"Christos Rodakis?" Gregory asked, appearing pleasantly surprised. "So, Christos lives here. I knew him years ago, back in Heraklion, Crete, when he made the famous wine. He is the one who sent his son-in-law, Captain Kouris to me. Tell him to come and see me. We have much to talk about."

"I will do that," Tony said, nodding.

"Oh, and don't forget, we leave at two."

"I know," Tony replied. "I'll be back before then. By the way, when would you like to get together to talk about the business?"

"We can talk about it on the way back to Piraeus," Gregory said, smiling. "You go and enjoy yourself, because I promise you, it's going to get busy after today."

Without notice, Gregory teetered, losing his balance. His arms shot up, grasping the air wildly, and he almost fell in the water if Tony hadn't grabbed him in time.

Tony's heart raced as he tried to steady him. He kept a strong grip on his arm. "Are you all right?" he asked his father, studying him with concern.

His father's typically robust features had turned pale as a sheet of paper. His aquiline nose was flared, and his eyes were hidden under the fluttering of the eyelids. When he finally opened his eyes, he stared blankly in front of him.

Tony repeated his question.

Gregory focused his eyes on Tony. "Yes, I'll be fine," he said, standing upright shakily. "You can let go."

"Let's come away from the water."

Gregory complied, and Tony let go of his arm.

Gregory passed his hand over his eyes, shaking his head and frowning. "I've been getting these spells more regularly now."

"I think you should have someone with you all the time now that you are experiencing these blackouts," Tony said sternly. "Why don't we head back to the hotel so Michael can look at you?"

"I'll be fine, don't worry," Gregory said, having regained his balance.

"Father, I don't think you should be out here alone in case another spell comes along," insisted Tony.

"If it'll ease your mind, you can walk back to the hotel with me," Gregory replied. He appeared shaken by the spell.

Tony conceded and walked with him slowly. He saw Michael leaving the hotel. "There's Michael."

Michael came toward them and greeted them.

Tony told his friend what had happened.

"Here, Mr. Plakis, why don't you come with me?" Michael said.

"Tony, I'll be fine with Michael," Gregory said, shooing him. "Go finish with what you were doing."

Tony watched the two men walk slowly towards the hotel. He admired how his friend could make everything all right. When Michael asked to join them on the trip, little did he know how much they would need him.

With a troubled heart, Tony turned and resumed his journey.

CHAPTER 8

Searching for the proper way
To give her back her book today.

Tony approached Pericles's coffee shop. Two older men sat at one of the small tables, drinking coffee and talking under the shade of the nearby tree. The younger of the two wore a black captain's hat and was flicking a string of worry beads every few seconds.

Mr. Pericles leaned against the door, talking with the men. It seemed as if he had just said something funny, for laughter erupted from the small table. When he spied Tony, he approached him eagerly, his large belly still shaking from the deep laugh.

"Good morning, Mr. Tony. I see you made it, my friend," Mr. Pericles boomed, his wide grin and hearty handshake confirmed the words of friendship.

"Good morning, Mr. Pericles," Tony replied, grinning. "I took your offer and decided to come by this morning to see Mr. Rodakis. Is he here?"

"Yes, he's been waiting for you."

Mr. Pericles led him to older, white-haired man who was chuckling and wiping his eyes with a handkerchief. He looked like he could be Ipatia's grandfather, for he was handsome, with large, olive-green eyes and a firm chin.

As the introductions were made, Christos Rodakis rose to shake his hand, smiling. "Sit down, sit down and join us," he said, pulling a chair for him.

"Nick Kalogeorgos," said the other man, standing and shaking hands with Tony.

"Stellios, a cup of coffee for Mr. Plakis," Christos said, motioning to the shop owner.

Mr. Pericles turned to Tony. "How would you like your coffee?"

"Thick and sweet," Tony said.

"Right away!" Mr. Pericles went inside the shop.

Nick was still standing.

"Nick, aren't you going to stay awhile longer?" Christos asked.

"Barba Christos, you know my wife. If I don't leave now, she will surely come looking for me. She has been eager to get the supplies, you know. I just stopped to say a brief hello," he said. Then he turned to Tony and said, "I hope you enjoy the island during your stay. Yiasou, Barba Christos." He slapped Christos heartily on the back, then walked away, flicking the worry beads.

"Mr. Rodakis, I rescued your granddaughter, Ipatia, yesterday from a snake," Tony offered.

"Ah, so you are the Tony she talked about. You have my congratulations for helping her out of her delicate predicament," Christos said, laughing.

Tony laughed along with Mr. Rodakis, feeling comfortable. The coffee shop was beginning to get busy, as a few more people arrived. Mr. Rodakis greeted each newcomer with a hearty welcome, apparently on familiar terms with them. The Turkish coffee arrived shortly, and Tony sipped the dark brew, savoring its sweet, delicious flavor.

"I came by to see you because I found a book belonging to your granddaughter. She dropped it in her haste to leave," Tony said. He handed it to him.

"Yes, thank you. Stellios had mentioned something about it. Ever since she was young, Ipatia loved to read. She even persuaded Dr. Thanassis into borrowing his medical textbook," Mr. Rodakis said, leafing through the slim volume.

"It seems as though you have a scholar on your hands," Tony said, smiling. The more he heard about Ipatia, the more intrigued he was.

"Yes, but a girl her age should be thinking about marriage, not about books," Mr. Rodakis scoffed. He shut the book firmly and pushed it toward Tony.

Tony decided to change the subject. "Mr. Rodakis, I'd like to ask you a favor. I understand that you gave the vase sitting by the door to Mr. Pericles over the matter of a horse?"

Christos turned and looked at the vase. "Yes. Ipatia's father gave it to me as a gift, God rest his soul, but it belongs to Stellios now."

"I am interested in ancient vases. This one in particular," Tony replied. "I also understand one needs a horse to travel up the hill to your house?"

Mr. Rodakis turned to Mr. Pericles, who stood nearby listening intently. "Stellios, my good man, why do you tell nice people like this gentleman that one needs a horse to visit my home? Are you trying to sell him your infamous horse?" He winked and everyone laughed. He turned to Tony and said, "Our friend here has been trying to sell his horse for a very long time. But the price has been so high that no one would buy him."

"Is the horse here?" Tony asked Mr. Pericles.

"Certainly, Mr. Tony," Mr. Pericles replied.

Tony followed him to the back, where a white mare was standing, tied to a pole. After looking the horse over carefully, Tony nodded his satisfaction at the horse's condition. She was young and healthy.

Tony gently stroked the mare's mane, thinking for a moment, then turned to Mr. Pericles and made his offer. "Here is payment for both this horse and the vase in the front, the one near the door," Tony said, pulling out his wallet and placing a wad of bills in the man's outstretched hand.

Mr. Pericles counted them and thanked him profusely. He eagerly saddled the horse. "I will give you the saddle, no extra cost."

When Tony and Mr. Pericles returned to the front with the mare, Tony found Christos seated on his wagon.

"I did not want to leave without saying good-bye to you," Mr. Rodakis said to Tony, gazing in awe at the horse. "I see you agreed on the price."

"Thank you, Mr. Rodakis. Are you leaving already?" Tony asked, mildly disappointed at the man's departure.

"Yes, I must hurry home. My granddaughter is leaving today on the ship for Piraeus, and I must bring her to the harbor."

"Before you go, I wanted to tell you something. Did you know the vase you gave to Mr. Pericles was much more valuable than the old horse he gave you?"

"How could an old vase like that, which sits around collecting dust, have more value than a horse?" Christos scoffed. "Why, the horse could breed more horses. I can travel everywhere with it, and it could help carry supplies and even help till the soil."

"The cost for this white horse is much more suited to what your vase was worth than the old horse he gave you," Tony insisted, handing the reins to the old man.

"What is this?" Mr. Rodakis said, appearing surprised. "Don't you need the horse?"

"No. I am leaving today for Piraeus. This horse belongs rightfully to you. I plan to place the vase in the museum in Athens," Tony said firmly.

Mr. Pericles whistled in surprise.

Speechless, Mr. Rodakis stared at Tony for a moment, realization dawning in his eyes. Dismounting, with reddened eyes, he shook Tony's hand vigorously and patted him on the back. "A thousand thanks, Mr. Tony. You are a true *Leventi*. How can I ever repay you?"

"If you could direct me to a good restaurant, that would suffice," laughed Tony. "I haven't eaten since yesterday morning."

"Why don't you come to my house for lunch? That is the least I can do to repay you," Mr. Rodakis cried.

Tony hesitated, thinking about the long trip up the hill and back.

"Mr. Tony." Mr. Pericles took Tony aside, whispering, "We *Lipsiotes* are very hospitable people. It would be an insult not to accept his invitation."

Tony nodded, appreciating Mr. Pericles's tactful suggestion.

It would also be a good opportunity for me to return the book to Ipatia.

"Thank you, I will accept your gracious offer," Tony told Mr. Rodakis.

"Good," Mr. Rodakis said. "You can ride up the hill with the white horse. Just follow me."

Tony pulled Mr. Pericles over. "Please prepare the vase for me and wrap it in a cloth. I will return shortly for it."

"Don't worry, my good friend. I'll have it ready for you."

Tony mounted the white horse and followed Christos up the narrow, cobbled street, past the various shops, past the pedestrians. Several people waved to Mr. Rodakis. A couple of times, he stopped to talk with them; one was an older, toothless woman with a cane, who wore a long black dress, her head covered with a black cloth, and the other was a tanned man wearing a hat and work clothes. After the greetings, Mr. Rodakis kept the conversation brief and then moved on.

Tony expected that by the end of the day, the whole town would have heard about him.

The road continued to slope upward and eventually led them outside the town and to the main road. Tony recognized the tree and water trough from the day before. He smiled, remembering the scene with Ipatia.

The road became wider, allowing them to ride side by side and making it easier to have a conversation.

"Mr. Rodakis, I've been meaning to tell you something. My father, Gregory Plakis, says he knows you from Heraklion. Is that true?"

"Ah-ha," Christos said, looking smug. He shook his finger at Tony, saying, "I thought there was some resemblance. The apple falls from the apple tree."

Tony was surprised to hear this. People had often said he resembled his mother more than his father. "How did you meet my father?"

Christos chuckled, "We grew up in the same neighborhood of Heraklion. My family had a wine business, and my father often gave wine to relatives and friends. Your father happened to taste our wine at a friendly gathering and asked who made it. Next, he came looking for us."

"Yes, that sounds like Father. Was he trying to start some business with you?" Tony said, smiling.

"You know him well. He was single then and interested in the way we made the wine. He almost convinced me to start a business with him, but I had other plans. Who knows, he may have ended up in the wine business rather than in the shipping business."

"What made you come here?"

"I was already engaged by the time I met your father. My fiancé was from Lipsi. Her uncle from Crete arranged the marriage. I came to see her and fell in love with her and Lipsi Island. My Maria was a beautiful and virtuous woman and lived with her mother, a widow. I had made plans to leave here after our wedding, but she didn't want to leave her mother who was frail. So we stayed here."

"You must have loved her to leave Crete and come here," Tony said softly.

Christos nodded. "I did. She was kind, compassionate, and always helping people. After we married, I bought the property next to her mother's house and started a grape orchard. Later, I added an olive orchard. My wife was a hard worker, working steadily by my side. We began making olive oil. I sold bottles of wine and oil, enough to make a living," he said, with a shrug of his shoulders. Then he remained silent after that confession.

They passed rows of fig and almond trees, their branches reaching out to the road, forming sketchy shading over their heads.

"Whatever happened to your wife?" Tony asked.

"She died of pneumonia, God rest her soul. Our daughter, Irene, lived with her husband Manolis in Piraeus and was pregnant at that time. So, she could not come to comfort me. I left for Crete, to get away for a while, but nothing was the same. My parents were gone by then. I had a cousin who had lived in our house all these years. He is a bachelor, older than I am, probably in his upper seventies by now. I realized that my home was here, in Lipsi, so I returned," admitted Christos.

"How did your son-in-law happen to work for my father?"

"Manolis had just received his captain's license when he married my daughter, but he didn't have a job. I knew about your father's shipping business, so I sent Manolis to him, with several bottles of my best wine. Your father remembered me and hired him on the spot. I heard that Manolis became one of his best captains."

"I know. I met Captain Kouris," Tony said sadly. "We were good friends."

"Oh yes, Manolis was a good man. I not only lost my daughter, but the best son-in-law I could ever ask for," Christos said. He took out a handkerchief and wiped his reddened eyes. "Now I'm also going to lose my granddaughter who is leaving for Piraeus today. God be with her on the trip. I don't want anything happening to her. She's all I have."

"Why is she leaving?"

"Her Aunt Sophia is there, and she wants to go to the university there. I have mixed feelings about that."

"Is she traveling alone?"

"Mrs. Xilouris was to travel with her, and now she cannot go because of her son's condition. I must stay behind to manage my olive trees and vineyard. I feel that Ipatia is still too young to travel by herself."

Tony silently listened, remembering the image of the girl swinging like a monkey from the tree. "I'll be taking the same ship to Piraeus, Mr. Rodakis. If it's all right with you, I'll make sure she gets to her aunt."

"That's kind of you, young man. Is your father traveling with you? For if he is, then I would love to give him some of my best wine," Christos said, delicately using the excuse of the wine to ensure his granddaughter would be traveling with older chaperones.

"Yes, he is, and now that I remember, he asked to see you. He is down at the dock. I can lead you to him later," Tony said.

"Good. We'll go after lunch," Christos said heartily.

Their discourse continued on general topics; they covered the history of Greece, its politics, the making of wine and gardening. Impressed by Mr. Rodakis's knowledge, Tony enjoyed their lively discussion. Soon, the topic switched to fishing.

"I am not a fisherman," admitted Christos. "I get seasick. But if the sea is calm enough, I do fish for squid. It's a peaceful feeling as the boat sits out there, and the sun is setting, and all around you is quiet. Have you ever gone fishing for squid?"

"No," Tony said, liking the idea.

The path finally led them to the house. Its simple white color, blue shutters and red flowers were inviting to the eye. The shady courtyard felt refreshingly cool after the warm trip. White trellises that lined its stone borders were laden with climbing grapevines. Tony immediately liked it here.

"Welcome to our humble home."

CHAPTER 4

My heart did lead me to your door,
Your book to give and you adore.

Ipatia had finished scrubbing the floor in the kitchen and was wiping it dry with a rag, humming a tune, when she heard knocking on the door.

"Ipatia, Ipatia."

"Yes, *Pappou*," she sang out, rising. "I'll be right there."

She opened the door and rushed outside to greet her grandfather. Seated on a large white horse next to him was Mr. Tony, the man who rescued her the other day.

Ipatia stopped in her tracks, feeling speechless. She was reliving the dream she had the previous night, of a knight arriving on a white horse.

"Ipatia, my dear, I believe that you have already met our guest, Mr. Tony," Grandfather said, gently reminding her of her manners.

"Good afternoon, Mr. Tony," Ipatia said, regaining her voice and nodding politely. Mindful of her disheveled appearance, she nervously pulled back strands of loose hair from her face. This man made her feel tongue-tied.

"I am pleased to see you again, Miss Ipatia," Tony said, in a ringing voice. He dismounted lightly in one swift stroke. "You will be happy to know that I came to return your book."

"Thank you," she exclaimed, reaching out for the book that was in his outstretched hand. Her fingers brushed his lightly. She held her breath, stepping back, clutching the book close to her

70

chest, feeling surprised that he would come all the way here to return her book. *Why didn't he give it to Pappou to bring it to me? Where did he meet Pappou, at the coffee shop, or on the way here?*

"My pleasure," Tony replied, smiling.

Christos gestured towards the open door saying, "Please come in."

Tony followed him into the cottage. His tall height forced him to stoop as he entered the doorway.

"*Pappou*, what about the supplies?" Ipatia asked, trying to find an excuse not to go in right away. The young man exuded a powerful force that made her tremble slightly.

"They can wait. Mr. Tony is joining us for lunch."

She followed him silently.

Mr. Tony sat at the table, his tall frame making the room appear small. Ipatia offered him a glass of water.

While he talked with her grandfather, Ipatia dutifully prepared the lunch, moving rhythmically with the chatter. She was constantly mindful of not bumping into Mr. Tony, for the kitchen was small.

In a matter of minutes, the table was decked in a colorful display with a large salad of sliced tomatoes, cucumbers and onions drizzled with olive oil dressing, along with plates of black olives, sliced *mizithra,* and stuffed grape leaves. She added *Nona*'s cheese-pies and a fresh loaf of bread.

Grandfather went into his bedroom and returned with a bottle of red wine. "This simple house, Mr. Tony, is old and has weathered several years of storms and use, but it has seen some fine wine," he said proudly.

He poured wine into three small glasses, handing one each to Tony and Ipatia. Then he lifted his glass.

"Ahh, I am looking forward to trying your famous wine," Mr. Tony said, raising his glass.

"A toast for you, my kind man, who helped me bring our supplies up and for the magnificent horse. We are indebted to you," Christos said, saluting him.

They drank in silence.

Ipatia touched her glass lightly with her lips as a token. She rarely drank wine. *She wondered what Grandfather meant about a horse.*

"Yes, this is excellent wine," Mr. Tony said, appearing pleased.

"There's no greater joy than seeing a guest in my house enjoying my wine," Christos said, appearing pleased.

As they ate lunch, Ipatia remained quiet, observing the two men as they conversed.

"The *dolmades* are tasty. Miss Ipatia did you make them?" Mr. Tony said, pointing to his plate of stuffed grape leaves.

Ipatia looked up, surprised at the compliment. She nodded shyly. Cooking was something that was expected of her, and she rarely received compliments from her grandfather. "The grape leaves are fresh, from our vineyard, and the herbs are from our garden."

"All the girls on the island are taught to cook at a young age," Grandfather said matter-of-factly.

"The women I know rarely cook," Mr. Tony said. "Even my sister and stepmother don't know how to cook."

"The land has much value and provides for our needs. We use the grapes for the wine and the grape leaves for the *dolmades*. We also make our own olive oil and have about one hundred olive trees. Every year, starting in early November, the Tsatsikas boys help me pick the olives."

"I used to help also when I was young," Ipatia piped.

"Let me tell you a story about her. When Ipatia first visited the island during the summer with her parents, she was around five or six," Grandfather said with a gleam in his eye. "One day, the little girl came up to me, looking quite important. She tugged on my sleeve, confiding that she saw many black olives on the ground and that maybe we should pick them up. When I looked down, I saw her pointing at a group of goat droppings."

Everyone broke out laughing.

"Ipatia became my best helper," Grandfather said, wiping his eyes from the laughter. He continued, describing the preparations in making the olive oil.

Tempted in joining the conversation, Ipatia hesitated, recalling Doctor Thanassis's visit a few months ago. She had eagerly jumped into a discussion with him about medicine and her grandfather had reprimanded her afterwards. He said her time would come when she was married. Meanwhile, she was supposed to be quiet, or else people would label her a bold, vain girl.

"Ipatia, do you have your clothes packed? We must leave shortly to buy the tickets. The ship leaves at two."

"Yes, *Pappou*."

"Good. Mr. Tony and his family are also traveling on that ship. He said that he will see that you get to Piraeus safely."

Ipatia's eyes opened in wonder. *Was that the reason why Grandfather was so friendly to this man?* Her grandfather didn't think she could handle the trip alone but needed assistance.

She excused herself and fled to her bedroom. She was feeling slightly remorseful. Her grandfather's tone of voice was that of an adult speaking to a naughty child, and here she was almost eighteen. She shut the door and stood there a moment, waiting until her heartbeat slowed. She had never felt this way before. She could hear them talking.

Curious, she nudged the door slightly open, hoping that they didn't hear it creaking, and peered into the kitchen. Mr. Tony's back was towards her, and to his right sat her grandfather.

As she changed her clothing, Ipatia observed Mr. Tony through the crack in the door. His handsome features came alive as he talked with Grandfather, gesturing while talking. Was it her imagination, or did the kitchen appear warmer and fuller, as it filled up with his vibrant voice ringing out in laughter.

Then, just as quickly as it started, the conversation died. She shut the door in haste, not wanting them to notice that she had been eavesdropping. She caught the last words her grandfather was saying. "I need to unload the supplies from the cart so we can put Ipatia's trunk in it."

It became quiet after that. The men must have gone outside.

Ipatia finished dressing and bundled her long, wavy hair into a bun, securing it with two large pins. Checking the mirror, she placed the hat on her head. When *Nona* had presented it to her, she had said knowingly that all women in Piraeus wore them.

Ipatia winced as the hat engulfed her head. Perching it more carefully on her head, she prayed there would be no wind today.

She checked her purse for the money and key for the trunk. Everything was there. Then she remembered the gemstone. She found it and held it up, gazing at it and cherishing its beauty. She carefully placed it back in her purse.

Her black, Sunday shoes came next. She slid her feet into them. She had outgrown them, for they pinched a little, but she had no other shoes other than her sandals. She walked around the room, trying not to wince. She will remove them when she got on the ship, she promised herself.

She peeked out the door. The kitchen door was wide open and boxes of supplies were already stacked in the kitchen. She could hear the men talking outside.

Mr. Rodakis busily arranged the wagon and donkey.

"I will bring a box of my wine to give to your father," Mr. Rodakis promised Tony.

Tony thanked him and watched him go back into the house to retrieve the bottles. He took a deep breath of the clean air and looked around him, realizing that this simple, secluded house situated on a hill boasted a panoramic view of the orchard-studded hills, the valley below, the blue sky above, and the sea beyond. The scenery opened his heart, releasing an inexplicable sense of joy.

Moments later, Ipatia came out of the house pulling her trunk. She had a pinched look on her face.

"Here, let me help," he said, going to her.

As Tony took the trunk from her, she looked up, smiling, but her hat plopped down, covering her face. She pushed the hat up, frowning, and her purse slipped from her hand and fell to the ground.

Tony laughed heartily as she stooped to pick up the purse, which caused her floppy hat to fall to the ground and her hair come tumbling down. Blushing furiously, Ipatia turned her back and gathered her falling hair back into a bun.

His laughter died as he sensed her quiet desperation at remaining dignified. He had done an ungentlemanly thing by laughing at her. Feeling a sense of guilt, Tony stooped down and retrieved her hat, shaking off the dirt from it. He waited until she finished placing her hair up.

"You have a nice, large hat," he said solemnly, handing it to her.

"Thank you," she murmured, her eyes lowered. She put her hat on more securely, pulling it down over her eyebrows. She peered at him from under it. Her eyes shimmered with unshed tears and injured pride.

Tony's heart melted. "I'm sorry if I laughed. Everything happened all at once, you see," he explained, gesturing comically and trying to make her feel better.

She started giggling and then her purse fell a second time, causing them both to break out into laughter.

After the laughter subsided, Tony carried the trunk to the back of the wagon. She followed him. He placed the trunk in the wagon.

"You have a wonderful view of the water, even better than my father's house." Tony commented. "Is it safe to swim in these waters, Ipatia?"

"Yes, it is," she replied. "We usually swim close to the beach, though. Sometimes sharks have been seen farther out."

"Dolphins are good to have around," Tony said. "They help keep sharks away."

"Once I saw a group of dolphins playing nearby," she said, grinning. "They were the prettiest sight one could see. They were so playful, and they looked as if they were having fun."

Tony smiled at her openness.

"Oh, I almost forgot." Ipatia's fingers dug inside her purse. "I would like to give you this," she said, proudly placing something in his hand.

Tony gazed at the brilliant gem, which was the size of an almond. Light-green in color, with specks of yellow, it glittered intensely. "That is kind of you," he replied, touched by her gesture. "It has an interesting color."

"Father gave it to me, from one of his trips to Russia. He called it the cat's eye. He said it reminded him of my eyes, although I think my eyes are greener. I've seen it change color from a light green to a red, depending on how much light it receives."

Tony glanced at her eyes and then studied the stone, his interest piqued. There was a resemblance, although her eyes were more beautiful than the gem. "Ahh, yes. This could even be an Alexandrite gem," he said, "which has greener than the yellow observed in a cat's eye."

"Alexandrite?" she prompted.

"I believe so. Discovered in the Ural Mountains, it supposedly was named after the future Russian Tsar, Alexander the second, for his coming of age in the 1830's," he replied.

He looked at it again and was about to give it to her, but she shook her head.

"It is a gift," she said.

He hesitated, wondering if she knew its value. "I don't know if I should accept this since your father gave it to you."

"Oh, you should," she blurted. "I mean, I owe you so much for saving me and for bringing back my book. It's the least I could do. Please accept it."

He thanked her and then placed it carefully inside his pocket. Her father evidently picked good souvenirs, first the ancient vase, and now this valuable stone. He would check into it, but he believed this type of stone was not common.

Christos carried a box on his shoulders, heading toward them. "Here is the wine for your father," he said proudly.

Tony thanked him. He pushed the trunk to the side to make room, and then helped Christos position the box of wine next to it.

Ipatia hopped on the wagon and settled herself on the small seat, keeping one hand on her hat.

They ambled down the small path with Tony following them on the white horse. When they reached the main road, Tony moved to the front and began talking with Christos.

As they approached the coffee shop, Tony remembered the ancient vase. "Mr. Rodakis, I need to stop here for a moment to see about the vase. You go ahead."

"We'll see you down at the dock," Christos said, and they moved on.

CHAPTER 10

Life's cycles, one by one,
Unfold like an onion.

Ipatia spilled all the questions she had bottled up inside her. "How did Mr. Tony come here with the book, and who paid for the horse? Why were you so nice to him, and why did you-"?

"Wait, wait," Christos said, laughing. "I'll answer them one at a time."

He talked about Mr. Tony's visit in the morning at the coffee shop to return the book, and how he talked him into coming for lunch. He also informed her that Mr. Tony bought both the ancient vase from Mr. Pericles so he could put it in a museum, and he also bought the horse.

"I was surprised when he offered me the horse, saying that the value of the vase was much more than the old horse that Mr. Pericles had given me. Mr. Tony must have heard that the old horse had died, and that I needed a new horse. He is a good man," he said, shaking his head.

"Yes, he is." Ipatia nodded, piecing the puzzle together.

Her grandfather looked at her thoughtfully.

They stopped a short distance from the passenger boat. Her grandfather removed the trunk from the wagon and handed her the canvas bag. "Wait here while I see about your tickets."

Ipatia looked around. People were slowly arriving, gathering in small groups along the harbor. To her far left, a few weathered men sat on the ground with their fishing nets spread around them like spider webs. They skillfully mended the nets, chatting to each other while others removed the fresh catch of the day from their boats.

Her gaze rested on a group standing near the passenger boat. Ipatia recognized Melissa, Tony's sister, Bonnie, and Dr. Hatzis.

Her heart raced when she spied Tony arriving on the white horse, appearing pleased. He carried a large, wrapped object.

"Ipatia, guard these well. This one is for the passenger boat, and the other one is for the ship," Christos said, interrupting her thoughts. He handed her the tickets.

"Yes, *Pappou*."

"What did you do with your money?"

"It's in my purse."

"Good. Now listen carefully. Here are the legal documents your aunt sent after your parents' death. When you turn eighteen, you will meet with the banker in Piraeus. Your father has placed money in a trust fund there and the papers have the account number on them. Guard these well."

Ipatia carefully placed them in her purse.

"Look, *Pappou*. Mr. Tony is coming here, and he's bringing someone with him," she whispered, watching Mr. Tony approaching with a shorter, older man.

"Gregory Plakis. It must be at least fifteen years since I last saw you, and you haven't aged one bit," Christos exclaimed, slapping him on the back.

"Christos Rodakis. Old friend. It's good to see you," Gregory shouted, grinning boyishly.

They shook hands vigorously.

"Tony told me you were here, and I couldn't leave without saying hello to an old friend," Mr. Plakis said. He stared curiously at Ipatia.

"Meet my granddaughter, Ipatia," Christos said proudly.

Ipatia smiled and extended her arm to Mr. Plakis, saying, "How do you do?"

"She's the daughter of Captain Kouris," Christos explained.

"Ah, yes, yes. I thought you looked familiar. You've grown into a beautiful young lady since I had last seen you," he said, first shaking, and then holding her hand warmly. "You are tall like your father, but your bone structure and delicate features bear a strong resemblance to your mother. I could never forget your mother's beauty."

Ipatia blushed from the compliment. "My father worked for you?" she asked.

"Yes, thanks to your grandfather. Your father was one of my best and most courageous captains. A good man he was. We were sorry to lose him."

Mr. Tony stood silently by, observing this exchange.

"Thank you, Gregory. But more important is her character. Beauty is only skin deep," Christos replied, his eyes twinkling. "And now I'm going to be losing her. She is traveling to Piraeus to stay with Sophia, her aunt."

"Not Sophia Kouris?" Mr. Plakis asked. "She was the best seamstress we ever had."

"Yes, that's my aunt," Ipatia said.

"You tell her Gregory Plakis said hello."

Ipatia nodded shyly.

"Tony was kind enough to offer to see that Ipatia gets there safely. Now that I know that you also are going on the trip, I feel even more confident that my granddaughter is in good hands."

"Yes, my son has always been one for helping people out. Don't worry, my friend, you can trust that she will get there safely," Gregory said, somewhat dryly, looking at Mr. Tony.

Mr. Tony smiled back and then gazed at Ipatia.

"Are you traveling with the rest of your family?" Christos asked.

"Yes, my wife Christina and daughter are over there with some friends of the family," Gregory said, gesturing towards them.

Christos looked at the group and nodded appreciatively, saying, "You have a lovely family. Now look what I have for you,

Gregory. Several jugs of my finest wine." He proudly displayed the box filled with the wine.

"Thank you, my friend," Mr. Plakis said, patting Christos on the back with gusto.

"It is my pleasure. I heard you visited Heraklion. How is life there?"

"Where shall I start? Things are not the way they used to be."

They exchanged news, discussing the deaths, marriages, and births of the people they knew.

Ipatia stood awkwardly nearby, listening. Mr. Tony stood close to her, tuned in to the conversation. She could feel his warmth emanating towards her, almost as though his arms were embracing her. Her grandfather had said that Tony was going to see that she got to Piraeus safely. She wondered what that meant. *Is he going to sit with me and keep an eye on me?* She liked the idea. *What if he has a cabin and asks me to go with him there?* She pushed that anxious thought from her mind.

The sound of the ship's horn blasted in the distance.

"The ship has arrived," Ipatia announced, pointing to it. "I hope we're not late."

"Don't worry, it won't leave until the passenger boat arrives," Mr. Tony said, looking at her and smiling.

A woman's voice called out from a distance, "Tony, Tony."

Ipatia saw Bonnie and Melissa waving to them. They were joining the line of people that had formed to board the passenger boat.

"Father, they are boarding the passenger boat," Mr. Tony said.

Mr. Plakis shook Grandfather's hand one last time and said, "If you need anything, please don't hesitate to let me know."

Mr. Tony shook Grandfather's hand next. "I am pleased to have met you, Mr. Rodakis. Here is your horse. I'll return for your granddaughter."

"Thank you for everything, and God bless you," Christos replied, taking the reins from Mr. Tony's hands. He led the horse to the wagon and tied him to it.

Mr. Tony picked up the box and said to Ipatia, "Wait here for me."

Ipatia admired the ease with which he carried the heavy box. She watched as he whistled softly, walking with his father towards Bonnie who had remained behind, waiting for them. When Tony grabbed Bonnie's luggage with his other hand and walked with her up the ramp to the boat, Ipatia looked away, feeling disappointed. She didn't want to see anymore.

"Come, let's get closer to the passenger boat," Grandfather told her.

They walked slowly toward it, her grandfather carrying her trunk.

"Remember to write, and let me know what happens," he said.

"Don't worry, *Pappou.* I will write."

They reached the ramp to the passenger boat. She hugged him tightly, the tears flowing freely.

"It's all right, my dear, now don't you cry, or else I'll cry also. We will see each other soon, won't we?" Grandfather said, patting her on the back. He took out a handkerchief and wiped his wet eyes with it.

Mr. Tony loomed over them. "We'll make sure she gets to her aunt. Here, let me carry her trunk."

"Thank you, Tony, for your reassuring words," Christos said.

Mr. Tony smiled as he gently led Ipatia up the side ramp, carrying her trunk. They handed their tickets to the attendant. The front of the boat was packed with people. Ipatia glimpsed Mr. Tony's family there.

"Let's go to the back where it's less crowded," Mr. Tony told her.

As they headed to the back of the boat, the crew pulled the ramp and slowly the small boat chugged forward.

Ipatia gripped the handrail as the boat rocked. She could see her grandfather in the distance and waved to him, feeling a wave of sadness engulf her. He waved back. Why hadn't she thought about his being alone before? *Who would wash his clothes and cook for him?*

Tony placed her trunk down. The boat slammed against some waves, causing Ipatia's stomach to roil. She gripped the rail even more tightly and leaned forward as a wave of nausea overcame her. She had not inherited her father's sea legs

"Are you all right? I can stay with you, if you'd like," Mr. Tony said, gazing at her with concern.

She took a deep breath. "I'll be fine. It's just a short ride," she said shakily.

"Here, why don't you have a seat?" His touch was soothing as he took her hand and led her to her trunk.

Ipatia thanked him and sat on it. The nausea returned and she bent over. He continued holding her hand while talking softly. She didn't remember what he said, just that his warm touch felt good, and his pleasant voice was soothing to her ears.

Afterwards, Mr. Tony went to the front to check on his family.

When the boat reached the ship, Ipatia rose shakily, eager to get off. She wobbled forward, pulling the trunk. Up ahead, a ramp from the ship had been lowered unto the boat and the other passengers slowly walked up the ramp and onto the waiting ship.

In a few moments, Mr. Tony appeared in front of her. "Ah, here you are. I see we don't have to carry you off the boat. Follow me," he said cheerfully, walking ahead, carrying her trunk.

She followed him up the ramp, her stomach still reeling.

"How do you feel?" he asked, turning slightly towards her.

"I'll feel much better now that I'm getting off that small boat."

He laughed, saying, "The ship is much bigger and doesn't rock like the boat."

As they boarded, Ipatia observed the passengers on the ship: they were tourists with colorful clothing, carrying cameras and speaking foreign languages; Greek families strolled with their children; and groups of college students laughed and chatted. Some people hurried past her with boxes of squawking chickens.

She was pleased that this ship was larger than the one she traveled to Rhodes with.

"Ipatia, do you have your ticket?" Mr. Tony asked.

She pulled out the stub and handed it to him, feeling nervous. *Why does he want to look at my ticket?*

He looked at the ticket and bit his lip. "Your grandfather bought you a class C ticket. Would you rather go into a cabin? It's not too late to get one for you."

"A cabin?" she asked, suddenly seeing red. *What does he take me for? I am a good girl. How dare he try to get me into a cabin?* "No, no, thank you. This ticket is fine."

Mr. Tony raised an eyebrow, looking skeptical. "You should sleep in a cabin, especially if your stomach is sensitive to any rocking."

"Could you give me back my ticket?" Ipatia insisted, almost shouting.

"All right. All right. Let's go this way," Mr. Tony said, handing her the ticket reluctantly.

Ipatia followed him up the stairs while he carried her trunk. Several people coming down the stairs stopped to let Tony pass with the trunk, and then flew past him, breezing by Ipatia. Some men, dressed smartly in white uniforms, slowed their pace, staring at her boldly.

She quickly lowered her head, blushing and focusing on the steps instead.

They entered a large lobby and made their way to an outside corridor. Tony whistled as they walked slowly through the corridor.

She glanced to her left, toward the island and the dome of St. John crowning the harbor and relaxed when she saw the church. She made the sign of the cross. She saw the white boats bobbing up and down in the water, embracing the dock like a coral necklace, while the sea sparkled like diamonds on a blue oil painting. *I must remember to describe that image in a poem one day.*

"Here we are," Mr. Tony said.

They stepped into a huge room to their right. Chaos reigned. Filled to capacity with people either sitting or standing everywhere, Ipatia and Mr. Tony juggled their way through the crowds, looking for an empty seat.

At the back of the room, Mr. Tony found an empty seat next to an old couple. He placed the trunk down.

"This looks like a good place for you," he said to Ipatia. "Please stay in your seat. I will be downstairs in a cabin. Try to get some sleep if you can."

"Thank you," she said brightly. She settled in the seat, looked up at him, and smiled.

He returned her smile. "You're welcome."

Ipatia watched him leave, feeling a sense of pride at having been escorted by him. He was tall and handsome and exuded a powerful air that made heads turn his way. The old couple smiled at her, making her feel comfortable with her seating arrangement.

When Tony reached the door, he turned and looked at her, and waved. Embarrassed at being caught staring, she looked down, her hat shielding her face.

Afterwards, Ipatia removed her hat. The tight shoes were the next things to come off. To her right, the older couple quietly discussed things, their voices lowered.

People seated in front of her were arguing about politics, gesturing emphatically, trying to make their points. To her left, a group of college students, boys and girls, were joking and laughing, as if they had no care in the world. She observed them and was filled with admiration. Maybe one day she would be a college student, traveling in a group like that. They appeared to be returning from some field trip. *Yes, but what makes me think Pappou would let me travel with boys?*

In the front of the room, a man played a santouri and sang folksongs, while another played a violin. After the ship began its journey, the noise stabilized into a low hum.

After some time, Mrs. Poditis, the woman next to her started a conversation with her. Ipatia learned her life story. She was traveling with her husband to Piraeus because his health was not doing too well. "And what about you? Why are you going to Piraeus?" she asked Ipatia.

Ipatia related her story to her.

Mrs. Poditis promised Ipatia that she would let her know when they arrived in Piraeus.

A uniformed man interrupted them, asking for their tickets. After he moved on, Ipatia resumed her conversation with the woman.

CHAPTER 11

My dear, sweet aunt did not appear,
But you did care and drew me near.

Tony sauntered into the ship's dining room with his family and guests. They sat around a large table, eating and talking.

Later, the group filtered off in different directions, and Tony stayed behind, talking with his father and making arrangements regarding his transition into the family business.

"May I join you?"

Tony looked up. Chuck Daras stood there, calm and suave.

"Of course," Gregory said, appearing pleased to see him. "We were discussing the shipping agency. You came just in time."

Chuck Daras thanked him and sat down. He removed a pack of cigarettes from inside his shirt pocket and after offering it to them, lit a cigarette.

"I hear you are going to be your father's right arm," Chuck said to Tony.

"Yes. May I ask who told you?"

"Your little sister," Chuck said apologetically. "We were upstairs on the deck, discussing the shipping business. I admit she is knowledgeable about the business. She almost sold me a ship just now."

"Hahahaha," Gregory laughed, slapping the table excitedly. "I tell you, that girl can run this business." He expounded on Melissa's beauty and accomplishments, making her appear almost superhuman.

Tony listened quietly to his father's creation of an angelic Melissa, one who took care of stray animals and wanted to help others. *Father was up to something.*

"Melissa has not only been a good daughter, but a son to me," continued Gregory, nodding his head emphatically. "She has been more dedicated and devoted to the shipping business than Tony here. From the beginning, he wanted nothing to do with ships, but instead, wanted to go to the university."

Tony had heard enough. He excused himself and went to his cabin. His large frame sank into the soft mattress. He needed to calm down. *A few minutes before Chuck Daras showed up, Father was praising me about getting involved in the family business. As soon as Chuck showed interest in Melissa, Father was just as willing to cut me down so Melissa could look good in Chuck's eyes. Father has not changed. No matter how much I try to see him in a good light, he will always be a self-centered, thick-skinned man, thinking only about himself and his business.*

Afterwards, Tony strolled outside, appreciating the resplendent sunset, while lovers walked past him, hand in hand. Noisy sea gulls glided in the air, following the ship. He gazed at the frothy water flowing out from the back of the ship. He felt as turbulent as the water.

The plans he discussed with his father regarding the business appeared solid, but when Chuck Daras showed up and brought his sister into the picture, his father's attitude changed. Tony wondered about his sister's role in this.

He stood there for an indefinite amount of time, mulling over the mixed feelings that threatened to engulf him. This transitional period was not going to be easy. His father's business could control his life, destroying everything he had worked for, his education and his freedom. *Yet, it is my duty as the first born, to be in charge.*

He thought about Ipatia and walked up the stairs to her floor. Sidestepping a group of people flowing out of the large room, he entered the room. He could see that Ipatia had removed her hat and was sleeping peacefully. He wasn't about to interrupt her sleep.

He decided to visit the lounge, and on his way, bumped into his sister. She appeared happy.

"Where have you been, Tony? I have been searching everywhere for you. Look what I have on my hand," Melissa exclaimed. She held out her hand proudly.

"What about your hand?"

"Can't you see the ring on it, you silly? Michael proposed to me. We're going to be married."

"Congratulations, little sister. Does Father know?" Tony asked, surprised at the timing. He knew his methodical and logical friend well. Michael was not the type to propose this readily, especially on a ship. He pecked his sister on the cheek.

"Not yet. I wanted you to be the first to know. Now that I have your approval, I know Father would be just as pleased."

"Yes, and why shouldn't he? Michael is the best friend I've known," he reassured her.

She beamed up at him.

"Where is the lucky bridegroom?" he asked, looking around expectantly.

"He went to the lounge. He's expecting you."

Tony found Michael in the lounge, seated at the bar. He appeared to be nursing a drink. Tony congratulated him.

He made a toast, raising his glass. "This is for the happy couple. May you have many, many years of happiness together."

They drank and conversed into the night, reminiscing about the past and their friendship.

The sound of the horn blast woke Ipatia. She rubbed her eyes and met darkness. As her eyes became accustomed to the dark, she could see people gathering their belongings and leaving. Soon, others arrived. The old couple seated next to her slept soundly.

Ipatia stretched, and her stomach growled in return. Minutes later, she was munching on a cheese pie, thinking about her grandfather and her godmother, and wondering what would be happening back on the island. After she finished, she realized she was thirsty. She had forgotten to bring water with her.

Ipatia remembered passing the lobby on the way here. Someone there could direct her to some water. She placed her bag on her seat and walked out into the hallway. The lobby was quiet, except for a uniformed man who sat behind the counter. After asking him directions, he pointed politely towards the lounge.

She wondered what had happened to Mr. Tony. She got her answer when she approached the lounge. It was empty except for Mr. Tony and Dr. Hatzis who stood at the bar, their backs to her, having a conversation. She stood awkwardly at the doorway, not wanting to intrude.

Dr. Hatzis was saying to Mr. Tony, "I've wanted to ask you what your plans were for Bonnie. Melissa's told me the girl is in love with you."

Ipatia became flustered, not sure whether to stay or leave. If she walked in, she would be intruding on their private conversation, and if she left, she would still be thirsty. Something held her there a little while longer.

"I made it clear to Melissa that I am not interested in a long-term relationship with Bonnie," Mr. Tony replied.

"Bonnie is a nice, attractive girl."

"I can see her one day marrying someone rich and making him happy, but I am not that man. I am too busy with Father's shipping business."

Michael raised his voice. "Tony, you've been a good friend all these years, the best friend a guy could ever have. You've helped me a number of times when I needed it, and I appreciate it. But there's something you need to know about yourself. You seem to attract beautiful, wealthy women with your good looks, and there's nothing wrong with that, but-" He stopped, guzzling down his drink, as if to give him courage for what he was about to say.

"Go on," prompted Tony.

"You're the perfect gentleman, treating Melissa's friends like queens at first, with your undivided attention, your compliments, your smiles, always making them feel special. Just when they start falling in love with you, another girl comes into the picture, and you seem to lose interest in them. Then they run to Melissa for help, telling her all about it, and then she comes to me, telling me what happened. You are probably doing that to Bonnie right now. She is not like the others, you know. She's got class and her father's so rich, he could buy your whole shipping business."

"I did not treat Bonnie or any other of Melissa's friends like queens, as you say, and my compliments are not meant to make them fall in love with me. If it appears that I lose interest in them because another girl comes into the picture, it's because there was nothing there between us in the first place."

"What about this new girl, what's her name, Ipatia? I saw how she looked at you the other day, and she looks like she could get hurt if you decided to dabble with her."

"Ipatia is not a topic for discussion. She's in a totally different class of people," Mr. Tony replied in a raised voice.

Ipatia fled the room, her heart racing.

I'm in a totally different class of people.

She slipped back to her seat, trying to make sense out of all that she heard. She didn't know who to believe, Dr. Hatzis or Mr. Tony. One thing was clear, Mr. Tony's sister was involved.

Michael quickly apologized. "Tony, I'm sorry if I offended you. I realize when I drink a little too much, I sometimes say things that may be offensive."

Tony forgave him instantly. He patted him on the back, saying, "No, no, that's all right, Michael. I think I drank a little too much myself. We have been friends too long to let something like that get between us. Everything is all right. I think I'll call it a night."

Michael agreed with him, and the two separated on friendly terms. Tony went to his cabin and stayed there for the rest of the trip.

After some time, the horn sounded for Piraeus. Tony and his family were one of the first groups of people to exit the ship. Tired and sleepy, no one in the group did much talking. Once on the dock, Tony obtained cabs for his family.

Mr. Daras was the first to leave. He appeared quiet, even upset about something as he bid the group farewell. The next to leave was Bonnie, who looked sleepy and tired. She yawned as she waved to them.

The drivers finished loading the Plakis luggage into the trunk.

Gregory pulled his son to the side and talked quietly to him. "Tony, what's the story with Christos's granddaughter?"

"I passed by earlier in the evening to see her, but she was sleeping. She is in the third class, and they haven't come out yet. I promised her grandfather to see her safely home."

Gregory appeared skeptical as he got into the taxicab. Christina and Melissa were already inside the cab, waiting for him. Christina peered out the window and asked Tony if he were coming.

"I'm coming later."

Tony watched as the cab sped onward, towards Kifissia. Michael stood next to him, silently waving to them as they left.

Tony said to Michael, "You better get home before your own family wonders about you."

"Fine, fine. I'll be seeing you tomorrow then. Good-bye, good friend."

After Michael left, Tony found a taxicab and began his search for Ipatia, driving around slowly, looking for a tall girl with a large, silly hat.

—◈—◈—◈—

Mrs. Poditis nudged Ipatia awake. "Come, Ipatia, we've arrived in Piraeus."

Ipatia's watch showed ten o'clock. Had she slept through the horn's blast? She groggily rose and followed the couple, dragging her trunk behind her.

Several people waited in line ahead of them, and many others soon arrived behind her, as they waited for the large door to open.

After what seemed like a long time, the big ramp resembling a mouth with wide jaws slowly opened. Ipatia followed the crowd and walked down the ramp. People spewed out of the ship, like a big tidal wave, going off in different directions.

The cool, dark night descended upon Ipatia as she pulled the trunk, feeling weak and tired. She had been standing for a long time in the line and her tight shoes pinched her feet, causing her to inch slowly down the ramp. People behind her pushed and juggled past her, making her lose her balance and fall forward.

"Watch out for the girl," barked a man's voice. Several others clamored in unison.

Ipatia was lifted by strong arms and carried down the rest of the ramp and to the side, away from the crowd. Someone placed her trunk next to her. She groggily thanked the two men who had helped her. They were middle-aged and smiled back. She watched them return to their families and disappear into the night.

Mrs. Poditis and her husband saw her and hurried to her side, asking her if she were all right.

"Yes, thank you," Ipatia said. "I'm all right. I am going to wait for my aunt to come get me."

They left in a taxicab after she reassured them twice that she would be fine.

Shivering from the cool evening, Ipatia hugged herself as she sat on the trunk, looking around, feeling somewhat lost. She ignored her thirst and tiredness as she began to concentrate on the people around her. After the ship emptied its passengers, the cars and small trucks slowly rolled off the ramp, one by one.

Ipatia strained her eyes, constantly searching for her aunt, trying to spot a tall, thin woman with a long face and short hair among the crowd. A nagging thought found its way at center stage. *Aunt had not replied to my letter. How do I know if she even got it?*

Her heart started racing when she saw a car roll to a stop in front of her. She arose, expecting her aunt to come out of the car. Instead, Mr. Tony came out of the car. He seemed concerned.

"Ipatia, why are you still here? Wasn't your aunt supposed to come and get you?" Mr. Tony asked sharply.

"Yes, and I am waiting for her," she replied firmly.

"It's late. I can drive you to her house," he offered.

"No, thank you, for if she comes and I am not here, then she will worry," she said, shaking her head.

Mr. Tony insisted that she leave with him, but she adamantly refused any assistance, explaining that her aunt was somewhere around there.

He sighed and left in the car.

Time passed, and the place became so deserted that Ipatia began to worry. Maybe something did happen to her aunt. She was beginning to question the wisdom of traveling alone without Mrs. Xilouris. *Now what am I going to do?*

Her watch showed eleven o'clock. She began to contemplate about getting a taxi. She arose, wondering where she would find one.

Someone tapped her on her shoulder. She turned and faced the short man who wore a uniform and hat.

"Are you Ipatia Kouris?"

Aunt Sophia must have sent him. He knew my name.

"I am to bring you to your Aunt Sophia's house," he said briskly. "Can you please give me her address?"

Feeling relieved, Ipatia dutifully produced the piece of paper with her aunt's address and read it aloud. The driver nodded and took her trunk, whisking it into the car

They drove into the night.

When they stopped at her aunt's residence, the two-story house that Ipatia used to live in, she attempted to pay him. The driver refused the money. He removed the trunk from the cab and followed her.

Ipatia knocked on the door, but no one answered. She knocked again. Thinking that her aunt might be sound asleep, she hesitated. A thought occurred to her. She turned to the cabdriver, her voice quavering, "Sir, did my aunt send you?"

"No, miss. Mr. Tony Plakis did," he admitted. "I am his chauffeur. He asked me to drive you to your aunt's house."

"Oh." Ipatia dug inside her purse, pulling out some coins. "Sir, I insist that you accept the money for the ride and tell your Mr. Tony that I can take care of myself."

Tim took the money sheepishly. "Thank you, miss, but I have instructions to stay with you until you enter the house. I'm to help you with the trunk. Orders are orders."

He waited while she knocked again.

The door opened slightly and Ipatia cried out her aunt's name with joy and crumpled into the woman's outstretched arms, having fainted from sheer exhaustion.

When Ipatia awoke, she was lying on a couch. She lifted herself, then rubbed her eyes, blinking. In front of her sat her aunt, talking quietly to the cab driver. Ipatia studied her more carefully, realizing to her dismay that she was not her aunt.

"Is my aunt here?" Ipatia asked, glancing around, wondering who this woman was.

"I'm sorry, dear child, but you see, she is not here. That is what I was explaining to the driver. I'm renting the downstairs apartment. My name is Marika. I know we look alike, and I understand how you mistook me for her, but please understand that she is not here."

"She's not here?" repeated Ipatia, feeling a rush of anxiety. Then without warning, she broke down, sobbing uncontrollably.

"Here, now don't cry, poor girl. Please don't cry," said Marika, wringing her hands together.

Ipatia's crying slowed down. Sniffling, she asked, "How can I get a hold of her?"

"All I know is that she is in America and she'll be back in three weeks. She didn't mention that you were coming," Marika replied.

"She's in America? What is to become of me?" Ipatia cried. She buried her head in her hands, sobbing.

"Miss, please listen to me. I have orders to drive you to the Plakis residence if your aunt is not here," Tim informed her.

Ipatia looked up at him, still in a daze. He walked with her down the stairs and back into the cab.

Feeling exhausted, she dozed off as the cab sped along into the night.

"Miss, we are in Kifissia. We've arrived," announced Tim. Moments later, the car pulled to a stop.

Ipatia could barely make out the white outline of a large villa in the darkness. She slipped her feet back into her shoes. Yawning, she got out of the cab and shuffled behind Tim as he pulled her trunk to the front door.

Even through her tiredness, she smelled the soft scent of jasmine wafting toward her like a palliative balm, soothing her soul. She swayed yet did not notice her legs giving way from under her and the ground rising up to meet her; she had already faded away into a deep sleep.

CHAPTER 12

I sing with the birds a merry tune,
Because I know I'll see you soon.

Ipatia dreamt that her parents were alive and well, and walking in a large, green pasture away from her and through an open door. She ran after them, but the door shut behind them. She tapped on the door and it opened, but instead of her parents, Mr. Tony was standing there, smiling down at her. Behind him was a room full of food, and the scent of warm bread made her mouth water. He was bending down to kiss her when Ipatia awoke from the dream.

Snuggling further in her bed, Ipatia buried her face into the pillow, trying to finish the dream, but to no avail. Mr. Tony had vanished, and she was left hugging the soft, fluffy pillow instead. Her eyes fluttered open, greeted by the daylight streaming through the window.

As she stifled a yawn, she heard a door close.

"I'll be right there, *Pappou*," she said, stretching lazily.

There was no answer.

Ipatia's eyes shot open. Her eyes saw daylight, and she became worried that she was late in milking the goats. She bolted out of bed, losing her balance and landed on her left foot. Sharp, stabbing pain shot up her leg, and Ipatia cried out in agony. She sat on the cold marble floor, rubbing her throbbing ankle.

I am not in Lipsi, and Grandfather is nowhere in sight. I fell because I had slept in a strange bed that was much higher than my cot.

The Swiss cuckoo clock on the wall chimed twelve o'clock. Had she slept all this time? An aroma of freshly baked bread tugged at her hungry stomach. She looked around and found the source of the scent.

A small round table stood to the side of the room, laden with food. Someone must have brought it in. *Had the dream been real?* She almost believed that Mr. Tony had been in the room a minute ago, bending down to kiss her. She blushed at the idea.

Her stomach growled in anticipation.

As Ipatia arose, she tripped on her large, white cotton nightgown and almost fell forward. Balancing herself in time, she carefully folded the ample material around her small body and limped towards the table.

Her eyes feasted on the thick slices of fresh bread, butter and jam, biscuits, two boiled eggs, cheese, and red plump grapes. A glass of milk also rested on the table.

Nearby, lay a folded note with her name on it. The English handwriting was bold and clean.

"Dear Ipatia, I hope you slept well. After you eat, please don't leave, for I wish to speak with you. Tony."

Ipatia froze, wondering if Mr. Tony had brought the food in with the note. *Stop imagining things.*

Her stomach growled once more, reminding her of the late hour. After saying her prayer, Ipatia feasted on the meal. As she munched on the juicy grapes, she tried to recall what had happened the previous night. She drew a blank after she arrived at the Plakis house.

Questions formed in her mind. Who undressed her and whose nightgown was she wearing? Who brought the food in this morning? Where was her aunt and why hadn't she written to let them know she was in America?

Afterwards, Ipatia searched in her trunk for clean clothes to wear. She pulled out a yellow, silk dress with short sleeves that her godmother had bought for her, insisting that she stop wearing black.

Ipatia hadn't worn it yet. The rest of the trunk held work clothes and her black garb. She stroked the silk dress, picturing herself in it. Maybe she should wear it.

She looked around for the wash basin but did not see any. Maybe they had a washroom, as in Rhodes, where there were sinks and even bathtubs. Her sprained foot, now swollen, didn't fit into the shoe.

Carrying her dress and clean underclothes in one arm, Ipatia peeked out the hallway. There was no one in sight. Good. No one would notice that she was barefooted. She veered right, hobbling carefully down the grand hallway, hearing the rhythmic chiming of a clock coming from somewhere ahead.

"May I help you?"

Startled, Ipatia turned and saw an older woman standing in a doorway, staring kindly at her. She was fair and plump and wore an apron. Her blonde braid was wrapped tightly around her head. She appeared to have been stirring something in a bowl.

"Hello. Who are you?" Ipatia asked.

There was a hearty chuckle, followed by a thick foreign accent. "I am Gilda, the housekeeper and cook. This house belongs to the Plakis family. We were worried about you last night when you fainted."

"I fainted? I don't remember anything."

"*Yah*, you fainted right there in front of the door, and the professor, I mean Dr. Tony, picked you up ever so gently and took you straight into my bedroom. As he was leaving, he asked me to dress you a nightgown."

"Thank you, Gilda," Ipatia said, wrapping the nightgown around her body.

Gilda chuckled. "I had nothing to give you but one of my nightgowns. Miss Melissa was already asleep, so I couldn't ask her."

"Thank you for everything."

"You are welcome, but you should thank the professor. He stayed up late just to make sure you arrived safely."

Professor?

"Oh, that was kind of him. Is he here?" Ipatia asked, pulling her nightgown around her more protectively as she looked around. She didn't want to be seen in her nightgown.

"No, no, don't be afraid. He left a few minutes ago with Tim, the driver. He said he would return shortly. There is no one else here but Miss Melissa, and she is upstairs in her room."

"May I ask you something Gilda?"

"*Yah.*"

"Who made the breakfast?"

"Why, was anything wrong?" asked Gilda, her eyes widening.

"Oh, no, everything was delicious," Ipatia said, nervously. "Thank you for making it. I'm just not used to eating so much."

"*Yah,* I did put a little more food on the tray because you looked like you could use it. I asked the professor to carry it because it was heavy."

"He did?" Ipatia said, feeling weak in the knees.

"Ah. Don't worry. I knocked and checked to see if you were presentable first. You were asleep when he brought the tray into your room," said Gilda, beaming broadly.

"Why is he called professor?"

"Oh, that's because he has a doctoral degree and taught economics at the university in England," said Gilda proudly. "Now his father is sick and wants him to manage the business." Her voice had dropped down to a whisper.

"His father is sick?" echoed Ipatia.

"*Yah,* I heard him tell Mrs. Christina that he wasn't feeling well, and they left for the hospital in Athens," said Gilda, her eyes opening wide.

"Oh, I'm sorry to hear that," Ipatia said. She liked Tony's father. "Who is this Mrs. Christina?"

"His second wife, of course," said Gilda. "Is there anything else that you will need?"

"Yes. Where could I wash?"

"How silly of me, talking with you like this and you standing there in nothing but a nightgown," Gilda said. "Come, follow me to the study. That is the closest one here."

They went down the hallway, past several rooms, and stopped in front of two glass doors. Gilda opened the doors, and Ipatia immediately liked the sunlit room. The two windows allowed views of a flower garden and a glimpse of the verandah. A beautiful Persian rug graced the center of the room and on top of it stood a large desk with a comfortable chair.

Her heart filled with joy when she saw a baby grand piano standing in the far corner of the room. A vase filled with cut flowers was on top of it. She wondered who played the piano in the family.

Bookcases, filled with various books, lined the wall to her left, while the other wall boasted expensive oil paintings depicting different eras and exotic worlds.

Ipatia's eyes widened when she saw the telephone on the desk. Telephones were difficult to come by on the island, and people who requested them had to wait years to get one. Except for her aunt, she didn't know anyone else who had one in their home. The only telephone on the island was at the post office, and they charged a heavy price to use it. Maybe she could call her grandfather on the telephone. She would ask Mr. Tony.

Gilda pointed to a door on the right. "This is the washroom. I see you have your clothes with you, so feel free to bathe. The towels are over there. I will have your other clothes washed later, but now I must get something out of the oven before it burns."

Ipatia thanked her, and then stepped into the washroom. She gazed in awe at the alabaster white porcelain bathtub. To her left, the entire wall was one large mirror. She turned on the water, and then undressed. She stepped into the bathtub and slowly lowered herself into its inviting warmth. She shivered as she felt a breeze. It came from the partially opened window on the other side of the room. Oh well, she was not getting up to close it, not now.

She began humming, enjoying the warm, sudsy water. The humming turned into a song, and she could hear the birds chirping outside, accompanying her. The water they used on the island was well water, and she could never get it warm enough like this.

When Tony returned home from the hospital, he went to the back and sat on the verandah, reading the newspaper. On beautiful days like today, this was his favorite area to read and think. He stopped his reading to focus on his father, who was undergoing a battery of tests, and was obviously upset about the whole thing. It turned out to be a short visit. The nurse had interrupted their conversation every few minutes, and after they took his father for testing, Tony returned home.

He resumed his reading. Someone was singing, and he looked curiously in its direction. Occasionally, Gilda would sing, but this was a higher pitch. It couldn't be his sister. She never sang this cheerfully.

Curious, Tony walked slowly towards the sound. His glance fell on the open window that faced the rose bushes. He smiled. Ipatia was awake.

He returned to his seat and tried to resume his reading, but his thoughts wandered towards the girl. He had spoken to his father about her, and he grudgingly said she could stay with them temporarily.

Ipatia gingerly stepped out of the bathtub. She dried her hair first, then her body vigorously with the large bath towel, humming softly. She studied herself in the mirror. She had never seen herself in a full-length mirror before. She was pleased to see that she was filling out nicely in all the right places.

After dressing, Ipatia gazed at herself in the mirror again, this time appreciating the dress which made her look fuller and a little older. She combed her fingers through her wet hair. Out in the hallway, she could hear women's voices. She recognized Gilda's voice but not the other woman's voice. That was probably Melissa.

Ipatia went to the window, gazing at the large jasmine bush that faced the window. She opened the window, allowing the breeze to sweep the intoxicating scent of the jasmine into the room. Then she sat at the piano, tapping her fingers nervously on the keyboard. She didn't know what to do now.

When was Mr. Tony coming back so they could talk? Hearing the sound of a car, she went and looked out the window. She could see Tim leaving with Melissa in the car.

The house was quiet again. She was alone.

The sun's rays poured generously into the room from the open window, inviting her to play. Content, she leafed through the sheets of music, picking a Mozart piece. Within a few minutes, she had run through it enough times and gained enough confidence to pick up speed and expertly weave the notes in a smooth succession.

As Ipatia played, she was transported back in time to when she was young again, happy and carefree. To a time when her parents were alive and she had felt loved.

She was finally at peace.

CHAPTER 13

Love notes floated like the kiss
To plant themselves upon my lips.

The last notes echoed in the room as Ipatia's fingers rested on the keyboard. She searched through the sheets of music for something else that was easy enough for her to play when her keen ears picked up a movement behind her.

Ipatia turned and saw Mr. Tony sitting at the desk, studying her with an odd expression on his face.

"Oh," she said, feeling her face become hot. *How long had he been here?*

"Sorry to have surprised you. The door was open, and I heard you playing. I couldn't resist coming in to see you play."

Concerned that she had overstepped her boundaries, Ipatia shot up. "Ouch," she exclaimed, wincing from the pain of her ankle. She slumped down on the bench and rubbed her ankle.

"Is everything all right with your foot?" he asked, jumping up and striding toward her.

"I fell on my foot, and it's a little swollen," she confessed.

"Here, let me have a look." He bent down and touched her ankle gently.

"Ouch."

He arose. "It appears swollen. You probably should see a doctor. Meanwhile, you should stay off it, if you can."

"Yes, sir," she said meekly, not knowing what to do, not able to tear her eyes away from his. Should she get up and leave, or sit there? She wasn't used to being alone in a room with a young man before.

"You play the piano well, Ipatia. My congratulations on your fine performance."

"Thank you for the compliment although it's been many years since I had last played," Ipatia said, smiling. "Do you play?"

"I haven't played in a long time either, but let me see now," he said, leafing through the sheets of music. "How about a little Beethoven? What do you say about 'Fur Elise'?"

Feeling pleased, she said, "It's one of my favorite pieces."

He sat down on the bench next to her and rolled up his crisp, white sleeves. He touched the keys softly at first, stroking them, caressing them, then more boldly he cruised through the music, his fingers moving fiercely.

Ipatia shut her eyes, enjoying the swelling and ebbing of the music. Her eyes fluttered open when she felt him touch her. He had leaned over, reaching for the low notes. The music ended, leaving the room filled with a fullness of spirit it didn't have before.

"Well, how did I do, *Maestro*?" he asked huskily, his hands resting on the keyboard as he gazed at her with half-closed eyes.

Breaking the spell, she arose and leaned against the wall. "You did well except for the middle section. You need to practice it more often. It needs to flow, like ripples in the sea. My music teacher used to say that to me, for that is the most difficult passage in the piece."

He arose, leaning towards her.

Ipatia tensed, for there was nowhere to go. He was blocking her path.

"It seems to me the most difficult passage has still to be lived," he whispered. He kissed her softly on her lips, lingering before moving back.

She savored the moment, feeling pleasant and warm all over. *But it was not right.* "Why did you do that?" she managed to whisper, after she came back to earth.

His eyes glowed with a special charm of their own. "I've been meaning to thank you for your beautiful gift, the Alexandrite stone. It changes color, as you said. Ipatia, I can't help noticing, but your green eyes, they're a different color now, almost hazel."

"You didn't have to thank me with a kiss," she scolded lightly. "I mean, you don't kiss men when you want to thank them, do you?"

He laughed at her rebuttal. "Ipatia, you have never been kissed by a man before, have you?"

She shook her head defiantly, fighting back the tears. He was treading too closely into her personal life.

"How old are you?"

Ipatia blinked. She wasn't used to men asking her bold questions. *But he isn't an ordinary man.*

She regained her courage, and straightening herself up, looked him squarely in the eyes. "First of all, thank you for the nice compliments, Mr. Tony. However, where I come from, it's considered impolite for a man to kiss a girl before they are engaged, and even more impolite to ask a girl her age."

"*Mia culpa,*" he said. Stepping back further, he bowed his head slightly.

Ipatia grabbed the opportunity to limp away, her movement limited by her sore ankle. She wasn't about to stay around and fence with this man. She felt herself dangerously lapsing further and further away from her upbringing every time she was near him.

"I don't know what that means, but I do think you are taking advantage of my situation," she retorted, inching her way to the door.

"Ipatia, I assure you, my intentions up until now have been purely philanthropic," he said. "I apologize if I offended your sensitivities. In the future, you can rest assured that I will not get closer than a *foot* from you." He looked down at her swollen foot comically.

She giggled at the pun. "Thank you," she managed to say.

"Now, regarding your stay here."

"Yes?"

He paced the room. "I understand your aunt is to return in three weeks?"

"That is what the renter told me."

"I spoke with Father, and we agreed that you could stay here the three weeks," he said, stopping briefly at the window to gaze outside, his back to her.

She paused. Before his kiss, she would have been eager to accept his offer. All she could picture now was having to fence daily with his affections. Could she maintain her distance? *But I have nowhere else to go.*

"Thank you," she managed to say. "Is your father here so I can thank him also?"

"No, he went to the hospital this morning because he wasn't feeling well," Mr. Tony admitted. "I returned not long ago from visiting him."

"Oh, I'm sorry to hear that he is in the hospital," Ipatia said, recalling Gilda's words earlier that morning. "I would like to speak with my grandfather first before I give you my answer."

"All right. If there is a telephone on the island, we can call there," he said stiffly.

"He asked me to call him at the post office when I arrived safely. I have the number in my purse."

She quickly limped out the door.

Tony watched her leave the room. He wondered if he should have a doctor check her foot before they did anything else. He was curious about her age. Although she had the beginning signs of breasts and hips, she lacked the social graces of a young woman. She was impulsive, stubborn as a mule, and so shy, that she blushed every time he talked with her. How many young women swung around in trees yelling for help, and then ran away from their rescuer? *Am I upset because she asked me not to kiss her?*

He shook his head, smiling. She looked and acted young, yet a part of her showed an older, gentler, kinder Ipatia. Besides, her grandfather did say she should be thinking about marriage and not about books.

Then he remembered how he felt this morning, almost like a school boy, entering her bedroom with the food tray and going to her bed, curious to get a glimpse of her. The image of her peaceful, angelic face with the golden curls billowing around her was still fresh in his memory. Enchanted by her beauty, he gazed down at her, tempted to steal a kiss, but when she stirred, he withdrew quickly. His own heart had raced as he left, for he thought he had heard her speak out his name.

Let's face it, he was used to older, more sophisticated women making the first moves, falling in love with him and encouraging his kisses. To them, it was just a game. He had no experience with young, naïve girls. To Ipatia, a kiss was probably as good as a proposal of marriage.

From now on, I should be more careful around the girl.

Ipatia returned shortly, handing Mr. Tony a piece of paper with a telephone number on it. "Grandfather doesn't usually go down to the post office except in the mornings," she explained.

"Let's arrange for him to be there tomorrow morning, around nine-thirty?"

"Yes, that's a good idea. I know he's down at Mr. Pericles's coffee shop by nine o'clock, so it wouldn't be much of an effort to go to the post office from there, and-" Ipatia stopped, appearing thoughtful. "I forgot to ask, how much will it cost?"

"Don't worry about it." Mr. Tony laughed as he dialed the telephone number. He arranged with the postal clerk to inform Mr. Rodakis of the telephone appointment.

After he hung up the telephone, Tony looked at Ipatia. "It is done. Tomorrow morning, we will telephone your grandfather.

Meanwhile, would you mind joining me for a cup of coffee on the verandah? It's as pretty as the view you get from your home in Lipsi, I guarantee it," he ventured.

Ipatia was still feeling excited about the prospect of speaking to her grandfather and said impulsively, "Yes, I mean, I don't know. What did you mean yesterday when you said *mea copa*, or whatever that was?"

"I thought you would ask," he said, chuckling, thoroughly amused. "But where I come from, it's impolite for a girl to ask."

Ipatia blushed, realizing he was fencing again.

"No, seriously, *Mia Culpa* means my mistake, or in other words, forgive me," he replied.

"Oh," she replied, liking the explanation.

She limped alongside him down the hallway. They had reached her room. "Will you excuse me for a moment? I have something to do first, and then I will meet you in a little while outside."

He looked at her for a moment, and then nodded graciously and left.

Ipatia slipped into her room, catching her breath. This man was going too fast for her. She clutched the slip of paper with the telephone number on it, and sat down on the bed, thinking about everything that had happened this morning. She wasn't used to spending so much time alone with a young man, and on top of it, being kissed.

Was it because she had talked boldly with Mr. Tony in the studio, that she had inadvertently encouraged his advances? *Remember what Pappou said about conversing with young men.* She should be more careful in the future.

Tony stopped at the kitchen and looked inside. "Gilda? Oh, there you are. Can you please bring two coffees and a few pastries out to the verandah?"

"*Yah*, professor," said Gilda, smiling broadly. "I want to let you know that Miss Melissa told me that she and Dr. Hatzis are coming for dinner."

"Thank you for telling me. Please make sure there is ample food and set the table."

"Will the girl be joining you for dinner?"

"I assume she will. Go ahead and set an extra plate for her anyway. Also, chances are that Ipatia might be remaining here for three weeks, so you will also need to move her into the guest bedroom before you leave today."

"She is staying here? Oh no, no," Gilda cried, shaking her head. "Today, I leave for my vacation. The new housekeeper will not be here until tomorrow. Who will watch her until then?"

"My sister and step-mother will be here."

Didn't Miss Melissa tell you? She is leaving after dinner with Dr. Hatzis to visit his family. They plan to stay there overnight, and Mrs. Christina is staying in the Athens hotel close to your father. No one else is going to be here."

"I forgot about your vacation," he said, rubbing his forehead. "I didn't know Melissa was going to Michael's home, either."

"Also, you are a single man, no? She is only a girl and shouldn't be left alone in this house with you. What if her parents find out?"

"She has no parents. She has only a grandfather who is living far away on Lipsi Island. There is no one else for her right now. We are her family for the moment, until we figure out how to get her to her aunt."

"Oh, how sad. The poor girl has no family. *Tsk, tsk*," said Gilda, wagging her head. "Maybe I can see if my niece Olga can come and stay over tonight."

"Gilda, you are a gem," Tony said, pecking her on the cheek. He whistled as he went out to the verandah.

Ipatia sat on her bed, thinking about everything. Someone knocked on the door. She wondered if it were Tony. "Come in."

Gilda peeked in the room. "Miss Ipatia, the professor told me that you are staying tonight. I will show you to another room because the new housekeeper is coming tomorrow and is going to use this room."

"A new housekeeper? Are you leaving?"

"Only for four weeks. I will ask my niece, Olga, to come and stay over for the night, in case you need anything. Please come with me and don't worry about anything."

Ipatia followed her slowly down the hallway. They went past the kitchen and turned down into another hallway, going towards the entranceway. At the front lobby stood a great stairway that wound upstairs to the second floor. She looked around in awe at the marble floors, the white columns in the doorways, the busts of Greek statues, and the beautiful paintings on the walls.

They turned left and continued down another hallway and finally stopped in front of a door.

"Here we are. This is the guestroom and is even bigger and nicer than my room, Yah?" said Gilda, smiling, as she opened the door. A stream of sunlight met them, bathing the room in the early afternoon glow.

"It's wonderful," Ipatia exclaimed. She had never witnessed so much beauty and elegance in a bedroom before. It even had a private washroom. "I will need to bring my trunk of clothes here."

"Don't worry, we'll get them moved. I heard you playing the piano and the beautiful music filled the house again. You play well, too." Gilda's face had a joyful expression as she clasped Ipatia's hands together.

"Thank you, Gilda," Ipatia said, smiling. She heard the cuckoo clock chiming four o'clock.

"There I go again, talking, and there is so much work to do before I leave," said Gilda, shaking her head and waving her hands in the air. "Oh, Mr. Tony said to tell you that he is waiting for you outside. I will bring the coffee and pastries in a minute."

Gilda left a breeze behind her as she swooshed out of the room, her plump body moving surprisingly swiftly down the hallway.

Ipatia was feeling better already. The cheerful room was large, with two windows that held elegant gold drapes over white lace curtains. A Persian rug covered the marble floor and there were landscape paintings on the wall. A beautiful, crystal vase, filled with flowers, sat atop a white dresser. The bed's satin, ivory bedspread had intricate embroidery that resembled two large, colorful birds.

Ipatia limped towards the window and looked outside. It overlooked the large verandah that boasted several pots of beautiful flowers and life-sized Greek statues. Mr. Tony was sitting alone at a table, reading a newspaper. He appeared to be in deep thought.

Beyond, she could see a glimpse of the sea.

She slowly made her way outside, following the path that led to the back verandah. She would have normally enjoyed the walk, savoring the scents and beautiful array of flowers, but her foot hurt every time she pressed on it.

As she approached Mr. Tony, she could see behind him the steps leading down to the large swimming pool area. Tall cypress trees surrounded the pool area, providing privacy, and nearby was a tennis court. Beyond, the land sloped downward, lending a spectacular panoramic view of Athens and the sea.

He looked up, appearing surprised to see her.

Ipatia had resolved not to be the first to start the conversation. She was aware of and nervously anticipating, what he was going to say or do next.

"I thought you had changed your mind," he said, smiling.

"Gilda moved me to the guest bedroom, and it took some time. Thank you for the beautiful room."

"I'm glad you like it. I hope you can stay the three weeks so you can enjoy it more," Mr. Tony said, his eyes smiling.

"Thank you for your hospitality, but I do need to speak with my grandfather first, to see what he will say," she replied stiffly, suddenly feeling shy again.

Gilda arrived, carrying the tray with the refreshments "Here you are," she said, serving the coffee and pastries."

CHAPTER 14

You talked about your life to me,
It opened possibilities.

After Gilda left, Tony watched Ipatia sip her cup of warm coffee quietly and timidly eat her pastry. He sensed the girl's nervousness and picked up his newspaper, trying to immerse himself in the news. *I must remember to maintain a respectable stance so she can feel comfortable with me.*

His eyes fell on an article about a possible merger between Chuck Daras and John Meriklis, who was Bonnie's father. It took him a moment to realize the implications. "I can't believe it," he exclaimed unexpectedly. Meriklis was a supermarket tycoon. Wasn't Daras supposed to have worked some deal with his father instead? He would have to tell Father about this.

He folded the newspaper and tried to compose himself. He typically did not overreact like this. *Is it because I want to talk to her but don't know what to say after that scene in the study?*

"What is it?" Ipatia asked, looking at the back of the paper.

"The news is always the same, either there is a scandal, or someone dies, or someone buys someone else's business," Tony said, more calmly.

"My grandfather used to say the same thing," she offered.

He smiled, struck by her innocent beauty. "Ipatia, let's talk about something more pleasant. For one thing, tell me a little about yourself."

"You won't believe this, but I was born in America."

"You were?" he asked, arching an eyebrow.

"My father had gone to Baltimore on one of his trips, hauling cargo. My mother often traveled with him, and she was a little over seven months pregnant when her labor pains began the same time the ship was docking in Baltimore. I was born two hours later in the hospital in Baltimore and had to remain there for six weeks because I was a premature baby."

"Is that so? How did you return to Greece?" Tony asked, trying to picture this healthy-looking girl as a tiny, premature baby.

"My father had already left, so Mother and I flew back to Greece by airplane." She continued her story. "My parents called me "Amerikanaki," which was a pet name they gave me from being born in America. Mrs. Rodos, an English teacher who lived down the street from us in Piraeus, taught me English. She is the one who gave me the English book that you found.'

"Yes, I remember," he said. "How did you end up in Lipsi?"

"We visited Lipsi every summer. The summer that I was eight, my father received news from a relative visiting from Crete. Grandfather Kouris lived in Crete and had suffered a severe stroke and was lying in bed on the verge of dying," she said. Her voice began to tremble. "My parents left immediately for Crete, leaving me behind with my grandfather. A month later, we learned that on their return trip from Crete, their ship was caught in a storm at sea and had sunk. There were no survivors."

"I'm sorry to hear that."

The sound of heels clicking on the pavement interrupted their conversation. Melissa, Bonnie, and Michael were approaching them.

Ipatia arose quickly. "I'm feeling somewhat tired. I'd like to go and lie down for a little while."

"Please stay for a few minutes more. I want Michael to look at your foot, if that's all right with you," Tony said softly, touching her arm before standing to greet the group.

The girl sat resolutely back down in her seat.

"Hi Tony," Melissa said, kissing him lightly on the cheek. "We came back from visiting Father. He's expecting you tonight. He said he had something to tell you. It's about business."

"Oh?" he replied quietly. He greeted the others.

Ipatia smiled at them and remained quiet, while the group stood around talking.

Tony went inside and instructed Gilda to bring more drinks and refreshments. Then he called Michael into the house to help him bring more chairs out to the veranda.

"How is it going with Ipatia?" Michael asked curiously, as he picked up a chair.

Surprised by his friend's question, Tony became alert. *Michael rarely showed interest in women.* "She fell on her foot and it appears swollen. She hasn't seen a doctor yet."

"I should look at it then," Michael said promptly.

They brought the chairs to the table and everyone sat down. Tony noticed how Bonnie and Melissa ignored Ipatia and chatted about the latest fashion.

Gilda arrived with a tray of refreshments, placing it down on the table and serving the refreshments.

"Ipatia, Dr. Hatzis knows about your swollen foot and would like to examine it," Tony said.

Ipatia blushed as Michael bent down and examined her swollen foot.

"How did it happen?" Michael asked her.

"When I awoke today, I didn't know where I was and jumped out of bed and landed on my foot."

"I can't tell for sure if you sprained it or fractured it," he said, standing up. "You need to go to the hospital tomorrow and get it x-rayed and then come to my office afterwards," Michael said. "Tony can you bring her?"

Tony nodded. His car was in the shop. He would have to borrow Tim's car.

"My love, you promised me that you wouldn't see patients tomorrow," Melissa said to Michael. "We were supposed to go shopping in the morning for the engagement rings."

"Oh. I completely forgot. Sorry," Michael said, wincing at the reminder. "I didn't inform my staff, and they've already scheduled patients. How about the day after?"

"You keep putting it off," Melissa complained.

After some haggling, they arranged to meet tomorrow afternoon for the rings.

"Will you please excuse me? My foot is hurting a little, and I'd like to rest it," Ipatia said, getting up.

"Put some ice on it to remove the swelling, and try to stay off it," Michael said.

Bonnie rushed forward and grabbed Ipatia's arm. "Here, Ipatia. I'll walk with you," she said sweetly.

Tony watched in amazement. There was a sweet side to Bonnie that he hadn't seen before.

Ipatia and Bonnie walked slowly, entering the house. Ipatia felt Bonnie's sharp nails digging into her arm. She eased away, but the painful grip was tight.

They reached the bedroom.

"There," Bonnie said holding tightly to Ipatia, guiding her to the bed. "You lie down and rest. If you need to move around, call for me, and I'll come and help you."

Ipatia thanked her with reservation and watched her leave, her heels clicking on the floor. Ipatia rubbed her sore arm and spied the indentation marks caused by Bonnie's sharp nails. She felt uneasy. Was Bonnie putting on an act for Mr. Tony? *Was Bonnie jealous of me spending time with him?*

As Ipatia rested in bed, she watched the sun's rays pouring into the room. A peaceful feeling washed over her. She was beginning to like this room.

Gilda came with a bowl of ice cubes and a towel. "Miss Ipatia. Mr. Tony told me to get you some ice for your foot."

She liked Gilda, and she liked Mr. Tony. She smiled dreamily back.

"Will you be joining them for dinner?" Gilda asked.

Ipatia tensed, remembering both the edgy conversation Melissa had with Dr. Hatzis and Bonnie's deceptive behavior. An uneasy feeling replaced the peace. She didn't feel comfortable being in their company.

"The doctor said I needed to rest my foot, so I think it's best to remain here."

"I am leaving right after dinner to go on my vacation. My niece, Olga, will stop by later and see if you need anything."

After Gilda left, Ipatia wrapped the towel around the ice and placed the ice pack on her foot. She rested in bed, feeling the breeze from the window and the sound of the birds chirping cheerfully outside. It felt so peaceful. She thought about what happened today and how she felt being with Mr. Tony. She smiled when she pictured herself sitting with him on the verandah, talking about her life. He had appeared interested, gazing at her with his large, chocolate-brown eyes and prompting her with questions.

A knocking on the door aroused her. She opened her eyes. *I must have dozed off.*

"Hello? Hello? I am Olga," a woman said, opening the door and carrying a tray of food. She was a younger version of Gilda, except she was thinner and her dark-blonde hair was shoulder length.

"Hello. I'm Ipatia."

"I know. You're the lovely young lady that my aunt talked about," Olga said cheerfully, putting the tray of food on the table. "I brought you some food. I am only here for tonight. I work in a beauty salon and have to be at work early tomorrow morning by seven-thirty."

"You do? What do you do?"

"Oh, everything," Olga began, sounding important. She described the work she did as an apprentice, and how she had plans one day to open her own beauty salon. "Well, I will leave you then, so you can eat."

"No, wait. Why don't you join me for dinner?" Ipatia asked, desperate for some company.

"Thank you, but I ate already. I can just sit here and keep you company, though."

Ipatia hobbled to the small table. She said her prayer and began to eat.

Olga studied her for a moment. "You know, Miss Ipatia, you could use a haircut. The style these days is much shorter, and although it might make you look a little older, it will make you look more sophisticated."

"I've always had my hair long. I wouldn't know how to handle it short."

"Why not?" Olga said, shrugging her shoulders. "It's less work and easier to comb. Even if you don't like it, it'll grow back again."

While Ipatia ate her dinner, Olga continued expounding on the virtues of having short hair and finally persuaded Ipatia to cut her hair.

Olga went and retrieved her shears and comb and started cutting Ipatia's curls. Soon, Ipatia's long tresses lay on the floor while Olga snipped the final touches.

"There, I hope you like it," Olga said, giving her a mirror.

Ipatia gazed at herself in the mirror with mixed feelings. She was used to her long hair, but on the other hand, Olga had been right, her short hair bobbed around her face, making her look older. She couldn't decide if she liked this haircut.

"In case you don't like it, I brought you a scarf that you can put on," Olga said, half-joking as she retrieved it from her pocket and gave it to her.

"That was thoughtful of you," Ipatia laughed. She unfolded the scarf, admiring the bright colors "How can I repay you?"

"Don't worry about it," Olga said, taking the tray with her tools and going to the door. "I am staying in my aunt's room for the night in case you need anything. The new housekeeper is supposed to arrive tomorrow morning. Otherwise, have a good night."

***

That evening, right after dinner, Melissa and Michael excused themselves, intent on leaving.

"Melissa what are your plans for the night?" Tony asked.

"I'll be visiting Michael's family and should be back late morning. Michael has appointments tomorrow morning and I have shopping to do."

Tony nodded, bidding the couple farewell as they left.

"I must be going also," Bonnie said.

Tony walked with her towards the entranceway of the house, his hands in his pockets.

"Now that you'll be here in Greece, I hope we'll be seeing more of each other," Bonnie said lightly, tossing her hair back.

"The reason I chose to stay here is because my father is too ill to run the business."

Bonnie turned and glared at him. "I hope your decision wasn't swayed by that island girl who is staying here."

She was gone before Tony could reply, her heels clicking angrily down the driveway and out into the street. He stared at her retreating figure, stung by her toxic remark, yet admitting silently there was some truth in what she said.

When Tony entered his father's room, he found him sleeping. Christina was sitting by his side, reading a magazine.

"How is everything with Father?" Tony asked. He pulled up a chair next to her.

"They gave him some medication to help him sleep. He's still been complaining of those spells," she said quietly.

"Do they know what is wrong with him?"

"No, not yet. They are running more tests on him. He's scheduled for a needle biopsy tomorrow."

"They still don't know what he has yet?" Tony asked incredulously. "Do you know how long he'll be here?"

"No, they haven't decided that either. I'd rather have him here for the time being, so he doesn't fall and hurt himself," she said, shrugging.

"Good idea. Melissa said he was upset about something and wanted to see me?"

She paused. "He received a business call this morning, and seemed upset afterwards, but did not tell me anything about it."

"I can talk to him tomorrow when I visit him again."

"He'll be disappointed that you came and he was asleep. He did want to talk to you."

"That's all right. It's better that he gets well. I'll return tomorrow."

"Come late morning, after they've done the biopsy. You can also talk to the doctors then if you have any questions."

Tony stayed a while longer, hoping to speak with his father, but he did not awaken, so Tony returned home.

CHAPTER 15

Two gentlemen spent time with me.
I wonder where all this will lead?

The next morning, Ipatia awoke to the sound of birds chirping outside her window. She rubbed her eyes and stretched. Her thoughts turned to yesterday's events. She smiled dreamily, remembering playing the piano, and Mr. Tony's kiss. *Stop those thoughts right now. It was wrong of him to kiss me.*

She pulled the covers away from her body. About to get out of bed, Ipatia remembered her swollen ankle. How foolish she had been to jump out of bed yesterday and injure it.

A knocking on the door interrupted her thoughts. Her heart jumped, as she imagined Mr. Tony bringing her the tray like yesterday morning. She did not want him to see her in her nightgown. She scrambled under the covers and pulled them up to her chin. "Come in."

"Good morning, Miss Ipatia. I am Soula, the cook, with your breakfast," Soula said. She was a friendly, middle-aged woman, with sturdy arms strong enough to carry the heavy breakfast tray into the room.

"Good morning, Soula."

"I hope I didn't wake you, but Miss Olga told me before she left this morning that you would want your meal early."

"Thank you," Ipatia said, smiling and sitting up in bed, feeling special. "Is anyone else awake?"

"Oh, you mean Mr. Tony? I think he left with Tim, the driver earlier this morning, and Miss Melissa still hasn't returned," Mrs. Soula said, as she left the room. "Enjoy your meal, Miss Ipatia."

There was no note today on the tray. Ipatia felt slightly disappointed, secretly hoping that Mr. Tony would have written again. She ate her breakfast, wondering how she was going to telephone her grandfather if Mr. Tony wasn't there to place the call.

Someone rapped on her door.

Ipatia's heart started racing again, wondering if it might be Mr. Tony. Instead, a thin, nervous woman stood at the door and introduced herself as the new housekeeper, Mrs. Katina.

"Miss Ipatia, do you need anything?" she piped.

"No, thank you. Everything is fine."

Mrs. Katina appeared relieved and excused herself, saying she was busy, since she was new and trying to get everything in order.

Ipatia washed and dressed into a black skirt and black, long-sleeved blouse. She wanted to hide the nail marks and the black and blue areas around them that were caused by Bonnie. She waited anxiously until nine-thirty. She limped towards the study, wondering if Mr. Tony would remember the telephone call that he was going to make to her grandfather.

The double doors to the study were open. Feeling hopeful that Mr. Tony would be there, she peeked inside.

The study was empty, compounding her anxiety. She knew that her grandfather did not like to wait, but what could she do? She could not place the call without Mr. Tony.

Ipatia perused the bookshelf, looking through books, but did not have to wait long.

"Good morning, Ipatia, sorry I'm late," Mr. Tony said, walking briskly into the study. "I had to pick up my car." He stopped in his tracks when he saw her. Surprise was written all over his face. "What happened to your hair?"

Ipatia touched her curls, remembering her haircut. "Oh, uh, Gilda's niece, Olga cut my hair. She thought it would look better short."

"I liked it better long. You shouldn't let others influence you," he said curtly.

Her face turned red and she pulled herself up stiffly. "Mr. Tony, we had an engagement to call my grandfather, didn't we?"

He gazed steadily into her eyes. "Please call me Tony," he said huskily.

She softened. "All right. *Tony.*"

He cleared his throat. "Before you telephone him, I would like to remind you that you are more than welcome to stay here, Ipatia. Melissa is back today, so you can tell your grandfather that you won't be alone. Do you have the number? I can dial it for you."

She handed him the paper with the telephone number on it.

After he finished dialing, he handed her the telephone, and then picked up a book from a shelf and walked out of the study.

"Hello, this is Ipatia Kouris. Is my grandfather there?"

"One minute, please," said a young man's voice.

"Ipatia, my girl, how are you?" Grandfather asked. His voice was shaky from emotion.

Ipatia was glad to hear his voice. She told him that she was at the Plakis house and explained how she ended up there. When she finished, she asked him, "What should I do? Should I remain here?"

"If I had only known that your aunt would not be there, I would not have let you leave," he scolded her.

Feeling penitent, Ipatia didn't know what to say. *He is right.*

"Listen to me. You are to go to Cousin George's house. He lives in a suburb of Piraeus with his family."

"Isn't he the one who visited us a couple of times with his wife Paula?"

"Yes. I don't know if they are there, though, because they travel often, but at least give it a try," he said. "Now, get a pen and paper, because I am going to give you their address. If they are willing to have you, gather your belongings and go and stay there until your aunt arrives."

She wrote down the address. "What if they aren't there or cannot have me staying with them?"

"Then so be it. You will have to stay with the Plakis family," he said, sighing. "Let me know what happens. By the way, give my greetings to your cousins if you see them, and to Mr. Tony and his family."

"I will do that. How are things there?"

"Fine, fine. We all miss you, and everyone's been asking about you," he replied. His voice was beginning to soften.

She asked him about Mrs. Xilouris and little Nick.

"I saw them this morning. As far as I could see, the boy was doing well, and Mrs. Xilouris asked about you."

"Good. How are you doing being alone, *Pappou*?"

"Your godmother and her family have been helping me. Thomas will come later today to help me with the chores. How has Mr. Tony been toward you?"

She told him about her foot, and that he was going to drive her to the doctor to get it checked. "He is very kind to me. Did you know that he is very educated and a professor at a university?"

"Hmm," her grandfather said. Then he sternly reminded her to behave like the good girl that she was and not to talk too much in the presence of Mr. Tony.

"We don't want them thinking that our girls from the island are too bold," Christos said. "Now I must say good-bye because there are others here that need to use the telephone."

Ipatia made her tearful farewell. She went into the hallway and found Mr. Tony leaning against the wall, reading the book.

"How did it go?" he asked, studying her closely.

"My grandfather has a cousin who lives somewhere in Piraeus, and he gave me his address. I am to stay with them," she said, trying to sound cheerful.

"I want you to know that you are always welcome to remain here."

"Thank you, but I am to stay with my cousins."

"Fine, but first we need to see about getting your foot x-rayed and visiting the doctor."

"All right, and can we stop afterwards and check on my cousins?" she insisted.

"I think we can manage that."

As they drove down the road, Ipatia noticed a bus stopped ahead at a bus stop.

"Where does that bus go?" she asked curiously.

"It goes all the way to the docks in Piraeus," Tony said, pointing in the general direction. "Why?"

"I was curious," she replied. She remained quiet after that, looking at the scenery, mindful of how masterfully he drove. She realized they had been high up on a hill, for the winding road led them slowly down its slope, past beautiful large villas with spacious properties.

Tony pointed towards the sprawling city below them. "That is Athens where the hospital is."

She gazed at the famous city, with its cluttered tall buildings, busy streets and busy way of life, so different from Lipsi Island's pastoral setting and slower pace.

Tony turned on the radio, and they listened to the music. She was too shy to speak, and she sensed that he was more reserved than usual.

Soon, they arrived in the city. Tony made driving look so easy, as he expertly maneuvered the car around the busy streets of Athens.

They stopped at the hospital to get her ankle x-rayed. Walking through its corridors teeming with people and nursing staff, Ipatia felt overwhelmed. She had not been in such a big hospital before. Her eyes opened wide with wonder as she saw patients walking, limping or being wheeled around.

"Here, let's get you to the right place." Tony guided her to the x-ray department.

"I'll be back shortly. I need to do an errand," he said, after depositing her in the room.

After what seemed like a long time, a technician called Ipatia to get her x-ray. The x-ray room was cold and dark, and Ipatia shivered throughout the procedure.

Afterwards, she sat waiting for Tony's return, her anxiety mounting. He had left her abruptly at the hospital, and she wondered if he were upset with her. Maybe he did not want to help her, and she had become a burden to him, yet her heart felt that was not the case. He did arrive on time for the telephone call and he did ask her to call him Tony. He even brought her here. Was he reserved with her because of her haircut? She touched her hair thoughtfully. Feeling miserable, Ipatia sat and waited.

"Ipatia."

Ipatia turned toward Tony's voice, her heart swelling with joy. *He came.*

He approached her, smiling in that charming manner of his that made her feel special. She returned his smile. Somehow, he made everything feel all right.

"We need to visit Dr. Hatzis and see about the test results," Tony informed her, helping her limp down the corridor.

Tony drove her to Dr. Hatzis's building, not far away from the hospital.

The lobby felt cool with its marble floors as they entered the building. The office was on the first floor.

Tony held the door open for her as she limped into the waiting room. The plain, sterile room was small and held a few chairs where an old couple and on older woman sat in them. To the side was a bookshelf with magazines.

Dr. Hatzis came out of the examining room and greeted them. "It might be a while before the x-ray records are in. I hope you don't mind waiting," he said.

"I need to go see about my father. Would you like to wait here, Ipatia?" Tony asked Ipatia. "I'll come for you later."

Ipatia's anxiety returned. *Tony is leaving me alone again in a strange place.* She nodded.

"I will phone you when she's finished," Dr. Hatzis told him.

A nurse called Dr. Hatzis into the office.

After Tony left, Ipatia read the medical journals that were lined up on the bookshelf. Time passed, and patients came and went as she focused on her reading.

Ipatia was beginning to feel hungry. She yawned. Shortly thereafter, a nurse came into the waiting room and called her name. Dr. Hatzis's office was down the hallway and when they entered it, he was busy writing something in a medical chart.

He looked up and smiled.

"I have good news, Ipatia. The films show you don't have any fractures or breaks in any of the bones in your foot," he said. "You'll be back to normal quickly."

"Oh, that's wonderful, Dr. Hatzis! You don't know how happy that has made me," she exclaimed joyfully.

"I am happy for you, too, Ipatia," he said softly. He discussed the proper care for her swollen ankle, reminding her to rest it. "If you need anything else, let me know."

Someone knocked, and a nurse entered the office. "Dr. Hatzis, you are needed."

"I'll be right there."

"Before you leave, doctor, could we telephone Tony?" Ipatia asked.

"Yes, of course." Dr. Hatzis dialed the number for her.

Ipatia appreciated the doctor's attentiveness towards her. After he handed her the telephone, he excused himself to examine the patient.

Katina, the new housekeeper at the Plakis house, answered the telephone. She said that Mr. Tony was not there. Ipatia asked her to tell him to phone her at the doctor's office when he arrived.

Ipatia returned to the waiting room. She sat and read some more magazines. Finally, the waiting room was empty. Her foot was throbbing and she was feeling miserable.

Dr. Hatzis came out of his office and was surprised to see her there. "Wasn't Tony supposed to pick you up?"

"When I called his house, Katina told me that he hadn't arrived yet," she mumbled.

"If you don't mind waiting, I can drive you back to the house later in the day when I'm done seeing patients. I'll be going there anyway to see Melissa."

"It's not so easy. I have to go somewhere else after I finish here," she explained, blushing at his invitation. She told him about her cousins.

"I know George Mastroyiannis and his family," he said, his blue eyes lighting. "Last time I saw them was a month ago, and he mentioned they were going to Italy for a visit, but I don't remember when they were leaving."

The telephone rang and Dr. Hatzis answered it. "Oh, hello, Katina. Yes, she is waiting here for Tony. I will tell her. By the way, is Melissa there? Please let her know I wish to speak to her."

Ipatia listened curiously to his conversation with Melissa. It seemed like his voice tightened slightly.

"Yes, we can go for the rings. I think we should try several places before we decide, don't you?" Dr. Hatzis hung up the telephone, then turned to Ipatia and said, "Tony will be here around one o'clock to pick you up. I finished seeing my last patient. Why don't we have something to eat until he arrives?"

"Oh, I don't know," Ipatia began, blushing once more. Although she felt comfortable being with him, the idea of having lunch with him sounded too intimate.

"I know your foot is not well and you are probably hungry, so I will go next door, get some souvlakia and bring them back here. Will that be all right with you?"

She nodded silently, wondering how in such a short time, she had been left alone with two single young men, and she did not feel that bad.

Within minutes, Dr. Hatzis returned with the savory souvlakia nestled in pita bread. They sat down and ate their lunch.

Ipatia asked him about his profession, and he responded by relating his experiences in medicine. Enraptured by what she heard, Ipatia admired the little miracles he performed on people, helping them to live. They were laughing over an incident he had with one of his patients when the glass door to the office flew open.

◆━━━◆ ◆◆━━━◆ ◆◆━━━◆

Tony was surprised to hear laughter coming from the office. When he entered the room, he saw Ipatia and Michael laughing heartily. His radar went up.

"Hello you two. What have you been up to?" Tony asked, trying to sound cheerful. He had never seen Michael look so boyishly happy. Was Ipatia infecting him also with her youthful cheerfulness?

"I was telling Ipatia that story with the old man who had a hearing problem, remember that story?"

"Oh, yes, and you asked him to sit down, and he dropped his pants down instead?"

The room erupted with laughter once more.

"How is your foot, Ipatia?" Tony asked, after the laughter died down.

"Very well, thank you. Dr. Hatzis said there are no fractures, and in a short while, I'll be back to normal."

Michael walked with Tony and Ipatia outside, heading towards Tony's red convertible sports car. "By the way, how is your father?" Michael asked.

Tony sighed. "When I arrived at the hospital, the nurse told me he was having tests done."

"What about Christina?"

"She wasn't there, either. I learned from the nurse that she had left earlier for the hotel. I waited awhile, hoping I would see Father, but he did not show up by the time I left. I'll find out later when I return in the afternoon."

Tony opened the door for Ipatia, and she sat in the car. He waved to Michael as they drove away.

Tony looked at Ipatia. "Could you give me the address where we are going?"

She took the paper out of her purse and read it aloud.

"I know where it is. It's near my office," he said.

"Oh, that's nice," she replied dreamily, and then stopped. "I meant that it's nice that you know where they live."

He pulled down the top of the car. They rode through the busy streets, weaving smoothly in and out of the cars. He glanced at Ipatia's beautiful profile with her straight nose and small, firm chin, as she gazed quietly at the buildings and people walking the streets. She was more subdued than usual.

Tony turned on the radio, thinking about how he had criticized her for cutting her hair, and afterwards, when she told him about going to her cousins' house, he had been quiet with her. He also had left her alone in the hospital and at Michael's office all morning. *Did I treat her the way Father would have treated me, with indifference?*

He glanced her way again. Still quiet. *Too quiet.* Moments earlier, he had found her laughing heartily with Michael.

A favorite song was playing.

"*Asta ta malakia sou,*" he sang along. His rich, baritone voice blended well with the song, drowning out the sounds of the noisy streets. The lyrics were about a woman's hair and the seasons of life.

He glanced at Ipatia and caught her staring at him, making her blush prettily. She pushed the curls of hair from her face, and then searched her purse. Retrieving a scarf from it, she wrapped it around her head.

"I heard you speaking with Dr. Hatzis about your father," she began. "I hope it isn't an inconvenience that I stayed at your house while your father was at the hospital."

"Your visit isn't an inconvenience at all. My father often invites people to stay with us even when he's not there."

A short time later, they arrived at her cousins' address. They entered the courtyard of the three-story building and found an older woman sweeping the adjacent courtyard.

"Excuse me, madam. Do you know where the Mastroyiannis family lives?" Ipatia asked her.

"Yes, they live downstairs, but they aren't here. They left two days ago on a trip and won't be back for a month."

She thanked her and timidly turned to Tony, looking at him expectantly.

"Then it is settled. You stay with us for now," he said, feeling a rush of unexplained happiness.

Ipatia smiled as she returned to the car with him. "Thank you."

They pulled out into the main road and traveled a few blocks, entering an area that had shops and stores. When they stopped at the light, he pointed to the tall, modern looking building on the right-hand side. "That is our office building."

"It's a large building," Ipatia exclaimed.

"Yes, now that you mention it," he replied, nodding appreciatively, "we own the whole building. My office is on the third floor and we employ thirty staff."

Tony turned a corner, thinking about what would happen next. Once he dropped Ipatia off at the house, he would have to leave to visit Father. He didn't want this time with Ipatia to end just yet, plus he needed to speak to her.

"There's a place nearby where they make the best *loukoumathes* (sweet donut balls). Let's stop there and bring some back for my father. I am visiting him later at the hospital. It will perk him up. He goes crazy over *loukoumathes*." He chuckled.

Ipatia laughed along with him.

A few minutes later, they sat at a small table outside the loukoumathes shop, enjoying the sweet doughnut balls with a glass of cold coffee frappe under the shade of a tree. The chirping sounds of birds provided a serene atmosphere.

"Hmmm. You were right, these are the best *loukoumathes*," she murmured, chewing one of the honey-dipped doughnuts that were still warm. "Thank you so much."

The sun's rays filtered through the leaves soaking them with a cozy ambiance.

Ipatia pulled up her sleeves and took off her scarf and put it in her purse. Her fingers combed through her short hair, pulling it down as if to make it longer.

That simple act tugged at his heart. "Ipatia, I wanted to talk to you about today."

That got her attention. She stared at him wide-eyed.

"First of all, I'm sorry for making comments about your short hair earlier. I was out of line."

"That's all right," she said, fingering her hair nervously. "I also am not used to having it cut so short."

"Also, you experienced a long day, from your phone call to your grandfather, and then having your foot x-rayed and waiting all these hours at Dr. Hatzis's office. I apologize for leaving you alone for so long."

Tony wasn't prepared for the tears that welled in the girl's large eyes. She stared at him, her beautiful light-green eyes shimmering with tears, and then she looked down, shamefaced.

I had touched a chord.

Ipatia wiped her eyes and sniffed. "I don't normally cry like this," she muttered, feeling miserable and vulnerable at the same time.

"That's all right, you're probably tired. Maybe I shouldn't have brought you here but driven you home to rest," he said, gently touching her arm.

"Oh, no," she exclaimed, pulling her arm away and shaking her head. "I'm enjoying this, truly I am."

Ipatia noticed his glance settle on the welt marks left from Bonnie's nails on her arm. She had forgotten about them.

A shadow passed over his face. "Ipatia, how did you get these marks?" he asked, pointing to her arm, his voice dangerously low.

She covered them with her hand. "It's nothing, really. It happened when Bonnie helped me to my room. Her nails were a little sharp," she said.

He muttered something darkly under his breath.

After they finished, Tony ordered a large batch of *loukoumathes* to take with them. As he drove home, he sang along with the radio, making the trip amusing and fun for Ipatia.

Ipatia enjoyed listening to his singing. They arrived back at the Plakis house around three-thirty.

"I won't be coming in," Tony said, getting out and opening the door for her. "Father's expecting me, and I need to see him."

He waved to her as he sped away.

She felt a surge of happiness as she strolled into the house. Tony had a way of making a woman feel special. Even her foot felt better. *Yes, but he treats all the girls like that. Remember his kiss the other day, and Dr. Hatzis's conversation with him in the ship's lounge.* Feeling somber, she entered the hallway, limping towards her room. Her foot was feeling quite sore. She must remember to rest it and keep it up. Melissa saw her and came toward her.

"Ipatia, was that my brother that drove away?" Melissa asked somewhat abruptly.

"Yes, he was going to visit your father in the hospital."

"Hmmff," Melissa said, narrowing her eyes. "I wanted to speak with him first before he went to the hospital." She walked away, muttering to herself.

Ipatia sensed that things were not right and went to the safety of her room. She lay on the bed, feeling disturbed. Melissa was so much different from her brother.

Ipatia quickly fell into a light sleep.

CHAPTER 16

I heard your family's wish for you.
Goodbye for now, dare it be true?

Tony hiked up the hospital stairs to his father's floor and walked down the dimly lit corridor, sensitive to the rank smell of formaldehyde that permeated the air. He gingerly carried the box of *loukoumathes*, appreciating their sweet scent. They were a nice reminder of another world that he had just come from.

He found Dr. Vaskanos speaking to the nurse in the hallway. He asked him about his father.

"We need to speak privately. Please follow me," Dr. Vaskanos replied seriously.

Tony followed him into a private room. They sat down.

"Let me speak frankly, Dr. Plakis," Dr. Vaskanos began. "We are still obtaining results from the tests and cannot be one hundred percent sure until they are finalized. What I can tell you, is that, given your father's symptoms and what the films show, there is a high probability that he has a brain tumor in the lower base of the brain. We won't know for sure until the biopsy results are in."

Tony was troubled with the news and asked several questions. They talked for a while. He thanked the doctor, shaking his hand and slipping money into it.

He found his father sitting upright in his bed, alone and awake, wearing his reading glasses and reading the newspaper.

Tony tried to be cheerful as he presented his father with the box of loukoumathes. "For you, Father."

His father grudgingly took them and then put them aside. "Can you explain yourself, Tony? You were supposed to come this morning and speak with the doctor. Instead, you were traipsing around town with an island girl almost half your age. You spent more time with that, that girl than with Bonnie." Gregory took off his glasses and rubbed his eyes.

"I gather you spoke with Melissa," Tony said quietly.

"I just got off the telephone with her," Gregory grumbled. "She said you were gone all day with Ipatia."

"For your information, I dropped Ipatia off at Michael's office in the morning because of her swollen ankle and came immediately here, but I was told you were getting tested and Dr. Vaskanos was not in yet. Then I went back to Michael's office and brought Ipatia to the house before coming here."

"And the *loukoumathes*?" Gregory demanded. "I know your fondness for taking girls there."

"They were for you. I know you like them."

"Hmmf. What did the doctor say? I've got a brain tumor, don't I?" Gregory grumbled, changing the subject.

"All the tests are not back but given your symptoms and the spot on the x-ray film, he thinks that's a strong possibility," Tony replied, trying not to use the word "brain tumor."

"I knew it. When he kept stalling, I guessed right that he was hiding something serious from me," Gregory said, tightening his mouth. "Did he mention surgery?"

"Treatment does include surgery, if the tests come back positive, but he doesn't recommend you having it done here. Instead, he gave me the name of a top neurosurgeon in the United States. They have these surgical machines that are much more advanced there."

"I thought he would say something like that. I'm going to get a second opinion before I decide anything," muttered Gregory. "Sit down, I wish to speak to you."

"Yes?" Tony asked, making himself comfortable in the large armchair near the bed. This was a special purchase made by his father for Christina so she could sit comfortably by his side.

Gregory coughed nervously before he began speaking. "When I promised Christos Rodakis that my son was going to help his granddaughter to come to Piraeus, I kept my promise. I didn't realize however, that my son was going to make a fool of himself spending all day with her showing her around the town. Did you forget you are practically engaged to Bonnie?"

Tony waited until his father stopped his ranting. He quietly said, "I helped Ipatia, just as I would have anyone needing my assistance, and for your information, Bonnie knows my true feelings about her."

"Melissa told me. She says Bonnie was crying to her on the telephone and had taken tranquilizers to calm down. Obviously, the girl is in love with you. What's wrong with marrying Bonnie? She comes from a good, rich family, she's attractive, and she's a nice girl."

"I didn't intend to hurt Bonnie's feelings," Tony said thoughtfully. "She is a lovely girl and has good characteristics, except for one."

"And what can that be?"

Tony tightened up. "Bonnie is a jealous person. I witnessed the nail marks she gave Ipatia the other day, pretending to escort her to her room. There were bruises around them, too."

Gregory chuckled. "That shows she's interested in you."

Tony's mouth settled into a thin line. "I am not interested in marrying Bonnie."

"You're going on thirty, son. That's a good marriageable age," Gregory countered.

"Yes, but you didn't marry until you were thirty-three," Tony retorted.

"Ah yes, and I remember my father pressuring me to marry a certain heiress when I was also thirty," Gregory recalled. "I was stubborn then, like you are now, and didn't give in. I married the most beautiful woman on Crete."

"Yes, and she wasn't an heiress either."

"You got me on that one. I guess I can't force you to do something you don't want to do," Gregory replied.

Tony changed the subject. "Did you read the newspapers recently?"

"That Chuck Daras is playing games," Gregory replied. "He said he would consider signing a contract with us, and now he wants to do business with Meriklis who has a supermarket empire. I think he did it after he learned about Melissa's engagement to Michael."

"Who knows why he did it," Tony said, feeling exasperated. "Also, Bonnie's father is a shrewd man and won't make any deals with Chuck Daras unless he's sure he'll get a good bargain."

Gregory leaned back and placed his hand on his forehead. He shut his eyes.

"Should I call the nurse?" Tony asked, getting up.

"No, no, the dizziness will pass," Gregory said, breathing deeply. "Don't leave yet. I have to speak to you about something else. I received a telephone call from the port of Thessaloniki. They are holding one of our cargo ships for questioning. I do not know the details, but I need you to go and investigate the problem. Typically, I would go, but as you can see, I'm in no shape to be traveling. Also, you may need to consult our attorney if the need arises."

"Oh?" Tony said, digesting the information. "When should I go?"

"Make arrangements to leave on the first airplane for Thessaloniki. We've already delayed a day and every minute that passes by while that ship sits at the port is costing us money."

When Christina arrived, he discussed with her his father's health. Later, Tony went to the travel agent's office and made the necessary arrangements for the trip. He was scheduled to leave the next morning.

Ipatia awoke later that afternoon to the sound of voices coming from the hallway. It took her a moment to realize where she was. She arose, careful not to step on her sore foot, washed and dressed, then went and stood near the window. The sun was setting and covered everything with an orange glow. There was something comforting about a sunset. She took out a few papers from her trunk and began to write her thoughts down.

Mrs. Soula came and told her dinner was being served. Ipatia set aside her writing and followed her to the grand dining room.

The elegant room with its wine-colored velvet curtains, large Persian rug, and long dining room table boasted of expensive taste. The lit chandelier reflected its light in the large, gold-framed mirror on the wall.

Melissa and Dr. Hatzis were the only ones seated at the table. Ipatia greeted them.

"I see you are walking better," Dr. Hatzis said, smiling at her.

Melissa stared at her.

Ipatia wasn't used to having all this attention focused on her, and blushed, nodding silently.

The cook entered the room, pouring white wine into the crystal glasses.

The dinner consisted of baked grouper smothered with tomato sauce, baked potatoes, salad, and crusty bread.

"Where is Tony?" Dr. Hatzis asked, looking at Melissa.

"He couldn't make it for dinner," Melissa said, wiping her mouth with a napkin. "He is busy preparing for a business trip. Father's health is not the best these days, so Tony represents the company now."

Dr. Hatzis gave Melissa a puzzled look. She leaned over and whispered in his ear, saying, "I'll tell you later."

Ipatia had looked forward to seeing Tony again and was crestfallen that he wouldn't be there. The dinner went by quickly, with Dr. Hatzis and Melissa doing the talking. It seemed they couldn't agree on a number of things regarding their wedding.

Ipatia quietly ate her food, listening to the couple have a heated discussion about the rings. Dr. Hatzis was content with a simple, gold ring, asking what was wrong with that since he had spent a considerable amount on the engagement ring.

"The large diamond ring I set my heart on is the one I want," Melissa insisted.

"How much does it cost?" he countered.

When Ipatia heard the price of the diamond ring, it caused her to drop her fork. She apologized while the couple stopped to stare at her.

In addition to the diamond ring, Melissa wanted to travel around the world for their honeymoon. He preferred going to Paris, or one of the Greek islands for their honeymoon. Melissa insisted on a world trip. She wouldn't have it any other way.

After dinner, the couple arose to leave and Ipatia excused herself, saying she needed to go and rest her foot.

Melissa said, "Come, Michael, let's stroll out into the verandah. I feel like going outside."

He grudgingly followed her as she led him outside.

Ipatia went into her bedroom and immediately felt the evening's cool breeze coming from the open window. She shivered as she went to close it. She stopped when she heard Dr. Hatzis conversing with Melissa outside on the verandah.

Ipatia moved away from the window but could still hear their conversation.

"What do you mean that Tony had a quarrel with your father?" Dr. Hatzis asked.

"I called Father shortly before dinner to see how he was doing, and he appeared upset that Tony had spent the whole day with the island girl, you know. They had even gone to the loukoumathes shop and ate there, and Tony brought *loukoumathes* back for Father," Melissa said.

"What's wrong with that?"

"Did you forget about Tony and Bonnie? Father wanted him to stay here not only to run the business for him, but because he wanted him to be near Bonnie."

"Yes, but I don't think Tony is interested in her."

"How can it be? Bonnie told me Tony kissed her on the trip," Melissa persisted. "I know Tony. He doesn't typically kiss women unless he's very interested."

"Are you sure Bonnie wasn't the one doing the kissing?"

"Anyway, Father says if Tony marries Bonnie, that marriage can bring much money into the family."

"I'm beginning to understand everything now," Dr. Hatzis said.

Ipatia had heard enough. She went into her washroom and closed the door, trying to shut out the conversation. She didn't want Tony quarreling with his father over her. .

Afterwards, she lay in bed, thinking about things, unable to sleep. She went over the couple's conversation several times in her mind. Each time she went through it, she ended up thinking the same thing. She didn't feel comfortable staying here any longer.

I must leave this place.

If Tony's fate was to marry a rich girl, why should Ipatia get in the way of his destiny? Where could she go? Her cousins were away on a trip and her aunt was in America. Then the option presented itself. She sat up in bed, feeling excited.

She pictured the renter talking with her and telling her that her aunt was not there and would return in three weeks. *I could stay with her until my aunt returned.* The only way to be sure was to visit her.

Ipatia arose swiftly and began packing her clothes, making sure everything was ready, making sure she didn't leave anything behind. She retrieved a pen and a piece of paper from her purse.

Sitting down at the little table, she mused for a moment, hesitating, and wondering if this were the right thing to do. *I must let Tony know what happened.* Yes, but what if someone else found this letter? She could seal it.

Without further thought, she began to write, "Dear Mr. Tony, thank you so much for all you have done for me, and in making my stay here a pleasant one. I will never forget it. I think it is better that I leave. Yours truly, Ipatia."

After she folded the note, she searched in her trunk for an envelope. She had brought some along to write letters to her grandfather. Finding what she was looking for, she inserted the note, then wrote Tony's name on the envelope and left it on the table.

In bed, Ipatia tossed and turned, unable to sleep for a long time. When she finally did sleep, the tears were still wet on her cheeks.

⟡ ⟡ ⟡

Tony returned home late that evening. He had spent the rest of the day purchasing his airplane tickets and meeting with their attorney. The house was quiet as he made his way upstairs to his bedroom. Inside his bedroom, he changed and then lay on the bed, unable to sleep. Light filtered in from the moon, casting its magic glow into the dark bedroom.

Tony remembered the gemstone Ipatia had given him. He arose and went to get it, standing near the window, holding it up against the light from the moon. It glowed red in the dark room as Ipatia glowed in his own life. He smiled softly.

His little Ipatia had aroused deep emotions in him. He had truly felt happy when he heard her yesterday, first singing merrily, and later, playing the piano. The kiss he gave her was a spontaneous overflowing of those deep emotions. He didn't remember feeling this way towards a woman before. When she asked him not to kiss her again, he realized how much that comment meant to him. Also, he realized now that she had worn the long-sleeved blouse to hide Bonnie's nail marks. *This girl had values.* His happiness had continued as he sang beside her in the car, then afterwards, when he saw her enjoying her *loukoumathes.* He felt as if he was a boy again, without a care in the world.

He had lived in a structured world for as long as he could remember where everything operated like clockwork. His classes, his schedules, his summer vacations all had a sense of ritual woven into their fabric. These rituals had choked out any feelings he had, replacing them with a boring complacency that lacked spirit.

Within the last few days, all that had changed. Fate or a higher power had made their yacht run into bad weather, forcing them to land on the island. Was it so he could save the girl from the snake or to help a young boy who cut his arm? Or was it to bring the girl to his house?

Now, fate again caused his father to fall ill, requiring Tony's help, forcing him to leave for Thessaloniki. He gazed at the stone again, wondering if a girl named Ipatia, who had a fondness for running away, was going to be there when he returned or was she to become just a beautiful memory?

●●• ——— ◆ ●●• ——— ◆ ●●• ——— ◆

The next morning, Ipatia arose promptly at four-thirty. She had been used to getting up early to milk the goats and had learned to move around in the dark. She had packed everything the night before.

As the clock in her room struck five, Ipatia stole out the room quietly, her heart racing at the thought that she might bump into somebody. She tiptoed down the hallway, quietly pulling the trunk behind her, stopping occasionally to relieve the ache in her foot and to make sure no one was coming. It seemed forever before she reached the large, front door. With relief, she found herself outside, carefully shutting the door quietly behind her.

By the time she reached the bus stop, she was breathing heavily and her foot was hurting.

Ipatia sat on the trunk and prayed the bus would come quickly so no one would drive by and recognize her.

The bus arrived after twenty minutes. Ipatia, aided by one of the passengers, boarded the bus with her trunk. She showed her aunt's address to the driver.

The bus driver nodded. "I'll let you know when we arrive."

•••———◈ •••———◈ •••———◈

Six o'clock that morning Tony arose from a sleepless night. Ipatia had been on his mind all night. He was feeling guilty that he had invited her to stay at their house, and now he was leaving again. The nagging feeling that he was following his father's footsteps was beginning to bother him, yet he had no choice.

As he washed and dressed, he toyed with the idea of writing Ipatia a note to explain his absence. That was the least he could do. He decided he wasn't going to let Melissa know his plans. She had been interfering in his life too much lately.

An hour later, Tony paused in front of Ipatia's door, holding the note. He was tempted to wake her and talk to her. *What would I say?* He would probably shock her with his feelings. Instead, he slipped the note underneath her door before leaving for the airport.

CHAPTER 17

Life brought me back to Piraeus
To teach the English languages.

The bus pulled to an abrupt stop in the middle of somewhere. Ipatia peered out the window, gazing at the darkness. The trip had been a long one, and she had fallen asleep along the way, yet somehow felt refreshed. A few passengers remained in the bus, and it appeared they also were sleeping.

The bus driver turned and looked at Ipatia. "You get off here, miss," he said, opening the door.

Ipatia gathered her belongings and hurried to the front. The bus driver placed her trunk on the pavement, and then pointed towards the parked taxis. She thanked him. The bus turned the corner and was instantly out of sight.

Ipatia slowly walked across the street, pulling the trunk behind her. Her ankle still ached. She found a taxi, and the journey continued for a while longer. The early morning darkness began to wane. They passed groups of children carrying their books, evidently going to school. At the top of the hill stood a small grocery store.

"We're almost there," Ipatia said excitedly, recognizing the store. "It's down the hill. There, where the playground is. You can drop me off there."

Moments later, she knocked on her aunt's door, wondering what she would find. To her delight, her aunt opened it.

"Aunt Sophia," Ipatia exclaimed, surprised to see her.

"Ipatia. I almost didn't recognize you," Aunt Sophia said, as she hugged her niece with emotion. She wiped the tears of joy from her eyes. "I'm so glad you came back. I returned yesterday, after Miss Marika, the renter, sent me your letter. She told me all about your visit. But she wasn't sure where you were staying."

"I'm sorry. I wasn't thinking clearly that night to tell her," admitted Ipatia sheepishly. "But I am so glad you are back."

"That makes two of us," Aunt Sophia said, her eyes moistening. Then she became businesslike. "Well now, let's get you settled first. Is this all you have?"

"Yes, Aunt, just me and my trunk. Oh, I almost forgot. Here is the wine that my grandfather made. It's for you," Ipatia said, retrieving the bottle from her handbag.

Her aunt thanked her and helped carry the trunk inside. The two-story house consisted of two living quarters. One suite was downstairs and another one upstairs.

"Marika, the tenant you met, is renting the downstairs. So, we will be living upstairs," Aunt Sophia informed her. "Here, let me help you carry this."

Aunt Sophia carried the trunk upstairs.

Ipatia walked slowly up the winding marble stairs, mindful of her sore ankle.

"The house is too big for me, and I've rented the downstairs whenever possible and resorted to living upstairs."

As her aunt unlocked the door, memories of Ipatia's youth came rushing in, overwhelming her. She stifled a cry, trying to compose her emotions. "I remember this so well," she said, feeling excited.

Ipatia eagerly followed her aunt into the living quarters. To the right of the entranceway was the kitchen, and to their left, was a small hallway that led to the sleeping quarters.

Ipatia entered her parent's bedroom and could almost smell her mother's perfume lingering in the air, a reminder of a time of leisure and prosperity, and a reminder of her father's expensive gifts. The white dresser, imported from France, with the large mirror, still stood against the wall.

Two porcelain female dolls, dressed in exotic clothes, sat on the bed. "Aunt Sophia, you kept my dolls. Thank you so much." Ipatia rushed to the dolls and touched them fondly.

"I kept them so you can give them to your children one day."

Ipatia went to the dresser and picked up the gold comb resting there. She gazed at it nostalgically. "This was my mother's comb. I would pester her to comb my hair with it when I was a child. I wanted to do and use everything she did."

"I didn't touch anything," Aunt Sophia said, gesturing around sadly. "At one point, you will have to decide what you want to do with them. By the way, you will sleep here, and I will sleep in the other bedroom, the one that used to be your bedroom."

Aunt Sophia left to prepare the meal.

Ipatia unpacked and reverently placed her parents' pictures on the dresser, then checked the drawers. Filled with her parent's clothes, she carefully removed the contents and replaced them with her clothes. The ache in her heart was becoming unbearable.

"Ipatia, food's ready."

"I'll be right there." Ipatia hurriedly changed into other clothes, hung her Sunday dress in the closet, and joined her aunt in the kitchen. The round table held plates of scrambled eggs and toast, biscuits, feta cheese, and black olives. Her aunt poured the coffee into the cups. They said a prayer and began to eat.

"Ipatia, tell me the news from the island. How is your grandfather and your godmother?"

Ipatia obliged her aunt and chatted about her grandfather, the people and life on the island. "Grandfather almost didn't let me come. He was worried that you had not gotten my letter," Ipatia finished.

"I was in America when your letter arrived here. Marika forwarded all my mail to me. So when I received it, I made airplane arrangements to return right away. She didn't know I was coming until a few days ago."

"Oh, that explains why she said you would return in three weeks," Ipatia said. "So, what made you go to America?"

"We have cousins in Chicago, Antonios and his wife Stasoula, who visit here often and kept inviting me to go there."

"How are we related?"

"Well, Antonios's father and my father are brothers. So I am first cousins with Antonios. They wanted me to meet someone there. So I accepted their offer and went this summer."

"Did you meet him?"

"Yes," Aunt Sophia said, her eyes shining. "His name is John, and he is a good friend of Antonios's and lives next door. He is Greek and a widower, with no children. He recently celebrated his fiftieth birthday with a party. We were all invited and I went along."

"Do you like him?" Ipatia asked her.

"How about I tell you some other time," Aunt Sophia replied, smiling fondly at her. "Your grandfather stated in his letter that you wanted to further your education. Tell me about that, Ipatia."

Ipatia explained how her teachers in Rhodes recommended that she continue her studies at the university because she had done well in school.

"It's difficult to enter the universities here in Greece. My friend's son took his entrance examinations last year and even though he received high marks, he was not accepted in any of the universities," Aunt Sophia warned her. "He is studying in Italy."

"Really?" Ipatia asked, gulping her milk down nervously.

"Yes, but then again, Marika's niece made it to the university here, so one never knows."

"I hear the entrance examinations are given in late spring."

"Yes, sometime in June. We can get all that information before the time comes," Aunt Sophia remarked. "So, tell me, was your trip a nice one?"

Ipatia nodded, describing the few days before the trip and her involvement with the Plakis family. "I went to their house in Kifissia," Ipatia finished.

"I happen to know the Plakis family."

"That's right. Mr. Plakis said he knew you," Ipatia exclaimed, her eyes widening. "You were their seamstress, weren't you?"

"Yes, but first, why don't you finish your story?"

Ipatia continued, telling her about everything. She ended with the conversation she heard between Melissa and Michael outside her window.

"Melissa is loyal to her father and will do anything he says," Aunt Sophia said thoughtfully, crossing her arms. "Do they know that you came here?"

Ipatia shook her head. "I left a farewell note but didn't say where I was going."

Her aunt raised her eyebrows. "I think we need to place a call to the Plakis residence right away and let them know where you are, young lady. The pharmacy has a phone down at the corner. Follow me."

"Can we also call *Pappou* so he knows what has happened?" Ipatia asked, grabbing her purse with the telephone number in it.

Her aunt nodded.

Their walk to the pharmacy was a pleasant one. They passed some residential buildings with pots of bright flowers lining their entrances. They crossed the street and entered the two-story building located at the corner.

The pharmacy was empty except for a young man standing behind the counter and wearing a white lab coat.

"*Yia-sou* Vassili. I need to use the telephone," Aunt Sophia said cheerfully.

"Over there, Miss Sophia," Vassili said, smiling and pointing to the telephone. "Pay me when you are done."

Aunt Sophia looked through the telephone directory and then dialed the Plakis residence.

"Hello, I'm Sophia Kouris, Ipatia's aunt." Aunt Sophia paused, listening. "Oh, you are the new housekeeper? Is anyone from the Plakis family there? No? Could you inform them that

Miss Ipatia has come home to her aunt safely, and we'd like to thank them for everything."

After she hung up, Ipatia handed her the paper with the telephone number on it. "This number is for the post office in Lipsi. We can leave a message with Mrs. Xilouris's nephew, who works there, to tell my grandfather that we will call back tomorrow morning at nine-thirty."

Aunt Sophia nodded and proceeded to dial the number, leaving the message with the young man.

They walked quietly back to the apartment.

"So, tell me, Aunt Sophia, how did you get to work for the Plakis family?"

"We go a long way back with that family. First, your grandfather knew Gregory Plakis back in Heraklion, Crete. Then your father worked for them as a captain, and he put in a good word for me. I ended up sewing clothes for the whole family and anyone else they referred me to."

"What about Mr. Plakis's first wife?"

"She died before I started working there. I did see pictures of her, though. She was a beautiful woman, and Tony resembles her, with his dark, handsome looks. Melissa, on the other hand, has her father's short height and fair hair. She was a mischievous one, though. Many times, I could not find my threads or needles, for she had hidden them," Aunt Sophia said, laughing.

"Was Tony mischievous also?"

"No, not like his sister. As a young boy, he was the perfect little gentleman, always saying thank you and helping me out. I remember thinking that with those handsome looks, he would probably break many women's hearts one day." Aunt Sophia chuckled.

"Really?" Ipatia asked, her heart racing at the memory of Tony's features. "Who took care of the children?"

"They had a nanny. Tony, the older of the two, went to a boarding school in England. His father wanted him to learn the English language because of the shipping business. Mr. Plakis kept saying his son would be in charge of the business one day. I never saw Tony after he left for the boarding school, but he used to write and ask about me occasionally. I still sewed for the family and sometimes his nanny would tell me his news. I worked up to the time when your parents died," replied Aunt Sophia, sobering up.

They reached the house and climbed the stairs.

"Things are much better now. I sew for a few good patrons," Aunt Sophia said, unlocking the door. "Here, let us go into the living room."

They went through a glass door that led into the living room which had a sofa the color of ripe peaches and two, creamy white upholstered chairs. A glass coffee table with a small crystal bowl sat in the center of the room. On the wall were several framed pictures.

Ipatia thought she recognized her father in one of the pictures. "Is that my father?"

"Yes, he was twelve years old in that picture. There's something else in this room, Ipatia. Have you forgotten?"

Ipatia looked around. Behind the opened balcony door, somewhat hidden, stood an upright piano. She ran to it joyfully. "My piano," she cried, running her fingers over the keys.

"I have been saving it for you all these years, for I knew you would return one day," Aunt Sophia said.

The room filled with lively notes that flowed in succession, transporting her back to another world where there were no cares, no worries, but beautiful feelings. When Ipatia finished playing, she was rewarded by the sound of clapping.

CHAPTER 18

Your search for me did make me start,
A note you sent did touch my heart.

Ipatia and her aunt sat outside on the balcony, enjoying their refreshments, the breeze, and the view. To her left, beyond the tops of the buildings, Ipatia saw a slice of blue. "That must be the Piraeus harbor," she said, pointing to it.

"Yes."

To her right, Ipatia glimpsed the playground and open field, a reminder of her youth. A few children ran around, shouting and laughing. Their mothers stood nearby chatting.

Sounds of a bouzouki playing strains of Rembetiko music drifted toward them from a nearby residence. The soulful song penetrated Ipatia's soul, making her feel a sadness she could not shake off.

"There's old Mr. Damaskis playing his bouzouki again," Aunt Sophia said. "He lives alone; he lost his wife and daughter in a car accident a few years ago."

"It probably does him good, playing the music." Ipatia listened a while longer. "Aunt Sophia, how did you come to live here?"

"A young man from Piraeus is to blame," Aunt Sophia said. "I was not much older than you when a cousin of my girlfriend's visited Heraklion for the summer. He hung around us, and was a likable and charming young man. We became engaged and he wanted me come to Piraeus with him at the end of the summer."

"You went with him?"

Aunt Sophia nodded her head emphatically. "My father saw how much in love I was, so he came with us to Piraeus. Your father, Manolis, helped Father buy this house as a dowry. The suite downstairs was mine, while this suite here belonged to your father. But at the last minute, my fiancé decided he didn't want to marry."

"Oh dear, that must have been awful for you," Ipatia said. "You know Aunt Sophia, I don't think I want to marry."

"Don't be silly. Don't let an old maid like me influence you. If someone good comes along, you grab him, because those chances don't always come your way. I know," Aunt Sophia retorted.

"I want to go to the university and get an education in order to help people. Maybe I'll choose nursing or a health science."

"Haven't you considered marriage?"

"Yes, but I don't think I would make a good wife," Ipatia said, shaking her head. "I'd be worried all the time that something might happen to him."

"In nursing, you will meet all kinds of sick people. Not everyone survives their illness, for one reason or another."

"I know. That is why I am interested in nursing, because I want to help people live longer."

Aunt Sophia sighed. "Yes, helping others is wonderful, but what will you do when the sick person is better off than you. They will have their family gathered around them to show their love and support. You will go home tired from working all day, and who will be there to meet you, to love you, and let you rest your head on his shoulder?"

Ipatia became thoughtful, picturing what her aunt said.

"Aunt Sophia, you would have made a good lawyer." Ipatia laughed, breaking the somber atmosphere.

"No, thank you," Aunt Sophia said, chuckling. "Ipatia, my girl, I'm going for a nap. You probably are dusty from the trip. Why don't you bathe before resting?"

Tony arrived in Thessaloniki Tuesday morning and met with the captain of the ship. The captain complained that the port authorities were holding the ship for no good reason.

When Tony went to check with the port officials, they were not around. He was told that the officials would be in touch with him. With nothing else to do but wait, he returned to the hotel later that morning.

At eleven-thirty, he called his home and spoke with the housekeeper. Melissa was out and his father in the hospital. He asked about Ipatia's whereabouts.

"I don't know, sir," said Katina. "I haven't seen her all morning, and today Soula has the day off."

"Can you check her room, please?"

Tony waited for a few minutes.

"Mr. Tony, the girl is not in her room. I found an envelope addressed to her laying on the floor near the door."

Tony was worried. That was the note he had left her. *She must have left before I did.* "I'd like to speak with Tim, the chauffeur."

Moments later, Tony explained the situation to Tim. "She's my responsibility, as you well know, Tim. She disappeared without saying where she went to."

"If I may make a suggestion, sir, Olga, our housekeeper's niece may know something about Ipatia's disappearance."

"Good idea. By the way, why don't you also pass by Ipatia's aunt's house and check there in case she decided to go there. Call me when you find out any news."

"Is there anything else you may need, sir?"

"Oh, I almost forgot, a letter addressed to Ipatia is in her room. Please see that she gets it."

"All right. Where can I reach you?"

Tony gave him the telephone number to his room. After he hung up, he dialed the hospital. He asked the nurse how his father was doing. She said he was still sleeping. Tony asked to speak to Christina.

"One minute, please," said the nurse.

"Hello, Christina. This is Tony. How is Father?"

"Your father is the same, only a little more irritable. Anyhow, they think they know what is wrong with him. He will tell you when you return. Meanwhile, they will discharge him tomorrow."

Her voice sounded tired. Tony briefed her on his status. He planned to contact Mr. Spithas, their lawyer, after he found out what the problem was with the cargo ship. He anticipated that he should finish in a day or two. After he hung up the telephone, he went to the restaurant across the street for lunch.

After bathing, Ipatia made her way to her bedroom. Her aunt's door was shut, indicating that she was napping. After Ipatia dressed, she didn't feel sleepy, so she searched for something to read. She found the English novel given to her by Mrs. Rodos. Ipatia took the book out on to the balcony and sat reading it, feeling the breeze ruffling through her wet hair as she escaped into another world.

A bell rang somewhere, startling Ipatia from her fascinated absorption with the story. Ipatia arose to answer it, realizing her aunt was asleep. She opened the door and was surprised to see Olga, Gilda's niece. "Olga, what are you doing here?"

"Tim, the chauffeur drove me here," Olga explained, looking pleased. "He called me at work, you know, to tell me you had disappeared, and if I knew anything about it. Of course, I didn't, but I felt responsible for you, so I asked to come along. You see, he remembered your aunt's address."

Tim came up the stairs and joined them. "Hello, Miss Ipatia. We were worried about you," he said, removing his hat.

"Thank you for taking the trouble to look for me. I did leave a note for Mr. Tony, and we telephoned the house not long ago, telling the housekeeper where I was."

"I didn't get the news. I may have already left by then," said Tim, scratching his head.

"Please, why don't you come in?"

"Thank you, but we must be going. We only stopped by to see if you were all right," Tim said hurriedly. "Oh, I almost forgot. This is from Mr. Tony." He handed her an envelope.

Ipatia became flustered, thanking him as she took the envelope from his outstretched hand.

After they left, Ipatia went into her bedroom and read the note. It said:

"Dear Ipatia, I'm sorry I won't be able to see you today. I had to go away on a business trip. I don't know how long I will be gone. I truly enjoyed hearing you play the piano. It brought back memories of my youth. In case you've already left for your aunt's by the time I return, good luck with everything, Tony."

She read it several times, and then clutched it to her bosom. Her heart started racing at the thought that he cared enough to write her a note before he left for the trip. *How did he know I would be at my aunt's house? It's as if he could read my mind.* She was blissfully happy.

Then she remembered Melissa's conversation with Dr. Hatzis about Bonnie, and suddenly her happiness didn't ring true. How could she be happy with a playboy, who went from one woman to another as if they were used clothes? He had kissed Bonnie, just as he had kissed her. Now Bonnie was crying because she loved him, and he was spurning her to make Ipatia happy. *How do I know one day he won't turn around and do the same thing to me, make me cry while making another woman happy?*

Ipatia's happiness turned into tears.

Tony returned to the hotel late in the afternoon after meeting with the port officials. He telephoned his lawyer and told him the news. Their ship did not have authorization to be hauling the cargo that it carried, and there were stiff penalties involved. After a long conversation, he hung up the telephone.

Mr. Spithas assured him that he would handle it from now on and would keep him updated on the situation.

After removing his suit and tie, Tony gazed out the window, thinking about everything that had transpired that day.

The telephone rang.

"Mr. Tony, Tim here," said Tim. "I found Miss Ipatia. She is at her aunt's house and her aunt has returned from her trip. Miss Ipatia said she left you a note, and they also telephoned the Plakis residence earlier today to inform you of her whereabouts."

"Thank you, Tim. Make sure you place her note in my bedroom."

Later that afternoon, Aunt Sophia had arisen from her nap and found Ipatia sitting out on the balcony, reading her book.

"Oh, there you are," Aunt Sophia said, stifling a yawn. "I keep wanting to sleep during the day and less at night. I think it may be caused by the jet lag." She sat down next to her.

Ipatia told her about the incident with Tim and Olga.

"That's strange that the housekeeper didn't tell them."

"Tim said he had probably left before we called."

"Yes, that may be the case."

The sound of Ipatia's book dropping to the floor startled her. It had slipped out of her lap.

"What were you reading?" Aunt Sophia asked, looking curiously at the book.

"An English novel given to me by Mrs. Rodos years ago. The heroine ends up with the man she loves."

"That sounds like a nice story," Aunt Sophia said. "You were always interested in books, Ipatia, ever since you were a young child. How is it you read love stories, yet you won't think about falling in love and marrying?"

Ipatia laughed, saying, "It's much easier to experience this through a book than to live it."

"By the way, I bumped into Mrs. Rodos before I left for America, and she asked about you."

"How nice of her. I would like to see her again," Ipatia said wistfully.

"Why don't we visit her today? She would be happy to see you," Aunt Sophia said impulsively.

Ipatia eagerly jumped up and hugged her aunt once more. They left shortly after that. Along the way, they stopped at the bakery and chose a chocolate torte.

A few minutes later, they rang Mrs. Rodos's doorbell.

Mrs. Rodos came to the door wearing the same gray dress she always wore. Her keen gray eyes peered at them through her silver, rimmed spectacles.

"Greetings, Mrs. Rodos. Look who I have brought to see you," Aunt Sophia said, proudly moving Ipatia forward.

It took Mrs. Rodos a moment to recognize her. "Ipatia Kouris. I can't believe it's you," she exclaimed. "After all these years, you have finally come to visit me."

After their warm greetings, Mrs. Rodos eagerly led them inside the house. They sat in the parlor. Ipatia observed the bookshelves with the familiar musty smell of the books while her aunt and Mrs. Rodos conversed in small talk. Nothing had changed here. She felt that only she had changed.

"Excuse me for a moment. I'll make some tea. We can have it with some of your delicious cake," Mrs. Rodos said. She was gone before they could resist.

Minutes later, Ipatia sipped the tea and sampled a small slice of the torte.

"Tell me, Ipatia, have you finished school yet?" Mrs. Rodos asked in English.

Ipatia nodded. Replying in English, she recounted her story of having gone to Rhodes Island to finish her schooling.

"Miss Sophia, you should be proud of your niece. She is a talented girl, and her English is impeccable."

"I always knew Ipatia was a bright girl."

"I would like to ask Ipatia something, with your consent, of course," Mrs. Rodos said. "You see, my assistant quit a few days ago and I need someone to help me out. The classes are every Monday, Wednesday, and Friday evenings, from five-thirty to about seven o'clock. Ipatia, what do you think? We will pay you for your services."

"I would love that," Ipatia cried out. Then embarrassed by her outburst, she sheepishly looked at her aunt for approval.

Her aunt nodded, smiling at her.

"Good. Come tomorrow at five o'clock. That will give us time to go over things before the students arrive," Mrs. Rodos said, back to her brisk manner.

CHAPTER 19

My eighteenth year I found I must
My money earn without a trust

The next morning, Wednesday, Ipatia and her aunt went to the pharmacy and placed the telephone call to her grandfather. He had been waiting for her call. He sounded relieved that she was with her aunt.

Soon, Ipatia and her aunt were returning home.

"Ipatia, I've been meaning to talk to you about what clothes to wear for your English class tonight. You've been wearing black since you arrived."

"That's all I have to wear," Ipatia explained.

Her aunt stared at her feet with a bewildered look on her face. "Those sandals don't go, do they?"

"I wear them because my foot is still swollen."

"Then that settles it, young lady. Today, we go and buy some clothes more suitable for you, and a new pair of shoes."

"Thank you, Aunt Sophia, but wouldn't it be better if we sewed my clothes? I mean, I'd like to learn how to sew, like you, and it'll probably cost much less to do it ourselves."

"Of course, my dear, but you need clothes and shoes for tonight."

They took the bus downtown, and Ipatia's exuberance was unchecked. The bustle of the city invigorated her, with all types of people, buildings, and commotion keeping her on high alert. Aunt

Sophia expertly guided her through the busy streets to where there were several clothes shops.

The first store was small and dark, and filled with clothes racks everywhere. Ipatia and Aunt Sophia looked at the clothes on the racks. Ipatia didn't see anything she liked. Aunt Sophia lifted a mini-skirt from the rack, showing it to her.

"That is more suitable for a younger girl," Ipatia whispered.

"You're right." Aunt Sophia put it back. "I think these are the new styles and this shop is geared to shorter women."

Eventually, they found a store that suited their taste and budget. The shoes were also difficult to find, since Ipatia's feet were larger than normal. Finally, they settled for a pair of brown, leather walking shoes. After they finished shopping, they stopped off at the fabric store and bought some fabrics and supplies.

They arrived home early afternoon. Ipatia took a light nap and afterwards, started to get ready for her class. She hummed as she put on her new white blouse and blue skirt.

Her aunt knocked on the door. "Ipatia, just so you know, it's almost five o'clock, dear," Aunt Sophia reminded her.

"Come in, Aunt," Ipatia said. "How do you like it?" She twirled around the room in her new outfit.

"Splendid choice." laughed Aunt Sophia, clapping her hands. "You look like a schoolteacher, I may say. All you need are those spectacles Mrs. Rodos wears."

They both laughed at the picture.

The walk to Mrs. Rodos's house was a brisk one, as Ipatia was mindful of the time. She quickly immersed herself in her new job. She was responsible for handing out the materials to the children and in aiding them with their lessons if they needed help. The class session flew by quickly, and Ipatia enjoyed herself immensely.

Tony arrived in Kifissia earlier that day. Katina answered the door. "Greetings, Katina. Is my father home?"

Katina nodded fearfully. "Yes, he is, in the verandah."

Melissa rushed to greet him. "Tony, I'm so glad you're home," she cried.

"What's going on? Is everything all right?" Tony asked, studying her tear-stained face. She rarely greeted him at the door. *Something had happened.* He heard yelling coming from the direction of the verandah.

"How can it be?" burst out Melissa, sobbing uncontrollably. "I broke up with Michael this morning, and Father's upset about the whole thing."

"One would think that he'd be happy," Tony remarked dryly, remembering Father's preference for Chuck Daras. He was about to ask her why she broke up with Michael when Melissa cried out, "*Ohhhh,*" and fled to her room.

"Melissa, Melissa," Tony said, immediately regretting his words, but she had already vanished. Melissa had a habit of falling in and out of love quickly and this wasn't the first time she had broken off an engagement. What made it troublesome this time was that Michael was his best friend.

Tony found his father sitting outside, moving his arms about in an agitated fashion while Christina tried to soothe him.

"In the end, she will have no one," growled Gregory.

Tony greeted them.

"Tony, you returned just in time to hear the good news," said his father sarcastically.

"I heard."

"Your father is upset because Melissa didn't want to marry Chuck in the first place because of Michael, and now she broke off with Michael because she felt he was too cheap. Your father thinks Melissa will become an old maid and have no one to marry. I was telling him she is still a young and pretty girl and –."

"She is not so young at twenty-seven," interjected Gregory. He turned to Tony. "I'm a sick old man, Tony. My years are numbered. I don't have the stamina I used to have before."

"Don't worry, Father. Everything will be all right," Tony said, patting him on the back. "Melissa is your daughter, a true Plakis, and will not let you down."

Early Sunday morning, Ipatia and her aunt decided to go to church. Marika joined them. The three women walked up and down a steep hill that eventually led them to the great church with the round dome.

After service, they stood outside, munching on their *antithoro*, a small piece of blessed bread.

Aunt Sophia chatted with some women from the church. A client of hers introduced her to another person who wanted to have something sewn for her. She arranged an appointment with her.

"Why don't we visit the Mikrolimano?" Aunt Sophia suggested to Ipatia and Marika. They both agreed.

They grabbed a taxi, heading for the popular harbor. It teemed with singles, couples, families, and tourists. As they approached the restaurant section, Ipatia enjoyed watching the white, picturesque boats docked along the way. They contrasted well with the azure canvass of the calm water.

The enticing scent of fried *calamari* (squid) emanated from a nearby restaurant. They decided to eat there. The calamari were fresh and succulent, and they enjoyed it with fried potatoes, feta-topped tomato and cucumber salad, and fresh bread.

Ipatia asked Marika about her teaching, and Marika talked merrily about her classes. Ipatia mentioned her own plans for the university.

Marika appeared skeptical. "The University of Piraeus might not have the program you are looking for. It's geared more towards industry rather than medicine," she informed Ipatia.

"Oh, I didn't know that."

"I'm afraid so. Why don't you stop by sometime, and I'll tell you more about it," Marika said. "I have some materials that may be useful."

Afterwards, they continued their walk, returning to the teeming harbor. Ipatia spied a large ship docked at the harbor that resembled her father's ship. She wondered who the captain was. She wondered if he also had a family waiting for him when he returned from his trips. Just then, a man got out of a cab and walked purposefully toward the ship. He was tall and dark. He looked like Tony. Her heart raced as he disappeared into its bowels.

"Ipatia. Ipatia, is everything all right?" Aunt Sophia asked.

Ipatia blinked at her aunt. "What?"

"Is everything all right? You look like you saw a ghost."

Something held Ipatia back from telling her what just transpired. "I, I remember when we used to come here often with my parents when I was young."

"Let's go and have some ice cream at the café. I know it will perk you up. Come on," Aunt Sophia said, hooking her arm in Ipatia's arm.

She was right. Soon, they were chatting and laughing away, and the rest of the day turned out pleasant enough.

Three days later, it was Ipatia's eighteenth birthday. That morning she peered into the mirror and saw the same face that she had been seeing all her life. The same almond shaped, light-green eyes, and the small, straight nose. Her lips were too full, especially after she ate. She pursed them together, trying to make them thinner. She laughed at the image in the mirror. She picked up the comb and began combing through her thick curls. Tony had said that he preferred it to be long.

The day went by quickly, and soon, Ipatia had returned from the English class. She was surprised to see Marika when she arrived home.

"Happy eighteenth birthday, Ipatia," Aunt Sophia said, hugging her. "I have something for you."

A few minutes later, she returned with a chocolate torte. Lit candles sat on top.

Touched by her aunt's thoughtful gesture, Ipatia clasped her hands. "Thank you, Aunt Sophia," she exclaimed. "I don't normally celebrate my birthdays."

"I know, Ipatia," Aunt Sophia said. "But you don't celebrate a name day either, and I thought a birthday would be appropriate."

"She does have a name day, Sophia. It's St. Hypatius, and it is celebrated on March 31st," Marika informed them.

"I have a name day?" Ipatia said, feeling wonderful. She had always felt left out when other people celebrated their name days but she didn't have a name day.

After Marika left, her aunt presented her with a wrapped package.

Ipatia emitted an exclamation of joy when she removed the white, cotton summer dress from the package. She proudly held it up in the air. "It's beautiful."

"I'm glad you like it," said her aunt, hugging her. "You should have seen me. Every time you went to class, I stopped whatever I was doing just so I could finish sewing it."

Ipatia tried the dress on. The straps and open neckline showed off her slim neck and the sash around her waist gave her curves. "It looks great," she said, showing it to her aunt.

They spent the rest of the evening with much laughter as Ipatia shared funny stories from the English class.

At some point, Aunt Sophia brought up the discussion of Ipatia's trust fund. "Ipatia, in the letter your grandfather wrote me, he mentioned that when you turned eighteen, he wanted me to make sure you went to the bank to see about the trust fund. I think I sent you those papers after your father died?"

"Yes. *Pappou* gave them to bring with me."

"Good. I also wanted you to know that your father loved you and wanted you to have the best." Sophia paused. "This upstairs suite is to be your wedding dowry when you marry. He told me so."

"Really?" Ipatia asked, feeling the blood rush to her head from the news. "But I don't have plans of marrying."

"It won't go away. Whenever you decide," Sophia said firmly. "What do you say we go to the bank tomorrow morning to see about the trust fund?"

The next morning, they entered the large bank, their footsteps echoing on the marble floors.

They presented her papers to the trust manager, Mr. Prasinakis. He was a thin man, balding, with large glasses. He left and returned shortly with documents in his hands.

He peered at Ipatia from above his spectacles. "Miss Kouris, you were correct in saying that your father opened this trust fund and that you would access it once you turned eighteen. It's in American dollars, and the balance on the account is fifty-seven thousand, seven hundred twenty-three dollars, which includes the interest it has accrued over time."

Ipatia was surprised at the amount.

"When can Ipatia withdraw funds?" Aunt Sophia asked.

He cleared his throat. "I think there is one condition that has to be met first," he said, reading the papers carefully. "Ah, here it is. Miss Ipatia needs to marry."

"What?" Ipatia cried.

"This money is to be used for your dowry, and it requires the signature of your husband before it can be released," he explained.

"My father wrote that?" Ipatia asked incredulously.

The manager showed her the paper with her father's signature. It was dated two years after the opening of the account. Her father must have added this as an addendum to the original paper. She read where it said that her husband sign also before the moneys were to be released.

Ipatia handed it back to him, biting her lip.

On the way home, she sat quietly next to her aunt in the taxi, musing about everything.

"I was just as surprised to hear about this as you are," admitted Sophia. "I think that your father's decision is a good one. What amazes me is his foresight in setting up your dowry when you were so young."

"If a man loves me, he loves me for myself," Ipatia muttered, "not for my money. It can stay there for all I care."

"Ipatia, your father worked hard during his lifetime. He was doing what he thought best for your future."

"It can't bring my parents back, and I don't want it to buy me a husband."

"One day, when the right young man comes along, you will think differently."

Shortly after they returned home, a client came to pick up her clothes, and Aunt Sophia became busy with her.

Ipatia excused herself and retreated to her bedroom. She thought about her aunt, alone and single, sewing for women for the rest of her life. Ipatia did not look forward to the same fate. *Let's face it, I'm confused.*

Ipatia shut her eyes, picturing her parents, trying to communicate with them. *I've always loved you and obeyed you, but I hadn't known how much you wanted me to marry. I want to ask forgiveness for going against your wishes, but I want to go to school first. Then I promise that one day I will marry.*

For some reason, the image of Tony Plakis came to her mind. Her heart quickened. She found his notes and reread them. She wondered what relation he had with Bonnie. She wondered how it would feel being married to someone like Tony. She fell asleep with Tony's notes in her hands.

Tony rubbed his eyes, feeling tired. He had been in the office all day working steadily. He looked out into the room, his eyes resting on the small table next to the window. The ancient vase with the geometric designs from Lipsi Island was on it, but not for long. Arrangements had been made to have it copied; the original was to be placed in the museum in Athens.

Curious about Ipatia's father's accumulation of expensive items, he had spoken with Captain Sardelis, one of the older captains in the company a few days ago. "How easy is it to get a hold of a vase or item of worth?"

"I know someone who deals in those things. He likes to collect vases and items of value. Traveling to other countries gives us opportunities to buy and trade. What is cheap in one country has value in another. You do understand."

Looking at the vase again, Tony realized that the girl's father had made some good choices in his travels. The image of the vase at the coffee shop in Lipsi Island popped into his head, followed by the image of a frightened Ipatia running away from him with her long tresses flowing behind her. He was startled and rubbed his eyes once more. She had changed so much from that first encounter.

Tony thought about his father's health. The verdict had been that the malignant tumor was located in a location of his brain that was dangerous. However, the procedure to remove it surgically could cost him his life. There was a specialist in Chicago who had a good reputation for this type of tumor, but his father, always cautious, said he wanted to see if there were any other options available first.

CHAPTER 20

No matter how much we try,
Our hearts cannot keep a lie.

September arrived, and one day, as Ipatia was helping her aunt with her sewing project, her aunt said, "Ipatia, it would be a good idea for you to work on your mother's clothes. It's a shame to have them waste away in the closet."

A week later, Ipatia's mourning period officially ended when she walked into the living room wearing one of her mother's finished dresses.

Her aunt's pleased expression was rewarding to see. "You remind me so much of your mother."

Ipatia wore it to class that day and received compliments from the children. After class, she talked with Mrs. Rodos about her dreams of a higher education. To Ipatia's delight, she found a staunch supporter for education in Mrs. Rodos.

"You see, Ipatia, I received a degree in languages from Oxford University in England where I had specialized in the Greek language," Mrs. Rodos said. "After that, I came to Greece to visit some friends and to practice my Greek. I met my husband in a restaurant in Greece. He was the cook there and had a habit of singing loudly while cooking. I went a couple of times to that restaurant before I got the nerve to tell him I liked his singing. Whenever I went there, he sang a special romantic song for me, and the rest is history," Mrs. Rodos said, starry-eyed.

"That sounds romantic," Ipatia said.

"Yes, but one cannot live on love alone. He did not make that much money, and we struggled the first few years," Mrs. Rodos said, nodding her head sadly. "I helped pay the bills by teaching English. We lived with his parents at first. Then our son was born two years later, and we moved into a small apartment. A friend of the family found him a job as a cook on one of those cargo ships that travel long voyages. They were paying well, so he took it. When the war started, an enemy ship struck his ship. I lost him then."

"I'm sorry to hear that," Ipatia said, biting her lip.

"I do miss him, but I know he's up there somewhere watching over me. We all have to go someday. Some people go sooner than others do. Anyhow, I am thankful for my education, because I supported myself and my son with my teaching."

"Where is your son?"

"Robert is in England with his family," Mrs. Rodos said. "I visit them during the holidays."

"So, what made you remain here in Greece?"

"Greece is my second love, as one might say," Mrs. Rodos said. "I studied the Greek language and the Greek culture and became fascinated about ancient Greece. The Acropolis and the Parthenon are such great architectural wonders. I've also read the works of Greek philosophers like Aristotle and Socrates, with their wisdom and logic. I could not help but fall in love with Greece."

"You know, I would love to visit the Acropolis and the Parthenon," Ipatia said wistfully.

"Then so be it," Mrs. Rodos said. "We can plan an outing to go there soon. Before I forget, let me give you some books useful for your university exam."

As Ipatia walked home, carrying the books, she reflected upon Mrs. Rodos's story. Her husband had died, something that Ipatia dreaded. Yet, she was doing fine. Ipatia started thinking about Tony, imagining him being a cook and singing romantic songs for her in a restaurant. For some reason, she could not see him doing that.

A car honked. The sun had set and she could not see well. Dr. Hatzis waved to her from the car. She stopped and gazed at him in surprise as he pulled to the side. *What is he doing here?*

"Hello, Dr. Hatzis," she said. She had mixed feelings as she slowly approached the car, remembering the last time she had seen him with Melissa outside her bedroom window, talking about Tony and Bonnie.

"Do you need a ride?" he asked.

"No, thank you. I live down the block with my aunt."

"Oh, that's nice. You are probably curious to see me here," he began. "A colleague of mine, Dr. Demetrios recently retired, and I have replaced him. I came by today to have a look at the office."

"So, Dr. Demetrios retired," Ipatia said, remembering the kind, old doctor. "We visited him a few weeks ago because my aunt needed to refill a prescription."

"I plan to take over his office and would like for you and your family to continue coming. By the way, how is your ankle these days?"

"It has healed nicely, thanks to you."

"Good. I see you are carrying books. Are you taking courses?"

"No, I'm helping teach English at a school down the road," she said awkwardly, "and Mrs. Rodos, the English teacher, lets me borrow her books. I am reading them for the university entrance exam."

"Come to think of it, I remember you showing interest in medical topics that day you came to my office. You can stop by my office anytime, and I'd be delighted to loan you some medical journals."

After that day, she played with the idea of going to his office to get the medical literature he mentioned but didn't feel comfortable enough to do that.

••————◈ ••————◈ ••————◈

Tony sat in the airplane, gazing pensively out the window. They were about to land in Greece. Yesterday in England, he received a telephone call from his father. He sounded weak and complained about his deteriorating health. This prompted Tony to leave England immediately and return home.

His father's offices in England and New York made it necessary to travel to these sites often to ensure everything was in order. He was beginning to get tired from all that traveling.

When he arrived home, he met Melissa and Christina waiting for him. They appeared worried.

"Where is Father?" Tony asked, looking around. He noticed the dark rings under Christina's eyes, a sign that she hadn't been sleeping well.

"He is napping," Christina said wearily. She explained how his father was becoming weaker and his limbs were becoming spastic. "He doesn't have control over his movements."

"We have to do everything for him now," Melissa complained.

"Then we need to do something, before it is too late," Tony said firmly.

"We found a specialist for this type of brain tumor in Chicago," Melissa said hopefully. "Father has agreed to be seen by him."

After much discussion, Tony was convinced that this was the best option for his father. The next morning, he telephoned the physician's office in Chicago. The physician was available and they covered the pros and cons of surgery. Tony hung up the telephone, deep in thought.

When he walked into the living room, he found his father sitting on the couch, his arms jerking uncontrollably. Christina and Melissa sat next to him, holding on to him.

"Well, what did he say?" Gregory asked, gesturing feebly, unable to control his movements.

"The doctor spoke frankly. He needs to see all your tests and records before promising anything."

"That can be done easily enough," Melissa said.

"Did he say anything else?" Gregory asked, his hand jerking uncontrollably.

"If he operates on you, he cannot guarantee you will be totally well from the operation," Tony said slowly, trying to put it more gently to his father than what he had heard from the doctor.

"That's what the doctor here told us. What can this doctor do for me that's better?"

"As you know, the location of the tumor is dangerous. In the past, these types of operations were risky, and they still are. He uses state-of-the art technology, which has helped a number of patients live who would have died otherwise. The operation may give you a fighting chance of living a decent life. If you don't do anything about it, then you forfeit that chance."

"What about chemo and radiation? Aren't they also treatment options?" Melissa asked.

Tony shook his head. "I don't know. The doctor said surgery is the best option right now."

"I've made up my mind. I'm going to America to get rid of this thing once and for all. I'm tired of being sick," Gregory grumbled, striking his hand forcefully on the table. Christina and Melissa jumped at the sound.

"So be it. We are coming with you," Tony said.

Two weeks later, they left for America.

On a gray, rainy Monday in October, Ipatia took an umbrella with her to class but she forgot it in the classroom when she left, and by the time she reached home, she was soaking wet.

The next morning, she awoke with a sore throat and felt tired all day. By Wednesday morning, Ipatia was coughing and had an earache. She slept through the morning, waking up only to eat some warm *avgolemeno* soup that her aunt had made. She fell promptly asleep again.

Midday, Aunt Sophia said, "Ipatia, you feel hot and may have a fever. You need to see a doctor."

Later that day, Ipatia sat in Dr. Hatzis's office.

"Open your mouth wide. That's good," Dr. Hatzis told her. "Your throat is red and swollen."

He checked her ears next. She winced when he touched her left ear. "You have an ear infection."

"She wanted to go to class tonight, but I felt she needed to see you," Aunt Sophia explained.

"You did the right thing, Miss Sophia. With antibiotics, expect about a week for her to get over this," he said, reading the thermometer. He prescribed antibiotics and told Ipatia to get plenty of liquids and rest.

A nurse came to the door and spoke to him.

"Please wait here," he said to Ipatia before leaving the room.

Ipatia wondered if she should ask him about Tony but decided not to. It would seem too bold.

Dr. Hatzis returned a few minutes later, holding a couple of medical journals in his hands. "Ipatia, if you still are interested in reading medical topics, I saved some to give you."

"Oh, yes, doctor. I would love to read them."

"When you are finished reading these, bring them back, and I'll loan you a whole set of new ones to read."

"Thank you, doctor," Aunt Sophia said, looking surprised.

When Ipatia and her aunt left his office, they stopped by the pharmacy to get her medicine.

"I must remember to tell Mrs. Rodos that you are sick and won't be coming to class for several days," Aunt Sophia said.

When Ipatia awoke later that day, her aunt greeted her, holding several books in her hands. "Mrs. Rodos sends you her best wishes. Look at all these books she gave for you to read."

The next day, her aunt made it a point to say nice things about Dr. Hatzis. Ipatia agreed and thought nothing of it. She stayed inside, resting and reading. A few days later, she felt well enough to sit and watch her aunt sew.

"Ipatia, I haven't heard you cough at all today. Dr. Hatzis is a wonderful doctor. He knew just what to do to make you well," Aunt Sophia said, handing her the medicine and a glass of water.

"Aunt Sophia, a day doesn't go by without you mentioning his name," Ipatia said, laughing.

"Oh, I didn't realize I was doing that. I never had a young, eligible doctor treating my niece before," she chuckled. "He is handsome, isn't he?"

"Aunt Sophia, *really*. Dr. Hatzis is engaged to Melissa," Ipatia exclaimed. She was beginning to feel annoyed at her aunt.

"My dear, I was only making an observation."

After that day, Sophia avoided mentioning him.

A week passed before Ipatia was well enough to return to the English class. She stopped by Dr. Hatzis's office on the way there. The waiting room was empty, but she could hear the doctor in the examining room with a patient. She scribbled a note and left it with the literature he had loaned her and a plate of baklava. In the note, she thanked him for the material and said, "The homemade baklava was a token of appreciation from Aunt Sophia for everything you have done."

The next day, Sophia received a letter from America.

"Who is it from? What does it say?" Ipatia asked her.

"It's from John. He wants to pay me a visit. He'll be in Greece during the holidays to see his parents," replied Aunt Sophia, starry-eyed. "Isn't that wonderful?"

"Is that the man you met in America?"

"Yes, and you know what? Something tells me he's serious."

CHAPTER 21

My father's health took up my time.
I returned to Greece, my love to find.

Tony and his family returned to Greece in early November. He immediately went to work in the office the following morning.

The first person he greeted was Rita, the front desk receptionist.

"Good morning, Rita," Tony said, smiling at her. His hands full of gifts, he placed the packages on her desk. "These are souvenirs from America. Can you please have them distributed to everyone? Please keep one for yourself."

"Good morning, Mr. Tony, how was your trip?" asked Aristotle, coming out of his office.

"Hello, Aristotle," Tony replied. He shook hands with the bookkeeper. "The trip was better than expected, thank you."

They walked toward his office.

"Sometime today, I'd like to go over everything that happened while I was away."

"Certainly, Mr. Tony," replied Aristotle. "I'll be free in an hour if that would be fine with you. Oh, and the vase you ordered has arrived. I put it in the office. The original vase is in the archaeological museum's possession."

Tony nodded, feeling pleased. Later, he studied the vase in his office. It looked exactly like the original. The images of Ipatia swept before him. *Sweet, innocent Ipatia, this vase belongs to you.*

He thought about their trip to America. The brain surgeon had not guaranteed anything. He had stated bluntly that his father could die during the operation, or if he survived, could remain disabled for the rest of his life.

After the operation, Tony's father did not die, but the future would show whether he would walk again.

That same moment, Ipatia and Mrs. Rodos were visiting the archaeological museum in Athens.

Ipatia walked slowly around the rooms, stopping to observe each artifact, moving on to the next object. "Just think. People thousands of years ago were making these objects," she exclaimed, fascinated by the ornaments worn by women in ancient times.

They reached a room that held various vases. At one point, she spied a familiar looking vase. She pointed to it. "This looks like the vase my father had given my grandfather. It has the same lines and figures."

They moved closer and read the inscription below the vase. Ipatia's heart began to race. "Gift from Dr. Antonios Plakis. In loving memory of Captain Manolis Kouris," she read aloud. "He remembered my father." Her eyes filled with tears.

"That was nice of him," Mrs. Rodos said. "He not only has a good eye for beauty, but the logic to know what to do with it."

At the end of November, Ipatia received a letter from Grandfather.

"What does it say, Ipatia?" Aunt Sophia asked.

"*Pappou* is doing fine," Ipatia began. She continued to read. "He apologizes for not having answered my letters, but he's been busy. Tom and another boy gathered the olives this year, and he had a good crop. He says he misses me because I could pick olives quicker than both those boys could."

They laughed.

Ipatia excused herself and went to her room. She finished reading the rest of the letter. He wrote that her godmother came over with food periodically, and things were quiet now that Ipatia was not there. The horse Tony had given him was helping him greatly.

Ipatia reread the letter several times. She sat down and wrote to him about her news, particularly the news about the vase.

Aunt Sophia received another letter from John, this time stating that he would be visiting the week before Christmas. That week was full of excitement as Ipatia helped her aunt prepare for his arrival. Ipatia helped clean the house while her aunt went to the hairdresser's. Later that week, they went shopping and she helped her choose a new dress. As the day approached, they also stocked the refrigerator well. Her aunt told her that she intended on cooking a special meal for him.

On the way to class one day, Ipatia stopped at Dr. Hatzis's office to return his medical journals and to give him a package. She found him locking the door.

"Hello, Ipatia," he said, looking surprised. "You made it just in time. I was closing the office early today."

"Dr. Hatzis, I brought back the journals you loaned me," she said breathlessly, handing them to him.

Blushing at his steady gaze, she handed him the wrapped package she carried. "My aunt and I made some Vassilopita. You can freeze the bread until New Year's Day."

"That's kind of you and your aunt," he said, taking it. "Why don't you keep the journals as my gift for the holidays?"

"Thank you," Ipatia said, feeling pleased, as he handed her back the journals. She turned and headed for the stairs.

"Here, let me walk with you downstairs," he said, touching her lightly on her arm.

For the first time, she noticed he was the same height as her, if not slightly shorter. They walked down the steps.

"How did you like the reading this time, Ipatia?" he asked.

"Some technical words were a little difficult to understand," admitted Ipatia. "I think the medical research on leukemia and cancer is amazing."

"Yes, isn't it?" he asked. "There is still much more to be discovered in those fields. We are just beginning to scratch the surface."

They had arrived outside.

"Before you leave, I would like to wish you the best for Christmas and the New Year. Will you be spending them with your aunt?"

"Yes. Are you going to spend your holidays with Melissa?" Ipatia asked. She had been curious about Melissa all this time, for he had not mentioned her.

"I'm afraid not," Dr. Hatzis said, looking slightly amused, putting his hands in his pockets. "Melissa and I are no longer engaged. We had too many differences that couldn't be resolved."

"I'm sorry to hear that. I didn't know."

He was staring at her in the same analytical and dissecting manner in which he had studied her the first time in the yacht. Suddenly she knew why he had been interested in giving her the journals.

Ipatia shifted uneasily away from him, ready to bolt, not wanting to face the dawning reality of his intentions.

"By the way, the office will close for the holidays and will reopen in three weeks. If there is any medical emergency, here is my telephone number where I can be reached."

She took the piece of paper shyly, afraid to look at him. "Have a Merry Christmas." She sped away before he could say anything.

He stood there, gazing at her wistfully.

Sophia rested on the sofa, reading a magazine. The doorbell rang. She glanced at the clock. It showed six-thirty, too early for Ipatia to have returned from class. She jumped up excitedly, fixing her hair, and hurried to the door.

John stood there, handsomely dressed in a dark-navy suit, white shirt, and blue silk tie.

"Hello, Sophia," John said warmly, taking her hands in his and kissing her lightly on her cheek. "I am glad to see you again."

"John, I'm so glad you could come," she said just as warmly. She caught herself gazing into his eyes, and then looked down, abashed at the emotions she was experiencing.

John stepped to the side to reveal a young man standing behind him. "This is my nephew, Stellios. He lives in Athens."

"Welcome," she said, shaking his limp hand. She gestured inside. "Please come in."

John entered the suite with his nephew. "I thought you lived downstairs, but Miss Marika told me otherwise."

"Yes, I've rented the downstairs to her," Sophia said, leading them into the living room. "This used to belong to my late brother. I like it better up here. It's roomier and has a nice view from the balcony." She pointed to the sofa. "Please have a seat. Would you like some coffee?"

"No, no, some other time," John said, smiling. He gestured for her to sit down. "Tonight, I am treating. I'd like to invite you and your niece out to Diamond's. Stellios says good things about it. Right, Stellios?"

"They have great entertainment and a lake in the back," Stellios said.

"That would be lovely, but my niece hasn't returned from school. She helps teach English classes three times a week and I'm expecting her any minute."

The class had just finished and Ipatia and Mrs. Rodos were giving books as presents to all the children. To Ipatia's surprise, several children presented her with their own small gifts. Ipatia gave Mrs. Rodos her own gift, a framed poem she had stitched on canvas.

"Thank you Ipatia. The poem you wrote about me and the English class is lovely. I will hang it here in this room so everyone can read it. I hope you enjoy the book I gave you," Mrs. Rodos said.

Ipatia thanked Mrs. Rodos in turn for her present. When Ipatia saw the time, she excused herself and left quickly.

"Aunt Sophia, sorry I was late," Ipatia said, bursting into the house.

"Hello, Ipatia," Aunt Sophia said, interrupting her. She hurried to her and whispered into her ear. "We have guests."

By her aunt's glowing demeanor, Ipatia immediately realized who their "guests" were. She placed the children's gifts to the side and followed her aunt into the living room.

Her aunt introduced her to two male visitors. John gave her a hearty handshake and flashed her a boyish grin. She smiled cheerfully back, immediately feeling comfortable. The younger man, thin and pale in color, gave her a cold, limp hand to shake.

"Ipatia, John has invited us out to a nightclub," Aunt Sophia said. Her face glowed with anticipation.

"Oh," Ipatia said. "I don't think *Pappou* would approve my going."

Aunt Sophia became flustered, "Her grandfather was very protective of her on the island, you know," she explained to John.

"Oh, I see," he said, winking knowingly at Sophia. "Ipatia, this one is suitable for families, and it has a wonderful lake."

Ipatia liked what she heard. "That sounds nice."

The women excused themselves, and Aunt Sophia followed Ipatia to her bedroom.

"What should I wear, Aunt Sophia?"

Aunt Sophia pulled out a black, sequined evening gown from the closet and showed it to Ipatia.

"How about this dress? I sewed it for your mother. It should fit you," Aunt Sophia said.

Ipatia stared at the glamorous dress, with its low neckline and thin straps, trying to picture her mother wearing it. "I'm doing this just for you, Aunt," she said, chuckling, as her aunt left the room.

Ipatia felt exposed with the low neckline and pulled on the thin straps trying to make it go higher. She swept up her hair and secured it with a few hairpins. She put on her mother's long, diamond stud earrings, appreciating the way they sparkled.

Her aunt returned, also wearing a dark-blue evening gown with a shawl on her shoulders.

"You look lovely, my dear. Worth a million drachmas," Aunt Sophia said approvingly. "It's a little cool outside, so here is a shawl."

Grateful for the shawl, Ipatia placed it over her bare shoulders. "Thank you, Aunt Sophia. You look lovely yourself," Ipatia said, observing how her aunt's elegant evening gown was becoming on her.

John appeared pleased at the transformation of the two women.

When they reached the nightclub, Stellios went to park the car. Aunt Sophia conversed with John, while Ipatia stood quietly nearby, appreciating the exceptionally mild temperatures for December. Tall, swaying palm trees lined the perimeter of the property. Plush landscaping with scented flowers added beauty to the place.

Stellios arrived soon thereafter, leading them into the carpeted lobby.

"The entertainment isn't until later, but we can get good seats now and watch the show from there," Stellios said.

They went into a large ballroom that had a stage extending into the center of the room with tables encircling it. A wet bar was stationed in the corner.

John ordered appetizers and drinks for everyone.

Then the show began. Singers, dancers, and acrobats took their turns on stage. Large, spinning balls that hung from the ceiling, flashed bright colors on the performers, making them appear magical. After the show, the floor was opened to the public for dancing. It became noisy, so they strolled outside.

A walkway led to the large, oblong lake and circling its perimeter were soft lights, illuminating it romantically. Ipatia could see couples standing on a bridge that stretched across the lake. Soft romantic music was coming from somewhere above their heads.

"Oh, look over there," Aunt Sophia exclaimed. She pointed to the boats that glided slowly down the lake.

John persuaded Aunt Sophia to go with him on one of the boats.

Stellios asked Ipatia politely if she would like to join them, but she declined. Feeling the cool night air press upon her exposed arms, Ipatia pulled her shawl around her, shivering slightly as they strolled forward.

They found a bench and sat down. Stellios talked about his last year at the PolyTech Institute while they watched the boats gliding by.

Ipatia noticed a familiar looking man, sharply dressed, standing on the bridge. He was talking with a woman. She strained her eyes, desperately trying to catch a better glimpse. As he moved closer to her view, she stared.

Tony Plakis had come to the nightclub with his sister.

"Melissa, are you sure you want to continue to wait for this Daras fellow? We've already been here over an hour and I need to rise early tomorrow morning for my flight to England," Tony said, checking his watch. It showed ten o'clock.

"I'm positive he's here somewhere. Now don't be a sour face. He said he'll be here, and he will," Melissa said, smiling back at him. She continued to look for Chuck Daras.

Tony's eyes searched the area once more, noticing a young couple sitting on a bench across the lake. What caught his attention was that the woman was taller than the man. On closer inspection, the young woman was exquisitely beautiful yet appeared oddly familiar. He stared for a moment and his heart quickened as he realized her features were similar to Ipatia's. He shook his head. Ipatia wouldn't be dressed in a sophisticated evening gown, sitting alone on a bench with a young man. *Not the Ipatia I know.*

"Oh, there he is," Melissa said excitedly, pointing with one hand and tugging on Tony's sleeve with the other.

Tony turned and spied Chuck waving to them.

"See, I told you he'll be here. Come on, Tony, let's go meet him."

"All right," Tony said. He smiled down at his sister. He had never seen her so excited before, not even with Michael.

As they walked slowly off the bridge, Tony glanced once more at the bench where the girl had been sitting, but she had disappeared.

ᚲHAPTᛌR 22

There she stood, elegantly dressed,
A dream unfolding, he confessed.

Ipatia became excited when she saw Tony standing there with his sister. She rose nervously from the bench, saying shakily to Stellios, "I'd like to wait for my aunt and your uncle at the boat dock."

The small boat area was located near the back entrance and the walkway. As they left, Ipatia furtively glanced behind her, hoping to see Tony. She felt slightly disappointed when she saw that he had disappeared.

"Here they come," said Stellios, interrupting Ipatia's thoughts.

They watched the boat, which her Aunt Sophia and John were in, returning from the excursion.

"Ipatia, you should have come," Aunt Sophia said, laughing, as she got out of the boat with John's help. "We had so much fun."

They walked around for a few minutes more, while Aunt Sophia chattered about their little adventure. "We almost fell into the water when another boat bumped into us," she said. Then she noticed the time. "Oh, look at the time. It's been a lovely evening, but I think we should be going. The trip back is close to an hour."

John nodded and said, "Whatever you like."

They reached the front of the club.

John said, "You two ladies wait here and we'll bring the car. It's parked down the road."

They were gone before Sophia could protest.

185

"Aunt Sophia, I wanted to tell you-" Ipatia began, intending to mention Tony's presence.

"I'm sorry, Ipatia. Can it wait?" interrupted Sophia, touching her arm briefly. "I need to excuse myself one minute. It is a long trip back to the house, and I don't think I can wait. Do you want to join me?"

"No, thanks. I'll wait here in case the men come looking for us," Ipatia said, laughing.

Her aunt left hurriedly, and Ipatia stood there, daydreaming of a tall, handsome young man who had saved her from a snake once. She strolled down the sidewalk, enjoying the evening breeze, the palm trees and the quietness after all the loud music inside. Seeing Tony's sister there had dampened her excitement. The memory of what Melissa had said to Michael, regarding Bonnie and Tony, was still fresh in Ipatia's mind.

•••————◈ ••• ————◈ •••————◈

Tony walked through the double-glass door, his hands in his pockets, thinking about his trip tomorrow. He left his sister and Chuck alone to discuss things. It appeared that their relationship was becoming serious, and Tony didn't want to be in the way.

Could I see Chuck Daras only as a brother-in-law? No. He was also a businessman. Tony had a premonition that if allowed, Chuck would waste no time in managing Father's shipping business. He was that type, and it would be just like Melissa to promise him that position.

Tony's thoughts wandered towards his own future. What would happen after Chuck joined the agency? He could either stay or return to his former position at Oxford. He had requested a one-year sabbatical. He could always return there.

Tony stopped in his tracks when he saw the same girl. She had her back turned to him, walking slowly, as if she were deep in thought. Her shawl had slipped down her shoulders, revealing her slim neck and bare, white shoulders.

He stood there, studying her, and feeling unsure whether to approach her or not. If she wasn't Ipatia, he could get in trouble with the girl's family.

When she turned around, he got his answer. As her steps brought her closer, Ipatia began to show signs of recognition.

"Hello, Ipatia," Tony said, striding toward her. His father had been right about her beauty. She was like a walking dream in that shimmering black dress. Her long legs, slim hips, creamy white shoulders and graceful neck all were exposing an elegance and sophistication that had been hidden in her black garb from the island. She was not the peasant girl he remembered. *She was a princess.*

Ipatia was mesmerized by Tony's pleasantly rich voice and handsome looks. That same person was looking deeply into her eyes, into her soul.

"Hello," she managed to say. Her cheeks felt flushed.

Time stood still, and they stared at each other, sucked up by a great force pulling them together.

"I thought I saw you by the lake, but when I looked for you, you had vanished. You always seem to be vanishing on me, Ipatia," he said, taking her hand. "Now I'm going to hold your hand so you don't run away this time."

Tony's action caught Ipatia off guard. She trembled slightly from his touch. *I must not let him get so close.*

"You know, *Mr. Plakis*, where I come from, it's not considered proper for a young man to be alone with a girl at a nightclub, and even more so, to hold her hand," she said firmly.

"Is that right?" Tony asked. "Then I will respect your wish, *Miss Kouris*, on the condition that you promise you won't run away."

They both laughed nervously.

"But now that we're on the topic of what is proper, may I ask how is it that you were sitting with a young man all alone on the bench?"

"Oh, Stellios? Let me explain. It's, it's, not like it seems," Ipatia said, stammering lightly. "He's the nephew of John Stavrakis, the man who invited us to come with them here. My aunt and John went on a boat ride, and I didn't feel like going along because I get sick on boats, so Stellios stayed behind with me."

"Where is everyone? Why are you alone?"

"Stellios left with John to get the car, and my aunt left for the lady's room."

"What would your dear grandfather say if he learned you were out here this late hour, all alone at a nightclub?"

"He wouldn't like it," she admitted.

"I am only teasing," he said, laughing. "How have you been, Ipatia? You know the house felt empty after I returned home from Thessaloniki, with everyone gone. I had been hoping to see you still there."

His warm gaze settled on her, speaking volumes.

"I apologize for my impulsive behavior. My grandfather always scolded me for it. I didn't feel comfortable staying there while your father was in the hospital, and you were about to leave."

"Is that the only reason?" he asked gently.

"No, but that was the chief reason," she managed to squeak out, unable to move.

"You're forgiven," he said, his voice husky, as he bowed. "I hope that someday you will trust me enough to confide in me what the real reason was."

Ipatia froze, unable to say what she truly felt inside. *He had said someday for me to confide in him. That means he wants to see me again.* She had the odd feeling he was about to kiss her, but someone coughed, and he stepped back slightly and turned to look.

Aunt Sophia had been standing on the side all this time. She went up to him. "Tony, do you know who I am?" she said, smiling and excitedly shaking his hand.

He smiled. "Of course. You are Miss Sophia, the nice lady who sewed for us when we were children, and who always gave us candy."

"How have you been?"

"I'm doing fine, thank you," Tony said. "You look much younger than I remember."

"You were always one for saying such nice things," Aunt Sophia replied, chuckling. "What have you been doing lately with yourself? Last time I heard, you were somewhere in England, teaching at a university."

Ipatia was amazed at the familiarity between her aunt and Tony.

"I am staying with my family in Kifissia for the time being. Father's shipping business is keeping me busy."

"You're working for your father?" Aunt Sophia asked.

"Yes. He's recuperating from a surgery, and I am helping him with the business."

"Sorry to hear that. And your sister?"

"She's somewhere around here with her new beau, Chuck Daras."

John and Stellios arrived in the car and honked at them.

"Please give our best wishes to your father and say hello to your sister for me."

"We'll have to talk another time, I see your escort has arrived," Tony said, somewhat dryly. "Have a pleasant evening."

Ipatia bade him farewell, disappointed that they were leaving. She watched him walk away, his hands in his pockets. He was not his usual, carefree self. Something had changed.

"Why don't you two women share the back seat?" John suggested, opening the door for them.

Ipatia sat in the back with her aunt, and the car drove on into the night.

"Tony has turned out to be such a handsome young man," Aunt Sophia remarked.

"He's engaged," Ipatia said dryly. She knew what her aunt was thinking. *Where was Bonnie tonight?*

"Oh, I didn't mean it that way, you know, having known him when he was a child and everything," Sophia explained, appearing flustered. "I was just noticing the difference."

Then everything became silent and the sound of the car's tires droning on the pavement made Ipatia feel sleepy. She began to doze off.

"Ipatia, did Tony say Melissa had a new beau?"

"Yes," Ipatia murmured, half-asleep.

"Wasn't Dr. Hatzis engaged to Melissa?"

"Oh, that's right, I forgot to tell you," Ipatia exclaimed, bolting up from her sleep. She rubbed her eyes. "Today when I went to drop off the Vassilopita, the doctor was closing the office for the holidays. I asked him if he was going to spend his holiday with Melissa, but he said he no longer was engaged to her."

"That makes him available," Sophia observed.

"What do you mean?" Ipatia asked, drifting off to sleep, unable to stay awake.

After that evening, John visited them almost daily, and there was much gaiety and laughter when he was around. He had a good sense of humor, and his boyish charm was appealing to Ipatia. She felt her aunt's happiness every time he visited.

One day when Ipatia arrived from class, she found her aunt alone in the living room, sewing.

"How was your day?" Ipatia asked, joining her aunt on the sofa.

"Oh, fine, fine. John stopped by later this afternoon and he was his ever-charming self," replied Aunt Sophia, smiling. She threaded a needle. "He had something to do, so he couldn't stay that long, but he invited us to his parents' house for New Year's Day. Do you know what that means?"

"It means he likes you."

"And I like him, but I think it's becoming serious," Aunt Sophia said, beginning to sew a hem on a skirt. "I hope his parents like me."

"They will," Ipatia exclaimed, hugging her aunt. "You are such a lovely and kind person. They are lucky to have a daughter-in-law like you."

"Ipatia, whatever gave you that idea?" Aunt Sophia asked, appearing pleased.

The days whizzed by and New Year's Eve arrived. Aunt Sophia fussed with her hair and clothes all day. Ipatia helped her bake the traditional Vassilopita, kneading the dough and making sure that she placed a coin in it.

John came by and picked them up later that evening. His parents turned out to be pleasant people. They embraced Sophia and Ipatia as if they were family. Ipatia and her aunt had such a good time that they didn't get home until early the next morning.

Ipatia woke up late the next day, feeling tired and groggy. She found her aunt already in the kitchen busily preparing breakfast and humming. She was in an unusually cheerful mood.

"Good morning, Ipatia. I hope you slept well. I hardly slept at all. I was going to tell you the wonderful news last night, but you were so sleepy, I thought I'd wait until today to tell you." Sophia said, her eyes shining.

"Yes?"

"John proposed to me last night. Your aunt is going to be married."

Ipatia jumped up with joy, hugging her aunt with all her might. "Congratulations, Aunt Sophia. I'm so happy for you."

"Thank you," Aunt Sophia said, hugging her back. "I know this is sudden, and at my age, but when God gives me an opportunity like this one, I can't refuse it."

"Isn't that wonderful? So, tell me, dear Aunt, what are your plans? When are you going to be married?" Ipatia asked, settling back down in her chair. Amidst her happiness, a small doubt entered her mind, and it began to nag her. *How am I going to fit into this new couple's life?*

"Last night, we didn't have much time to discuss all the details, but we did manage to agree on the wedding date to be in February. That allows me two months to prepare for it. I need to order my wedding gown and send out invitations and do a number of other things that one needs to do when one marries."

"I can picture you looking dazzlingly beautiful in a long, white wedding gown, standing at the aisle with uncle John handsomely dressed in a tuxedo. You will make the perfect couple."

"Thank you, Ipatia, that's so sweet of you."

"Where do you plan to live after the wedding?"

Sophia cleared her throat and looked Ipatia squarely in the eyes. Her voice trembled slightly as she said, "As you know, John lives in a suburb of Chicago, and his house sits right next to Antonios's house. Once we are married, he wants us to go back to America and live there."

"America?" Ipatia asked, her voice ending in a high pitch. She stared at her aunt. She had mixed feelings about the idea. She was happy for her aunt's marriage but going to America to live was another story.

"Yes, America," replied Sophia, nodding her head. "Isn't that amazing? Me going to America to live. I was up all night just thinking about it. Anyway, I thought about you and felt it wrong to just get up and leave you. Therefore, I'd like you to know that you can come and stay with us. With your English, you'd get along fine."

Ipatia thought for a moment before replying, "What does Uncle John say about this?"

"I haven't discussed it with him yet. It came to me last night as I was thinking about everything, but I'm pretty sure he won't say no to the idea."

"I don't know what to say," Ipatia said slowly, feeling overwhelmed. "I did have plans to take the entrance examination in the spring and visit *Pappou* during the summer, but the thought of going to America is exciting."

Sophia hesitated. "First of all, you can continue your studies in America. You understand English, so it will not be a problem. There are also plenty of universities there for your studies. You can still visit your grandfather in the summers. It'll just be a longer trip."

Ipatia was silent, digesting the information.

"Why don't you think about it for a while? There's no rush," Aunt Sophia said, patting her on the back. "We have two months until the wedding anyway."

"Is it all right if I speak with *Pappou*, to see what he has to say?"

Her aunt readily agreed.

Later that day, Ipatia walked to the pharmacy and placed a call to speak with her grandfather the next morning. She spent the rest of the day thinking about everything her aunt had said.

The following morning, Ipatia spoke to her grandfather and relayed the news about her aunt's wedding and her plans to move to America with her husband.

"Your aunt is getting married?" His voice sounded surprised. "That's good news. Give her my congratulations, Ipatia."

"Yes, I will. Meanwhile, what should I do? She has invited me to go live with them in America, but I have plans to take the entrance examination in the spring."

"The idea of going to America is out of the question. First of all, you don't have the money for the trip and don't expect to live off charity all your life, young lady."

"I know," she admitted. "That means I would remain here. I won't be by myself, because Miss Marika rents the downstairs."

"Under no circumstances am I going to allow you to live there alone. If your cousins, George and Paula, are willing to have you, then you can stay with them. Otherwise, you come back here and stay with me."

"I tried going to the cousins before, remember? They weren't there. They like to travel."

"Try them again. I don't think they travel all the time," he replied firmly.

Ipatia walked slowly back home, deep in thought. She discussed her conversation with Aunt Sophia.

"I understand you have your own life to live, and I wish you all the best. We'll see about visiting your cousins one of these days. However, the invitation still stands for you to come and live with us."

After that day, her aunt was like a teenager, excited about everything, glowing and happy all the time. John left for America a few days later, kissing Aunt Sophia and promising her that he would write often. He needed to go and prepare for his new bride to be.

CHAPTER 23

Michael's story begins to unfold.
Ipatia is seeing him, I am told.

One Saturday in early January, Tony sat in his study, conversing and joking with Michael, who had dropped by unexpectedly.

Michael said, "How long has it been? I haven't seen you for at least three months. Ever since-"

"Michael, Michael," Tony said, laughing at his friend's complaint. "The reason why I haven't been by to visit you is not because of anything that happened between you and my sister, but because I have been busy with our business, and with Father's health. I've been traveling back and forth to our various offices. There's always something that needs attention."

"You're telling the truth now," Michael said, half-jokingly.

"Yes. This pile of papers is from the office," Tony said, pointing at the stack on his desk. "I haven't read them yet."

"You know, Tony, I remember when you'd return from England during your summer breaks and we'd attend social events so we could meet women," Michael said. "You've changed somehow."

"Things *are* different," Tony said, nodding at his friend's description of him.

"All this work and no play, it's not healthy. I'm speaking to you as a doctor and a friend."

"You have a good point," Tony admitted. "But don't worry about me, old friend. I have a feeling that things will change for me after April."

"What do you mean?"

"Look, you've been such a good friend and everything, I don't want there to be hard feelings for what I'm about to say."

Michael's eyebrows went up. "I can handle it."

"Melissa is engaged to Chuck Daras. Their wedding is planned for April."

Michael became solemn. "I wish them all the luck in the world. Melissa had acquired expensive tastes and didn't want to give them up. I couldn't afford that lifestyle, not with the salary I was making."

"I understand."

"You said things will change for you?" Michael asked.

"It seems Chuck Daras is not only interested in my sister, but in our shipping business. With Melissa's encouragement, he has begun managing the company while I was away on this last trip. Yesterday, when I returned, I found him sitting at my desk with my sister, going over papers."

"Did you speak to your father about this?" Michael asked. "Chuck doesn't waste time."

Tony nodded, thinking about the conversation he had with his father earlier that day. He had asked him about Chuck.

"Now that Chuck is going to be part of the family, I think it best that he become involved with our company," Gregory replied. "He has many years of experience in the shipping business. I think he'll make a good manager."

"I remained here because you wanted me to help you out, but if Chuck is to be in charge, then it seems you won't need me much longer," Tony told his father.

"No, please don't look at it that way. I want you to stay and oversee things."

"Only for a few months, until Chuck Daras is ready to manage," Tony said before hanging up.

Tony turned to his friend, sighing. "Yes, I spoke to him on the telephone this morning. I made it clear to him that I would only stay for a few more months until Chuck took charge. My heart was never in this line of work, I'm afraid."

"Oh," Michael said, raising an eyebrow. "Where's your father now?"

"He's in Crete with Christina, and he'll probably stay there until he gets better. He doesn't want his old business associates seeing him so ill."

"Good luck with everything," Michael said, getting up. "By the way, I came by not only to see how you were doing, but to also ask if you wanted to join me and some cousins of mine. We're planning to go to Diamond's tonight, you know, the nightclub with the lake."

"Thanks for the invitation, but I'm afraid I'll have to turn you down. I'm meeting with our attorney this afternoon and those sessions last a while."

"Don't say I didn't try," Michael said, laughing.

"By the way, I went to Diamond's with Melissa, back in December," Tony said, leaning back in his chair with his arms behind his head. "A funny thing happened. I bumped into Ipatia, the island girl, and her aunt. She looked so different, so much older."

"Who, her aunt?" Michael teased.

"No, I meant Ipatia," Tony said. He smiled when he noticed his friend's teasing look.

"Tony, you've been away so much, I haven't had the chance to tell you the latest news. She's been coming to my office for several weeks now," Michael said, looking Tony squarely in the eyes.

Tony sat straight up in his chair. "How did this come about?" he asked cautiously. Michael had confirmed a suspicion in his mind. *His friend was smitten by Ipatia.*

"She visited me once with her aunt when she had an ear infection," Michael said nonchalantly. "I loaned her a few medical journals, and now she occasionally comes for a few minutes to drop off the old ones and pick up the new ones."

"She's a unique girl," Tony said, feeling odd about the whole thing, trying to picture her being interested in medical journals.

"I know, I know," Michael said, laughing. "That's what you say about all the women you meet."

"This one is different," Tony said, shrugging.

"Remember, I'll be waiting for you to visit me in my new office," Michael said, at the door.

"All right then, how about in a couple of weeks when I get back," Tony said, bidding his friend farewell.

The attorney arrived a few minutes later, and Tony became busy with him. Then Melissa popped her head in the door to let him know she was going out on a date with Chuck.

Afterwards, Tony sat alone in the living room, gazing absentmindedly at the flames in the fireplace and thinking about things. Was Tony enamored that time he saw Ipatia at the nightclub? Is that the reason it bothered him that Michael was interested in Ipatia? Yet he did nothing. He was too busy with his father's business, and all for naught, because after all is said and done, Daras was going to replace him and be in charge. But isn't that what he wanted? To go back to England and teach?

"What would I be going back to? The college walls and dusty books that hide me from the world and will keep me away from Ipatia?" muttered Tony aloud. Then he remembered his father's negative reaction when he learned that Tony had spent time with her. "How could I get past his anger if I were to marry the girl?"

Father never thought about my plans or my dreams. All he cared about was himself and his business. That is why he chose Bonnie, to bring in more money for the business. Tony realized that if he continued allowing his father to control his life, he was going to lose Ipatia if he didn't do something about it.

The fire was almost out, and he added a few more logs in the fireplace, watching them feed the fire. He stood there, deep in thought, gazing at the flames.

Two weeks later, Ipatia and her aunt decided to visit her cousins, George and Paula. The taxi rolled to a stop in front of the residential building. The same old woman was sweeping outside. This time, she nodded when Ipatia asked her if the Mastroyiannis family was home.

Moments later, Paula answered the door. Ipatia and her aunt introduced themselves, followed by hugs and kisses. Paula escorted them into the cozy apartment.

Ipatia immediately liked the couple. George was a stout man, with a jovial nature. He laughed at everything, whereas Paula, although sweet, tended to be the more serious of the two.

"Mrs. Makroulis next door, mentioned about a girl coming here looking for us, but we had no idea that you were that girl. Do you remember us, Ipatia?" George asked, smiling whimsically at her, as he observed her. "You were a little girl then, when you and your parents visited us that one time. I don't remember seeing Sophia then. Your grandmother and I are first cousins. My mother and your great-grandmother were sisters."

"Yes, you do look familiar," Ipatia said, shyly nodding her head. His nose was small and straight, like her grandmother's, but that was the only feature that had redeeming qualities other than his good-natured self. His large eyes bulged, and his mouth moved loosely, as if all the years of laughing had gotten it loose around the seams.

"I've had health problems, which have caused me to grow these white hairs and this stomach," George laughed, his large stomach heaving with the laughter. "After Dr. Hatzis left, we have had to deal with a young, inexperienced doctor who's always trying different medicines on me."

"Is that Dr. Michael Hatzis you are talking about?" Aunt Sophia asked, perking up.

"Yes, do you know him?" George asked, curiously.

"Yes. He moved near us and treated Ipatia recently," replied Aunt Sophia, nodding her head emphatically. "I was so impressed with this young man. His new office is near our house. He is so kind, that he lends Ipatia medical journals to read."

"Dr. Hatzis had mentioned he knew you," Ipatia said.

"Ah, really? We need to pay him a visit one of these days," George said, nodding his head with pleasure. "What a good doctor. We had been going to him for several years. Now that he moved, Dr. Savas has replaced him. He is no good."

"Now, now, George, give him time. When Dr. Hatzis first became our doctor, he was also fresh out of medical school, don't you remember?" Paula said, coming in to the room with a tray full of refreshments. "You see, we have a special place in our heart for him, because he and our Christos are the same age, thirty years old. They served in the army together. When Christos broke his leg during training, Dr. Hatzis helped treat the leg. They became good friends."

Paula picked up a framed picture of Christos in his captain's uniform and gave it to Sophia.

"Christos lives in Thessaloniki with his family," explained George. "We spend half the time there, so we can be near the grandchildren."

"You also have a daughter?" Sophia asked, showing the picture to Ipatia before handing it back to Paula.

"Yes, she's four years older than Christos. Popi lives in Athens with her husband and two children," Paula said, showing them a picture. "Her husband owns an appliance store."

"Very lovely," Aunt Sophia murmured.

"Excuse me for asking, Sophia, but do you have family?"

"Not yet," Aunt Sophia said, smiling. "You see, I'm getting married in a few weeks."

George and Paula congratulated her warmly, and then Paula asked her how she met her husband to be. Aunt Sophia discussed the topic with enthusiasm and ended the discussion by inviting the couple to the wedding.

"Thank you for the invitation. We would be delighted to come," George said, nodding his head energetically.

"You said that John is from America. Will you be staying here after the wedding?" Paula asked.

Sophia replied, "I'm glad you asked that question. After our honeymoon, we plan to live in Chicago, where John owns a house and has a real estate business. Ipatia prefers to stay here and enter the university, but her grandfather doesn't want her staying here alone. Christos asked if she could stay with you."

"Ah, good old Christos. He was one for values. There's no one like him," George said, guffawing and slapping his knee with enthusiasm. "I remember one year we visited your grandparents, Ipatia. My Popi was sixteen or so, and lovely, I might add. Anyhow, we had gone to a festival, and a boy asked her to dance the waltz. With our permission, she got up and danced with him. He must have been not much older. Christos wasn't too happy about that. We learned later that Christos reprimanded the boy's parents afterwards, just because their son danced with our daughter."

"I can see that happening," Sophia said, nodding emphatically.

"We'd love to have Ipatia come and stay with us. There's plenty of space," Paula said, smiling also. "When is the date, my sweet?"

Aunt Sophia told them the date.

"February 12?" echoed George, scratching his head. "Just wait a minute and let me check the calendar. There's something about that day that reminds me of something."

He came back with his calendar and his reading glasses.

"Isn't this the week we're going to be in Thessaloniki for the baby's baptism?" George asked to Paula, pointing to the calendar. After studying it closely, Paula nodded.

"Christos is baptizing his son on February 16, so we may be able to come to the wedding after all," Paula said. "However, we were planning to stay over their house for a few weeks after the baptism."

"Ipatia can come with us," George said, taking his reading glasses off and looking at the girl. "Ipatia, what do you think about that?"

"I'd like to meet my cousins," Ipatia admitted.

"Now wait a minute, George," Paula said. "We need to check with Christos and his wife first. We don't know if they have anyone else coming there for the baptism that week."

"Ah yes," George said, stroking his fleshy chin thoughtfully. "I hadn't thought about that."

"Is it all right if we get back in touch with you first, before you make any concrete plans, Sophia?" Paula asked. "I don't want to make any promises until we hear from my son first."

George and Paula promised to let them know as soon as they found out.

Later that evening, back at home, Ipatia sat in the dining room, writing to her grandfather the news. He had been right. The cousins willingly received her. As she sealed the envelope, her aunt entered the dining room.

"After you're finished, could you help me with the wedding invitations?" Aunt Sophia asked. "I've put them off for too long, and I need to send them out."

"I'd love to," Ipatia said.

"Good. Here is the list of the people I'm inviting to the wedding," Aunt Sophia said, handing her a piece of paper with names on it, an address book, and a bunch of envelopes. "Write their names and addresses on the envelopes. When you are finished, give them to me. I'll do the rest."

An hour later, Ipatia came across the Plakis name. She looked at her aunt curiously, almost excited and asked, "Are we inviting the Plakis family?"

"Yes. They were kind enough to house you when I wasn't here, and it's a small way to show our gratitude," Aunt Sophia said. "Oh, and I also want to invite Dr. Hatzis, but we don't have his home address. Could you do me a favor, dear, and drop off the invitation at his office tomorrow when you go to class?"

"You're inviting him?"

"Why not? He's done so much for us and that's the least we can do in return," Aunt Sophia said firmly.

"I'll try to remember," Ipatia said, resigning herself to the task. She took the invitation from her aunt and placed it inside her handbag. Lately, she had been having mixed feelings about Dr. Hatzis. She had a hunch that he was interested in her. As a doctor, he was a nice man, but she recoiled whenever she tried seeing herself getting close to him.

CHAPTER 24

The invitation brought you to me
I walked you home and stayed for coffee

The next day, Wednesday, Sophia had several clients coming and going. Mrs. Sarkidis arrived shortly after breakfast, followed by Mrs. Vardis who dropped by to pick up a finished dress. Aunt Sophia asked Ipatia to pin the hem on Mrs. Sarkidis's dress while she went to attend to Mrs. Vardis.

As Ipatia worked, she enjoyed listening to Mrs. Sarkidis chat about her grandchildren.

In the hallway, Aunt Sophia was reassuring Mrs. Vardis by saying, "Yes, yes, it's just the right fit." She saw her to the door, and then returned to the living room.

Ipatia arose, saying, "I finished the hem, Aunt."

"Good. Mrs. Sarkidis, dear, if you can slip out of that dress, I'll have it sewn quickly. There are refreshments in the dining room, please help yourselves."

"I'll only stay for a little," Mrs. Sarkidis said, eyeing the refreshments.

They drank coffee and ate the sliced chocolate torte that Mrs. Sarkidis had brought, while Aunt Sophia sewed the hem of the dress, conversing with Mrs. Sarkidis.

"Ummm, this is decadent chocolate," Ipatia exclaimed, appreciating the chocolate torte.

"That's an interesting way to describe it, Ipatia. It's one of my favorite tortes," Mrs. Sarkidis said, nodding eagerly.

"Speaking of decadent, my dear Mrs. Sarkidis," began Aunt Sophia, tying a knot. "Can you imagine my shock when we went shopping for a skirt the other day for Ipatia and found the prices much higher than I ever remembered them to be, and the skirts so much shorter. They're using less material and charging more for it. I couldn't imagine my niece wearing one of those things. There is no decency in our society these days. The women are baring it all."

"I've seen women wearing those short skirts, and it's disgusting. What about those bikini swimsuits one sees on the beach these days. They keep getting smaller and smaller. Some women aren't even wearing the top parts. Why, I remember when I was young, we couldn't even show our ankles," Mrs. Sarkidis said, gesturing comically toward her plump legs.

"You know what I think?" Ipatia said. "I think people who do these things have something lacking in their lives. Maybe they feel they aren't pretty enough, or don't get enough attention from people, so they show more skin in order for someone to pay attention to them."

"My philosophical Ipatia," Aunt Sophia said, laughing. "In my days, even if someone had that idea in their silly head, they wouldn't think about doing it, because society didn't accept it. People would shun them. Yes, my dear, times have changed."

Then they went on to the topic of Aunt Sophia's wedding. Mrs. Sarkidis suggested having her grandchildren participate in the wedding ceremony.

"They would be perfect for the flower girl and ring boy," Mrs. Sarkidis said, taking out photos of her grandchildren from her purse and showing them to Sophia. "Anna is four and Peter is five."

Aunt Sophia nodded, saying how lovely they were. She asked her if they should check first with her daughter, Toula.

"Don't worry, my Toula will go along with it," Mrs. Sarkidis replied. She glanced at her watch. "Oh, look at the time, it's almost twelve o'clock. I have to be back by two-thirty. I hope I make it."

"How did you get here?" Ipatia asked.

"With the train and the bus," Mrs. Sarkidis replied. "Mind you, it took me over an hour to get here. But I had to come, knowing Sophia is leaving, and this dress needed to be finished."

Ipatia asked her where she lived and when Mrs. Sarkidis told her, Ipatia recognized the town; it was the same place where her cousins George and Paula lived.

After Mrs. Sarkidis left, Ipatia discussed at length with her aunt about the commute from her cousins' house to Mrs. Rodos's classes. Her aunt agreed that traveling back and forth in the evenings presented a problem.

With a heavy heart, Ipatia walked to class later that day. She didn't look forward to telling Mrs. Rodos she would no longer work for her after she moved.

After class, Ipatia straightened up the room and waited for Mrs. Rodos to finish her writing.

Mrs. Rodos looked up inquisitively. "Yes?"

"Mrs. Rodos, I wanted to tell you some good news. My aunt is getting married and you are invited to the wedding," Ipatia said. "We mailed out the invitations this morning."

"How wonderful," Mrs. Rodos cried. "Weddings are such nice events. I love to attend them."

"Now, the bad news," Ipatia said, more soberly. "My aunt is leaving for America right after the wedding, and I will have to move in with some cousins who live on the other side of town."

"Is that right?" exclaimed Mrs. Rodos, taking her glasses off and looking at Ipatia with wonder.

"Yes," Ipatia said, nodding. "At first, I thought I could continue coming here to the classes, but I found out today that I would need to travel by train and bus to get here. I won't be returning home until late at night."

"I wouldn't have you doing that," Mrs. Rodos said, shaking her head emphatically. "Although you've been an excellent help to me, and I will miss you, you need to do what's right for you.

"Thank you."

"I almost forgot your pay." Mrs. Rodos handed her the paycheck.

As Ipatia placed it in her handbag, her fingers brushed against the white envelope inside. "Oh dear, I forgot to pass by and give Dr. Hatzis the wedding invitation. Good-bye Mrs. Rodos."

Ipatia fled toward the doctor's office. The late hour gave her concern, but she could easily slip the envelope underneath his office door. The pharmacy's well-lit sign loomed ahead, a signal that she was nearing her destination. She pulled on the door handle and was pleased when the door opened. She ran up the dark stairwell, stumbling on the last step as she entered the hallway. She winced, rubbing her foot and muttering softly. That foot always felt sensitive after the sprain.

When Ipatia arrived at the office, she was surprised to see the light on and the door open. She stopped in her tracks, ready to leave, for inside were Tony and Dr. Hatzis, standing and conversing.

Ipatia's heart raced when she saw Tony's tanned face. It contrasted well with his white, pressed shirt. His sculpted Grecian profile with his firm chin revealed a stunning likeness to an era in Greek history where gods and goddesses ruled.

Dr. Hatzis stood next to Tony and appeared shorter and foxier tonight, with his brown mustache and pointed chin. Maybe he had always been that way, and she hadn't noticed it before.

"Hello, Ipatia," Dr. Hatzis said, looking pleasantly surprised, as he gestured her in.

Tony smiled tightly when he saw her.

"Hello, Dr. Hatzis, hello Mr. Tony," Ipatia said breathlessly. "I had forgotten to drop this by earlier, so I came now."

She nervously handed Dr. Hatzis the wedding invitation, mindful of Tony's eyes watching her.

"What is this?" Dr. Hatzis asked, his slim, pale fingers opening the invitation and reading it.

"My aunt is getting married and would like to invite you to her wedding, but she didn't have your home address, so she asked me to drop this off."

"I appreciate the invitation. What a pleasant bit of news," he said, peering at her from behind his spectacles.

Ipatia then turned and spoke to Tony, saying, "We mailed your family an invitation this morning. Your fiancé Bonnie, is also invited, Mr. Tony."

"Thank you," Tony said slowly. "My parents are in Crete, and if I were to come, I would be coming alone. Bonnie is not and has not been my fiancé. When is the big day?"

He was not attached to Bonnie.

"It's February 12," Ipatia said, feeling flushed again. Suddenly, he appeared nicer and more approachable, as if the barrier that had been between them was no longer there.

"Ahh, just a few days from St. Valentine's day," Tony remarked. "I don't know if I'll be in town then, but if I am, I will try to make it. Thank your aunt also for the invitation."

"I must be going. It's late and my aunt is expecting me," Ipatia managed to say, although her feet did not want to move for some reason.

"You'll probably want to read this," Dr. Hatzis said, breaking the spell. He picked up a new medical journal and handed it to her. "There's a section there about a new treatment for cancer."

"Is that the treatment you had mentioned for my father earlier?" Tony asked him.

"Yes."

"Thank you, Dr. Hatzis. Good night," Ipatia said, regaining her momentum. She took the journal, and bidding the two men farewell, left quickly before they could say anything. She hurried down the hallway, mindful of the time.

Ipatia heard footsteps behind her.

Tony joined her.

"It's too dark for you to be walking alone."

He took her arm gently and her heart soared at his touch.

They walked slowly down the steps. She felt as if she were living a dream, even as her heart's racing beat reminded her how alive this moment was. This time, she did not want to run away. Instead, she wanted to melt in his arms.

When they reached the ground floor, he opened the front door for her. The cool air smacked her soundly, bringing her back down to earth. She shivered.

"Are you cold?" Tony asked. "I can drive."

"No, thank you. I'll be all right," she murmured.

They strolled slowly down the sidewalk. Another couple passed them, and for the first time, she felt like one of them. Only Tony did not have his arm around her shoulder. She wondered how that would feel. The soft streetlights cast a magical glow around them.

"How have you been, Ipatia? The last time I saw you was at the nightclub," Tony said softly, breaking her concentration

"Yes," admitted Ipatia, coming back to reality. "We've been busy with the preparations for the wedding. This past week, I didn't have time to read Dr. Hatzis's medical journals, and I don't know if I'll have time to read this one either."

"I was curious to find out how you and he started this little exchange."

"One day, he saw me walking home from English class and stopped to say hello and told me about his new office. Then he noticed the books I was carrying and I told him Mrs. Rodos gave them for me to borrow-"

"Sorry for interrupting, but who is Mrs. Rodos? I've come across her name before," Tony said.

"My English teacher. Her name is inside the English novel you found that day I dropped it," Ipatia said, nodding her head. "She has an English class down the street from Dr. Hatzis's office, and I work for her three days a week."

"Ahh, that's interesting," Tony said. "But don't let me stop you. What were you saying about Dr. Hatzis?"

"What was I saying?" echoed Ipatia, starting to wonder why he was so interested in him.

"You told him about the books Mrs. Rodos gave you," prodded Tony.

"Oh, yes, sorry. Then he said I could also borrow his medical journals. I didn't accept the offer, because I didn't think it proper. When I had the ear infection, and we visited him, he gave me a medical journal. That is how it started. I had to return it and then he had another one waiting for me." Ipatia stopped abruptly, feeling she had spoken too much. She looked down bashfully, not sure what to say next.

Tony thought about what she said. The girl's story seemed plausible enough. His friend Michael was behind this, spinning his web and drawing the girl closer to him. Now her aunt had become involved. Why else would she invite him to her wedding?

"Do you often visit Dr. Hatzis at this late hour?" Tony asked quietly, his body tensing up in anticipation. How far had this gone?

"Oh no," Ipatia retorted, shaking her head emphatically. "Typically, I drop the magazine off before English class, during daylight. Today I had forgotten the wedding invitation in my purse until after class, and Aunt Sophia asked me to deliver it because she didn't have his home address. Anyway, I thought I would slip it under the door and leave quickly, but I did not expect Dr. Hatzis, or you, to be there."

"I find it interesting that you like reading medical journals and English novels in your spare time. Somehow, I thought girls your age were not interested in such things," Tony observed. He was thinking of Melissa and her girlfriends when he said that.

"What do you mean?" Ipatia asked, her fingers nervously brushing back invisible strands of hair from her face.

"Girls your age typically spend their time dressing up and going out with their friends so they can meet young men to marry," he replied softly.

"Yes, it's odd, isn't it? I was always different from my girlfriends," she said shakily. "Ever since I was a child, I have spent much time reading books and learning things. As I became older, I saw my girlfriends getting all dressed up for the boys and I would tease them about it. And do you know what?"

"What?"

"They were all married."

"So why didn't you marry?" Tony asked. "It seems to me, there are plenty of young men that would be interested in you if you gave them a chance. Like Dr. Hatzis for example."

"Dr. Hatzis? Now you are beginning to sound like my Aunt Sophia," Ipatia retorted. "I see him as a doctor, someone who treats people and not someone to marry." She became silent. "Why haven't *you* married?"

"What?" Tony asked. *She is throwing the ball back at me.* He thought for a moment, then said, "I guess because I was too busy having fun to settle down. Besides, up until now, the right girl hadn't come along."

"Oh?" Ipatia asked, raising her eyebrows.

"So, tell me, what's your excuse for not marrying?" Tony asked, enjoying this immensely. He gazed at the beautiful girl, with her high cheekbones, her soft, full lips, open and inviting, and her wide-open, honest, light-green eyes. In this magical moment, suspended in time, he had entered another world, filled with truth, beauty, and love.

"If I marry now, then I won't have the opportunity to go to the university. My husband would want me to stay home and have children," she said firmly.

"Is anything wrong with that?" he asked, liking the picture of her surrounded by babies.

"No, but I am different," she said defiantly. "I will always wonder what I missed if I don't do it now."

"I see," Tony said. "You think if you marry now, you would not be able to do all that. Hmm, so if the right young man came along today and asked you to marry him, you would choose the university over him?"

"I know this sounds ridiculous, but yes, I would," Ipatia said forcefully. "If he truly loved me, he would wait until I finished my schooling. True love is patient and lasts forever, just as in that English novel you found and gave back to me."

"English novels don't always represent real life," Tony said dryly, remembering the story in the book. The heroine had pursued a career and still had gotten her man by the end of the story. "I suppose you would do the same for him, if you had to."

"If I really loved him, I suppose I would," she said, hanging her head.

Tony decided to change the subject slightly. "Don't get me wrong, Ipatia. I think what you are doing is admirable. I presume you are interested in medicine?"

"I had thought about becoming either a nurse or a doctor," she said, perking up. "But the sight of blood makes me sick to my stomach, so I'm going to get a degree in a health science, like microbiology, and work in a laboratory. This way I can still help people who are sick."

"Yes, one's health is important," Tony said thoughtfully. It appeared she was determined to get an education. "We need people like you to study microbiology so they can fight diseases. Look at my father, for instance. He has all the money one could ever wish to have, and it still cannot bring him back his health. He will probably depend on doctors for the rest of his life."

"How is he doing?" Ipatia ventured.

"Thank you for asking. He's had his surgery recently and is still recovering," Tony managed to say.

"If there is anything I can do to help, please let me know," she gushed forth.

Her kind offering touched him. "Right now, he's getting all the help he needs."

They were silent for a while.

"By the way, how is your aunt?" Tony asked.

"Very busy preparing for the wedding. Last night, we were up until midnight writing the invitations," Ipatia replied. "Next, there's the flowers to order for the wedding and the reception, the dresses to be sewn, and the photographer to be chosen."

Tony nodded, as if he wanted to hear more.

"Aunt Sophia is sewing her wedding dress, and everything has to be just perfect. I sewed the little pearls on the dress the other day. Now she has all this shopping still to do for her trip. I am afraid everything won't fit in her luggage. Already her suitcase is full, and she even had me sit on it while she closed it, trying to squeeze everything in. I almost fell off, because I was bouncing so hard on it." Ipatia giggled.

Tony burst into laughter.

"We're here," Ipatia said, as they approached the house.

The walk ended too soon, Tony thought.

Ipatia turned slightly towards him, ready to bid him farewell.

"I have been meaning to pay your aunt a visit, and this time is as good as any," Tony said, almost whispering. He took her hand, gazing ardently into her eyes. He had a difficult time holding back his feelings and not taking her in his arms. *I promised her I would keep my distance.*

Ipatia gazed back, then removed her hand and fumbled for the key in her purse and slowly unlocked the door.

He stood there, watching.

She turned towards him. "Will you please come in?"

He felt unexplainably happy.

They walked up the winding staircase together.

CHAPTER 25

You took me home to visit my aunt.
You offered me work, what more do I want?

Aunt Sophia opened the door. "Tony. What a pleasant surprise," she exclaimed when she saw Tony.

"Hello, Sophia," Tony said. He pecked her lightly on her cheek. "I was visiting my friend, Dr. Hatzis, when Ipatia stopped by the office. I didn't want her walking home alone."

"That's right, Aunt Sophia. I went to Dr. Hatzis's office after class to drop off the wedding invitation. I had forgotten to do it earlier. Mr. Tony asked if he could walk me home," Ipatia said nervously, not sure how her aunt would react, but her aunt seemed fine with the news. She was not at all like her grandfather, who would have been upset to see her walking home at night with a young man.

"How nice of you to do that," Aunt Sophia said, leading him into the living room. "Please come in and make yourself comfortable."

"Thank you," Tony said, sitting down.

"How do you like your coffee?"

"Don't go to all that trouble," Tony said, smiling at her.

"No trouble at all," Aunt Sophia said. "This being your first time here, shouldn't I offer you at least a cup of coffee?"

"All right then, how about making mine sweet," he replied.

Aunt Sophia went into the kitchen with Ipatia right behind her.

"How did this happen? Tony Plakis here?" Aunt Sophia asked, in a hushed voice.

Ipatia summarized everything in a few short sentences.

"He wanted to come and visit me?" Aunt Sophia asked, looking surprised.

"Yes," Ipatia said, nodding resolutely.

"I'll find out soon enough. Now be a good girl and help me with the refreshments," Aunt Sophia said. She took the chocolate torte from the refrigerator and placed it on the counter.

"May I cut the torte?" offered Ipatia. "Isn't it great that Mrs. Sakellarias brought this in today?

"Yes, we do have her to thank, don't we? Oh, and remember, the good china and silverware are in that cabinet," Aunt Sophia said, pointing in that direction. "He wants his coffee sweet, as we do, so make ours all in the same pot. We can pour the coffee at the table. I know I sound nervous, but I'm going back now. It's not polite to leave our guest alone too long."

•••——◆ ••——◆ ••——◆

Sophia found Tony at the piano, playing a soft, romantic tune, while gazing out at the balcony view. She sat down in one of the armchairs, admiring his fine playing.

A sense of pride came over her, as if she were seeing him through the eyes of a mother. Even when he was a young boy, he held a special place in her heart. Maybe because his mother had died, she had felt that way. *No, that was not the only reason, Sophia. His sister was also without a mother, and she didn't feel the same way about her. She lacked the noble qualities that he had.*

Whenever Sophia would visit his home, the boy would be happy to see her, bringing his toys to show her. Then he would sit next to her, telling her all his news of the day, while she worked on her sewing. Melissa, on the other hand, was not accommodating at all. Whenever Sophia wished to try a new dress on her, Melissa whined, wanting instead to play with her dolls.

The music stopped, and Tony turned around and saw her.

"Superbly done. You played a favorite tune of mine. It brought back fond memories of my youth," Sophia said, clapping in admiration.

Tony came and sat on the sofa. "I haven't played this song for years, but it felt appropriate somehow."

"By the way, how is your father doing these days?"

"Unfortunately, he's been in a wheelchair since his surgery and cannot walk or lift his hands. Although he speaks and thinks clearly, he needs help with everything. Christina feeds him and helps dress him."

"I didn't know that," Sophia exclaimed, feeling shocked with the news. "Is he here in town, so we may pay him a visit?"

"No, he's in Crete with Christina. He felt it better to remain there. He doesn't want his old business associates to see him in the state he is in."

"Please give him my regards next time you talk to him."

"Surely," Tony replied, nodding. "By the way, what is this I hear? You are planning to marry?"

Sophia explained to him how she met John and how one thing led to another.

"Congratulations are in order. You look happy," Tony said, smiling fondly at her.

"Yes, I feel happy. Everything has gone smoothly, almost as if some greater force is helping us. We did send you an invitation to the wedding. I hope you and your fiancé can make it."

"Dear Sophia, how did you ever come to the conclusion that I have a fiancé? Even your niece said the same thing earlier," Tony said, laughing aloud.

"I apologize for the mistake, but I think Ipatia had overheard someone mentioning it," Aunt Sophia said, afraid to reveal the source.

"I see. Could that someone be a short blonde, named Melissa? Anyway, I hope it will not disappoint you if I come alone," Tony said, raising an eyebrow.

"Not at all," Aunt Sophia said, appearing flustered.

Ipatia entered the dining room with a tray.

"Let's sit in the dining room for some refreshments," Aunt Sophia said, rising, appearing relieved. "Tony, why don't you sit here?"

He willingly obliged her.

Ipatia poured the thick, sweet Turkish coffees into the small cups.

"Thank you for all this fine preparation," he said.

"You are welcome," Ipatia replied cheerfully. She handed him his cup of coffee.

"By the way, Sophia, what are your plans after the wedding? Will you remain here?" Tony asked.

"We'll be leaving for Chicago shortly after the wedding," Sophia said. "John has a real estate business, and he also owns a house there."

Tony's eyebrows raised, surprised with the news. "He has a real estate business?"

"Yes, he buys and sells homes," she said proudly. "He has done well with his business. He told me he owns several houses and a few apartment buildings. Some he rents and others he remodels and sells them at a higher price."

"Very interesting," Tony said, stroking his chin thoughtfully. "And what does Ipatia plan to do?"

Sophia stared at him in surprise. *He wants to know what will become of Ipatia. That means he's interested in her.*

"I plan to stay with my cousins, George and Paula Mastroyiannis, who live on the other side of town," Ipatia replied.

"Ah, yes, the cousins who like to travel," Tony said, gazing poignantly at her. "Will you continue to work for Mrs. Rodos?"

"No, it's too far to travel in the evenings," Ipatia said, shaking her head, appearing puzzled.

"You are probably wondering why I am asking," Tony said slowly. "I've been thinking about getting a personal assistant to help me sort through the pile of mail that has accumulated in the past few months. It's too much for me to handle, and it's difficult to find people who know the English language as well as you."

"What are you proposing?" Aunt Sophia asked, putting down her cup, intrigued by this young man's suggestion.

"I'm offering Ipatia an opportunity to practice her English and to get paid for it," he said. "She could come and work for me, for my father's shipping agency."

"Thank you, Mr. Tony," responded Ipatia, perking up at the compliment. "I do need to find a job to meet my expenses." She looked expectantly at Sophia, who was silently digesting the news.

"Where is the shipping office?" Aunt Sophia asked slowly, a thoughtful look on her face. She had a premonition there was more to this than met the eye.

"Close to my cousins' house, so I won't need public transportation," Ipatia replied.

"Is that right, Tony?" Aunt Sophia asked, raising her eyebrows.

"Yes," Tony said, looking amused.

"What about Ipatia's studies at the university?" Aunt Sophia asked.

"Mind you, it'll probably be only for the summer," Tony said quickly. "After that, things may change."

Aunt Sophia paused. "If Ipatia wants to do it, then I'll go along with it."

Ipatia's response was immediate. "Yes, I would, Aunt Sophia."

"Stop by the office when you can, Ipatia. I will have Rita, the receptionist show you what to do," Tony said, giving her his business card.

"Ipatia, one more request, if you may," Aunt Sophia said, somewhat nervously. She gestured to the piano. "Could you play a little music for us?"

Tony flashed his bright smile, saying, "Yes, play for us. How about Beethoven's 'Fur Elise'?"

Ipatia granted their wishes. She went to the piano and started playing.

After a few pregnant minutes of anticipation, Sophia spoke softly to Tony. "I appreciate what you are doing for my niece. However, I am leaving for America in a few weeks, and I want to leave with peace of mind that Ipatia will be all right. Ipatia's grandfather does not approve of men dallying after Ipatia without serious intentions, if you know what I mean."

"I was expecting that," Tony said. "Don't worry, you have nothing to fear from me or any other young man. Your niece has made it clear she's not interested in any relationships now."

"Did she say that she wants to get her degree first?" Sophia asked, feeling a little perplexed. She had not expected this response.

Tony nodded and said wryly, "Four years is a long time to wait."

"Yes," Sophia said, wondering what he meant by that.

Sophia gazed at Ipatia's willowy frame, moving rhythmically with the music. She was so delicate and at the same time, so strong, so firm in what she believed.

"She plays well, and it's a shame to miss her performance," Tony remarked, settling his gaze on Ipatia.

They remained silent, listening to the music, and when it ended, Aunt Sophia and Tony clapped heartily.

Ipatia arose and smiled at them.

"Bravo, Ipatia, well done," Tony said, smiling.

"I also enjoyed your playing," Sophia said warmly.

"Now I'm afraid I must be going," Tony said, rising to leave. "I have an early appointment tomorrow morning. Thank you for your warm hospitality, Sophia, and your fine playing, Ipatia."

Afterwards, as Ipatia and her aunt cleaned up, their conversation inevitably turned to Tony Plakis.

Sophia reminisced about him. "He was such a well behaved young boy," she said, "Look at what a fine, young man he's turned out to be." She also mentioned how handsome he had become and how nice of him to walk Ipatia home.

"Thomas, my godmother's son, used to walk me home many times," Ipatia said.

"The funny thing is that he's not engaged to Bonnie after all," Aunt Sophia said, ignoring her niece's comparison with Thomas.

"That's right," Ipatia said, perking up.

"He won't be a bachelor for long, though, mark my words," Aunt Sophia said, nodding her head knowingly. "I can't see him waiting around for any girl. He's a good catch, and there are many beautiful rich girls ready to snap him up."

Later in bed, Ipatia went over everything in her mind several times. She admitted she felt a sense of relief when she learned Tony was not engaged to Bonnie. Maybe Bonnie had represented the type of woman a playboy would pursue. The shadows of his playboy past had disappeared.

However, when her aunt said he wouldn't be a bachelor much longer, Ipatia felt a knot form in her chest. Tony was handsome, intelligent, charming, and yes, handsome to other women.

Ipatia somehow wanted him to remain a bachelor forever, to remain single, so she could dream about him. *Aunt Sophia was right. I must stop living on dreams and face reality.*

Tony will probably be marrying soon, and she might as well accept that it won't be her. Also, she still had four years of university before she could even begin to think about marriage. Did she really need to go to school if it meant losing him? But he hasn't even said he loved her, or even proposed. *But I love him.*

George and Paula paid Sophia an unexpected visit two days later.

"We happened to be in the area and also had some good news for Ipatia," Paula said, smiling as she handed her a wrapped box.

Sophia thanked her and excused herself. In a matter of minutes, she had returned with coffee and a tray laden with refreshments.

"Is Ipatia here?" George asked, taking the coffee offered to him.

"You just missed her. She went to her English class. She'll probably be back shortly after seven."

"We wanted to let you know that Christos and Tassoula are looking forward to having Ipatia come to Thessaloniki with us," George said, sipping a cup of freshly made coffee. He took a bite of the baklava, savoring the honeyed dessert. He carefully wiped his hands on a napkin.

"Ipatia will surely be delighted with the news," Sophia said.

"Unfortunately, we will need to leave early the day after the wedding. Thessaloniki is a day's journey with the automobile and the baptism is scheduled the following morning," Paula said apologetically.

"That is no problem," Sophia said. "Would it be too much trouble for you to come by on your way to the church and pick us up? That way you can also get Ipatia's luggage."

"It's fine with me," George said, nodding. He looked at Paula. She nodded back.

They discussed the details of their trip and Ipatia's preparations. Then Sophia told them about Ipatia's new job with the Plakis agency. With a little prompting from a curious Paula, Sophia confided that the son was a handsome, eligible young man.

"Oh," Paula said, her eyes twinkling. "Maybe we'll be hearing some good news soon."

"I have my reservations," Sophia said, shaking her head. "I think because he knows our family, he felt comfortable in asking Ipatia to work there. Even if there was interest on his part, Ipatia stubbornly wants to go to college to get a degree. He's too good a catch to wait around all those years for her."

John came a few days later and things got busier. He visited them daily and they would stop everything they were doing so Aunt Sophia could spend time with him.

One evening, he asked Aunt Sophia to go out with him. Her aunt invited her along, but Ipatia felt awkward and declined.

"Why don't you visit with Marika downstairs?" Aunt Sophia offered. "She would love to have company and she knows so many things. I think you'll like her."

It turned out her aunt was right. Marika had an encyclopedic memory and there were discussions on philosophy, politics, Greek archaeology and all kinds of other topics. Their discussion was still going strong when there was a knock on the door.

"We're back," Aunt Sophia said at the door. John was standing behind her.

"We'll continue another time," laughed Marika as she bid Ipatia farewell.

Thus, started a new friendship. Ipatia began looking forward to those evenings when her aunt went out with John.

CHAPTER 26

Did you drop in to see me, dear?
A smile, a laugh, a dream to share?

Two days before the wedding, Ipatia attended her last English class. The children came up to her to give her their best wishes. A few of them hugged her, their small bodies pressed tight against hers. Ipatia thanked them, feeling emotional and ready to cry.

Mrs. Rodos said she was coming to the wedding and asked her to keep in touch afterwards. When she heard Ipatia would be working for Tony Plakis, she even gave her an English dictionary, saying that she probably would need it. Ipatia thanked her and promised she would visit her in the future.

Later than usual, Ipatia headed home, mindful of the time. She didn't like walking alone at night.

As Ipatia approached Dr. Hatzis's building, she crossed the street, carrying her books. She had stopped coming altogether to his office, ever since Tony's visit a few weeks ago. She had thought about Tony's probing questions about Dr. Hatzis and decided that she wouldn't encourage him to think she was interested in him.

"Greetings, Ipatia."

Ipatia looked up, surprised to see Dr. Hatzis walking across the street, heading towards her. He must have seen her from the office and followed her.

"Hello, Dr. Hatzis," she said.

"Here, let me walk with you. My car is further down the road," he said, joining her. "What have you been up to? You haven't come by the office for weeks."

Ipatia filled him in on the latest news, telling him about her impending move after the wedding.

"Will you continue working at the English class?"

"To be honest, today was my last day there," she said, shaking her head. "I'll be working for Mr. Tony, I mean, the Plakis Shipping Agency. Mr. Tony wants me to translate papers for him."

"I'm sorry to hear you are leaving this area." He paused, as if struggling for words. "But at the same time, I'm happy that you will work for Tony. He is a good person to work for."

"Isn't he wonderful?" Ipatia exclaimed, looking starry-eyed. Then she realized how it must have sounded and said, "I mean, although I'm also sorry to leave this area, I am looking forward to working at his company."

They stopped in front of Dr. Hatzis's car.

"Will you be coming to my aunt's wedding?" Ipatia asked, having come back down to earth.

A shadow crossed his face. "I'm afraid not. I am leaving tomorrow for Italy. I'll be presenting a paper at an important medical conference there and I could not get out of this engagement," he replied tensely. "Please give my apologies to your aunt."

Ipatia had expected the doctor's attendance at the wedding and felt disappointed that he wouldn't be there. "I guess this is the last time I'll be seeing you," she began, feeling as if she were ending a friendship. "I would like to thank you for all the medical journals you loaned me and for all the times you treated me."

"The pleasure has been mine," he said sincerely, taking her hands into his. "You also brightened many of my days with your youthful charm, intelligent questions and helpful comments."

She smiled at his compliment. "Please have a safe trip, Dr. Hatzis," she said, shaking his hand before leaving.

Ipatia awoke Sunday morning to the pitter-patter of raindrops on her windowsill. The rain didn't dampen her high spirits as she jumped out of bed and got dressed. Today, her aunt was getting married.

Aunt Sophia was in the same high spirits, chatting about everything and giggling like a teenage girl. They spent the rest of the morning making last minute preparations for the wedding. George and Paula stopped by earlier than expected, apologizing for being early, but saying they wanted to make sure there were no delays because of the rain.

By the time they arrived at the church, the rain had stopped and the sun's rays began to peek through the clouds. It seemed as if time had stood still, as if everything was in slow motion.

They entered the church and shortly thereafter, proceeded with the ceremony. Ipatia picked up the train of her aunt's long dress. She followed her Aunt Sophia who purposefully walked with measured steps down the aisle towards the altar, towards her destiny. The priest stood there, smiling gently. John stood to the side, looking at Aunt Sophia expectantly, poised and handsome in his tuxedo.

Ipatia was mindful of people staring at them, and of her own long dress that she wore. She almost tripped over it twice. It seemed forever before they reached the altar.

Ipatia went and stood to the side of the couple. The ring-bearer and flower girl, the grandchildren of Mrs. Sarkidis, stood by her side.

The church was packed and Tony wasn't anywhere in sight.

Tony arrived late. He stood in the back of the church so as not to attract attention. He immediately noticed Ipatia standing next to the couple. She was a vision in that long, satin pink dress. She held a rose bouquet in her white, gloved hands. Her hair was pulled up, and blonde curls framed her delicate face. He was pleased at the picture.

He looked at the bride. Sophia could never match the beauty of her niece, yet she glowed with happiness.

After a few minutes, their Koumbaro, the nephew of the groom, moved towards them and placed two wedding wreaths, joined by a satin ribbon, on Sophia and John's heads. In the Greek Orthodox tradition, he crisscrossed the wreaths above their heads three times, leaving them on their heads when he had finished.

The priest then gave the couple a cup of wine to share. This was followed by a procession with the priest, the Koumbaro, and children, three times around the small table. The chanter's melodic strains set the pace, and their steps were slow and sure. The priest blessed the couple shortly after that, and the wedding ceremony officially ended.

The couple kissed gently, and then walked down the aisle and into the small hallway to receive their guests. Ipatia followed them and kissed her aunt and uncle, congratulating them joyfully.

"Thank you Ipatia, now stay here next to us and greet the guests with us," Aunt Sophia said, pointing to the space next to her.

"What do I say?"

"Just nod your head and smile," Uncle John said, laughing. "People tend to move quickly, so there's no time to chat with anyone."

As the guests trickled out of the church, Uncle John and Aunt Sophia greeted them with handshakes and kisses, receiving their well wishes. Ipatia dutifully did the same. People left packaged gifts along the side of the hall. Mrs. Rodos finally came by, and for the first time, Ipatia saw her not dressed in gray, but in a nice, beige suit.

Ipatia daydreamed that Tony came to her and kissed her cheek.

And then it happened.

She smelled his cologne first before she saw him. Tony stood before her, his handsome face bending close to hers, his lips gently brushing her cheek as she gazed at him.

"Best wishes for your aunt and uncle. You looked lovely standing there," he whispered, squeezing her hand, his eyes shining brightly, and then he moved on.

She sighed, her knees feeling rubbery. He kissed her and she let him. *So what? Everyone kisses during this time.*

"Ipatia, come dear, the photographer wants us in the church for pictures," Aunt Sophia said, interrupting her thoughts.

The reception took place at a nearby restaurant, where only close family attended. Live bouzouki music played in the background for entertainment. After the meal, some people got up to dance. The evening went by quickly. People began leaving, and the cousins alerted Ipatia that they would be leaving also.

Ipatia went and hugged her aunt. "I'll write to you," she promised, with moistened eyes.

"I will, too," Aunt Sophia said, wiping her own eyes. "Ipatia, remember what I said about going to the house. You have the key. Please go with your cousins and check on it whenever you can. You can also visit with Marika and play the piano if you'd like. Also, please forward any mail that arrives to my address in America. We plan to visit Greece in late summer, so we will see you then. But remember you are always welcome to come and stay with us in America if you ever decide to do so. Don't worry about the money, you can come sooner if you want. Just let me know, and we'll pay for your ticket."

"Thank you, Aunt Sophia. I will miss you," Ipatia replied, hugging. "Have a safe trip to America."

Ipatia shook hands with her new uncle, who swept her up in a bear hug.

"You are always welcome to come and stay with us," Uncle John offered, stepping back.

After the farewells were completed, Ipatia prepared for her trip. Although she looked forward to traveling to Thessaloniki with her cousins, she mourned the loss of two people she had grown fond of, Aunt Sophia and Tony. They both would be far away.

Ipatia attended the baptism in Thessaloniki and enjoyed being with her cousins and their family, who were a fun-loving group. The chubby baby cried when the priest partially immersed him into the water, causing a stir in the church. Some people smiled, others cried, others giggled. Once he was placed into the dry towels, though, he quieted down.

The next two weeks were exciting times for Ipatia. Between George and Ipatia's natural knack for humor, they had everyone laughing at their antics. Ipatia became everyone's darling. Her cousins also took her on a couple of day trips. She enjoyed the sightseeing greatly. It helped take her mind off Tony, but in the evenings, when she rested in bed, his handsome image would reappear, beckoning her to hasten back. Every night, she thought about him before going to sleep.

Time passed quickly, and with wet eyes, they said their good-byes and left Thessaloniki.

The long ride to Piraeus was uneventful except in an instance when someone cut in front of them abruptly. Her cousin had good reflexes and swerved away just in time.

"Why can't they see where they're going?" George shouted, displaying a rare burst of temper.

Ipatia had been shaken by the incident.

"Don't worry dear, your cousin is a good driver," Paula said.

When they arrived home, Ipatia went straight to bed, feeling exhausted.

The next day, Tuesday, Ipatia unpacked her clothes and settled in her new bedroom. Afterwards, she sat at the desk in her room and wrote to her grandfather. She wrote about the wedding, and how much fun she had in Thessaloniki. She sealed the letter and went to look for Paula. She found her in the kitchen with George.

"Is there a post office nearby?" she asked her. "I need to mail a letter to *Pappou*."

"Yes, there is," Paula said, wiping her hands. She had been preparing the evening meal. "Go left on this street until you come to the intersection. There, you make another left and walk a while until you see it. Oh, and here, let me give you some money to buy stamps for us."

"Is it all right if I stop at some shops and browse? I feel like walking after that long trip yesterday."

"Surely," Paula said, retrieving a key from her purse. "This is an extra key to the house. We might not be here when you return. We have some errands to do."

Ipatia enjoyed the walk immensely. Spring was everywhere, in the pleasant morning, filled with sunshine and a gentle breeze, and in the lively people that went about their daily business, shopping, conversing at the street corner, or waiting for a bus. A sense of anticipation hung in the air, as if something new was about to happen.

She strolled down the street towards the shopping district. To her right, laborers in work clothes hammered and worked steadily on a new building.

One worker on the second floor crooned a familiar romantic song. Ipatia slowed down, enjoying the music.

The worker stopped singing when he saw Ipatia, saying, "Hello, my lovely girl."

Ipatia hurried away, blushing furiously. Behind her, laughter erupted from the workers, followed by the man's singing.

As Ipatia approached the post office, she saw the tall Plakis building further down the block. She hadn't seen Tony after her aunt's wedding in February. Her heart started racing at the idea that she would be working there soon.

Ipatia entered the post office. Several customers waited in line, and she joined them. Ipatia bought the stamps, plus a few extra for her cousins, and mailed the letter. As she ambled toward the door, intent on making room in her purse to place the remaining stamps, she bumped into a man and dropped her stamps.

"Oh, excuse me," she said, feeling clumsy as she bent down to pick them up. The man had already dropped to the floor and was retrieving the stamps. Ipatia looked up and caught herself staring into the smiling eyes of Tony Plakis.

"Hello." He handed her the stamps and gently helped her up.

CHAPTER 27

I changed into a business suit
Because now I will work for you.

Ipatia had not expected to see Tony in the post office. "Hello, Tony," she said shakily. She tried to compose her racing heart. "We just arrived back from Thessaloniki, and I was mailing a letter to my grandfather."

"I gathered that," Tony said, his eyes twinkling. "Could you wait here a moment? I need to mail something."

Ipatia nodded and watched him finish his business. He looked exceedingly handsome in the tailored beige suit and crisp white shirt. At one point, he turned and gave her a warm smile, nodding at her. He had singled her out, catching her off guard.

Ipatia blushed at his overture, nodding shyly back, noticing the women in the post office staring at her curiously.

"How was your trip?" he asked, moments later, walking outside with her.

Ipatia discussed the details of the baptism and her trip. She talked about how the baby began crying right before the baptism, and how they fed him a bottle of milk to stop his crying.

"And when the priest picked up the baby, he burped right there and then," she finished, laughing.

Tony laughed with her.

Ipatia noticed they had stopped in front of the Plakis building.

"If you have a few moments, I can show you where the office is and introduce you to Rita, our front receptionist," Tony said, touching her arm lightly.

"All right," she said timidly. She followed him into the building. They took the elevator to the third floor. She saw herself through a mirror that spanned the back of the elevator. It made her look down, afraid to look at herself. That was something her grandfather had instilled in her since childhood. *Vanity was not to be coveted.*

Yet her curiosity got the better of her. Ipatia furtively glanced at the mirror once more and found Tony's handsome eyes gazing steadily at her through the mirror. Their eyes locked, sending warm emotions fluttering in her stomach. She looked down again, blushing.

The elevator doors opened. Unable to shake the giddy feeling away, she followed him. They went through two double-glass doors and entered a large, carpeted room.

A middle-aged, smartly dressed woman sat at a large desk in the front of the room.

"Hello, Rita. This is Miss Ipatia Kouris, the young lady I was telling you about," Tony said proudly.

"Nice to meet you," Rita said, smiling warmly as she shook Ipatia's hand.

Ipatia immediately liked Rita and the office. The office was spacious and tastefully decorated. Also, there were large beautiful landscape paintings on the wall. Tall windows allowed plenty of sunlight into the room.

Ipatia said, "Those are beautiful paintings."

"I'll tell you a little secret. I'm not really a receptionist," Rita confided dryly. "I'm here to watch over the paintings so no one steals them."

They laughed.

"Will she be starting today?" Rita asked.

"Not today. I brought her here to introduce her to you," he said. "When can you start work, Ipatia?"

"Tomorrow," Ipatia said brightly.

"Good," he said, smiling at her. "We could use your help."

"The office opens at nine in the morning, and we close around two. Then we reopen in the afternoon at five and stay open until eight. You are working only in the mornings?" asked Rita.

"Yes," Ipatia said.

"Tomorrow I will show you around and introduce you to everyone, and we can go over your duties then."

"Thank you. I will see you tomorrow morning," Ipatia said, heading towards the door.

"Wait a minute, Ipatia," Tony said quickly. He turned to Rita and said, "I won't be staying. Is there anything I need to sign before I leave?"

Rita raised her eyebrows. "Only these papers," she said, picking up a stack of documents and handing them to him. "If these aren't signed by tomorrow, Sarkalos will have my hide. He's been hounding me to get these purchase orders out."

He read them carefully, then nodded and retrieved a pen from inside his jacket and signed the forms.

"There, have a nice evening and I will see you tomorrow, Rita," he said.

They took the elevator to the ground floor and when they reached the front entrance, Tony turned and asked Ipatia, "Will you be walking home?"

Ipatia nodded, having forgotten her plans to browse the shops.

"Would it be all right if I joined you?" he asked softly, opening the door.

She nodded, feeling a surge of happiness with his request.

They strolled down the street together, discussing a number of topics. Ipatia asked him about his teaching experience at Oxford.

"There are several colleges, each autonomous, like Balliol College, Hertford College, Magdalen College, and so on. Students belong to one college, as do the teachers."

She listened to Tony talk about his years at Oxford, first his own studies and later, teaching economics, and then issues of current events. She chimed in with her own ideas. Then they discussed ancient Greece. Fresh from her talks with Marika, she expounded on the philosophical, political and archaeological history of Greece.

"I believe that there are two facets of Greece, the modern and the ancient. Everywhere you go, you see modern Greece with its bouzouki music, its souvlakia, its cars and buses. Yet, at the same time, right around the corner, there is ancient Greece staring at you, with the beautiful architecture on the Acropolis, like the Parthenon and the Erechtheum, the pinnacles of that great society," Ipatia said dramatically.

"Which do you prefer, Ipatia, ancient Greece or modern Greece?"

"Why, a little of both, I guess," she said, gesturing around her. "I admire what ancient Greece has offered us. Democracy, the Olympics, the philosophers such as Socrates, and the Hippocratic Oath that the doctors use even to this day. But I also enjoy the wonders and comforts of electricity, modern medicine, and public transportation."

"It seems as though you won't need to go to the university," Tony commented. "You seem to know everything already."

Ipatia laughed, explaining her discussions with Marika. "She knows so much. She's been to the university. She also said that the food we eat in present day Greece has been around for centuries. It has been tested by time. Even the Americans are looking into our diet. They call it the Mediterranean diet."

"Speaking of food, I wonder whether the *loukoumathes* were made in ancient times?" Tony asked, his eyes twinkling.

"Maybe."

"Remember the loukoumathes shop we went to?"

"Yes. I enjoyed it," she said enthusiastically.

"I'm feeling somewhat hungry. Why don't we go there? It's just down the road, and it's still early."

"You should eat a meal first," she scolded him. "The *loukoumathes* may taste good, but they're not nutritious."

"Yes, you are right," he said. "I know a place where they make the best souvlaki. It's around the corner. But we must go for coffee and loukoumathes afterwards."

"All right," she said, laughing. When he offered her his arms, she felt as if she were walking on clouds. They strolled down the avenue slowly, browsing the shops and boutiques, discussing the items on display, heading towards the restaurant.

The rest of the day was like one long dream. They sat and ate souvlaki with Greek salad topped with feta cheese, talking about a number of things, amidst the bustle of people coming and going.

Ipatia couldn't tear her gaze away from his. He was a good talker, and she enjoyed listening to him. She learned that he liked playing tennis, attending classical music concerts, studying archaeology, going to museums and traveling.

Then they strolled to the loukoumathes shop, laughing and chatting. The little shops they passed were no longer a point of interest, for they had escaped into their own little world. They sat outside the loukoumathes shop, drinking iced coffee and biting into warm *loukoumathes*, enjoying the scenery and the sunset.

Tony began reminiscing about England and the way of life there.

Ipatia nodded, feeling stimulated by the conversation, and at the same time comfortable, listening to Tony talk.

"I used to go to a restaurant owned by a Greek, not far from the Oxford campus. I'd meet with a few colleagues of mine there. We'd joke around and have a laugh or two," Tony said. "The Greek food was exceptionally tasty, and the owner's company was even more so."

"Do you miss England?" Ipatia asked softly.

"I used to, but recently when I went there because of the shipping business, I felt that it wasn't the same. Maybe the damp, cloudy weather bothered me, or maybe it was the polite, cold indifference of the people I dealt with," he said ruefully.

Tony became quiet, staring out into the distance, deep in thought. He could not ignore the fact that he had been busy thinking about Ipatia lately, eager to see her again. He had truly missed her cheerful company these last few weeks. Today, he realized how much she meant to him, and how much he loved her. He didn't want to be without her and he didn't want to wait four years. *I don't know how to get out of this dilemma.*

"I truly must be going," she said reluctantly, getting up. "I told my cousins that I would be out shopping, but it's getting rather late, and they'll be worried."

He touched her arm. "Please, don't go yet. You probably noticed I am quiet, and I apologize for that. I am truly enjoying this. Tomorrow I return to the grind of the office, and sadly, don't look forward to it."

"Oh," she said, and sat back down. "I have enjoyed this time with you also."

"So, Ipatia, tell me, how are your plans for the university coming along?" he managed to ask.

"I've begun studying for the examination, although I'm not sure which university I will attend yet," she said.

"The universities here are difficult to enter."

"I've heard," she said, nodding. "Meanwhile, the job is going to be perfect, because I could work during the days and study in the evenings."

"I'm glad to hear it," he said.

The walk home was pleasant enough, with Ipatia talking about her cousins. Tony listened quietly, slipping his hand into hers. *It felt right.* He remained silent as his emotions played havoc with his heart and mind.

She stopped and looked at him.

"Are we here already?" Tony asked, looking around.

"Yes," she replied. "Thank you for a wonderful time."

"You are welcome. I enjoyed it also," he said. Dipping his head slightly, he kissed the top of her hand before letting it go. "I hope this little kiss didn't transgress the pact we made."

She shook her head, her eyes shining.

"I will see you tomorrow then, bright and early?"

"Yes, bright and early," she said breathlessly, slipping her hand from his and going quickly into the house.

When Tony arrived home later that evening, he found his sister and Chuck in the dining room having dinner. He joined them and the evening was spent discussing the shipping business. Tony found a good resource in Chuck, who knew about the ins and outs of the business.

The discussion led to the topic of computers.

"With your business reaching all parts of the world, you will need a better way of monitoring everything. Computers can do that, and more. They are the way of the future," Chuck said. "My business already operates with them."

As they covered computers and technical issues, Melissa said, "I hate to interrupt you two, but Chuck, dear, it's nine o'clock, and we're supposed to meet your friends down at the Club, remember?"

"Tony, would you care to join us? We can discuss it further at the Club," Chuck said.

"Yes," Tony said, pleased at the invitation.

Later, Tony entered his bedroom close to midnight, thinking about what had transpired. He had spent the evening discussing with Chuck the pros and cons of switching from paperwork to a computer system. After Tony began asking him for advice, the company's profits had increased considerably due to the cost-cutting measures Chuck had suggested.

Adding computers to their business could be one more idea worth pursuing.

The next morning, Wednesday, Ipatia chose her work clothes carefully. She must portray a business-like character. She wore a creamy white blouse and light beige jacket with matching skirt that used to be her mother's but tailored by Aunt Sophia to fit her. The outfit brought the highlights out in her light-green eyes. She also put on pearl earrings.

Ipatia left the house carrying the English dictionary. She enjoyed the brisk walk and looked forward to seeing Tony again. The early morning coolness was refreshing. As she passed groups of children carrying their schoolbooks and walking to school, she fondly remembered the children at Mrs. Rodos's class.

When Ipatia entered the double-glass door, Rita was speaking to two men dressed in business suits, "You need to see Mr. Psaris. His office is on the second floor."

After the men left, Rita rose and extended her hand to Ipatia. "Good morning, Miss Kouris. Let me show you to your desk."

Ipatia followed her to the end of the hallway, where she opened the door that had a sign titled *Gregory Plakis*.

Ipatia was pleased with the size of the room. Sunlight filtered in through the large window on the left side, warming up the room. Two tropical potted plants sat on either side of the window. The room had a comfortable, yet professional feel to it.

"This is your desk," Rita said, pointing to the desk to their right. A sizeable pile of envelopes and papers sat on it.

At the back of the room was a large door.

"Is that Mr. Plakis's office?" Ipatia asked, pointing to it.

"Yes," Rita replied, going and opening the large door in the back of the room. "Mr. Tony is using it now."

Ipatia peeked into the office and was surprised to see the Greek vase from the island sitting by the window. The vase, the paintings on the wall, and the exotic objects that lay in the bookshelf, revealed an appreciation of art. The mahogany desk itself was a work of art with feet shaped like an eagle's claws.

Rita shut the door. "Mr. Tony usually doesn't arrive until ten or eleven o'clock, and today he is coming later since he has a meeting to go to first. Once he is in, he works the whole day through until late afternoon. He goes by the English work day instead of the Greek, if you know what I mean."

After Rita went over Ipatia's duties, she said, "Before you get started, let me show you around the building and introduce you to everyone."

Ipatia followed her into the hallway, stopping to meet Aristotle, the senior accountant, and Stamatis, a junior accountant. Afterwards, they went to the other two floors, where Rita introduced her to people. Ipatia couldn't keep track of all the names.

They found Mr. Sarkalos, the fleet manager, in his office, speaking to someone. After Rita introduced Ipatia, the other man turned to stare at Ipatia. He was an older, heavy-set man with a thick, gray mustache and wore a black Captain's cap.

"You are Captain Kouris's daughter?" he asked, appearing surprised.

"Yes?" Ipatia answered timidly.

"I am Captain Sardelis," he said and shook her hand. "You probably don't remember me, but I knew your father well. We traveled the seas together. He was a good man. Many times, we sat down and shared stories over a bottle of wine."

"Very nice to meet you," she said, smiling.

"Welcome on board," he said, winking at her.

As they left, Ipatia noticed people entering Mr. Sarkalos's office. "Who are they?"

"They work for the company," Rita said. "Mr. Sarkalos will give them their pay." She looked at her watch. "Oh my. It's eleven o'clock. Come, we need to get back. There is work to do."

⟨HAPTER 28

My heart beats hard when I'm with you.
This work I do, just suits me true.

After returning to the office, Rita showed Ipatia how to use the telephone and how to answer calls. She also showed her how to buzz her whenever she needed to speak with her.

"Mr. Chuck and Miss Melissa are expected later this morning," Rita said, before leaving. "If they get here and I am away, please let Mr. Tony know they're here by buzzing this button. It goes to his office."

After Rita left, Ipatia looked around once more, appreciating her work environment. Mr. Plakis's office door was shut. She wondered what time Tony would be arriving. She also wondered how Melissa would react once she saw her there.

Ipatia sat down and began the arduous task of working on the pile of letters on her desk. She read the first letter in the pile, painstakingly translating it from English to Greek. She used the English dictionary she had brought along, for there were several unfamiliar words.

The telephone rang, and Ipatia jumped at the sound. She had never had a telephone ring so close to her ear before.

She picked up the phone. "Plakis Shipping Business, may I help you?" she asked, her voice trembling slightly.

"Hello, Ipatia," a pleasantly rich voice boomed.

"Oh, hello," she replied cheerfully, about to say "Tony" but remembered she was in the office. *Should I call him Mr. Tony since I'd be working for him?*

"I am in the office and wish to speak with you. Can you please come in?" Mr. Tony asked. "Please bring some paper and a pen."

Surprised that he was in his office, Ipatia nervously went to his door and knocked.

"Please have a seat," he said, gazing at her appreciatively. "You look nice today."

She blushed and looked down. "Thank you."

"I hope you don't mind if we shut the door. It helps me concentrate."

Ipatia tensed, not knowing what to say in response to that. This was something new to her, being alone in a room with a man. No, not just any man, but with Tony. She sat upright and remained motionless, almost not breathing, not trusting her emotions, which were sending all kinds of signals to her head.

He shut the door slowly.

"You are probably wondering why I wish to speak with you," he said softly, as he sat down.

She looked at him, her heart pounding. *Was this his way of seducing women?* She was ready to bolt.

"I know this is new to you, but we do this to everyone we hire. Rita probably took you to all the departments this morning?"

She nodded.

"Good, and now I will go over the operations of the business and how the different departments work together, and how you fit in."

"Oh," she said. She felt better.

He discussed each department and its interaction with the other divisions of the shipping business. She listened intently and with shaky hands took notes along the way. She was mesmerized by the change in him. In front of her was not a seducer, not the man who kissed her hand the day before, but a man who knew his business, tough-minded and knowledgeable. Here, there was no softness, but a steely, single purpose of running a business and doing it well.

"I admit I'm still learning about this business myself, as I've only been in it a few months," Tony said. "Do you have any questions?"

She looked at her notes briefly, shuffling the papers around. "It seems to me, trying to keep track of all the ships, their maintenance, and the cargo schedules is a considerably complex task. Is there an easier way of remembering all this? How do the departments do it?"

"The way I would do it, is make diagrams, like this," he said. He took the pad of paper from her hands and began drawing on it.

"I would draw the departments, the cargo ships, put them in boxes, and then connect them with lines. If the cargo ship needs maintenance, then it goes to this department, and when supplies need to be ordered, it goes here. Any papers needing to be signed come to me, here at the top. You can always come back to the diagram if you forget."

Ipatia watched his shapely hands drawing broad strokes on her paper, enjoying the moment. After he had finished, he handed it to her.

She looked it over, nodding her appreciation. "Yes, now it makes sense. What happens when a ship breaks down at sea? How do they communicate when the cargo schedule is affected?"

"Good questions," he said, nodding appreciatively. He answered as thoroughly as he could. "I will ask Mr. Sarkalos more about that topic." He jotted something down on a piece of paper.

"I also had a few questions on the papers I am translating," she said.

"Bring them in tomorrow morning at eleven. I am expecting some calls shortly," he said, glancing at the clock and rising, signaling that their meeting had ended.

"Thank you," she said, getting up to leave, feeling slightly disappointed. Somehow, his impersonal lecture on shipping was not what she expected. *What did I expect? To be seduced?* She should get those silly thoughts out of her mind.

"By the way, was everything all right last night when you got home?" he asked softly.

She nodded brightly, noticing the change in him right away. *This is the Tony I know.*

"Good," he said, smiling.

"Before I leave, how did you want me to address you in the office? As Mr. Tony?"

He was silent. "Yes, that would be appropriate."

After Ipatia returned to her desk, she answered a business call and sent it into his office. Ipatia had a hard time working after that. She sat at her desk, in a daze. She thought about her meeting with Tony and soon, she was daydreaming.

At one point, the telephone buzzed again, shaking her out of her reverie.

"Ipatia, this is Rita, I'm going out for a snack. Do you want anything?"

"No, I'm fine, thank you," Ipatia said. The only other interruption was a young man who came in the office, carrying a tray that held a cup of coffee and pastries. She showed him to Tony's room, and he took it in.

Ipatia started working after that, forcing any intruding thoughts out of her mind. Several minutes later, she heard people talking in the hallway, followed by laughter.

The laughter stopped.

"Ipatia?"

Ipatia looked up at Melissa. "Hello, Miss Melissa," Ipatia said, forcing a smile and standing. She didn't know how to react to Melissa's look of surprise.

The man standing behind Melissa was not much taller than her. His dark-brown hair, graying temples, and small mustache gave him a distinguished air. Even though there were signs of over eating, he disguised it well with his tailored suit and tie. Dr. Hatzis was much better looking, Ipatia secretly thought. She wondered what Melissa saw in this man. She quickly got her answer.

"This is Chuck Daras, my fiancé," Melissa said, somewhat reluctantly, hooking her arm around Chuck's arm.

Ipatia noticed he was gazing at her unabashedly, and she looked down, bewildered. She never could get used to men staring at her.

"My pleasure," Chuck said.

"I'll let Mr. Tony know that you are here," Ipatia said, trying to act professional. Her hand trembled as she picked up the telephone. Her mind drew a blank. She couldn't remember which button to push.

"Don't worry, we'll tell him ourselves," Melissa said, pulling Chuck towards Tony's office.

"Hello, hello," Tony said, sauntering out of his office to greet them. He shook Chuck's hand and kissed his sister on the cheek lightly.

"I'm ready to start whenever you are," Chuck said.

"Come, follow me, then," Tony said. As they began to leave the room, he turned and said, "Ipatia, please join us. We will review the different operations of the agency. This is a good experience for you."

He asked me to join them.

Ipatia glowed as she followed the group silently down the hallway and downstairs to the second floor. They went into different departments, and Tony and Chuck discussed issues, going over the pros and cons of using certain methods over others. Melissa seemed knowledgeable on the topic, because she piped in several times, offering her own advice.

Ipatia remembered some people from her tour earlier that day and greeted them. The time flew as they worked their way around the different departments.

They entered Mr. Sarkalos's office. Ipatia observed Mr. Sarkalos's interaction with the two men and Melissa as they reviewed sheets of paper, asking him questions. Ipatia tried to decipher their jargon but gave up after a few minutes. Her stomach growled loudly.

Ipatia glanced at her watch. It showed two o'clock which was her quitting time. She cleared her throat, trying to hide her complaining stomach in the small room. The others, caught up in their discussion, didn't notice but Tony noticed.

He smiled at her and said, "If you'd like, you can leave. These items are not that relevant to you."

Ipatia thanked him and made her way back to her desk. She was mentally exhausted from the sheer volume of information packed in so few hours. She quickly left and headed home.

At home, she found a note from her cousins. They would be back around three. They had gone shopping and were expecting people over for dinner. She slept soundly until a knocking on her bedroom door awoke her.

"Ipatia, are you awake? It's six o'clock," Paula said.

"I'll be right there." Ipatia jumped out of bed and freshened up.

She greeted Paula and George in the kitchen and told them about her new job over a cup of coffee and a snack.

"No wonder you were exhausted, my poor dear," Paula said. "I hope you are feeling up to having company for dinner tonight. John and Sylvia are coming over. They baptized our son and are kind people. We travel often with them. I think you will like them."

Ipatia did enjoy herself. The couple joked with George and Paula, and Ipatia joined in the laughter. They asked her if she liked to travel.

"Yes," she replied.

They talked about the various places they had visited with Paula and George, describing some funny situations they had gotten themselves into.

Later that night, the couples sat down and began to play a game of cards. Ipatia watched for a while. Feeling tired, she yawned. She excused herself and went to bed. She slept soundly into the night, unaware of the laughter and noise coming from the dining room.

••⟶⟶⟶ ••⟶ ⟶ ••⟶ ⟶⟶

The next morning proved to be just as exciting and stimulating as the first. Ipatia strove to do a good job at the shipping office, and her interaction with Tony and the rest of the staff was positive. He called her into his office after he arrived and asked her to go downstairs and pick up a few papers for him.

Ipatia went dutifully downstairs to the department and was met by a woman who said that Mr. Kapos, the person who had the papers was not there.

"He'll return in a few minutes."

Ipatia chatted with the woman who started a conversation with her. Mr. Kapos, a middle-aged man, finally arrived, and Ipatia asked him for the papers.

"Yes, I have them here," he said, reaching for some papers on the side of his desk.

He handed her the papers, and then chatted about them, explaining the ordeal he had to go through to get them ready.

Ipatia politely listened, but quickly realized he liked to talk. He chatted away for several minutes and then switched to talking about the weather and its effects on his joints. After a few minutes of this, she excused herself, saying, "Mr. Tony is waiting for the papers."

When Ipatia knocked on Tony's door and entered, she found Chuck Daras deep in conversation with him. She handed Tony the documents and greeted Mr. Daras, then went back to her desk. Melissa did not come that day.

The rest of the day, Ipatia worked diligently on her translations, waiting for Mr. Daras to leave so she could discuss her work with Tony.

However, when two o'clock came, time for Ipatia to leave, Mr. Daras had not left yet. The door to Tony's office remained shut.

As Ipatia walked home, she felt upset. If she hadn't spent time talking with people downstairs, she would have had time to discuss her work with Tony. Once Mr. Daras came, she realized that her opportunity had vanished.

The next morning, Ipatia couldn't concentrate on her work as she began daydreaming about Tony, and how kind, handsome and smart he was. He had been arriving earlier these days. Her glance fell on the pile of letters on her desk. Feeling guilty at her idleness, she became absorbed in her work.

Several minutes later, Ipatia heard footsteps and looked up, her heart racing.

Tony entered the room and smiled. "Good morning, Ipatia," he said cheerfully.

She returned his smile. "Good morning, Mr. Tony. Sorry I didn't have a chance to go over the translated papers with you yesterday."

"That's all right," he said, ruffling his hands through his hair, thinking. "Why don't we do it now? I'm expecting Chuck again later this morning, so I'll probably be tied up after that."

Ipatia followed him into the office. He read each translated paper aloud. Oftentimes, he would nod his approval, and once in a while, to her dismay, he would break out in laughter at some of her translations. He apologized, saying she had a creative way of looking at things.

"You are doing a good job with the translations," Tony said, after reviewing all the papers. "At this rate, you'll be finished much sooner than expected."

"Thank you," she said, beaming. "What will happen next to the translated papers?"

"They are distributed to the various departments and reviewed, depending on what needs to be done with them," he said.

They were interrupted by a knock on the door. Mr. Daras had arrived. Ipatia excused herself and spent the rest of the time translating more papers. Once more, Mr. Tony's office door was shut for the rest of the day.

●•————◆ ●•———◆ ●•———◆

The days flew by and two weeks had passed. Ipatia was becoming more familiar with the operations of the agency and with its staff. When she arrived in the office Friday morning, she got her first paycheck from Aristotle. Later that morning, she peeked inside the envelope and was amazed to see the amount. She had never had so much money in her hands at one time. She would have to see about putting it in a bank.

Ipatia went to work with renewed energy, feeling a surge of pride at having earned so much money. Slowly, the paper pile was whittling away.

Rita buzzed her later that morning, saying, "Mr. Tony is going to have a meeting, and he needs to have his office arranged for the meeting. I'll be there with some extra chairs."

Rita came shortly after that, carrying a chair. Ipatia helped bring chairs into the room.

When Tony arrived, he was not alone. An older man was with him.

"Good morning, Ipatia," Tony said. "Mr. Glaros, this is my personal assistant. Ipatia, we are having our meeting in here and do not want any interruptions. Please answer any calls and write down messages."

Ipatia nodded, noticing how reserved he was, and how aloof he appeared when he used his professional demeanor. She watched silently as they entered his office. More people trickled in his office. The last to arrive were Melissa and Chuck.

Around twelve o'clock, the young man from the coffee shop arrived, carrying several cups of coffee on his tray and several pastries. The office door opened, and he delivered the refreshments. Then Mr. Glaros left, returning a few minutes later carrying a big box. The door shut behind him.

The door remained shut when Ipatia left at two o'clock.

George Glaros began the computer demonstration. Seated in the room were Aristotle, Stamatis, Jimmy, the computer guru they had hired a few weeks ago, Chuck Daras, Melissa, and Mr. Sarkalos.

After Mr. Glaros was finished, Tony arose and turned on the lights. "Very good, Mr. Glaros. Your plan is well thought out, and we will strongly consider it," Tony said.

"Can you project how long before we are up and running?" Chuck asked Mr. Glaros.

George Glaros turned off the computer. "It all depends on what we find," he replied, shrugging. "At least two months are needed to assess your company's needs. After that, we can meet to discuss the implementation phase."

"I will contact you in a few days," Tony promised.

After Mr. Glaros left, Tony looked at everyone expectantly. "Well, what did you think? Can it be done?"

"The computers are top of the line, Mr. Plakis," Jimmy offered, nodding his approval. "Once installed, I can start training the staff to use them properly."

"Mr. Glaros said we would be able to communicate with each other and eventually with the outside world. That intrigues me," Mrs. Sarkalos said.

"By the end of this year, you will see what he means," Tony said, nodding. "Gentlemen, this is an important step forward for our company. Thanks to Mr. Daras, who suggested the idea, we will move forward in a capacity never done before."

"In order for us to compete successfully with the world, we need to incorporate this new technology in doing business. Not only will these computers aid the accounting department but also provide quicker processing of transactions and data," Chuck said.

Later, Tony sat in his office, thinking about everything that transpired at the meeting. Communicating via the computers meant less business trips on his part. His father had balked at the idea of using computers, not wanting to hear about it, but after Chuck spoke with him, his father reluctantly agreed with the idea.

CHAPTER 29

You asked me out on a date
To test my love and our fate.

Ipatia had settled into a pleasant routine. She would come into the office, work a couple of hours, then greet Tony as he arrived into the office. Later in the day, he would stop by her desk, smiling and showing interest as she discussed her progress and her translated papers. Often, he'd offer some advice. She enjoyed those sessions.

The first weekend in April, Ipatia and her cousins traveled to Loutraki, located an hour away, near Corinth. The famous Greek spa and resort area was known for its healing waters.

Monday morning, upon her return to the office, Ipatia shared her experience with Rita. "Have you ever been there?" she asked her.

"Yes, Loutraki is such a lovely place," Rita said, smiling. "I used to go there often. But now with three cats, two canaries, and an aquarium full of fish, it's difficult to get away. Who will care for them? They are my family."

Ipatia entered the office and went to work on her translations; her English vocabulary was growing daily, and she had made a list of words that she referred to often.

She also had wanted to tell Mr. Tony about her trip to Loutraki but his door was open and he wasn't in. *He might be at a meeting.*

At twelve o'clock, Rita phoned her. "Rita here. I'll be going for a snack. Did you want anything?"

"No, thank you," Ipatia said. She hesitated, wondering if she should ask. "Did Mr. Tony have a meeting this morning? I haven't seen him all morning."

"Oh, didn't I tell you? Friday, after you left the office, he received news that he had a business trip to go to this week. He'll be back on Thursday."

Ipatia continued her work, but her heart wasn't in it. The rest of the day dragged like molasses. Why was she feeling this way?

The clouds on Tuesday morning threatened rain so she took her umbrella with her. Working silently at her desk, Ipatia did not feel like talking to anyone. Her thoughts about Tony kept intruding all day, making it difficult to concentrate.

When she arrived home, a letter from Aunt Sophia had arrived. She tore the envelope open and read it eagerly.

"Ipatia, how is your aunt doing?" Paula asked, hovering around her.

George joined them.

"She is doing fine and misses everyone," Ipatia said. "She wants to know if I visited the house and not to worry about the mail because Marika is sending it to her."

"Oh my, we hadn't thought about visiting the house. We should go and check on it and visit Miss Marika sometime soon," Paula said, fretting.

"Why don't we go this Saturday?" George asked.

"I would like that," Ipatia said.

"Did she write anything else, dear?" Paula asked.

Ipatia told them about Aunt Sophia's life, the daily routines, the people, and her struggle with the English language.

"At the end of the letter," Ipatia continued, "she writes that she has some important news but wants to wait a little more before confirming it. Her telephone number is included in this letter. She wants me to call her in a few weeks."

◦•────◈ •◦────◈ •◦────◈

Thursday finally arrived and Ipatia felt excited. *Today, Tony is returning.* Paying careful attention to her wardrobe, she wore a peach-colored skirt and a matching jacket with a white silk blouse. She also wore her mother's pearl necklace with matching earrings.

Entering the glass doors to the office, Ipatia's heart began to race when she saw Tony standing and talking with Rita. Several packages were on Rita's desk.

She greeted them and headed for her desk, conscious of his eyes on her.

Tony joined her moments later.

"Here is something for you, Ipatia," he said, smiling and retrieving a small, wrapped package from his suit pocket. "Straight from England."

She hesitated.

"I typically bring back presents for the staff."

"Thank you," she said, surprised by his generosity.

"And you don't have to kiss me because I gave you a gift," he teased.

She giggled, feeling her face heat up as she accepted the small package.

"How is the work coming along?"

She showed him a legal document that she had been working on which was encumbered by unfamiliar terminology. "I made a list of difficult words and that's helping me. I'll be finished with it in a day or so."

He took the translated document and studied it. She was rewarded by his admiring glance. "Good work."

"Is there any more work for me?"

"Yes, there is, as a matter of fact," he said, looking at her. "I have a number of things I need to do today, but we can meet in my office tomorrow, around noon, and discuss it then."

○──────◇ ○──────◇ ○──────◇

Later, in the privacy of her bedroom, Ipatia eagerly opened the slim book of poetry by famous English poets. Her fingers reverently touched the beautiful artwork that embellished the front and back of the leather-bound book. She stayed up late into the night reading it, inspired by the poems.

On Friday at noon, Ipatia met with Tony.

"There are a number of issues relating to the business that I need to discuss with you," Tony said. "But first of all, I am pleased with your progress and quick grasp of things, Ipatia."

"Thank you," she said, her spine tingling from the compliment.

"The reason why I wanted to meet with you is that I would like for you to get involved in our new project," he said. "We are planning to add computers to our offices. We are behind from our competitors and need to catch up with their technology."

Ipatia liked the idea. "I've never used a computer before."

"Don't worry. You're bright. You will learn quickly."

He continued his discourse, explaining the usefulness of the computers; he appeared to be well informed on the subject. When they were finished, she arose to leave.

"Did you get a chance to read the English poems, Ipatia?"

There he goes again, making me feel warm all over.

Ipatia blushed and nodded. "Yes. Thank you so much. They were beautifully and nobly written."

"I'm glad you liked them. My favorite poem is the one written by Lord Byron," he said huskily. "She walks in beauty like the night."

When he spoke those words, Ipatia's face felt hot and strong emotions coursed through her body.

How does one walk in beauty like the night? By gliding?

"It sounds wonderful. I'll look for it," she said, trembling. As she turned to leave, her shoulders straightened and her steps became measured as she tried to "walk in beauty like the night."

She felt him touch her arm.

"Before you go, I'd like to ask you something else."

She turned and gazed at him. His face was too close for comfort. Her heart beat wildly. "Yes?" she breathed.

"Would you be free tomorrow?" he asked. "We could go to a nice place on the mountain where we can have a picnic."

Enjoying the idea of going on a picnic with him on the mountain, she smiled and nodded. "Thank you, that would be wonderful. I mean, thank you for the invitation but will it be just the two of us?"

"I understand. I can ask Tim to drive us there," he said dryly. "Could you be ready by eleven? I'll come, I mean we will come and pick you up at your house. I will bring the lunch."

"Thank you. That would be wonderful," she said shyly as she slipped out of the room, almost running.

That evening, she talked with Paula and George about Tony's invitation to go on a picnic on Saturday, and they looked at each other before nodding their approval.

"We can visit your aunt's house on Sunday instead," George said.

In the privacy of her room, she eagerly leafed through the poetry book that Tony had given her searching for Lord Byron's poem. When she found it, she read the title out loud, "She walks in beauty, like the night."

She continued with the rest of the poem until she reached the end, saying, "A heart whose love is innocent." She sighed, gazing off into the room. Was it possible that Tony was trying to tell her something?

Someone knocked on the door. "Ipatia, could I talk with you a minute?" Paula asked.

"Come in," Ipatia said, putting the book aside and sitting upright.

Paula sat on the edge of the bed, looking at her with a kind face. "I want to speak to you as if you're my daughter. You see,

George and I promised your aunt and grandfather that we would see to your welfare." She paused, as if trying to find the right words. "Ipatia, when a young man asks a girl out on a date, it's either one of two things. He either is serious about her or he isn't."

"What do you mean?"

"Simply put, has this young man said anything about his intentions towards you?"

"No," Ipatia said, blushing and shaking her head.

"If he tries anything, you just smack him with your purse and come home right away."

Ipatia laughed at the picture.

"Are you in love with him?"

The question fell on Ipatia like a bombshell. She shut her eyes, contemplating her feelings. After a moment or two, she nodded shyly. "Yes. To be honest, I'm a little confused. I mean, at first, I did want to go to the university, but now I can't stop thinking about Tony. He's on my mind all the time."

"Of course. You're seeing him every day now," Paula said. "Are you sure it's not infatuation that you are feeling? Do you think he feels the same way about you?"

"I honestly don't know. Tony gave me this gift when he returned from England," Ipatia said, lifting the book. "Now he's asked me out on a date. I don't know why he's showering me with gifts and all this attention, except that-"

"Yes?" Paula prodded.

"He's dated a number of girls and maybe might want another girlfriend. On the other hand, Aunt Sophia said that he's an eligible man, and that he wouldn't be waiting long to marry."

"Let me help you on that issue. Before your aunt left for America, she confided in me that she had spoken to him, and he said his intentions were honorable," Paula said, beaming. "However, he had also mentioned that you were more interested in getting a degree than in marrying."

"He did?" Ipatia asked, stunned by the revelation.

That night, Ipatia dreamt that she was with Tony.

Holding hands, he led her through a green meadow. They passed some trees and stopped at a cliff. Beyond, she could see a spectacular view of the sea.

"It is beautiful here like on Lipsi Island," she cried.

Ipatia felt happy as they placed a tablecloth on the ground and started preparing the lunch. Tony whistled as he helped her remove the food from the baskets. At one point their fingers touched, and she felt electricity run through her. Then he got up, saying he would be right back.

Tony returned with a bouquet of fresh flowers. "For you," he said, presenting them gallantly to her.

"How pretty." She took them and smelled them. "I feel so happy and peaceful as if we are in heaven."

"I know what you mean," he said, gazing into her eyes lovingly. "How long has it been since you came to Piraeus, Ipatia?"

"Seven months and two weeks," she said.

"Seven long months and two long weeks," he said.

"What do you mean?"

"I mean, my darling, that I love you, and I can't live another day without you. I'm asking you to marry me," he said softly, taking her into his arms.

"I love you, too," she whispered, melting into his arms.

CHAPTER 30

We drove into the mountain road,
No clue of what the day would hold.

Saturday morning, Ipatia arose feeling bright and cheerful, remembering the dream and thinking about her picnic date with Tony. She opened her window, allowing the breeze to enter the room. It was a sunny day and she decided to wear her white cotton dress for the occasion.

Paula entered the room, carrying a white, lace shawl. "You might need this," she said, handing it to her. "It can get cool up on the mountain. You can use it both as a shawl and a scarf."

"Thank you, it's beautiful," Ipatia said, admiring it and placing it on the bed. "Before you leave, could you tell me whether this looks too formal?" She pulled up her long hair and coiled it into a bun, revealing her long, slim neck.

"It does look a little formal for a picnic," Paula said, studying her "Why don't you leave it down and maybe just pull your bangs back a little."

"Good idea," Ipatia said cheerfully as Paula left the room. She pulled the strands behind her ears, looking at herself in the mirror and admitting that it looked better.

As Ipatia hummed a favorite tune, she picked up the white shawl to leave and then spied a black spider on it. She dropped it, recoiling. Her heart started racing. She never liked spiders, or snakes, or scorpions. The last time she had seen the scorpion was right before she found out that little Nick had cut his arm. *Was this spider another sign?*

Determined to fight her fear, Ipatia grabbed the shawl, ran to the window and brushed the spider off. She watched in silence as the creature sped outside.

"Ugh!" she shuddered, shutting the window. "Stay away."

The doorbell rang. *It must be Tony.*

Eager to see him, Ipatia hurriedly wrapped the scarf around her shoulders and opened the door of her room, and then hesitated, remembering what had just happened. Her fear had returned.

Calm down. It was just a silly little spider.

George answered the front door.

Tony introduced himself. He chatted with Ipatia's cousins, warming up to them. Ipatia arrived shortly and looked appealing in the summer dress and lace shawl. He smiled warmly at her, complimenting her.

"Don't forget these," Paula said, handing Ipatia a box of pastries as they left. "Have a nice time."

They thanked her, and Tony led Ipatia to his car.

Ipatia looked around expectantly for the driver. "I thought Tim would be here," she said flatly.

"I apologize, my sweet," Tony replied. "You see, my little sister borrowed Tim early in the morning to do her last-minute shopping for her wedding. She is leaving tomorrow for Crete."

She appeared thoughtful. "I remember how busy Aunt Sophia was for her wedding preparations.

"Also, my car needs to be driven," he declared, opening the door for her.

Ipatia smiled and sat in the car.

Tony felt as if he were floating on air after she smiled.

They cruised through the various neighborhoods of Athens, stopping and going slowly. "Have you been up there?" Tony asked, pointing to the Acropolis.

"Yes, with Mrs. Rodos," Ipatia replied. "It's amazing how the columns are positioned. They form one straight line from top to bottom. Mrs. Rodos pointed that out to me."

"Yes. The ancient Greeks' achievements in architecture is outstanding. Did you visit the archaeological museum?"

"Oh yes," she replied, becoming excited. "I'm glad you mentioned it. I saw the geometric vase from the island, the one that Father gave to my grandfather. I appreciate your kind and noble gesture."

"As you probably noticed, its replica is sitting in my office," he said, smiling. "The original vase is safer in the museum and should be shared with the public."

"You are right," she said nodding appreciatively.

He became silent as they drove through busy streets, past honking cars. Minutes later, they were on a large road, speeding along.

"Is that Mt. Hymettus?" Ipatia asked curiously, pointing towards the large mountain looming ahead.

"Yes. The picnic area is there."

"Can one see everything from there? The city, the sea?" she asked.

"The picnic area is near the foot of the mountain at the Monastery of Kaisariani, so the view is not the same. It was built around the eleventh century, it also has remarkable frescoes inside," he said, gazing at her.

"Oh."

"Would you prefer going higher, for the view?"

"That would be nice," she said, nodding her approval.

"We can visit the monastery later, then. Above the monastery is a spring that in old days used to be the sole source of water for Athens."

"How interesting," she murmured.

As they made their way towards the mountain, Tony turned on the radio. The air was cooler and the breeze ruffled his hair. He noticed that Ipatia had tied her shawl loosely around her head.

"Tony, I've been meaning to ask you something," Ipatia said. "What is opportunity cost?"

"Where did you learn that?" he asked amazed. "It's an economic term."

"I know. Miss Marika mentioned it during our conversations and I didn't have a chance to ask her what it meant," she replied proudly.

"We chose this ride, for example," he said, "instead of doing something else. We forfeited other activities for this one. That's called opportunity cost."

"Ahh, I see now. There's a cost for everything."

"Yes, and time is considered a cost," he said. "Like the time needed to get an education versus marrying and having a family." He glanced at her, trying to gauge her reaction.

She was quiet.

She understood.

"Time," she said. "Time controls our lives."

"Yes, and efficiency is one way of getting an edge on time," he said.

"Is that why computers are so important?"

"Yes. They can do so many things in the same amount of time as someone who does only one thing."

"And what does that gain you?"

"Why, more time to do other things, like go to picnics."

They both laughed.

"How is your medical reading these days?" he asked lightly.

"I read something recently about the cells in our bodies. Researchers have found out that the cells replicate only so many times in one's lifetime, and then they stop reproducing."

"Our lives are finite," Tony remarked. "Which makes time so important."

"Yes, but the good thing is that life doesn't end when we leave this earth. When we pass away, we move on to a new life, a new level, where time is no longer a factor."

"If we were to die, Ipatia, would our souls meet again someday?" he asked softly.

She looked at him, her eyes shining bright with hope.

They became silent.

A love song was playing on the radio. In a short time, he was singing along with the music and entering that magical moment that transcended time and space.

After the song finished, Ipatia said, "You know, Mrs. Rodos, the English teacher met her husband in a restaurant. He was a cook who sang songs like this one."

"Really?"

She continued, telling him about Mrs. Rodos falling in love with his voice and then marrying him.

"And they were happily married after that, right?"

"Yes," she replied dreamily, leaning her head back. She turned and gazed fondly at him.

He glanced at her, struck by her beauty. "Did you like my singing?"

Ipatia jerked her head up. "I think you have a wonderful voice."

"Does that mean you'll marry me, Ipatia? Tony asked, teasing her.

Ipatia blushed, and then smiled. "I don't know. Are you a good cook?"

He laughed.

They had reached the mountain, and their car began the arduous climb up the winding road. The road became narrow and Tony had to be careful. There wasn't much room for error here. He honked right before turning a bend.

"Why do you honk?" she asked curiously.

"It's a safety precaution. Someone might be coming down from the other side, and I want them to know I'm here," he replied.

"So, they don't run into you?" she asked, tensing slightly.

"Don't worry," he said, laughing. "Ipatia, how long has it been since you came to Piraeus?"

Just like in the dream.

"Seven months and two weeks," she said, almost whispering.

"Yes, that's right," he said. "That's how long we've known each other. But in fact, I feel I've known you much longer than that. You see, I took a trip once, with your father, years ago. On that trip, your father talked about you so much that I had to see for myself the bright, darling daughter of his. So, after the ship docked, I stood on deck, watching you and your mother reunite with your father."

"I don't remember seeing you."

"You were five or six then. That was the year your father bought you the piano, wasn't it?"

"Yes," she said, nodding. "How did you know?"

"When he told me how you liked to sing so much, I persuaded him to buy you a piano," he said, looking at her. "And he thanked me for it afterwards."

Someone honked their horn loudly, startling Tony, followed by the screeching of tires as a car rapidly bore down on them.

Tony desperately veered to the right to avoid a collision but he was too late. An explosive sound followed as the other car rammed into them. That was all he remembered for then he blacked out.

•••———◈ •••———◈ •••———◈

"Christina, quick, get Father for me. It's an emergency!"

Christina immediately went to Gregory's room and woke him up from his nap. "Melissa is on the telephone. She says it is urgent."

Christina helped him get into his wheelchair and pushed him to the telephone. He sat there and listened. Melissa received a telephone call from a hospital outside Athens.

Tony had been in a car accident and was in the emergency room. He was in critical condition. They told her they were not equipped to handle such a severe case. She immediately arranged to have him flown by helicopter to the main hospital in Athens.

Gregory was in shock when he heard the news.

"Father, please come," were Melissa's tearful words before she hung up.

Once she arrived at the hospital in Athens, Melissa was guided to the intensive care unit, where she saw several nurses and doctors hovering over her brother. She walked slowly towards the bed, afraid to look.

His face was bandaged and unrecognizable. Melissa almost fainted when she saw him. She leaned against the wall for support. Gaining strength, she managed to squeeze in between one of the nurses so she could get closer. There were tubes everywhere.

Melissa touched his hand, pleading, "Tony, Tony."

"It's best not to wake him, Miss," said the nurse to her left, sternly looking her way.

Melissa walked to a chair and sat down, numbed by everything. She gazed at her brother as if she were in a trance. A nurse nudged her awake and said that they didn't allow visitors to sleep in the intensive care unit.

Melissa arrived home at midnight. She unlocked the door and entered the dark house. No staff greeted her at the door, compounding the strange feeling. Where was everyone? Then she remembered. They had left this afternoon for the Easter vacation.

The empty house echoed Melissa's loneliness while her steps took her down the hallway and into the study. She must call Chuck. There would be no trip to Crete tomorrow. She telephoned him and numbly told him the news and then broke down crying. He said he'd be right over.

Ipatia dreamt that she was walking in a beautiful meadow, dressed in white. In front of her stood a gate and behind it stood Tony. When she saw Tony, Ipatia opened the gate and ran towards him, happy to see him.

"You're all right," she said.

He took her hand and kissed it, saying, "Yes, my Love. You can't stay here though, you need to return."

She felt sad, saying, "I don't want to go back, I want to be with you."

"I'll try to return," he promised. He turned around and walked away.

Ipatia woke to the sound of voices above her. She blinked her eyes, trying to talk. Her one eye wouldn't open. Her chest felt heavy, and she had difficulty breathing.

"There, there, Ipatia. You'll be all right, my dear," Paula said, patting her hand sadly.

"Where am I? What happened?' Ipatia whispered, looking around her. Light was streaming into the room from a window. Her mouth felt dry. She licked her chapped lips.

"You were in a car accident and were brought to a hospital by some kind people who stopped to help."

"Ouch," Ipatia exclaimed, as she tried to raise herself up. "What happened to Tony? Is he all right?"

"Now, now, try not to move," Paula said, helping Ipatia back down into her bed. "They said you have a couple of fractured ribs."

"Do you know what happened to Tony?" repeated Ipatia, feeling concerned.

"We honestly don't know," George said, shrugging apologetically at the girl's plea. "When we asked about him, we were told that no one by that name was admitted here."

"I hope nothing happened to him," Ipatia said. Tears rolled down her face as she remembered the dream. The thought of Tony not surviving the crash sent her reeling. *Dear God, don't let that happen to him.* Her breathing became labored, and her head was beginning to throb. The pain in her ribs was unbearable.

"I, I can't breathe," Ipatia rasped.

Paula rushed from the room, bringing the nurse back with her.

The nurse aided Ipatia, moving her into a more comfortable position and propping her pillows. She stayed with her until Ipatia felt better.

"Don't worry, everything is all right," George said, trying to sound reassuring, but his voice cracked midway. "If you'd like, we can call Tony's home and find out for you."

Ipatia thought it over, tears of relief wetting her face. "Thank you, that would be wonderful." She sniffled, trying to remember where she put her purse. "Oh. I forgot my purse at home and the telephone number is in it."

"Don't worry dear, we'll call him when we get home," Paula said, patting her arm gently.

Ipatia smiled, feeling grateful, and then brushed away the tears, wincing at the gesture. She delicately touched her closed eye, feeling its soft bulge. "What happened to my eye?"

"The doctor said that there is swelling in that eye, and that's probably going to be like that for a few days. Once the swelling goes down, then you will probably be able to see," Paula said.

"That's good," Ipatia said, cheering up. "How did you find out that I was here?"

"When night came and you hadn't returned, we were concerned for your safety," began Paula. She glanced at George.

"I have a friend who is a policeman," George said. "We contacted him around ten o'clock last night and told him where you had gone, and he began a search."

"I'm so glad you found me," Ipatia exclaimed. "It must have been difficult to find me. I didn't have my purse with me or any identification."

"Yes, that was the hard part. Somehow, he learned about a car accident in the vicinity where you were going. The girl in the accident had been hospitalized. We took a chance and came here to see if that girl was you," George said.

"We were worried about you," Paula said, nodding her head emphatically, her eyes reddened.

"Thank you." Ipatia started to drift off, her eyes closing.

"Dear, would you like that I stay with you overnight, in case you needed anything?" Paula asked.

Ipatia's eyes fluttered open. She managed to whisper, "I'll be fine, Paula. I just feel sleepy."

"Don't be afraid to call for the nurse if you need anything."

Those were the last words that Ipatia heard as she drifted off to sleep.

CHAPTER 31

Life is filled with lessons to learn,
Some to keep and some to spurn.

The next morning, a nurse awakened Ipatia. The curtain had been drawn around her bed, and she couldn't see anyone, but she heard sounds of commotion and people talking in the background.

"Good morning. My name is Maria. I am your nurse today. Is the pain medicine helping you at all?"

"Yes, and it's also making me sleep all the time."

"Good, that's what we want. You need to rest," Maria said, sticking a thermometer in Ipatia's mouth.

"Can you tell me what's wrong with me?"

"Your x-rays show two fractured ribs and bruising in your lung. That's why it's difficult to breathe."

"Hmm, you still have a fever," Maria said, appearing concerned. She jotted it down in the chart.

"Will I need antibiotics?" Ipatia asked.

"You are already on them. You see that tubing leading into your hand?"

Ipatia looked at the thin tubing. She was surprised to see it entering her hand. The tubing was connected to a large, plastic bag filled with liquid, that hung on a pole. Overwhelmed by nausea, she looked away.

"You're getting your food and medicine from here. By the way, I'll talk to the doctor about your fever. We don't want you to get pneumonia. Meanwhile, someone is coming to draw your blood. Afterwards, you will go to radiology for x-rays."

"X-rays? What for?"

"When you first came in, the x-rays showed a spot in your lung, so they want to see whether it's still there."

A spot in my lung?

"Thank you, Miss Maria," Ipatia managed to say. "Could you pull the curtains away from my bed as you leave?"

The nurse cheerfully complied, then left.

For the first time, Ipatia noticed that her bed was located next to a large window. It was a gray day outside. The room was equally cheerless with its gray floor and low lighting.

Three other women patients were in the same room. They were talking amongst themselves.

She observed them quietly, trying to ignore the pain radiating from her rib area. Two of the women appeared middle-aged, and one looked to be younger, around Ipatia's age. Ipatia didn't get a chance to find out more because a young woman dressed in white came towards her, carrying a box.

"I've come to draw your blood," she said, drawing the curtains slightly around them and preparing her tubes.

When Ipatia saw the needle, she almost fainted. Looking the other way, she held her breath. She tensed when she felt the pinch from the needle. "I'm afraid I can't handle seeing blood," she said, swallowing hard.

"Don't worry, we're almost done," said the technician brightly. "You can look now."

Ipatia smiled apologetically as she watched the technician leave. A few minutes later, two nurses came into the room rolling a small bed with them. They lifted Ipatia off the bed and placed her on the other bed, using the sheet that was under her to support her weight. She moaned lightly from the pain.

"We're going for your tests," one of the nurses said.

When Ipatia returned later that morning, she fell asleep. When she awoke, she was feeling better and decided to meet her fellow roommates.

Lula, the middle-aged, dark-skinned woman whose bed was closest to the door, had a mysterious intestinal problem. The doctors couldn't find the cause. Katina, the young, pale girl to her left, had her appendix removed due to appendicitis. Across from Ipatia was Georgia, a plump woman who was treated for pneumonia.

When asked why she was in the hospital, Ipatia's short reply was that she had been in a car accident. She didn't go into further detail.

"The good Lord works in mysterious ways," Lula offered. "Sometimes He puts us in situations because He wants us to learn a lesson or because maybe we can be an example to someone else."

"Maybe He wanted us all to be here at the same time so we could become friends," said Katina, the youngest of the group.

"The evil eye may have touched you," Georgia said to Ipatia. "Sometimes when one has beauty and youth, and good things happen to them, people may envy that. It also can come from someone who compliments you or admires you. It's happened to me many times."

"What did you do about it?" Ipatia asked, her eyes wide open.

"I had the spell removed," Georgia replied. "My mother could tell whether or not I had it. She filled a small bowl with water and poured a little olive oil on the water. She then made the sign of the cross in the oil. If the oil blended with the water, I had the evil eye. If it stayed separate, I didn't. Then she would say a special prayer to remove it. Within hours I was feeling better."

"Do you know the prayer?" Ipatia asked curiously.

Georgia made the sign of the cross and then began reciting the prayer. Afterwards, she shared her experiences when she had been afflicted by the evil eye.

The friendly discourse was interrupted when a group of people arrived. Ipatia watched as Lula received her husband with their two children. The show of affection between the couple was unsettling for Ipatia. She looked away, unable to watch them. For some odd reason, that scene evoked a bittersweet feeling in her. She didn't realize how much Tony's absence after the accident had meant to her until now. *Where was he?*

Ipatia began a conversation with Katina. She learned that Katina was only fifteen, and she would be leaving tomorrow. Their discussion didn't last long, for Katina's parents, grandmother and younger brother arrived.

The area near Ipatia's bed became crowded and noisy as they managed to settle themselves around Katina's bed. Katina introduced Ipatia to them, and Ipatia smiled sweetly back at them. She listened to their chatter and then felt tired. She shut her eyes.

Ipatia's thoughts inevitably turned to Tony; she thought about his smiles, the words they spoke before the accident, his gift, and his kiss in the study. The scenes flowed together like one long movie. She began to pray silently. She prayed that he was all right and for her to have a speedy recovery. She fell asleep amidst her prayers.

A light tap on her arm awoke her. George and Paula had arrived. Paula brought some baked goods along with her smiles, and George made everything appear all right, sharing jokes with her. Ipatia introduced her cousins to Katina and her family, and they exchanged pleasant words. The room had become crowded.

Paula said, "We contacted your grandfather. He was concerned about you, yet thankful that we were here to help you. He's happy that you are all right and doing better."

Ipatia thanked her.

"We also spoke with your aunt in America. The good news is that she is pregnant."

"She is pregnant?" Ipatia cried, sitting up and clapping her hands together with joy. "I can't believe it." A sharp pain shot up her chest. She winced from the pain and eased back into the bed.

"What is it dear?" Paula asked.

"I'm still a little sore," Ipatia said ruefully. More subdued, she asked questions about her aunt's impending birth.

"You should talk with her after you leave the hospital. She wants you to live with them in America after you are well enough to travel," Paula said. "With the baby, she'll be needing your help. What do you think?"

"I'll have to think about it," Ipatia said. "Did you get a chance to call Tony's home?"

George shook his head sadly. "No one picked up the telephone," he said. "We tried two times."

They chatted awhile longer, sharing the latest news from their children in Thessaloniki, the national news, the weather, and their friends.

Ipatia's eyes were beginning to close. She felt sleepy.

"We better be going," George said, looking at Paula. "Ipatia needs her sleep."

"I'm sorry, but I can't seem to keep my eyes open," Ipatia said. She drifted off to sleep.

The following day, the doctor visited Ipatia and examined her. He told her that there had been some internal bleeding and they were monitoring it. When she asked him about the black and blue areas on her body, he replied that the bruises were caused by the bleeding, and over time, should start to turn yellow, which was a sign of healing.

"All your internal organs are intact. The two fractured ribs need several weeks to heal," he said. He ended the visit by saying if everything continued to improve, she should be ready to leave the following Monday.

●•———◈ ●•——◈ ●•———◈

Gregory sat by his son's side, gazing sadly at the young man's bandaged face and waiting for the doctor's visit. Two days ago, he had arrived at the hospital in Athens late in the evening and was wheeled into the intensive care unit by Christina. There, he met with the doctor who led him to his son. He had wept uncontrollably when he saw Tony lying in the bed, his face bandaged and comatose. He hadn't slept well since then.

The doctor came into the room just then. "Good afternoon, Mr. Plakis."

Gregory asked heavily, "Doctor, tell me the truth. What are my son's chances of recovering completely?"

"Not good," replied the doctor. "Surgery is needed, but it cannot be performed until his blood pressure is stabilized, and there's no guarantee he'll come out of his coma even after surgery."

Gregory collapsed right there on the spot. The nurses and doctors rushed to help him. After he revived, he demanded in a raspy voice, "Find me the best doctors. My son is not going to die."

In what seemed like a miraculous show of renewed vigor, Gregory set out to find a doctor to save his son. He spoke with specialists in other hospitals. Not satisfied with the poor prognosis, he obtained names of top brain surgeons in other countries.

Finally, he found a top surgeon in England, Dr. Kildare, who was known for his high success rate in these special cases. He reached Dr. Kildare by telephone and spoke to him at length, regaining hope after their conversation. Dr. Kildare suggested using a new surgical technique he had invented that he felt could help Tony. Gregory decided to transport Tony to England.

At first, the doctors said that Tony might not survive the trip, but Gregory insisted that if Tony did not make the trip, he wouldn't survive anyway. With calls back and forth from the doctor's office in England, they were able to transport Tony to England.

As soon as they arrived at the hospital, the attendants wheeled Tony off to surgery. He was operated on seven times before he was stabilized.

Gregory looked up when he heard voices. The nurses outside in the hallway were speaking English.

Christina and Melissa entered the room.

"You need to get some rest, dear, before we admit you too," Christina said. She kissed him lightly on the cheek.

"Why don't we go back to the hotel? Melissa will stay here and keep an eye on him."

Gregory shook his head, muttering, "Not yet. I have the feeling that any minute now, he will awaken. I want to be here when he does."

"I understand, dear, but it has been two weeks since he had his surgeries. The doctor said that it might be months or even years before he gets out of his coma, if at all," Christina said, patting him on the shoulder.

"Tony means everything to me," Gregory said, brushing his wet eyes awkwardly. He rarely wept, but during these last few weeks, it had become a common occurrence. "Did Doctor Kildare have any word about his condition?"

"He performed the surgery and that's all he could do. Now it's up to Tony's body to recuperate and heal."

"Should we tell anyone back home or in the office?" Melissa asked.

"No, not yet," Gregory replied, shaking his head. "We will tell them in due time."

"What will happen if he doesn't come out of his coma soon?" Melissa asked. "I know this may not be the time to say it, but what about my wedding plans? What about the plans for the new house?"

Gregory did not respond right away but instead looked thoughtfully at Tony. Whenever he spent more time with him, Melissa's jealousy came forward, and she would start making demands.

After what seemed a long time, he nodded his head heavily and said, "Daughter, you will have your wedding and your house."

Easter Sunday finally came. All the other patients had gone and the room was now empty except for Ipatia. Time marched slowly with no one to talk with.

Ipatia spent the morning reading the bible that Georgia had left her. She could use both of her eyes for the first time without straining them. She read voraciously. The bible was an escape from the thoughts that kept threatening to engulf her and the stark loneliness that overwhelmed her. It brought her peace.

Maria, the nurse brought in a tray of food.

"How about that? A nice meal for a change," she said, placing the tray down. "Here, let me check your temperature before you begin eating."

Ipatia placed the bible aside and complied by taking the thermometer offered to her. A few minutes later, she watched curiously, as Maria read the thermometer.

"Congratulations. You don't have a fever anymore," said Maria brightly, as she shook the thermometer.

"That's wonderful," Ipatia said. "May I go home then?"

"Let me check with the doctor," said Maria.

She returned after a while and told her that the doctor wanted to be sure her fever was gone for at least twenty-four hours, so Ipatia had to wait one more day.

Ipatia picked up the bible and began reading more fervently. *Dear Lord, thank you for the blessing you bestowed upon me today, your day.*

Later that day, Ipatia's cousins paid her a visit. They brought a basket filled to the brim with red-dyed eggs, Tsoureki bread, roasted lamb, and other goodies.

After their meal, Ipatia took a red egg and held it in the palm of her hand, looking mischievous, exposing the one end of the egg. "Who will try it first?"

Paula took her egg and tapped the end lightly on Ipatia's egg.

"Ohh. Mine cracked," Paula said.

They laughed together. Ipatia's egg also cracked George's.

"I'm afraid to eat it now. This one's a winner," Ipatia said, placing it down. She was beginning to feel better.

"Here, have my egg and some more bread," Paula said.

"No thanks," Ipatia said, rubbing her stomach. "You've stuffed so much good food into me today, I don't think I'll be able to fit through that door. By the way, did you hear anything from Tony's family?"

"Everything is closed for Easter, so we weren't able to place a call," Paula said. "We're sorry, Ipatia, but maybe we can try tomorrow."

Ipatia felt disappointed. The light, cheerful feeling of a few moments ago had been replaced with a foreboding feeling that she couldn't shake off. *Something was wrong if Tony hadn't tried to contact me.*

"After you get well, we're planning on visiting our children in Thessaloniki," George said quickly. "You can come with us, Ipatia. It might do you some good."

"Maria, the nurse, told me I no longer had a fever and I could leave tomorrow," Ipatia said hopefully.

"How wonderful," Paula exclaimed. "I'll bring your clothes then, tomorrow morning."

After her cousins left, Ipatia took a nap and later that evening, walked around in her room, remembering her conversation with her cousins and the talks with her new-found friends. She wondered how they were doing.

Ipatia ventured into the hallway, walking slowly and carefully. The nurses and medical staff had left for the holiday and only a handful of staff remained

She returned to her room.

Her mind wandered to Tony, to their conversations before the accident and all the kind deeds he had done. *His love had felt real.* She wept quietly, brushing the tears away, feeling an inexplicable sadness. Deep down inside she was feeling the same pain as when her parents had died. *Like the pain of losing a loved one.* She thought she'd never experience it again. She thought she'd never love again. She knew she had been wrong.

She whispered softly into the night, "Tony, I love you. Where are you? How could you leave me alone?"

Inside her heart, a small voice whispered back, *"Do not fear, my love. You will never be alone again, because I will always be with you."*

She fell asleep, feeling peaceful.

CHAPTER 32

I cannot bear to think of thee
In Crete with your family.

Ipatia awoke early the next day in anticipation of her departure. Her cousins arrived later that morning. Paula helped her get dressed by pulling the sleeves over her arms and buttoning the back of her dress. Several nurses came by to see her off, wishing her a speedy recovery.

Once home, they had a pleasant lunch of spinach pie, chicken souvlaki, and salad. Afterwards, Ipatia walked around a little, enjoying the freedom of being out of the hospital. She was still a little sore yet was eager to get back to her healthy self. Music from the radio filtered through the house, and at one point, a sad song mourning the loss of a loved one was being played, triggering sad feelings about Tony. Her tiredness returned and she sat down, feeling exhausted. She tried to read a book but began dozing off.

"Ipatia, why don't you nap? You don't want to exert yourself too much," Paula said.

Ipatia lay in bed and before long, she was asleep. Afterwards, she found George and Paula in the kitchen, sipping coffee.

"George, could I ask you a favor? I need to go to the pharmacy to pick up my medicines, and I also want to call and see about Tony," Ipatia said.

"Sure, sure," George said, putting his coffee cup down.

"I'll get you Tony's number," Paula said, going to retrieve it.

George drove Ipatia to the pharmacy.

She fingered the paper with the telephone number, wondering what she would find when she called Tony's house.

When they reached the shop, George said, "I'll just drop you off and wait for you outside since there is no parking."

Clutching the prescription and her piece of paper, Ipatia slowly walked into the pharmacy, mindful of her sore ribs. She gave her prescription to the pharmacist and went to the telephone. She winced from the pain as she lifted the telephone. She was still experiencing some soreness in that area.

As she dialed the Plakis residence, her hands felt clammy. It rang several times. A man picked it up and her heart beat wildly. It was the wrong number. She mumbled her apologies and redialed the number. This time, no one answered it. She let it ring several times before hanging up. She was feeling dejected as she slowly headed towards the door.

"Miss."

She turned towards the pharmacist, a tiny thin man with a large nose and even larger ears. He looked distraught.

"There is a charge for using the telephone," he demanded. "Also, your medicine is ready."

"I'm sorry," she said, blushing. Her hand fumbled in her purse as she looked for the change. "I was thinking about something else."

She quickly paid and left hurriedly out the door, still thinking about Tony and shaking her head.

"What's the matter?" George asked her.

"I can't get a hold of anyone at the Plakis house, and I'm worried about Tony," Ipatia said, slumping down, feeling miserable. "There's always someone at the house, either the housekeeper or cook. There must be something wrong."

The pharmacist came running out the door with the medicine. "You forgot this," he said, thrusting the small package towards her.

"Sorry," she said. "I just got out of the hospital, and I'm not feeling too well."

"No problem," replied the pharmacist, his face softening.

They drove away slowly.

"You really were affected, weren't you?" George said.

"I guess I was," she said solemnly. "I'm puzzled about the whole thing and would like to know what happened to Tony."

"I could drive you to the Plakis office building, and you can ask there."

Ipatia perked up at the idea, and minutes later, George dropped her off in front of the Plakis office.

"I'll be waiting for you down here," he said.

For some reason, the building seemed much larger today. Moving around had become tiresome and the thought of walking up the stairs overwhelmed her.

Ipatia took the elevator instead, her heart beating quickly, as she thought about what she would find and what she would say. How should she act if she saw Tony standing in the office talking with Rita? Should she be quiet or should she speak up? She would be quiet.

Ipatia forgot her plan when she saw Rita sitting alone at her desk. Everything appeared normal.

"*Christos Anesti*. Christ is Risen," Rita said gaily, greeting Ipatia with the Easter greeting, which was customary after Easter.

"*Alithos Anesti*. Truly He is Risen," Ipatia replied, smiling fondly at her. She wasn't sure if she should mention her accident because it would reveal the fact she had been on a date with Tony. A strong, gut feeling told her not to mention it.

"How was your Easter vacation?"

Ipatia paused before she spoke, trying to choose her words carefully. "Easter was nice and quiet. I spent it with my cousins. Did you spend your vacation with family?"

"I visited my younger sister and her family," Rita began. "Every year we visit her place because she has the biggest house and can accommodate the relatives." Rita rambled on about her holiday experience. The telephone interrupted her gay chatter. "Yes, the office is closed for the holiday."

After Rita hung up, she said to Ipatia, "Mr. Tony didn't leave any instructions for me to give you any work. He's in Crete celebrating Easter with his parents. Miss Melissa and Mr. Daras went to Crete also. You know, they're going to be married there. There's nothing to do until they return in a few weeks."

Ipatia was stunned by the news. Tony was all right after all. He and his family were in Crete. She realized now why her phone calls to the house were unanswered.

A burning sensation raged in her chest and consumed her whole body. *How could he leave for Crete without checking on me?*

Ipatia felt faint and leaned on the desk. Trying to regain her calm, she managed to say, "Thank you Rita. I should be going. Have a nice day."

Ipatia entered the waiting car in a daze.

George asked, "Any news?"

"Tony's in Crete with his family."

"What?" George sputtered. "I can't believe it. These young men nowadays have no decency."

On the way home, Ipatia remained quiet, puzzling over one thing. *Why hadn't Tony tried to contact me?*

She voiced her concerns with Paula later in the day.

"Maybe he had a good reason to go to Crete," Paula said. "Sometimes there are things in life we don't have all the information for."

"I don't understand it," Ipatia said, shaking her head. "One minute, he's giving me gifts and asking me out on a date, and the next minute, he's gone to Crete with his family for Easter without a word. It's not right to do that."

"I know, dear, it does sound confusing," Paula said, nodding her head, looking puzzled.

Later in the evening, Ipatia lay in bed thinking about Tony. Like a broken record, she went over everything in her mind once more; the days before the date, the day of the accident, and the days following the accident. Then she remembered the dream she had the night before the date. She now realized how her expectations had arisen. She had been expecting Tony to declare his love for her. *Maybe he doesn't love me. Maybe he just sees me as he does other women. Just a friend.* That would explain his lack of interest the past week, and his leaving for Crete without a note to her. The spider was an omen after all.

Tears streamed down her face, soaking the pillow. Dr. Hatzis's words to Tony at the ship's lounge came back to haunt her. He had been right all along. Tony was a playboy, chasing one woman and dropping the next. Now she had become the next victim, like Bonnie. He was probably busy chasing another woman. Afterwards, she resolved not to think about Tony ever again.

Melissa gazed at her husband's profile. They were seated in the back of the car while Tim drove them to her father's house in Kifissia.

"You look tired, honey," she said. "Why don't you rest first before returning to work?"

"I wish I could," he chortled. "I have to return to the office and deal with some issues I found out about on the trip. If I wait until tomorrow, it may cost the company much money."

They pulled up in front of the house. Melissa kissed Chuck good-bye before getting out of the car.

"I'll try not to be too long," he promised, before speeding off.

Melissa waved to him. He had been helpful these past three weeks, working hard at the shipping agency and traveling on business trips, representing the business. During this time, she and her family battled with Tony's condition.

Planning her marriage had been difficult, but her persistence paid off. Her father didn't want to leave England, and Chuck didn't want to leave Greece. She finally managed to convince Chuck to fly to England, saying how much she missed him.

On a rainy, spring day in England, Melissa exchanged vows with Chuck. After their short honeymoon in Paris, they returned to England to be with Tony and the family. Soon, Chuck wanted to leave for Greece, putting pressure on her.

Melissa talked with her father. "I need to be with my husband in Greece, and besides, what would happen to their business?

"And what will happen to Tony? I cannot do this alone," he replied.

Melissa insisted that her father bring Tony back to Greece, saying she could not remain in England, now that she was married.

Her father finally gave in to her wishes, and they returned to Greece in the middle of May.

Melissa entered Tony's bedroom. She wasn't surprised to find her father there in his wheelchair by the bed, reading a newspaper. He had become Tony's shadow, following him everywhere.

"Where have you been all morning?" Gregory demanded. "The nurse came already and was looking for you. She needed to show you how to do some type of therapy on Tony. I had her show Christina instead."

"That's all right. The nurse will show me tomorrow. Chuck returned from his trip today, and I went to the airport to be with him."

Melissa's eye caught a movement coming from Tony's bed. She ran excitedly to the bed. "Tony. Tony."

His eyelids fluttered, and he slowly opened his eyes.

CHAPTER 33

I leave Greece to be with my aunt,
Your silence, dear, I can't understand.

The days flew by and Ipatia's health returned, but the painful memory of a betrayed love was to remain imprinted in her heart much longer.

Determined to remove any reminder of Tony from her memory, she decided to leave for America.

Her cousins were reluctant to let her go just yet. George was concerned about her welfare. He suggested she remain with them awhile longer to let her wound heal more. But she wasn't swayed. She wanted to get as far away from Greece as she could.

Ipatia telephoned Aunt Sophia to inform her of her plans.

"I'm so happy you're coming," her aunt exclaimed. They discussed the trip in more detail.

With money she had saved from her earnings, Ipatia bought her tickets and prepared for the trip. Paula also helped her shop for gifts and gave her luggage for the trip.

Her grandfather's response to her news was the opposite of Aunt Sophia's.

"Why did you decide suddenly to go on this trip when I specifically told you not to?"

"Aunt Sophia is pregnant," she informed him. "She asked that I go there to help her with the pregnancy."

"And who paid for the tickets?" Christos demanded.

"I saved enough money from my earnings to pay for my tickets," she said proudly.

"And what did George and Paula say about all this?"

"They are fine with it," she said. "Aunt Sophia already knows and is expecting me there soon."

There was a long pause.

"If you feel well enough to go on such a long trip, then so be it," he said finally.

•••———◈ ••———◈ ••———◈

Ipatia gazed out the airplane window, shocked to see the buildings of Chicago's O'Hare Airport covered with a blanket of white snow. She had never seen or touched snow before. She also didn't expect it to snow on a spring day.

Minutes later, Ipatia was relieved when she spotted her aunt and uncle waving at her from among the crowd of people near the entranceway. Her aunt was almost unrecognizable underneath the thick, winter coat and the woolen scarf that circled her hair. They hugged and kissed and everything seemed so much better.

They arrived at the house about an hour later and Ipatia immediately liked the red, brick colonial with its two, white Grecian columns in the front.

"Come, let me get you something to eat," Aunt Sophia chirped, leading her into the large kitchen.

"You didn't have to go to so much trouble, Aunt Sophia," Ipatia said. "I could have helped you."

"Don't you worry about a thing," Aunt Sophia said. "We have cousin Stasoula to thank. She came by and prepared the roast beef for us."

Ipatia looked puzzled.

"Antonios and Stasoula live next door," Uncle John explained. "They have two sons and own a catering business. They're friendly people. You will like them. You have to watch the sons, though. They like to tease."

"They're expecting us at their house tomorrow for dinner," Aunt Sophia said.

After the meal, Ipatia was shown to her room.

The beige carpeted bedroom had large, walk-in closets, the two curtained windows and a bathroom next door.

Ipatia lay awake that night, picturing herself living with her aunt and uncle and attending the university here. They seemed happily married and the house was large enough for them all to live comfortably together.

Ipatia also wondered what Tony was doing in Greece, replaying all sorts of scenes in her mind. A sad feeling descended on her as she recalled hearing the news from Rita that he was in Crete.

The next morning, Ipatia found her aunt in the kitchen reading a magazine. The clock on the wall showed eleven o'clock.

"Good morning. Hope you had a good night's sleep."

"Yes, thank you. The bed was so comfortable that once I fell asleep I had a hard time waking up," Ipatia said.

"You must have been tired also from the trip. By the way, there is toast, boiled eggs and sausages, and the milk and juice are in the refrigerator. Help yourself."

"Thank you," Ipatia said. "Is Uncle John going to join us?"

"You just missed him. He already had his breakfast and then had to go see about a house," Aunt Sophia said. "His business in real estate is such that he has odd hours. I'm still trying to get used to it."

Ipatia chatted with her aunt as she ate her breakfast. Then she talked about the women she met in the hospital and their stories.

"They had all these problems and were still happy," Ipatia said. "I felt my problems were nothing compared to theirs."

"By the way, I've wanted to learn more about how you got into this car accident. George and Paula didn't tell me the details, except that you were with some friends."

"It's a long story, and I'd rather not talk about it, if you don't mind," Ipatia said hurriedly. She didn't feel comfortable relating the story and reliving the pain. She just wanted to forget it.

"Oh, all right," Aunt Sophia said, appearing thoughtful.

Ipatia met her good-natured cousins the following day. Antonios and Stasoula were warm and generous people and gave of their time freely. The boys, Nick and Chris, were older than Ipatia. Nick, who was twenty-two, was finishing his last year of college, while Chris, who was twenty, had decided to work with his parents in the catering business.

The boys quickly took Ipatia under their wing and planned an outing to show her downtown Chicago the following weekend. They visited museums and other sites of interest. With their help, Ipatia slowly put aside the painful memory of a lost love and forge ahead to a new beginning. Soon, her usual joking and laughter returned.

The weeks flew by quickly, and Ipatia submerged herself into her new role helping her aunt with the chores and cooking. After her bouts of morning sickness, Aunt Sophia spent part of the day lying in bed, fatigued. Ipatia also visited her cousins' house often, becoming good friends with Nick and Chris.

One day, Ipatia asked Nick about the universities in the area, and the discussion led to Chicago State University, the university he was attending. Seeing her keen interest, he took her the following day to the campus and showed her around.

"This is a beautiful place," she said, walking alongside him. "What do I have to do to become a student here?"

Nick took her to the admissions office where she obtained helpful information.

"I need a thousand dollars to attend," she said woefully, having read the application form.

"I have an idea," Nick said. "Why don't you work with us in my father's business? You have two months left. You can earn that much, if not more."

Ipatia agreed, and with Nick's guidance, applied to the university.

Antonios's catering business was booming. There was always room for more help. Ipatia worked mostly on the weekends and occasionally during the week. She earned good money when there were several wedding receptions. Ipatia helped prepare the tables, serve the meals, and clean up afterwards.

Ipatia received a letter a few weeks later from the university. The admissions office needed transcripts from her former school, and she had to pass the English examination. She had brought all the papers with her. With Nick's help, she had her transcripts translated, then submitted the required documentation.

The next step was to overcome the task of taking the English examination. After a considerable amount of time and effort, she managed to pass it. Each day, she anxiously searched the mailbox for the acceptance letter from the university. It came one day in early July.

"Aunt Sophia, I got accepted to the university," she shouted, waving the letter at her aunt.

Aunt Sophia was happy for her and hugged her. "Ipatia, we are proud of you. You were determined to get your education," she said. "And you'll make it."

After Ipatia received her acceptance letter, she worked even more hours at her cousin's catering business. She was determined to save every dollar she earned. The work was hard, and often she would come home too exhausted to do anything else except go to sleep. Then she would help her aunt at home, cleaning the house and taking care of errands.

Ipatia was reminded of the work she did on the island. She'd catch herself having negative thoughts while peeling potatoes or stirring a stew. *Is this what I came here for? No, but this will help me get my education.*

When Ipatia received her paycheck and deposited it in the bank, the balance continued to grow, fueling her efforts, pushing her forward, closer towards her goal, and further away from the memory of a broken heart.

Even with her hectic schedule, she was able to attend the local Greek Orthodox church with her aunt and uncle on the rare Sundays that she didn't work. The first time she visited the church, she noticed the Byzantine choral music wafting down from somewhere above her head. She looked up towards the balcony.

"That's the choir," replied Aunt Sophia proudly. "Why don't you join? They're looking for new people."

Ipatia was moved by the choral music. She joined the choir that same day. Later, she wrote a poem describing her experience.

Woven together with the incense-laden air,
These beautiful, soulful melodies
Echoed within the church walls,
Permeating into the recesses of my heart.
Here it was I found peace.

On Ipatia's nineteenth birthday, she had to work for a wedding banquet. She came home later in the day, feeling tired. When she went to rest on the couch, she found an upright piano sitting against the wall in the living room.

"A piano," she exclaimed.

"Happy Birthday, Ipatia," Aunt Sophia said, smiling proudly. "Your uncle found it in one of the houses he was selling. The sellers didn't want it. They said he could have it for free."

Ipatia hugged her aunt, thanking her. She sat down on the bench and began playing cheerful Greek tunes on the piano. She was transported back to Greece, to her grandfather, to the island.

After a few minutes, she switched to classical music. At one point, she began to play Beethoven's 'Fur Elise.' As her fingers glided over the keys, the memory of Tony playing this same song in his father's study intruded her thoughts. The scene that followed, when he kissed her, was hard to ignore.

Ipatia stopped, unable to continue as strong emotions threatened to overwhelm her.

"Please keep playing. It's so beautiful," Aunt Sophia said.

Later that evening, her cousins joined them for dinner and they celebrated Ipatia's birthday. After the meal, her aunt invited her to play the piano for them. She played her favorite songs. She was brought back to reality by the sound of clapping.

"We didn't know you could play so well, Ipatia," Stasoula said, clapping her approval. "We must see about getting you to play at some banquets. They are always looking for someone."

Soon, Ipatia was playing the piano for special events. She started wearing a long black dress for the occasion, pulling her hair back. Her elegance and graceful playing didn't go unnoticed. She was becoming popular and in demand, and she started focusing her energies on her music, playing the piano rather than serving the meals.

The semester finally started, and because of the heavy class load, Ipatia stopped working altogether. The first day of classes, she took a bus to the university and quickly got lost finding her way in the large, sprawling campus. That day was the hardest, as she tried to locate her classrooms. Her courses included Biology, English, Calculus, Physical Education, and Introduction to Philosophy.

The most difficult parts of the courses were the professors' lectures. Her knowledge of the English language did not prepare her for the terminology spoken in the classrooms. Sometimes the professors themselves didn't speak clearly, or oftentimes spoke too quickly for her to comprehend what they were saying.

Whenever Ipatia had free time between her classes, she went to the library and rewrote her notes, trying to decipher what the professor had said. Many times, she came home frustrated, asking for help from her Uncle John or Cousin Nick. They turned out to be great resources.

A few weeks passed, and Ipatia finally settled down to a comfortable routine.

One day in late October, Ipatia walked briskly across the campus headed for the bus stop. A cool breeze ruffled her hair, and the brilliant sun splashed the red and yellow leaves of the trees with brighter hues.

A man passed in front of her, resembling Tony. When he looked her way, her heart beat wildly, then she noticed that he was thinner and his nose was wider. She lowered her eyes when she realized her mistake. He quickly disappeared into a building.

She remembered that Tony had been a professor once. *He is like the professors here, who teach my classes, with students looking up to them, admiring their knowledge, power, and prestige. He is one of them.*

She liked this new image of Tony, which lifted him from the low ranks of a rich, spoiled playboy and into the ranks of a professor. It brought Ipatia a sense of satisfaction. Her eyes had been opened by the books she read, by the knowledge she was gaining, day by day, just as the knowledge he once had at his fingertips. Suddenly she felt much closer to Tony, as though this process of being a student helped her gain insight into his own soul that also thirsted for knowledge.

If only he hadn't left me.

She brushed the moisture from her eyes and hurried towards the bus stop.

That evening, just before going to sleep, she retrieved the little poetry book that Tony had given her and sat on her bed, leafing through it, remembering Tony's words, desperately searching for some clue as to her true feelings for him.

As Ipatia read Byron's words aloud, the strong emotions that ran through her body brought tears to her eyes. She knew just then that he could never be erased from her mind. She slept with it clutched to her bosom.

••————◆ ••——◆ ••————◆

"Tony, it's time for your therapy," Melissa said, bending over and nudging her brother, who was sleeping. She arose, and feeling faint, took a step back to compose herself. Trembling, she went and opened the window, allowing the cool winter breeze to enter the room, ruffling the window curtains.

Melissa took deep breaths as she tried to compose herself. She had confirmed her pregnancy with the doctor a week ago and was not surprised to be experiencing this spell. She heard footsteps in the hallway. It must be Suzie, the housekeeper. She went to the door to call her.

"Hi, Melissa," Bonnie said.

"Bonnie. What a surprise. Weren't you in Paris or something?" Melissa asked, hugging her best friend.

"I returned last night. I passed by your father's house, but no one was there. Then I remembered that you had moved. I looked up your new address in a letter you wrote me recently."

"It's so good to see you."

"I have some good news."

"What is it? Did you meet with the designer you told me about, you know, the one you wanted to work with?"

"Yes, and it turned out I didn't go with him, because he had idiosyncrasies. Anyway, he introduced me to another designer, Pierre, and one thing led to another, and we fell in love. Melissa, I'm going to be married," Bonnie said, lifting up her hand to reveal an engagement ring.

"How wonderful," Melissa exclaimed. "Now I also have some good news to tell you." She told her about her pregnancy.

"Isn't that grand?" Bonnie exclaimed. "Now we can go shopping for the baby's new clothes."

They talked about Bonnie's wedding plans and Melissa's pregnancy. There was a chiming of a clock in the distance.

"I forgot all about Tony," Melissa said, fretting. "I need to wake him up. He has to get up for his physical therapy, and he's already late."

She went back into the room and bent over Tony, speaking to him softly at first, then seeing it didn't work, raised her voice.

Melissa looked down at Tony's handsome profile. The accident hadn't marred any of his handsome features, except for a telltale scar in the upper left corner of his forehead, which was hidden by his locks of hair. *Yet he had changed inside.*

His head injury had left him with amnesia, and he had not recognized his family when he had awakened from his coma. He didn't remember his Greek, and he couldn't read or write, or play the piano. Tony had to relearn everything.

Gregory, shocked by Tony's condition, began in earnest to help in his physical rehabilitation. He was on a mission to restore his son. He hired physical therapists, nurses, and doctors to come and treat Tony. He even paid private tutors to teach Tony how to read and write again.

Only now, months later, was Tony just beginning to understand things and starting to communicate. But he still needed to be guided in his activities and reminded gently of his appointments.

"Hello?" he asked.

Melissa looked at Tony, trying to keep her composure. He said it as if he did not recognize her. She said pertly, "I'm Melissa, your sister, remember? You need to get up because you have to go to therapy, for your walking."

She helped him sit up in bed, trying to remind herself to be patient.

Bonnie looked at him with pity.

Tony sat up in bed. He stared at Bonnie with a puzzled look. His hair was in disarray, and he had a shadow of stubble on his cheeks.

"Hello, Tony," Bonnie said awkwardly.

He nodded his head silently, and then turned his gaze on Melissa, ignoring Bonnie.

"I think he wants to be alone," Melissa said, finally realizing her brother's reluctance to be dressed in front of Bonnie.

They left the room.

"I must be going," Bonnie said awkwardly. "I still have a number of things to do."

"Before you go, I just wanted to let you know we'll be going to Switzerland after the holidays. Father felt the whole family needed to get away."

"How long will you be gone?"

"I won't stay long because Chuck has to be back at work, but Tony will probably stay there much longer with Father," Melissa said.

Before Bonnie left, they arranged a date to go shopping.

Melissa held Tony as he arose, steadying him. She led him to the bathroom to wash and shave, reminding him that he needed to soap his face first before shaving. Then, she grabbed his shirt and pants from the closet and helped him get dressed. She slipped the coat on him.

"Now you have to go to your therapy."

Tony arose, and Melissa led him to Tim, who was waiting outside to drive him to his therapy session.

CHAPTER 34

An independent man I want to be
To let go and build a family.

One day in December, when Ipatia returned home from classes, she found her aunt clutching her stomach. The color had drained from her face, making her look sickly and pale.

Ipatia rushed to her side. "Are you all right, Aunt Sophia?"

"I think the baby is coming," Aunt Sophia said, breathing heavily. "Can you call your uncle to come right away?"

Ipatia's fingers fumbled as she dialed Uncle John's number.

He dropped everything and came immediately.

Twelve hours later, Aunt Sophia gave birth to a beautiful healthy baby boy named Alexander.

A few days later, when Aunt Sophia entered the house with the baby, everyone hovered around them, admiring the beautiful baby. It also became a trial for everyone. The baby kept waking up in the wee hours of the night, crying and sputtering. The next day, he slept straight through the day, giving his mother a chance to catch up on her sleep. Then, again, he woke in the middle of the night.

It took several weeks before the baby's sleep schedule was synchronized with everyone else's.

"May I hold him?" Ipatia asked one day after she came home from school.

Aunt Sophia handed her the bundled baby.

Ipatia held him carefully, studying his small features, his uniqueness, and his vulnerability. He trusted her completely. He smiled when she teased his lips with her small finger. He opened his mouth wide.

"How does it feel?" Sophia asked, beaming proudly.

"It's a wonderful feeling," Ipatia said, smiling down at him and cooing at him. She touched the baby's cheeks lightly. He stretched delightfully and gave her a wide grin. "There he goes again, smiling at me."

"I hope your studies aren't suffering because of the baby," Aunt Sophia said.

"Don't worry," Ipatia said. "Upstairs, it's quiet when I shut the door to study."

Ipatia's duties were twofold now. Not only was she studying, but she was also spending much time with the baby. Even with all her workload, Ipatia did well in her courses. She passed them with high marks, amazing both her aunt and uncle.

The spring semester went by quickly and Ipatia finished her first year in college. The summer arrived with all its glory, hot and muggy.

Ipatia worked with her cousins that summer and saved more money for college. She also continued to play the piano at the banquets whenever there was a request for music.

Ipatia's twentieth birthday marked the beginning of the next school year. As a sophomore, she was familiar with the campus and her English had improved considerably. That year, she also signed up for a computer course and enjoyed it tremendously.

Besides the formal education she was receiving from her courses, the university also taught her another kind of education, one that did not need books but came from experiencing life.

The students at the university were from heterogeneous backgrounds, ranging from Americans to foreign students from other countries; there were various religions and cultures; and there were liberal thinkers and conservative thinkers.

One day in December, Sheila, a classmate in her philosophy class, asked her to join her and some friends to attend a party on the university campus.

Ipatia hesitated.

"Come on, don't be so prim and proper. You're living in America now."

The party was on a Friday night and Ipatia attended more out of curiosity than anything else. She had made plans for her uncle to pick her up at nine o'clock. The large, banquet room was on campus and a band played rock and roll music on the stage. She joined Sheila and her friends at a table and ate refreshments and listened to the music.

Eventually, Sheila invited some young men to their table, and they sat there, chatting with them.

Ipatia smiled politely when the young men talked with her, trying to draw her in, but she noticed that they didn't say anything of importance. She felt different from them as though she were their chaperone.

After some time had passed, one of the young men rose. "Let's go to my apartment. There is better action there," he said slyly.

Her friends complied, but Ipatia didn't feel comfortable and did not go with them, giving them the excuse that her uncle was going to pick her up any minute.

After that day, Ipatia avoided spending time with the girls, finding excuses of having much studying to do.

The cold winter days rolled into spring semester. One day in March, a young man asked Ipatia out on a date.

"No," she said.

Another one in another class asked her if she would like to go to Florida for spring break, and again she flatly refused.

These overtures happened enough times to shake Ipatia's naïve assumptions about people. She learned to be more cautious around the college students. They were raised in a different environment, where there were no boundaries, and people dated casually. This was a world where "anything goes."

Over time, Ipatia's cheerful, outgoing personality was replaced with a cautious, reserved outlook towards the young men and women on campus, waiting to see what their character revealed before she opened up to them.

Spring break came and Ipatia spent it quietly with her relatives, enjoying the baby and playing the piano.

She wrote a letter to her grandfather and her cousins, describing her life. She wrote about the various holidays and how they differed from those in Greece. For Easter, not all the businesses were closed, as in Greece. She had to attend classes on Good Friday. Then there were new holidays, like Thanksgiving and Labor Day.

***

Ipatia passed through her second year of college with excellent grades, and soon, May loomed ahead, marking the end of the school semester. One weekend, Ipatia was in the living room, studying for her final exams. Aunt Sophia was sitting nearby, sewing.

"*Tia. Tia.*"

Ipatia looked up from her studies. Being a little over a year old, little Alexander was teetering, holding on tight to the side of the couch. His pudgy face was scrunched up and his large brown eyes pleaded with her. He grasped the edge of the couch, swaying, as his feet fumbled their way to her. She held out her arm and he took it. They walked slowly together. He looked so proud of his accomplishment, giggling joyfully.

"Ipatia, you would make a good mother," Aunt Sophia said, smiling.

CHAPTER 35

Now that I'm well again
A new life will I begin.

Someone knocked on Tony's door on a Friday morning in May.

"Come in," Tony said, buttoning his shirt.

Christina opened the door and peeked in. "Good morning."

"Good morning, Christina. Thank you for the reminder, but you don't need to wake me up anymore. I know Jon is here. I know you have an appointment to go to with Father, and I also know that my birthday is today. I am thirty-three years old today, am I not?"

"Yes, to everything," Christina said. "I am pleased at your progress as is your father." She kissed him lightly on the cheek and said, "Happy birthday, Tony."

After she left, he thought about her and how helpful she had been to him the past two years. She had also become his father's right arm.

Tony walked down the hallway, whistling. He met Jon, his Swiss physical trainer, in the gym room. The gym, built for Tony, had tall windows surrounding it, allowing plenty of sunshine into the room and breathtaking views of Switzerland's mountains. Exercise equipment placed around the room had aided him in his rehabilitation. He sat on the padded bench, listening to the trainer's suggestions, and then began his routine of exercises.

After several sessions, Tony arose, feeling a little sore, yet content. He took a towel from the rack and wiped the sweat from his face and body.

"I am pleased with your progress," Jon said, smiling, as he put away the equipment.

"I want to thank you for all your help this past year. Now I can do just about anything. Is that right?"

"You are officially healthy, and I think ready for the Olympics as far as I'm concerned. You've worked hard, and we have seen great improvements."

"Thanks to you," Tony said, rubbing his biceps.

"What do you plan to do after this?"

"Return to Greece. Maybe go into business for myself."

"Meanwhile, continue to do your exercises on your own," Jon said. "And don't forget to stretch before and after the exercises."

After Jon left, Tony took a shower, then dressed into a casual outfit. A year ago, he needed the help of a nurse to do these activities. This affected his sense of dignity, and his pride stepped in. Instead of the twenty exercises he had to do, he would force himself to do thirty, then forty. Pushing himself to the point of pain, he kept telling himself that the daily exercises and routines were his tickets to freedom.

His motivation to improve, and the determination to succeed, helped him through the laborious process of rebuilding his body and mind. He read countless books in English and Greek, business journals, and newspapers. He even attended medical lectures whenever the opportunity arose.

He could recite poems in Greek and English, play the piano passably well, sing Greek songs, and knew how to use the computer.

His phenomenal achievements had impressed his doctors, nurses, and family.

Tony whistled as he combed his hair. There was still some soreness in his movements, but he learned to tune it out.

In the afternoon, he found his father sitting outside in his wheelchair with a blanket over his knees. The chalet was nestled high on a mountain and the view was spectacular from here.

"Ah, here you are," Gregory said, looking up from his reading.

"Today was the last session with Jon, the therapist. I've more than accomplished all my goals."

"That's good," Gregory said, lifting his eyebrows. "Then you will come to Crete with us next week?"

"I don't plan on returning to Crete with you."

"What's this?"

"I appreciate all you've done for me ever since my accident, and I don't think I would be where I am without your help," Tony said firmly. "However, I have had many hours to sit and contemplate about life, and about where I am going. I feel as though I've been a burden to you and Christina. I need to go on with my life, as you need to go on with yours."

"Are you planning to join Chuck in the business?"

"Chuck is doing well with the shipping company. The computer system is up and running, saving us time. I don't want to go in and upset that," Tony said.

"Will you return to your teaching?" Gregory asked.

"I toyed with that idea, but it seems too arduous at the moment. I want to remain in Greece, invest my money, the money I earned from teaching to buy property."

"Property?" Gregory asked, bewildered.

"Yes, buy a few villas or a few commercial buildings, fix them up and sell them or even lease them out."

Gregory looked keenly at his son as he expounded his idea. They discussed the pros and cons.

"It appears that you know what you are talking about. But you can do all that in Crete."

"I know, but you see, Father, you want me by your side all the time. I can't do that anymore," Tony said tensely. "I want to be my own man. It's impossible to accomplish that when you are making decisions for me."

A week later, Tony left Switzerland, with its snow-capped mountains and chalets and arrived in Greece, feeling wonderfully alive. He was a whole man and was grateful for his father's help, and for the respite, treatment, and rehabilitation that had been provided there. At the same time, he was excited to be on his own.

He took a taxi and visited Melissa's new home in Kifissia.

He arrived late morning and found Melissa busy feeding her baby. Chuck was away on a business trip. He spent some time with Melissa, discussing things and telling her his plans.

"You want to buy villas and properties, and rent them out?" she asked him, looking incredulous. "This is not at all like you, to go into business for yourself. What about working with Chuck or teaching at the university?"

"I've had considerable time thinking this past year and came to an important realization." He paused, trying to gather his thoughts together. "All my life, I had depended on Father to help me, and even more so these past few years. Now, I have decided that I want to remain in Greece and be my own boss."

"Is it so bad that Father wants to help you?" she asked. "He would do anything to see you get ahead."

"Father won't always be here, and I've got to prove to myself that I can stand on my two feet."

"Do you have the money for what you want to do?"

"Yes. I have enough to get started and plenty more saved in case I need it."

"Where do you plan to live?"

"I haven't thought about it."

"You can live with us for now," Melissa began, wiping the baby's face with a napkin.

"Thank you," he said, pecking her playfully on the cheek. He enjoyed watching Melissa play with little Gregory. He joined them, laughing at their antics.

That evening, when Chuck came home from work, he spent time with Tony, discussing various topics. Tony found out that

Chuck also had property and had considerable knowledge of real estate.

"That is how I got started in the shipping industry," Chuck said. "Through real estate."

The next few days, however, the house did not provide Tony any peace. The baby cried often, causing all kinds of commotion. Also, Melissa's next-door neighbor, Marina, and some friends kept popping in for coffee. Soon they were bringing their daughters with them.

A few days later, Tony met Sara, a friend of Melissa's who joined them for dinner. She was attractive and charming and made him smile. Something about her reminded him of his past, maybe her smile or impish look. Yet he felt that he wasn't ready for a relationship.

Whenever Tim drove Tony in the family car, a terrible knot formed in Tony's chest, especially whenever a car honked at them. Slowly, the burning, fearful feeling faded away, and one day, Tony drummed up enough courage to ask Tim for the keys to the family car. He practiced his driving faithfully, with Tim sitting in the passenger seat. In a short time, he mastered the technique and felt confident driving in the streets alone.

The next thing to do was to buy a new car.

His new car gave him even more freedom to move around. He was beginning to feel more in control of his life, driving around to several real estate properties, developing his business plan.

Sara began coming over more often, and he was beginning to feel comfortable with her. Over time, he noticed she had two sides to her, the charming, happy side and the moody, quiet side, as though she were hiding something. Her moods began when she started hinting about marriage. He told her he needed time to establish himself first in his business before he could commit himself seriously to marriage.

As the weeks passed, Tony felt he could no longer live in his sister's house. The baby's noise and the interfering mothers and daughters left him no peace. He began to search in earnest for a new home, trying to find the idea of marriage and family more attractive. Even though he had no wife, at least if he had a home, maybe a wife could come later.

He finally decided to build his own house. He purchased a piece of property on the outskirts of Glyfada. The land was on a hill, overlooking the sea. He hired a construction company and worked out some floor plans with them. Month by month, he watched as the villa slowly took shape.

In early August, Melissa received word from her father that he and Christina were returning to Athens. He wasn't feeling well.

Several days later, Melissa went to the airport to meet them.

"Father, Christina, it's so nice to see you again," Melissa exclaimed, greeting them as they exited the airport. She had brought little Gregory with her.

"How's my little Gregory doing?" Gregory asked, planting a kiss on the toddler's rosy cheek. He was rewarded with a bright smile.

After picking up the luggage, they drove home talking about everything.

"How have you been, Father?"

"Not well," he admitted. "I feel as though I'm deteriorating. My right hand is shaking all the time. I can't write or hold a spoon anymore. Anyway, I want you to make an appointment for me in Chicago so I can be tested."

"All right, Father."

"How's Tony?" Gregory asked.

"He's doing well with his business. He's building a house for himself in Glyfada."

"That's a nice area. It sounds promising," Gregory said, nodding. "Is there a bride in the picture?"

"You remember my mentioning to you about Sara, the banker's daughter? She lives next door. Tony's been dawdling with her, like he did Bonnie. She's been talking about marriage, but he's been slow in going to the altar. I don't know what his plans are with her."

"He's like me," Gregory said thoughtfully. "I was stubborn like him when it came to marrying, but when the right girl came along, there was no holding me back."

They had lunch at Melissa's house and then left for their home, which was a half hour away.

Melissa made an appointment for her father and arranged for his trip to the hospital in Chicago. Two weeks later, Gregory went there to be tested. Although his tests came out normal, after his return to Athens two weeks later, he consulted with his lawyers. The result was the writing of a will. The attorneys also suggested putting some of that money towards a foundation. He balked at the idea first and then decided to talk with his son.

A few days later, Gregory met with Tony. "Son, what would you think about starting a foundation?" he asked.

"It sounds interesting to me. What made you decide on it in the first place?"

"My attorneys thought of it," Gregory said, chuckling. "They said some of my profits should be slated towards a good cause."

"You mean for a tax break?"

They both laughed.

"All joking aside. I truly am for it," Tony said.

"I knew you would, with your philanthropic nature," Gregory said. "You were always one for helping others."

They discussed the foundation further, deciding on its mission and where they would allocate the resources.

Tony contacted the attorneys later that day and started the legal process.

CHAPTER 36

A memory, so sweet and fair,
A mystery unfolds, do I dare?

They named the foundation "Kalkinon Foundation," and its goal was to fund cancer research and help cancer patients who were unable to pay for their cancer treatment. By the end of the year, the foundation was finally formalized.

Upon the guidance of the attorneys, Tony became its president officially on December 10. His sister became the treasurer. A storage room in their office building, designated for the foundation, provided a physical location.

They hired a secretary and bookkeeper to help its operations.

Once this was accomplished, Tony telephoned his father in Crete and told him, "The Kalkinon Foundation is up and running. I am officially the president."

"Good work, son. The first place I want to make a donation to is the hospital in Chicago, where I had my surgery."

Soon, Tony was receiving letters from the hospital thanking them for their contributions. One day in February, Tony read about the hospital's plans to build a new cancer center. The hospital was desperately seeking funding for the center. He spoke to his father about donating funds. He suggested a dollar amount.

"What do you think, ten million dollars grows on trees?" Gregory growled.

"I am offering to pay half of that if you pitch in the other half. I know this is a drop in the bucket for you."

"A very large drop at that. Let me think about it," Gregory said before hanging up the telephone.

It took his father a couple of weeks before he agreed to do it. The contribution was dutifully sent out after that to the hospital.

***

By the end of March, Tony had finished building his house.

The two-story, spacious villa sat high on a hill. It had Grecian columns on the front, and in the back, a large swimming pool, and a verandah with a view of the sea.

Tony walked inside the empty rooms, his footsteps echoing loudly against the marble floors. The high ceilings and open floor plan gave him a sense of open space. Almost every room had a fireplace.

Afterwards, he sat outside, gazing at the sea below, listening to the sound of the waves lapping rhythmically against the rocks. A melancholy enveloped him, pulling him down.

Something was missing.

Maybe the house needed to be furnished. It needed character, a life of its own. Melissa could help with that part. She was good with those things. He telephoned his sister but she wasn't home.

Tony had to shake off this depressed feeling. One way to do that was to go to his father's house in Kifissia and gather his belongings together and start preparing for the move to the new house.

He drove to his father's house. He had been here once before but had not returned after he realized that he had no memories of it. His father had mentioned that he could live there, but Tony wanted to make a fresh start.

It was empty, like a deserted shell. Melissa had moved to her new home on the other side of Kifissia and his father spent most of his time in Crete. Gilda only came when his father was visiting, and Tim had become Melissa's chauffeur now.

Tony went into his bedroom and started rummaging through his closet. He found custom-tailored business suits, designer shirts, and expensive silk ties. He piled them all on the bed. They seemed foreign to him as though another Tony had worn them once.

The closet was empty except for a bag stashed in the back. Curious, he removed its contents. The tattered shirt inside was covered with dried bloodstains. The shirt was beyond repair. *It must have been worn on the day of my accident.*

His hands felt clammy and his breathing became shallow, as he stood there, trying to recall the car accident. *I can't remember anything.* He tossed it aside, feeling frustrated.

Next, came the pair of pants. They also were bloodstained and Tony was about to toss them aside, when he noticed something bulging from inside one of the pant pockets. His fingers pulled out a small jewelry box. He opened it. Inside was a gold ring with a magnificent, green gemstone.

"Whew," he exclaimed, gazing admirably at the jeweled ring. His heart started racing as he noticed its small size, suitable for a woman. Why was it in his pocket the day of the accident? *Who was it for? Was this an engagement ring?*

Tony shook his head, touching his forehead, feeling a headache coming on. His family had not mentioned anything about an engagement, nor did any woman come forth.

Feeling perplexed, Tony still couldn't remember the details leading up to the accident. Questions that he had been unable to answer were now coming back to haunt him. Why was he going up the mountain that day, right before the trip to Crete, and why hadn't his family known about it?

Prompted by the mystery of the ring and his curiosity, he went through the drawers, taking everything out, mindful of any clue that could help him solve this puzzle. His movements were like that of a thirsty man searching for that single glass of water that would satisfy his thirst. At one point, a piece of paper fluttered out of some clothes. He stooped to pick it up.

His heart quickened as he read the note, signed by Ipatia. The person who wrote it had lovely, delicate handwriting, thanking him for everything he had done.

"Ipatia," he said softly.

That was an unusual and pretty name. *Who was she?* Why did she say that she had to leave? Why didn't her name strike a memory chord in his mind?

He didn't remember any Ipatia.

Feeling perplexed, Tony folded the paper and placed it in his pocket. This will have to wait. His headache had gotten worse.

The bookshelves were next. All kinds of books, ranging from economics to art to philosophy were there. He wondered whether he had read them all. Once he was settled, he was going to go through them and read them. He diligently stacked them together, and then carried them to the trunk of the car.

He worked steadily, filling the car slowly with books and clothes. When he had finished, the bedroom appeared like an empty seashell deserted by its occupant, a hollow reminder of another time. It held no memories for him.

Something spurred him to look under the bed. He found a pile of letters from old friends, held together by a rubber band. He didn't recognize anyone's name. He will have to go through them another time. They will help him juggle his memory.

He drove back to his home in Glyfada.

Tony returned to his sister's later in the evening to find Melissa and Chuck having dinner.

"You came just in time," Chuck said, wiping his mouth. "We got hungry, so I hope you don't mind that we started before you."

"No problem," Tony said. "I admit I'm a little hungry myself." He sat down and joined them.

The meal consisted of roasted chicken and potatoes, moussaka, baked green beans, olives, and bread.

"How's your villa coming along?" asked Chuck.

Tony talked about his villa, and Melissa cheerfully piped in, advising him on what type of furniture he should buy.

Then he talked about his discovery when moving his belongings from their parent's house to the villa. "Tell me, Melissa, do you know of a person by the name of Ipatia?"

"Ipatia?" she asked, staring at him.

"I found a note written to me by an Ipatia," he said, becoming slightly agitated. His little sister wasn't making it easy.

"Oh, yes. She was just an island girl you met in Lipsi Island the one summer we got stuck in a storm and had to stay there."

"There's one other thing your sister didn't mention," Chuck said wryly. "Ipatia knew English, and you had her working at the office, translating your documents for you into Greek."

"Is that right?" Tony asked ruefully, shaking his head. "I don't remember her."

Melissa smiled sweetly at him. "There probably wasn't much to remember."

Tony had learned to read Melissa's actions over time and had found that she wasn't always honest with him. Her words jarred with something inside him. He suddenly realized now why he hadn't been told about Ipatia. He became cautious and decided not to mention the engagement ring. His intuition told him they wouldn't know about it. Instead, he changed the topic.

"Did Sara come by today?" he asked.

"Yes, she did, and she was asking about you," Melissa said lightly. "Sara is a good catch. She's not only pretty but she's rolling in money. Her father owns several banks."

"Melissa, I don't think you should interfere in Tony's personal life," Chuck said, somewhat jokingly.

"That's all right, Chuck," Tony said, laughing. "Melissa probably thinks that money will buy me happiness. For your information, I need to find out more about what happened to Ipatia before I continue any relationship with Sara."

That evening, Tony sat in his room, thinking about Ipatia's personal note and the gemstone ring. Who did the engagement ring belong to? Could it be linked to her? Why couldn't he remember her? What happened to her and why hadn't she come forth all these years to see him?

Tired from all the unanswered questions, Tony focused his thoughts on Sara. He realized how Melissa had subtly pushed this relationship on him. It dawned on him that Sara's wealth was probably the reason why Melissa had her as a friend. During these last months, as their relationship blossomed, and construction of the villa was becoming finalized, Sara had hinted that there was more to their relationship than just friendship. He had entertained the idea of sharing the rest of his life with her.

But how could he promise her, or anyone else, anything, when he had bought the engagement ring for someone else? His heart had not revealed itself yet. He needed to find answers.

The next day, Sara visited Melissa. She had brought with her a nail manicure set and was filing her nails while talking with Melissa.

They began talking about Tony.

"I need to tell you something about Tony," Melissa said. "You know that he had amnesia once. Well, there's an old flame in his life, Ipatia Kouris, whose name he recently came across. I don't know how much he remembers, and I don't want to see you hurt."

"Ipatia Kouris?" Sara asked. "Somehow that name sounds familiar. Was it serious?"

"I can't say, but he's interested in finding out more about her. Her father, Captain Manolis Kouris, used to work for my father," Melissa said importantly.

That evening, Sara mentioned Kouris's name to her father, asking him whether he could check to see if any of his accounts were with any of their banks.

A few weeks later, Tony walked into Michael's office, wondering whether it was the right thing to do. He got his answer quickly.

"Tony," Michael exclaimed, greeting him wholeheartedly. "How long has it been? Three years?"

"I'm sorry I didn't visit you sooner, Michael, but I was too busy rebuilding my life," Tony admitted, studying him. He seemed friendly enough.

"Sit down, my friend. Would you like something to drink?"

"No thanks," Tony said, sitting down in the chair.

Michael smiled and began to reminisce about the past, but Tony stopped him.

"It's no use talking to me about the past," Tony said apologetically. "You see, I had amnesia due to a car accident. I have no memory of what happened before the accident, of you or anyone else. I came across your name accidentally the other day, when I was going through a pile of old letters."

"Oh. I am sorry to hear that," Michael said, sobered by the news.

"When I asked Melissa about you, she told me where I could find you. She didn't seem happy."

"It's understandable. Your sister and I were once engaged to be married. But that's in the past now. I married a year ago."

"Congratulations."

"You had an excuse for not coming to see me because of the amnesia, but I must apologize for not keeping in touch."

"Why do you say that?"

"After I found out that Ipatia was in love with you, I decided not to come between you two, so I kept away. You see, I had been interested in her for myself."

"Ipatia?" Tony asked. He sat there, feeling stunned. *Why didn't my family tell me about her?*

"Ipatia, the island girl."

"The island girl." Tony racked his brain, trying to remember her. He shook his head. "I don't remember her."

"You don't?" Michael asked, looking surprised. "I guess the amnesia *was* severe."

"Michael, tell me about her. How did I meet her? What did she look like?" Tony asked eagerly. His emotions were mixed. He was excited to hear about her but perplexed why she had become such an enigma.

"She was tall and slim, with long, golden brown hair, and large, hazel-green eyes. She was beautiful and came from the island of Lipsi, where we met her. She moved here and lived with her aunt right around the corner from here, but last I heard, she had moved to the other side of town with her cousins."

Tony thought for a moment, shutting his eyes. "If only I had known sooner."

"I suppose no one in your family told you," Michael said dryly. "Are you seeing anyone?"

"Yes," Tony said, nodding his head heavily. "Sara lives next door to my sister's house and has been pressuring me for marriage, but something has held me back."

"Ah, I see now," Michael said. "Maybe you aren't in love with her."

"Michael, I was in love with Ipatia, wasn't I? I can just feel it," Tony said, looking helpless. "The problem is, I don't remember her, or know what happened to her. She just vanished."

Michael nodded thoughtfully. "I distinctly recall that she talked constantly about going to the university," he said. "She had been reading medical journals of mine, showing interest in the medical field. I gather, if anything, that she may be at some university, studying towards her degree."

"I see," Tony said, juggling his memory. The girl had been more intent on an education rather than marriage. He still felt fuzzy in his mind about her, but what Michael was saying was beginning to make sense. Ipatia's plan to enter college might be the missing piece to the puzzle.

A young, attractive woman with green eyes and brown hair entered the office. Tony gazed at her inquisitively. She resembled Michael's description of Ipatia.

Michael went to the woman and hugged her and introduced her. "Tony, I'd like you to meet my wife, Betsy."

Tony secretly wondered whether Michael had chosen his wife because she looked similar to Ipatia.

The conversation shifted to the newlyweds.

A few hours later, as he made his farewell, Tony invited them to visit him at his villa the following Sunday.

That evening, Tony rested on his off-white couch in his villa, thinking about the conversation with Michael. Soft, classical music from the stereo system drifted through the house, competing with the sound of the waves outside, as he searched in his mind, going over all the events, trying to piece the puzzle together. The notes that spilled into the room caressed his mind, stroking it, kneading it, coaxing it to come forth with the answers.

Tony stopped thinking for a moment, enraptured by the music. Something about this composition reminded him of Ipatia. After it finished, the radio announcer named it, "Beethoven's Fur Elise."

Tony's heart pounded in his chest when he heard it. *I know this piece. Intimately.* He bolted up as the image of him playing this piece on the piano entered his mind. He had played it for Ipatia. He began pacing the room excitedly as images upon images raced through his mind: Ipatia hanging from the tree, her long hair dancing in the wind as he pushed the snake away. Ipatia running away from him with her donkey. Eating *loukoumathes* with Ipatia and laughing. Ipatia dressed in business attire, working in the office.

Then he paused, staring out as if in a trance, recalling the ring he found in his pants. "Think, Tony," he said aloud. The image of Ipatia handing him the gemstone came to his mind. *Yes, now I remember.* Ipatia's gift to him was the gemstone, in return for the book he found. Tony had converted the beautiful gem into a ring, with the intention of presenting it to her as an engagement ring. The ring was a promise, a seal of his love.

Tony felt an incredible, happy feeling, lifting him to giddy heights. He floated in an ethereal cloud of joy for a while, thinking about Ipatia. *She had made me happy. I am sure of this.*

Then a sobering question ruptured the joy and Tony began to descend from the clouds. *What happened to her?*

More disturbing questions reappeared, pulling him down to reality. He continued his pacing, troubled by questions that still needed to be answered.

•• —— ◈ •• ◈ •• ——◈

The next day, in a desperate attempt to piece together this troubling puzzle of his past, Tony drove to Mt. Hymettus, the same mountain where he had his accident. Maybe by coming here, he could remember what happened.

He chose to come during the middle of the afternoon, when there was little traffic. He parked the car in a safe spot, further down the road.

Walking towards the edge of the curving road, Tony stopped and gazed at the scene below him. The police had told him that he had swerved his wheel to avoid headlong collision with the other car and had careened down the slope and into the woods. His car had rammed into one of the trees in the woods, causing his injuries.

He carefully made his way down the steep slope, and then looked around, hoping to remember something, anything. He found the tree that had the marks from the car's collision, and even a few pieces of glass nearby, evident signs of the car accident.

His eyes desperately combed the area, searching for any clues of Ipatia, maybe a purse or a wallet. An hour later, he came up empty-handed. He probed further in the forest, continuing his search, not wanting to give up.

As the sun began to set, Tony knew that he needed to leave before it became dark. Feeling disappointed, he turned, heading back. Along the way, he must have chosen a wrong turn, for he became lost.

He forged ahead and recognized the area. Moving forward, he glimpsed a flash of color among the bushes to his left, and then it disappeared again. He moved closer to have a look.

It turned out to be a woman's lace shawl caught between the branches of the bush. *Was it possible this shawl belonged to Ipatia?* His heart raced as his trembling fingers managed to untangle the tattered shawl from the bush.

As he stroked it, wondering how it got caught in the bush, the answer presented itself in a flash. In his mind, he could see a woman wearing this shawl and sitting in the car with him. The woman's face was not clear. *It had to be Ipatia who had worn the shawl and had been in the car with me. After the accident, the wind must have carried it away.* But what happened to her?

A searing fear that Ipatia might not have survived the accident overcame him. Deep feelings for her, buried all this time, rushed to the surface. *My dearest, sweet Ipatia. How can I live with myself, knowing that I caused your death?* Emitting an anguished cry, he buried his face in the shawl, his tears flowing uncontrollably.

With heavy heart, he trudged back to the car.

CHAPTER 37

My love for you, a door that closed,
The truth unlocks the door once more.

The next day, still troubled over Ipatia's shawl and her disappearance, Tony decided that he must find out what happened to her. She had worked in the office. Someone there might know what happened to the girl. He had avoided going there after the accident, feeling awkward that he couldn't remember anyone.

With a single-minded purpose, Tony scrapped his fears, determined to find out what had happened to the girl.

He remembered where the office was. Tim used to point it out to him whenever they would pass by.

Rita greeted him warmly, chatting away as though they were the best of friends.

"I know this may be awkward for you," he said interrupting her midstream, "but I had amnesia from the car accident, and I don't remember you at all or any of the people you are talking about."

Rita nodded understandably. "Your sister had mentioned something. I'm Rita." She told him what her job was. "We've missed you, Mr. Tony and hope you are doing better."

"Thank you. The real reason I came was to find out what happened to Ipatia. I understand that she used to work here. Have you heard from her?"

Rita's eyes opened wide. "The last time I saw her was four years ago, the day after Easter Sunday, around the time of your accident," she said, shaking her head apologetically.

Tony's heart soared with joy. "Are you sure?"

"Yes," Rita said emphatically. "She came to the office, and I remember we talked about how we spent our Easter. She mentioned that she spent it quietly with her cousins. I assumed she had returned that day to work, and I told her you had gone to Crete, so there was no more work for her. I told her to return in a few weeks when everyone was back from Crete. She thanked me and left and didn't return."

"Didn't you know about my accident?"

"No, I'm afraid not," Rita said, sighing. "I learned about it afterwards. Mr. Gregory didn't want us to know right away."

"One more thing. How did she look?" he asked. He had a gut feeling that he was about to find the truth.

"What do you mean?"

"Was she limping or did she look sick in any way, maybe a bruise here or there?" he asked.

Rita appeared thoughtful. "You know, now that you ask me, I remember thinking that she was going to faint on me. Also, one side of her face, around the eye, was a little swollen."

Stunned by the revelation, Tony's mind furiously pieced everything together. He stood there, deep in thought. *Ipatia was alive.* He was sure of that. Her injuries were not as severe as his were, so she had been transported to one hospital, while he had been flown to another. When Ipatia returned to work and learned from Rita that he was in Crete, and there was no work for her, she had left.

He figured that Ipatia had been upset enough to leave and not try to contact him all these years. All because his father didn't want anyone knowing about the accident.

"Are you all right? I'm sorry if I said anything wrong," Rita said anxiously, interrupting his thoughts.

Tony stared at her, coming back to reality. He noticed her concerned look and smiled. "No, don't feel bad. You helped me more than you know," he said reassuringly.

Rita smiled. "Are you returning to work?" she ventured to ask. "Everyone's been asking about you."

"Thank you for your interest," he said. "But Chuck is in command now. I've got my own business now."

He whistled as he flew down the stairs.

"I tell you, it's true, Father," Melissa said, pacing the kitchen, talking on the telephone. "Captain Kouris had accumulated a considerable amount of money. He had a dowry in the way of a trust, now worth over sixty thousand American dollars in Ipatia's name, to be withdrawn only in the case of marriage. Sara's father told me himself."

"Why is money so important to you?" Gregory asked.

"Father. *You're* the one who used to extol the virtues of money."

"Yes, money is important, but it isn't everything."

"Now that Ipatia has money, Tony can think about marrying her."

"Now you listen here, Melissa. Tony knows what he's doing, and it's about time you stopped meddling into his affairs. If he's in love with the girl, whether she has one dollar or sixty thousand dollars, it won't make a difference to him. I married your mother because I loved her, not because of her money, and if I hadn't married her, you wouldn't even be here today. Never forget that."

The following Sunday marked the beginning of April. Tony waited for Michael and Betsy to arrive, having prepared for the occasion by hiring a cook. The scents from the kitchen had permeated the house, giving it a warm, cozy feeling.

The doorbell rang and Tony eagerly went to greet them. "Michael, Betsy," Tony said, happy to see them.

They sat down to a pleasant dinner. After the meal, the couple shared their happy news with Tony.

"Congratulations. When are you expecting?" Tony asked.

"Sometime in November," said Betsy, smiling.

"We just learned this morning, so you're the first to know, old friend," Michael said. "We'd like you to be the baby's godfather."

Tony was stunned, realizing what good friends they must have been in the past, for Michael to entrust him with that honor. "Thank you. I am truly honored," he said. "I'd be more than happy to do it."

The conversation continued for a while, and then Betsy became pale and touched her stomach.

"Are you all right?" Tony asked.

Betsy nodded.

"She's fine," Michael said, touching her arm reassuringly. "She gets these spells. It's a phase of the pregnancy that she's experiencing."

Betsy smiled at Michael, then looked at Tony. "If you'll excuse me, I'd like to rest a little."

Tony showed her to the living room where she rested on the couch. After returning to the dining room, he conversed with Michael, putting the pieces of his past together.

"Have you heard anything about Ipatia recently?" he asked Michael.

"Now that you reminded me of it, George and Paula Mastroyiannis paid me a visit recently," Michael said.

"Who are they?"

"They are Ipatia's cousins and patients of mine. Typically, before trips, they would come and get prescriptions filled by me. This time they were on their way to Spain."

"Did they say anything about Ipatia, where she lives?"

"Yes, as a matter of fact, they mentioned that she lives in America, in a suburb of Chicago, with her aunt and uncle, John and Sophia Stavrakis."

"Chicago?" Tony asked. Was it fate or a coincidence that they would be there? His father had gone to Chicago for treatment and the Kalkinon Foundation had given money to the hospital there.

Michael nodded ruefully. "I'm afraid so."

"Did they mention an address or a telephone number?"

"To be honest, I wasn't thinking along those lines, now that I'm a married man," Michael said apologetically. "They did say that she is graduating soon from a university in Chicago, with a degree in microbiology."

"Ah yes, the infamous degree that she chose over marriage," Tony said, sighing.

"Mrs. Rodos, the English teacher might know more about Ipatia. She lives right down the block from my office."

A few days later, Tony received a letter from the hospital in Chicago. He read it aloud, "We are grateful for the ten-million-dollar donation and invite you to a banquet to be held in honor of the Kalkinon Foundation, on June 26, 1993. Dignitaries will be present."

This was just the thing I needed.

Tony had spoken to Mrs. Rodos and found out where Ipatia lived. He had planned to go to Ipatia's house and knock on the door. Or was it that simple? How would she react after all these years? Would he recognize her when he saw her?

* * *

On a sunny day in June, Ipatia walked on stage at the university. Dressed in her black robe and hat, she eagerly received her bachelor's degree in microbiology. Her aunt and uncle, along with little Alex, proudly attended the graduation ceremony. The speaker, a judge who had graduated from the university years ago, gave an inspiring speech.

She was exhilarated the rest of the day, enjoying the attention she received from her relatives. Aunt Sophia held a small graduation party for her, and Ipatia graciously played her part as the hostess. She served the drinks and talked with people, answering their questions and joking with them. Her cousins were there to congratulate her along with her friends from church and some friends of the family. Her uncle even invited a couple of young men from his real estate business.

After all the guests had left, and Ipatia had finished helping clean up, she excused herself, feeling exhausted. Yet that evening when she retired to her room, she could not fall asleep. She lay in bed thinking about her life and her recent accomplishment. She admitted that she had focused all her energies these past four years on getting her degree and had thought of nothing else.

She remembered the questions that people asked her today. Where was she going from here? Was she going to continue her education and get a graduate degree or apply for a job instead? She admitted that she had faltered in answering them. She wasn't sure what she was going to do next. She tried to think about the future but didn't feel happy when she imagined herself doing any of those things. Why not? Why was she feeling so sad? Did she want Tony to be there, to witness her moment of happiness, like everyone else? Did she want him gazing at her lovingly, the way her aunt and uncle gazed into each other's eyes?

Ipatia buried her face into the pillow, sobbing.

After a few moments, she wiped her tears. This couldn't be happening. She achieved what she wanted, and yet she wasn't happy. The people that she saw on a daily basis, her aunt and uncle, her cousins, and now Nick and his wife, all seemed happy with their life, and they were all married.

Oddly enough, no one asked her whether she had plans on marrying. How could they since she had shunned even the mention of marriage all these years?

Sunday morning, they attended church service and later, the social hour in the church hall. They returned home around one-thirty. After lunch, Aunt Sophia sat in the living room, finishing a dress she was sewing, while Uncle John read the Sunday newspaper.

Ipatia sat on the floor, playing with Alex, helping him set up his new toy train set that his father had bought recently. "Here, let me show you how it comes together," Ipatia said, putting the parts together.

Soon, Alex was pushing his train, saying "Choooo, choooo."

Later, two of Alex's friends who lived nearby, knocked on the door, and he went outside to play with them. Ipatia stayed awhile longer, chatting with her aunt, then excused herself and went upstairs to her room.

She reread Grandfather's letter. Tom Tsatsikas was engaged to an island girl and making preparations for the wedding. *Pappou* looked forward to Ipatia's visit this summer, stating that she would be in time for the wedding. If she hadn't found a young man yet, he had a few picked out for her.

She smiled at her grandfather's matchmaking efforts. To marry now after having accomplished her goals, was not so terrible. Yet how could she ever love so deeply any another man as she had loved Tony?

She began writing the letter to her grandfather. The sunlight streamed in from the half-opened window, bathing her in its afternoon glow. The sound of children's laughter outside interrupted Ipatia's writing. She looked out the window. Alex was playing with his friends in the back yard.

She continued writing her letter. She let *Pappou* know what day she was planning to arrive on the island. After sealing it and placing a stamp on it, she arose and stretched luxuriously. It felt good not having to study for any more exams.

Ipatia yawned, then caught her image in the full-length mirror, and smiled. She was no longer skinny. Her bust and hips had filled out, giving her curves. With her slim waist and long legs, her voluptuous body was always attracting attention, particularly from the opposite sex.

She picked up the comb and began combing her luxuriant hair slowly, looking at herself in the mirror. Although her hair was once golden, with yellow highlights from the sun, it had turned into a rich golden brown color. When she finished, her shining mane of hair fell gracefully below her shoulders, almost reaching her waist. She had refused to cut it after that time Olga had chopped it short, remembering how Tony had preferred it long. Yet in public, she wore it either as a ponytail, a braid, or in a bun.

The glasses had helped with the reading she had done these past few years and added a scholarly touch to her features. Sometimes she wore them to keep the young men away. She smiled and put them on her head.

Humming a tune, Ipatia walked out of her bedroom, skipping down the stairs into the living room. There, she found her aunt sitting on the couch, reading the Sunday newspaper. Her uncle had gone to an open house.

"Ipatia, my dear, can you read this section?" Aunt Sophia asked, handing over the newspaper. "My English isn't as good as yours."

Ipatia read the article. "On June 26, the University Hospital is hosting a banquet. It appears some foundation has given ten million dollars for a new cancer center that's going to be built there. The banquet is in their honor."

She handed the newspaper back to her aunt.

"Didn't Stasoula say something about a banquet you needed to play in around that time?"

"Yes, I believe so," Ipatia said. "With all my classes, I had forgotten all about it."

"When is your trip to Greece?" Aunt Sophia asked.

"June 27. It's the day after the banquet," Ipatia said, thinking about her preparations for the trip. The banquet would give her extra money for the trip.

"Do you think you can still play at the banquet? It's only for a couple of hours."

"Why not? The rest of the evening I'm free," Ipatia said, shrugging her shoulders. "I'll be packed before then anyway."

"By the way, must you wear those glasses when you play?" Aunt Sophia asked. "For some reason, they make you look different, much older than your age."

"I know, I know. You've told me several times, dear Aunt," Ipatia said, twirling around and making comical faces while wearing her glasses. "Only be happy that I don't have a mustache and a big nose."

They both laughed.

Later that evening, over dinner, Ipatia asked Stasoula about the banquet on June 26.

"Oh, yes, my darling, we are catering for that event, so of course we will need you to play," Stasoula said breathlessly, her short, plump body moving with her words. "Why don't you play the same music you played at the last banquet?"

"Seats one through twenty are now boarding."

"Here, give him to me," Melissa said. "You must not be late for your flight."

"Bye, sweet one," Tony said, planting a kiss on his nephew's chubby cheek before handing him to his sister.

"Bye-bye," little Gregory said, puckering his lips and smacking Tony with a wet kiss.

"Tony, there is something I've been wanting to tell you. I, I feel like such a heel for not mentioning Ipatia to you sooner," Melissa began, stammering slightly. "I'm sorry. I hope you'll forgive me."

"Don't worry, sis," he smiled, patting her on the back. "You helped me in your own way."

"What do you mean?"

"You didn't push Ipatia on me like you did your other girlfriends," he smiled. "Maybe that was all I needed."

"Tony."

"Good-bye, sis," he said, hugging her. "You know that I love you."

"I love you too," Melissa said, her eyes moistening. She brushed away a tear. "We'll see you in Heraklion in a few days?"

CHAPTER 38

The banquet was a huge success,
I played piano in my black dress.

Early Sunday afternoon, the day of the banquet, Ipatia helped unload the van, and then followed Stasoula into the large dining hall. Five servers arrived and they set the glasses on the table along with the plates and silverware.

"Could you place the flowers in the vases?" Stasoula asked Ipatia, pointing to bunches of red and white carnations.

After Ipatia was finished, she admired the carnations which gave a burst of color to the white tablecloth. Bottles of white and red wine arrived and a server placed them on tables.

Ipatia went to the baby grand piano in the corner and practiced some excerpts from the music she was to play that evening. Her playing earned her smiles from the other workers.

The hospital committee started filtering in. One woman from the committee began handing out brochures of the program. She handed one to Ipatia, who thanked her, then placed it in her purse. She didn't have time to browse. The banquet would begin soon, and she still needed to finish a number of last minute tasks.

Later, Ipatia went inside the kitchen, where her cousin Antonios and Chris were busy preparing the meal. There were juicy meatballs, broiled shrimp, stuffed grape-leaves, and small pastry shells filled with various cheese fillings. Another tray held black olives, cubed feta cheese, hummus and eggplant dips.

Ipatia was beginning to get hungry.

"Here, have some of this, *Skinny*," said Chris. He handed her a plate of appetizers.

"Thank you, *Potato*," she said, teasing him with his nickname. He was always looking out for her and teasing her about being too thin.

Ipatia sat down in a corner to eat the food. She watched as Antonios put on his gloves and removed the stuffed chicken breast from the oven.

Stasoula came into the kitchen hurriedly with bags of fresh rolls.

"Ipatia, my love, after you finish eating, get ready to play, because people are coming already," Stasoula said, appearing flustered. Then she told Antonios, "We are ready to serve the appetizers."

Ipatia quickly finished her meal. She picked up her black outfit hanging on the door rack and hurried down the hallway, heading for the restroom.

•••———◈ ••———◈ ••———◈

Tony entered the banquet room and was escorted to his table at the front of the room, by one of the women of the hospital committee. She chatted about being delighted that he could make it. He graciously thanked her, and then sat down at his table. It contained all the dignitaries, the mayor, the president of the university hospital, and members of the hospital committee.

After the introductions, Tony spoke with the mayor, who was interested in having contributions made to his political campaign. Then the president of the university hospital talked with him about funding.

Tony invited them to visit him in Greece.

"It's a different experience," he said, describing Greece, his eyes shining. "Once you visit my country, you'll always want to go back."

Ipatia quickly dressed into her long black skirt and blouse. The outfit reminded her of her days on the island, when she wore all black. She pulled her hair back, forming a small bun at the nape of her neck. She skillfully fastened it with bobby pins. A few strands came loose, curling oddly, and she wet them, trying to smooth them out.

She decided to wear the glasses tonight, not wanting to encourage any ardent beaus. Her ring was on her finger. Ipatia was ready.

Ipatia entered the ballroom. Several well-dressed people stood around, talking and drinking. In the middle of the room, sat a long row of tables covered with white tablecloths and on top of them, sat trays of steaming appetizers. Vases filled with red carnations sat in the center of each table.

Ipatia walked slowly and regally to the piano, focusing on her task. She had learned a long time ago not to look at the people in the audience, so she wouldn't lose her concentration. The piano sat to her left, at the far corner of the room, away from the tables.

When Ipatia sat down at the piano, she began to play softly, trying to pace herself with the sounds in the room. As she became involved with the music, everything around her disappeared. She was oblivious to the people arriving with their tuxedos and long, sequined dresses, until at some point the noise in the room escalated enough to compete with her music. She adjusted her playing accordingly.

The clanking sound of glasses and silverware alerted Ipatia that dinner was being served. She needed to remain focused and expertly shifted to dinner music, constantly mindful of the rising tide of voices. This usually happened around this time.

As the servers handed plates of baklava and cups of coffee to the people, Stasoula waved to Ipatia from the back of the room.

Ipatia recognized the signal to finish playing. She nodded her response and leafed through the sheet music. In a short while, she began playing the last song, Beethoven's 'Fur Elise.'

Although Tony listened to the committee chairman speaking, his mind was on the pianist. He had noticed her the moment she glided into the room, her attractive figure clothed in black garb as she headed for the piano. Something about her was familiar, but he could not place her. She had caught his attention. He entertained the notion that it might be Ipatia, but quickly erased the thought. The chances of coming across Ipatia were one in a million. *I don't even know how she looks.*

"What do you think about that, Dr. Plakis?" the chairman asked him.

"What? Can you repeat that again?" Tony replied, forced back into the conversation.

Ipatia finished playing the last song. As her fingers rested on the keys, she sensed someone staring at her. She looked up and saw a tall, handsome man sitting with the dignitaries and conversing with them. He wore a black tuxedo with a white shirt that contrasted well with his dark, handsome looks.

As she studied him more, Ipatia's heart began to race. Whenever she saw someone that resembled Tony, she would tremble with excitement. The memory of Tony could never be erased from her thoughts. The handsome man glanced at her a couple of time but didn't seem to recognize her. *It must not be him.*

Stasoula tapped her on the shoulder. "The speakers are getting ready to go on stage," she whispered.

Ipatia stopped playing and quietly followed her to the back of the ballroom.

She opened the kitchen door for the servers as they wheeled the carts laden with dirty dishes into the kitchen.

One by one, the speakers went on stage, and Ipatia stood silently by the kitchen door, listening. Occasionally, she would open the door for the servers.

The speakers talked about the ten-million-dollar donation from the Kalkinon Foundation. They talked about how the money would help build the new cancer center. Then there was a slide presentation of a model of the building. They displayed a picture of the plot of land where the building was to be built, followed by diagrams of the facilities to be constructed. The images looked impressive.

Another speaker got up and spoke about how the funds could help the cancer patients directly. He introduced a couple of cancer patients who would be helped by the foundation. One cancer patient was Brenda, a ten-year old girl, sitting in a wheelchair. Her hair was all gone and she looked pale. She spoke about her illness, simply and yet charmingly. She was a leukemia patient undergoing chemotherapy and was grateful for the donation.

Ipatia's eyes filled with tears at the girl's plight. She clapped heartily with the rest of the people after the girl ended her speech. Brenda's parents joined her and spoke their appreciation, and then her father wheeled her off the stage.

The other patient was Jeanne, an older woman in her sixties who had breast cancer. She also was grateful for the donation and spoke about her own plight.

"Now, we'd like to ask the president of the foundation to speak next," the chairman said.

Ipatia became alert, for the man that arose and walked confidently to the stage was that tall and handsome man that had been sitting with the dignitaries. As he was about to speak, the kitchen door opened from behind Ipatia and someone nudged her from the back. To avoid them, she moved away and inadvertently bumped into one of the carts. The sound of the dirty dishes crashing to the floor was so loud, that people turned and stared with annoyed looks.

Feeling flushed at this mishap, Ipatia hurriedly picked up the broken pieces, placing them blindly on the cart. Other workers came to help, but the dirty dishes kept falling, crashing to the floor. She could hear laughter coming from people in the banquet room.

Someone had placed them precariously on the cart. Mortified, Ipatia rushed to pick up the broken pieces.

Stasoula tapped her on the shoulder. "We'll handle this. Go to the restroom and clean up."

Ipatia arose and noticed her soiled skirt. She fled to the restroom, feeling ashamed.

As Tony joined the chairman on the stage, a loud commotion occurred in the back of the room. He glanced in that direction. It appeared that the piano player had bumped into a cart and had spilled everything on the floor, and the workers were rushing to help her clean it.

Laughter erupted in the room as they tried to clean up the mess, and the dirty dishes kept falling from the cart.

Tony felt like laughing aloud with the others at the comic scene. Instead, he chuckled inside.

After it became quiet again, the chairman spoke.

"I'd like to introduce Dr. Antonios Plakis, President of the Kalkinon Foundation," the chairman said, shaking his hand.

Tony began his speech, thanking the chairman and focusing on the salient points. He also talked about his father. "For those of you who don't know the story, my father, Gregory Plakis, was diagnosed with an aggressive brain tumor almost five years ago. It affected his life to the point where he became dependent on others. He could not control his movements and required help in his daily activities, like eating and getting dressed."

Exclamatory sounds came from the audience, and the room hummed.

"The doctors in Europe were pessimistic about his future, giving him only a few months to live. We heard about Dr. Bernard and came here to Chicago where my father had a successful operation at the university hospital. Thanks to Dr. Bernard, my father has been alive five years longer, and is living normally. The way he is going, he plans to outlive us all."

Laughter erupted, followed by much applause.

Tony stopped, waiting for the clapping to die down.

"Because of my father's cancer, he could not be here with you today, but I want you to know that he was the inspiration behind the foundation."

He waited for the clapping to die down.

"The Kalkinon Foundation not only will help in the building of the cancer center to aid in cancer research but will also focus its efforts in helping pay for the costs of health care for individuals with cancer who do not have health insurance or have depleted their resources."

More clapping ensued.

"In closing, I would like to add that donations from the foundation will continue in the future. We hope that you will join us in this fight against cancer, the scourge of the twentieth century."

Everyone stood, clapping enthusiastically.

The chairman joined him on the stage, smiling and clapping. The applause died down.

The chairman shook Tony's hand and handed him a plaque. "On behalf of the university hospital, we present you with this plaque for the generous ten-million-dollar donation that the Kalkinon Foundation has given towards the cancer center and its patients."

"Thank you. On behalf of the Kalkinon Foundation, I am deeply honored to accept this award," Tony said, taking the engraved plaque. He held it proudly in front of him for the people to see.

Applause broke out once more, and people stood and clapped, while others took pictures, their cameras emitting bursts of light. Tony bowed his head, and walked slowly back to his table, amidst the applause, feeling pleased with the response.

The mayor came and shook his hand heartily, and so did the others at his table.

Slowly, people sat back down in their seats, and the noise in the room returned to a low hum.

"We'd like to thank you for coming here tonight, and also many thanks to the hospital committee for their help in making this banquet a success. All proceeds will go towards the new cancer center. Have a good evening," the chairman of the committee announced.

The award banquet had officially ended.

Within a few minutes, people began rising, starting to leave. Tony spoke and shook hands with a number of people who congratulated him personally. He glanced a few times towards the back of the room, hoping to get a glimpse of the piano player. He felt slightly disappointed that she had left. He wondered what happened to her.

The mayor asked Tony politely whether he was staying after the evening.

"Yes, for a few days," Tony said. "There is some unfinished business I need to attend to."

"We'd like to invite you to my house tonight," the mayor said. "We've invited some important guests for a small party and would be honored to have your presence."

"Thank you for the invitation. I'd be delighted," Tony replied, nodding.

The next day, Tony didn't awaken until early afternoon. He rubbed his forehead. He had gone to the mayor's palatial mansion and met several prominent people. He hadn't returned to the hotel until four o'clock in the morning, and now he was beginning to feel a slight hangover. He lay back in bed, going over in his mind what he was going to do today.

He had made up his mind that he was going to call Ipatia's house and introduce himself. Just like that. Then he would ask to speak to her. *Would I recognize her voice?* If she invited him over, then he would visit her and find out for himself if the girl still had feelings for him after all these years. Yes, but what if she already had someone? *I will soon find out.*

Tony arose and washed. After shaving and dressing, he found the telephone number of Ipatia's aunt and uncle that Mrs. Rodos had given him. He would have to find a way to get there, but first, he needed to telephone them.

He dialed the number, his fingers trembling. He still nursed deep feelings for Ipatia, after all these years.

"Hello?"

The woman's voice sounded familiar. Tony's heart pounded in his chest as the familiar fear of the unknown rose up to choke him. "Hello, this is Tony Plakis," he began, and then stopped when he heard the woman excitedly interrupt him.

"Tony Plakis. This is Sophia, how is it you called, after all these years?" Aunt Sophia exclaimed.

The image of Sophia, when he was a child, swept through his mind, and he inwardly sighed with relief. "It's a long story," he said, laughing. "I am in town. I came for a banquet given by the hospital."

"A banquet? Oh, you mean the one given in honor for some foundation," she said, sounding pleasantly surprised.

"Yes, the Kalkinon Foundation," he said. "My father and I formed it about a year ago."

"Oh, that's wonderful. I'm surprised Ipatia didn't tell me about you being there."

"Ipatia? Why, was she there?" he asked, his voice catching in his throat. Immediately the image of the young woman dressed in black, wearing those glasses, playing the piano came to him. *If only I had known.*

"Yes, she played the piano at the banquet," she said, her voice sounding puzzled. "Didn't you see her?"

She had been right there in front of me, playing the piano last night, and I hadn't recognized her. I missed the opportunity to speak with her.

"I'm afraid I didn't recognize her."

There was silence. "What do you mean?"

"I was in a car accident years ago, and in a coma. As a result, I had amnesia and forgot everyone and everything, including my family and friends. It took me years to get back to normal."

"I'm sorry to hear that."

"It's behind me now. I am well. Is Ipatia available to speak?" Tony asked. "I know this is unexpected after all these years, but I must speak to her. It's important."

"Oh dear. I'm afraid it's impossible."

"What do you mean? Is she married?" he asked, fearing the worst.

"No, it's nothing like that," laughed Sophia nervously. "You see, she left for Greece two hours ago. She'll be visiting her cousins, George and Paula Mastroyiannis in Piraeus, and then she plans to visit her grandfather in Lipsi Island."

"She left for Greece?" Tony asked, digesting the news.

"Will you be here for a while? We would like for you to come and visit us."

"I'd like to, but I have a plane to catch. I truly enjoyed speaking with you, Sophia."

CHAPTER 39

Our love began five years ago
Now this ring to thee I bestow.

Ipatia's flight was delayed an hour because of the heavy storm. The rain began after she arrived at O'Hare Airport. She sat around, waiting for the announcement of her flight and gazing out the windows at the gray and stormy day.

She rummaged through her purse, searching for her passport and boarding pass. She looked them over carefully. Everything was in order. She placed them back in her purse. Her hand brushed against the brochure from last night's event. She had forgotten it.

Ipatia leafed through the pages of the brochure absentmindedly, reading the different projects going on in the hospital, and the advertisements. She was upset that they hadn't put her name in the brochure as the pianist. Then she came across the name of the Foundation and its generous donation. As she read more carefully, her eyes opened in wonder and her hands felt clammy. *It couldn't be, but Tony Plakis had been at the banquet last night.* He was the president of the foundation.

How could I have missed him?

Ipatia frantically ran over the events of last night's banquet in her mind. Then she remembered seeing the tall, handsome man who had reminded her of Tony. *I had been right.* Yet when Tony glanced her way, he didn't seem to recognize her.

She hadn't stayed because of the little accident with the cart. Having soiled her skirt, she had remained in the restroom, trying to clean it. Stasoula had arrived shortly after to help her.

"I can't get these stains off this skirt," moaned Ipatia, showing her the dirty skirt.

"Here, don't worry about it. The banquet is just about finished, and we have enough help," Stasoula said. "Chris can drive you home. I know you need to finish packing for your trip tomorrow."

Ipatia had gone straight home from there.

Then she had been busy getting her luggage ready for the trip. She had dropped into bed, feeling exhausted.

Ipatia's thoughts were interrupted by the loud speaker.

"We are now boarding passengers in seats 20-30."

She pulled her boarding pass shakily out of her purse, got up and went to stand in line.

Eight hours later, Ipatia landed in the Athens airport. The sunny morning was a sharp contrast to the stormy weather she left behind in Chicago. Her cousins were waiting for her and their warm reception was heartening.

They whisked Ipatia away from the hub of the airport and transported her back to their home. There was much chatter and discussion along the way.

When they arrived at the house, they chatted awhile longer over lunch, and then Ipatia excused herself and went into her bedroom to nap. She fell into a deep sleep.

She dreamt that she was dressed in white, and Tony appeared next to her. He was kind and gentle and kissed her. She felt happy. Then he went and sat outside on the terrace, drinking coffee. When she went outside to join him, he had disappeared. She felt disappointed and sad. Then he reappeared, sitting in a new car and taking her to a palace, saying, "This is your new home."

When Ipatia awoke, she lay there thinking about Tony. Something warm and wonderful had stirred inside of her when she read the brochure with his name in it. Was she hoping that he would return in her life and continue where they had left off? S*top fantasizing. After all these years, he's probably married.*

She found Paula in the living room. "Hi Paula, where's George?"

"He went to get me something from the store," Paula said. "He should be back soon."

They talked for some time.

The doorbell rang and Paula went to answer it. She returned a few minutes later, appearing flustered.

"That was George," she said. "He forgot the money. He'll be back soon. Anyway, did you get a chance to catch some sleep?"

"Yes, thank you," Ipatia said. "I had this strange dream. Tony Plakis was in it."

"I've been meaning to tell you something. We visited Dr. Hatzis's office recently and learned that Tony had been asking about you."

Ipatia's eyes opened wide. "What do you mean?"

"Tony asked for your address," Paula said carefully. "We also spoke to your aunt on the telephone while you were napping. She said that Tony telephoned her this morning. He was in Chicago, at the banquet. He asked for you, and she told him you were coming here."

Ipatia's heart started racing. "She did?"

He asked for me.

"What are your feelings towards Tony?" Paula asked.

"What do you mean?"

"If he asked you to marry him, would you?"

Ipatia was stunned. She had blocked him for so many years from her mind, and suddenly, there he was, trying to come back in her life.

She paced the room anxiously. "It's not that easy to begin loving him all over again. I mean, after what he did."

"Do you still love him?" Paula asked softly.

Ipatia stopped, silently digesting everything. Tony meant so much to her, even after all these years. She felt as though a ray of light was shining on her. She nodded numbly. "Yes, with all my heart." The tears swelled in her eyes.

Paula arose quickly, appearing excited. "Excuse me for a minute, dear. I think I hear George at the door."

Ipatia sat still, motionless, as if in a trance. She could not ignore anymore the deep-rooted love she had for this man.

"Ipatia."

Ipatia jumped at the deep voice. She could recognize his voice anywhere. The same voice that sang her love songs was now here, in the room. She turned around to face Tony. Handsome Tony.

Am I dreaming?

Ipatia felt her knees buckle under her as she drifted into darkness. Someone held her closely, talking to her softly, caressing her arm, and kissing her cheek, saying he loved her.

She responded, saying "Tony," and snuggled in his warm embrace. *It felt so good.*

Ipatia slowly opened her eyes and found herself gazing into Tony's beautiful eyes. She blinked as the memories of hurt returned with vengeance.

"Tony Plakis, how dare you come here and mock me, after all these years?" she exclaimed angrily, scrambling up, trembling all over. She pulled back the loose strands of hair from her face and crossed her arms. Four years-worth of tears welled up in her eyes.

Tony took her in his arms and said softly, "I love you."

"How could you say that after what you did?" she persisted. This time, she did not resist.

He hugged her closely.

"What did I do, my sweet one?" he asked, still holding her close.

He nuzzled her cheek, making her feel hot all over.

"You left me there in the hospital and went to Crete," she whispered, afraid to look at him, afraid to reveal her true feelings.

"Before I explain, please do me a favor," he said, tipping her chin up so he could look deep into her eyes.

"What?" she whispered. She got her answer, as he kissed her slowly, fervently. She did not fight it, but instead gave her heart and soul to him. All her illusions were shattered in that kiss. She knew no matter what happened next, that she loved him and would always love him.

"Tell me, Ipatia, exactly what happened right before the accident. It's important."

She told him, and when she got to the part where she heard a honk and blacked out, she stopped.

"You blacked out?" he asked, interested.

"Yes. I remember waking up the next day in the hospital," she admitted. "I had two fractured ribs and stayed there through Easter. I asked my cousins to call your house every day, but no one answered."

Tony frowned. "I'm sorry my sweet one, if I could, I would have been there by your side," he said, moaning slightly. "I didn't awaken until a month later."

Ipatia's breathing became shallow. "What do you mean?"

"I was in a coma from the accident and almost didn't survive. When I finally awoke, I didn't remember anyone, not even my family."

Ipatia was stunned. "How could it be? I thought you had gone to Crete for the Easter holiday. Rita told me."

"I'm afraid Rita didn't know what happened," he said ruefully. "Father didn't want anyone knowing about it. The doctors in Greece said I didn't have much of a chance to live, so my family took me to England, where I was operated on several times."

Ipatia's heart swelled with sympathy. She touched his face lovingly. "Is everything all right, I mean are you fine now?"

"Yes, my love. Now that I am near you, everything is fine," he said huskily.

"I'm so glad," she said, hugging him impulsively.

He swept Ipatia in his embrace and kissed her once more, murmuring sweet words in her ear.

Years of holding their emotions at bay dissolved into a timeless, passionate moment.

After what seemed like eternity, they separated.

He told her what had happened with her cousins. "When you were napping, I came and introduced myself. I told them that I came for you but wasn't sure if you'd still want me after all these years. Paula asked me to wait in the kitchen while she talked with you first."

"That was why she was asking all those questions."

"Before I go on, there's something else you need to know about me," he said solemnly. "I no longer work for my father's business. I have my own business."

"You do?" she asked timidly.

"Yes," he said. "And I haven't that much money. I got into debt trying to start the business."

"It doesn't matter. In my opinion, money does not make a man noble, but his character does. I am proud of you for trying to do something on your own, even if it means being in debt."

He kissed her tenderly, feeling happy with her response.

He took out a little jewelry box from his pocket and removed a ring. "Do you see this, my love?"

She stared at it, looking surprised. "Yes. It looks like the cat's eye stone that I had given you. It's beautiful."

"I found it in the pants that I wore on the day of the picnic. I had the ring made for you."

"On the day of the picnic?" she asked, trembling at the implications. *He had been meaning to propose to me, just as in my dream.*

"Yes. I like to finish what I start." He removed the ring from the box and slipped it on her finger.

"I wasn't worthy of it," she said tearfully, gazing at it. "I mean, I feel so guilty. That day of the accident, you had wanted to have the picnic at the foot of the mountain, and I selfishly wanted to go to the top. We probably wouldn't have gotten into the accident if it weren't for me. Maybe God didn't want us to be together then, that is why he separated us."

"No, my love. It is our destiny," he said firmly, interrupting her with a passionate kiss. She melted in his arms. He didn't want this moment to end. "We were meant to be together."

Ipatia's guilty feelings had vanished, replaced by a warm feeling that saturated her body.

"Yes," she said dreamily, leaning against him, feeling safe. She told him about the dream she had, where she had wanted to be with him, and he had told her not to go with him.

"Do not fear, my love. You will never be alone, because I will always be with you," he said quietly. "It feels like yesterday when I last saw you. Everything is coming back to me now, your face, your hair, your eyes, and even your stubbornness."

She laughed delightedly, as her eyes, mind, heart, and soul, joined his. They kissed once more, elevating their love to another understanding, another place where there was no time. She knew in the deepest part of her heart that she loved him unconditionally.

"Will you marry me?" he asked charmingly, gazing intently into her eyes.

She nodded, her eyes shining brightly in his. "Oh, yes."

He picked her up, twirling her around. They laughed together. "The stone from the ring matches your eyes," he said appreciatively.

"I'm glad you made it into a ring," she admitted.

"Your happiness is mine doubled," he said. His face became serious. "Now I have a confession to make."

"Yes?"

"I'm not as poor as I told you previously," he said teasingly. "I am doing considerably well in my business. I built a villa in a suburb of Athens. It sits high on a hill and has a beautiful view of the sea. It is waiting for you."

"Tony, how could you lie to me?"

"Sorry, but I wanted to see your reaction," he said laughing. "Your heart is richer than all the money I have. You proved it to me."

Ipatia softened. "I hope your family will like me."

"My dear girl, my love for you will overcome any reservations anyone has about you," he said. "Once they see you for who you are, they can't help but fall in love with you."

"I love you so much," she said, before melting into his arms.

Her happiness was complete.

THE END

Author Bio:

Patty Apostolides is an author and a poet. She has written five novels and a poetry book. When she retired as a cancer biologist in order to stay at home and homeschool her son, her second career as a writer began. She holds a BA in Biology from Case Western Reserve University with minors in music and theater, and an MFA in Creative Writing from National University. She is the director of the Hellenic Writers Group of Washington DC.

Ms. Apostolides has performed as a violist in several orchestras (Cleveland Philharmonic, Cleveland Women's' Orchestra, Fairfield Symphony Orchestra) and more recently, as a violinist with the Frederick Symphony Orchestra. She also composes music.

She lives in Maryland with her son.

Visit the author's website:
www.pattyapostolides.com

CPSIA information can be obtained
at www.ICGtesting.com
Printed in the USA
LVHW021448060819
626724LV00002B/208